Praise for *The Spinster, the Rebel, and the Governor*

"This was obviously a labor of love...This was well written and well researched. I was incredibly impressed with the ability to highlight not only political upheaval but the social issues as well. It was a powerful and tightly woven novel."
National Federation of Press Women

A historical novel inspired by the life of one of Maryland's earliest English colonists. Dietz, the author of *The Flapper, the Imposter, and the Stalker* (2017), fictionalizes the story of Margaret Brent, a wealthy Englishwoman who becomes a prominent figure in Maryland in the mid-17th century... Although little of Margaret's real-life history was recorded, Dietz does a good job of drawing on what's known about her and about the early years of Maryland's colonization to create a well-rounded, convincing portrait. Over the course of the novel, the author employs a great many vivid details that bring everyday life in both England and Maryland into sharp focus... The novel sticks closely to its protagonist's perspective... (and) the book is sweeping in scope, covering Maryland's foundational years from the perspective of a woman who played a crucial role in its existence. A robust imagining of the life of a largely unsung hero.
Kirkus Reviews

T0043244

Other Books by Charlene Bell Dietz

The Flapper, the Scientist, and the Saboteur
The Flapper, the Impostor, and the Stalker
The Scientist, the Psychic, and the Nut

The Spinster, the Rebel, *and* the Governor

A Novel

Charlene Bell Dietz

Artemesia
Publishing

ISBN: 978-1-951122-80-5 (paperback)
ISBN: 978-1-951122-81-2 (ebook)
LCCN: 2023947501

Artemesia Publishing
9 Mockingbird Hill Rd
Tijeras, New Mexico 87059
www.apbooks.net
info@artemesiapublishing.com

Second Edition

Dedication

This book is dedicated to my family, my cousins, their children, and other descendants of the brave men and women who labored and gave their hearts to settle Maryland.

CONTENTS

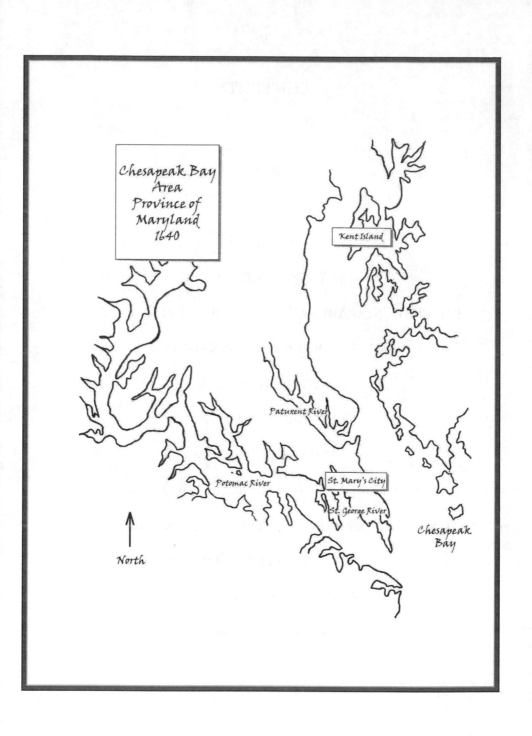

Chesapeak Bay
Area
Province of
Maryland
1640

Kent Island

Patuxent River

Potomac River

St. Mary's City

St. George River

Chesapeak
Bay

North

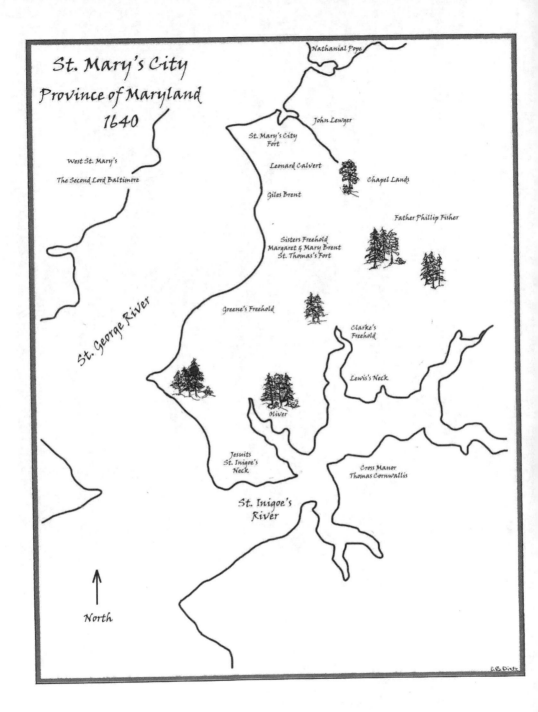

St. Mary's City
Province of Maryland
1640

Nathanial Pope

John Lewger

St. Mary's City
Fort

West St. Mary's
The Second Lord Baltimore

Leonard Calvert

Chapel Lands

Giles Brent

Father Phillip Fisher

Sisters Freehold
Margaret & Mary Brent
St. Thomas's Fort

St. George River

Greene's Freehold

Clarke's
Freehold

Lewis's Neck

Oliver

Jesuits
St. Inigoe's
Neck

Cross Manor
Thomas Cornwallis

St. Inigoe's
River

North

C.B Dietz

List of Characters

England

Margaret Brent: Protagonist of this story who insists on righting all wrongs.
Peter Coats: (Fictional) Young man who makes trouble.
William Keith: (Fictional) Angry itinerant merchant.
Pip: (Fictional) Brent's stableboy.
Dary: (Fictional) Brent's houseboy.
Crissa: (Fictional) Margaret's young maid servant.
Richard Brent: Father of Margaret, Mary, Fulk, and Giles.
Cecil, or **Cecilius Calvert**: Second Lord Baltimore. English proprietor of precolonial Maryland.
Mary Brent: Loyal younger sister of Margaret.
Fulk Brent: An older brother who protect his sisters.
Giles Brent: A younger brother looking for an exciting adventure.
Goodwin: Blacksmith who becomes an indentured servant.

Maryland

Simon: (Fictional) Quarter Master of the ship, *Charity*.
Leonard Calvert: Governor of the Province of Maryland and Cecil Calvert's brother.
Peasley: (Fictional) Governor Calvert's head servant.
Missus Davis: (Fictional) Governor Calvert's maid.
Henry: (Fictional) Freeman and musician.
John Lewger: Friend of Cecil Calvert and Secretary of precolonial Maryland.
Father Andrew White: Arrived in 1634 with Governor Calvert.
Father Phillip Fisher: Works closely with Father White.
William Claiborne: Early settler living on Kent Island who stirs up trouble.
Carrie Wells: (Fictional) Indentured servant needing Margaret's help.
Jacob Cole: (Fictional) Carrie Well's master.
Captain Thomas Cornwallis: Landholder who donates much to the welfare of the province.
Thomas Greene: Arrived with Leonard Calvert 1634. Margaret and Mary's neighbor.
John Morton: (Fictional) Freeman with wife, Bess, and toddler, John.
Chitomachen Kittamaquund: Tayac of the Piscataway Indians.
Mary Kittamaquund: Tayac's young daughter and ward of the governor and Margaret Brent.
Thomas Harris: (Fictional) Burgess from Sow's Creek.
Captain Richard Ingle: Merchant seaman for precolonial Maryland, from Virginia.

Thomas and John Sturman: Father and son Marylanders who fought against Catholics.

Nathaniel Pope: Freeman who, in 1642, purchases Leonard Calvert's newly built manor.

Edward Hill: A Virginian who, in 1646, took over governorship of precolonial Maryland.

Captain John Price: Head of Leonard Calvert's militia.

Genuine historical knowledge requires nobility of character, a profound understanding of human existence—not detachment and objectivity.

— Friedrich Nietzsche

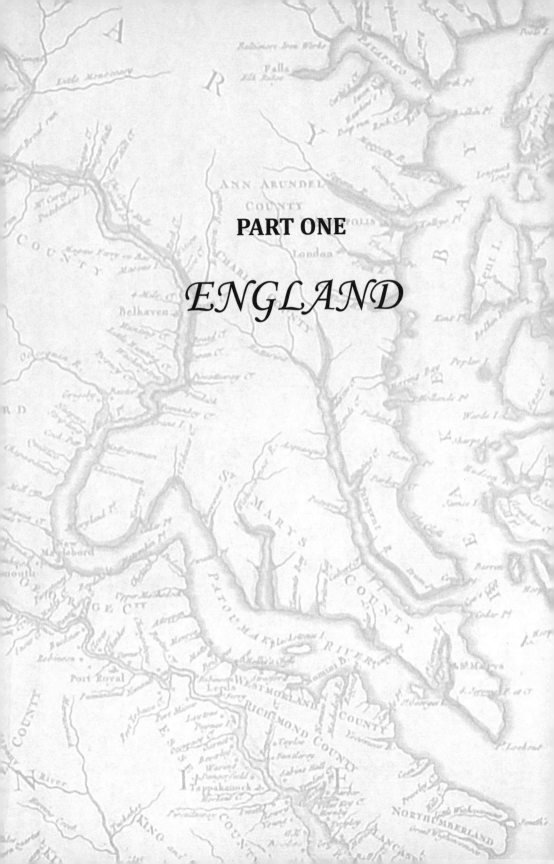

PART ONE

ENGLAND

Chapter 1

Gloucestershire, England
Spring 1638

There is no such difference between men and women, that women may not do great matters, as we have seen by the example of many Saints....
- Mary Ward (1585-1645)

ANYONE NOT LOST IN the loveliness of this fresh-washed spring evening could see trouble afoot. Margaret Brent glanced over her shoulder. Satisfied, she reined Gingo down from a canter into a trot. He flung his head in protest, then expelled a wet-sounding snort.

Margaret's mood matched his. She must not be caught riding in the countryside after dark, and now dusk crept over this gentle land with gray mist slinking along its valley floors. Yet an unusual sight puzzled her. A massive figure knelt in the shadow beside the doorway of a tiny, country chapel. She must investigate.

As misfortune would now have it, when darkness fell her father would be fraught with worry. Nevertheless, she could not ignore what made no sense or some ill deed she might prevent.

When she finished her work in Stratford, Margaret directed Gingo away from the closed shops and noisy taverns in the center of town. Poor Gingo navigated an unsure path, clopping down shadowed alleyways, picking his way over fetid garbage, excrement, and uneven cobbles until they reached the outskirts of the village. He hurried over the wooden bridge, making her cringe when his hooves thudded on the planks.

Margaret's life, or most assuredly her freedom, depended on her avoiding the curious townsmen who might question the business of Sir Richard Brent's spinster daughter riding alone so late in the afternoon. The hour required this detour, unless of course Margaret cared to degrade herself and lie.

Forgive me, dear Father, for the sin of these errant thoughts. I do endeavor to keep the folly of my falsehoods from finding a solid purchase within my heart.

Margaret leaned forward and gave the bay's rust-colored neck a scratch, worked a finger to untangle his black mane, then pulled him down into a plodding walk through puddles left by rain showers. Her loving little gesture would do nothing to help mollify his innate desire to speed. He displayed his unhappiness with another shake of his head. Regardless, she could not pass by this chapel and let some wrong transpire.

If anyone of importance encountered Margaret, she would need more than heaven's helping hand to protect her from unasked questions. In years past, her father had held the title of sheriff, but if the gentleman now holding this office had seen her in Stratford at this hour, her father's station would be of no help to her. She knew well the powerful authority of the sheriff and how fast speculative news traveled to the king's men.

Margaret directed Gingo off the main road and onto the sanctuary's path. She tugged him to a stop and recognized the huge figure as Sara Coates' boy. Man-like, with awkward elbows and knees, a voice still at the crackling stage, and haystack hair, he crouched beside the doorstep in the spring grass outside the chapel. The low sun would set within the hour. It washed a butter glow over the spire of this limestone house of worship but left the Coates' boy in shadows.

The boy held something close to his chest and shielded it from sight. Dark earth soiled one knee of his too small breeches. From inside the church, angelic voices concluded their hymn followed by a sonorous male voice.

Choir practice?

"Young man," Margaret called. "Show me what you are hiding."

He flicked a finger over his lips and scowled a warning to her. His too large chin sported several tiny, infected bumps—common of someone his age.

"Stop whatever this nonsense."

The sounds of her words carried no heart. Her attention involved weightier issues of the mind and soul rather than what appeared to be no more than a childish prank.

"Most boys your age leave their silliness at home and busy themselves in productive pursuits."

He needed hard work to make him sweat. Margaret touched the rein against Gingo's neck, her mount obedient, turned and trotted back onto the main path. Her father had changed their stable boy's life. Maybe he could do the same for this young man.

A screech, like the sound of a hawk plunging from the heavens and snatching some poor unsuspecting rabbit, caused her to spin back toward the chapel.

Exchanging shrieks for sobs and squashing her blue, satin gown and petticoats in fists, a diminutive girl danced tippy toed on the chapel step, her blonde curls bobbing. A slender, grass-green snake writhed before her until it found refuge in a crack under a stone.

"Ellie." The boy, howled with laughter. "Your coif's on crooked."

"And you, young Coates, your head is on crooked," Margaret scolded. This boy would come to no good. Someone must step in to redirect his actions. She would call this to her father's attention tonight.

Margaret pulled her gray, woolen cloak tighter, tucked a strand of hair under its hood, then nudged Gingo. He lurched into a gallop with hooves spraying mud flecks that slapped her cheek.

Margaret took the path leading down into the yew-tree forest.

As shadows elongated, another sense of urgency rose within her. The wise do not pass through woods after nightfall. Her father warned of increased treachery on lonely dark roads. She smirked. A younger and shapely lady with fine features might have more to worry about than a lady such as Margaret. She, now thirty-six years, of strong, firm, and tall stock, with unruly red hair, no matter her numerous suitors, felt certain to be thought of as plain. At this age, she would make an abductor's efforts a waste of both their time.

Yet thieves who might hide in this small forest concerned her more.

Gingo slowed of his own accord when they entered the darkened woods. Fallen, splintered branches, an abundance of gnarled roots that protruded above the barren ground and deep vegetative brambles made staying on the path imperative. Margaret clucked to Gingo, urging him on, but his ears twitched and his hesitancy sent shivers up her spine.

Margaret allowed Gingo to halt while she strained to listen. Something moved—heavy boots chewed down through soft mulch. She saw nothing but she could smell someone, unwashed with the rancidness of vomit. The oak bushes rustled.

A form emerged from the undergrowth, then lurched out from the shadows. William Keith stood in her path. He blocked her way.

Gingo reared and stumbled backwards. He regained his balance with a snort. Margaret patted his neck and whispered to stay calm. Gingo settled, but his withers twitched. Nervous smells from the horse's sweat rose into the damp air.

The man held something, but she couldn't discern what in the evening's poor light.

"William Keith, I am surprised to see you here." Margaret had left his wife and their five children less than an hour ago. "Are you sick?"

Her stomach knotted. Keith had waited for her here. He knew she would ride home through these woods.

"Sick of you, I'd say." He coughed up something, then spat. "Ye have no business talking to my wife. She's got you women plotting agin me. Since I figure you're their leader, I'm here to see an end to your doings." Keith cracked a long, black leather whip toward Gingo. The animal shied sideways. Margaret grabbed the pommel.

She might be able to gallop past him, but in turn he could trip Gingo by wrapping the whip around a leg. If she rode off the side of the path into the forest, Gingo's footing would be difficult. Her horse might stumble over some unseen, gnarly root and break his leg. Yet nothing prevented Margaret from turning back the way she came except the lateness of the hour. Her father would have a search party out soon enough.

"William Keith, please lower your whip."

A soft hollow *eeyhoe* with several brief snorts came from behind the bushes. Margaret's heart hurt. She knew Keith used that whip on his sweet and loyal donkey.

He continued to hold the whip at a threatening level.

"Your wife suffers under your unkind hand. Her swollen and split lip did not come from any fall. This afternoon we could see those bruises you left on her cheek. None of us said anything, but I know your temper when you take to drink. You have been a good man and have provided well for your family. Why do you not appreciate her toils to create a comfortable home?"

"Woman, ye know nothing. She deserves what I give her. I forbade her to go to this gathering of yours, yet she defied me." Sweat covered his forehead. "I know what goes on. Ye don't just sit and sew, mend, and stitch. All of you talk the faith. This afternoon, at the window's ledge, I heard each of you practicing Latin. Latin! What would the magistrate say to that? But I shan't tell him, because I can't be having them drag her off to prison, burning her at the stake, and leaving me with the young ones."

Margaret held her breath and kept a well-practiced dispassionate look. This drunken man's words would ruin them all.

"Listen, woman. Hear what I have to say to ye." He lowered the whip and wiped his forehead with his sleeve. "I'll continue to beat her as long as she continues on with this sham. We're not high born like you and your family. No one looks the other way for us. If the authorities uncover what she's doing, they'll think I approved of her behavior. They won't fine me. Na. They'll put us both under lock, take my lands, and both our heads."

Here stood a frightened, but dangerous, man.

She could understand his frustration, but no one held the right to determine another's spiritual devoutness. His wife would continue to practice Catholicism in this mandated Protestant world, and he would continue to beat her.

Margaret adjusted the angle of her knee into a more comfortable position around the pommel. Then she shifted her weight to her foot in the stirrup, smoothed her skirt, and took time to gather her words.

"William Keith, contemplate what I have to say—because this is true." She leaned forward and stared into his eyes. "I have no influence over the spiritual beliefs of your wife. I have seen few women as pious as she. Even if I never return to your town again, she will continue on with her studies." Margaret straightened her back, which signaled Gingo to get ready to move. "You may continue to abuse her with words, your fist, or your whip, but here is where I give caution. You will not change her, but any man who partakes of his wife's food preparation, or who sleeps soundly beside her at night would be well advised to treat this woman with affection and respect."

"Do not threaten me." He waggled the whip in her direction.

She waited for him to find the words she expected him to say.

"If she poisons me or stabs me in my sleep, she'll be off to prison and the chopping block. She'd never do something dumb as that and leave her children without their ma and pa."

"Except, as God's way, your wife's rounded stomach tells me she is carrying your sixth child. No matter how she chooses to serve her Lord, you must be kind to her. If you continue to incense her emotions to a high level, she might dismiss her pious ways." As drunk as he appeared, Margaret saw he still attended to her words. "Then if you are done away with, she will plead her belly in court. The odds say she will be home in no time, tending to the five other young ones. Your eldest son will inherit all your goods and earnings. He will care for your wife, and she will enjoy what your hard work has provided. The best part, your wife will no longer have to endure your cruelty."

She snapped the reins and Gingo lurched ahead.

Keith leaped aside as she had guessed.

"Good evening, William Keith. I am late."

* * *

In less than an hour, Gingo trotted up the familiar darkened lane and headed toward the comfort of his horse barn. Candle lamplights shining out from the downstairs windows of the manor gave the appearance of a ball or attendance of dinner guests at the least.

Margaret's uneasiness of the evening increased. Her father never entertained anymore, and visitors to this house would not be of the festive nature. She would have seen horses about the road if her father had called friends in to search for her.

The stable boy stepped from the doorway of the barn, swinging a lantern high. When the wedge of light caught Gingo and Margaret, Pip doffed his cap and took hold of Gingo's bridle with his other hand.

"Your father's been asking after you, m'lady. I tol' him you'd be making your presence afore dark."

Margaret slipped her leg from around the horn of the pommel and eased down off Gingo. Straightening her skirts and pushing back her hood, she gave Gingo's ear a quick scratch, his neck a pat, then nodded to Pip. As Margaret scurried along the moonlit path to the manor, she made out the shape of a carriage. Hurrying up to it, her confusion mounted.

Cecilius Calvert's horse and carriage stands unattended in our courtyard. What trouble brings the second Lord Baltimore here alone without a driver and after dark?

Chapter 2

ALERTED BY THE SOUND of her approach, the carriage horse twitched his ears, quivered, and blew air from his nostrils. Margaret skirted around the carriage. She whispered to the handsome beast and stroked his nose. Once he settled, she hurried across the cobbles and up to the massive hand-carved oak door. Before she could grasp the handle, the door opened, letting out a sliver of yellow light. Crissa peeked out.

"Lady Margaret." She held the door wide. "I feared you would miss an important family gathering in the drawing room with Lord Baltimore." She lifted her hands to remove Margaret's cloak.

Margaret nodded but swept past and hurried toward the spacious room off the passage near the ornately carved oak staircase. The last time she had seen Cecil Calvert was at his father's funeral five years ago. Cousin George's title of Lord Baltimore had been bestowed by King James, and after his death the title had passed down to this eldest son, Cecil. The Brent family enjoyed a sense of security, having the Calvert men as friends.

Her moment of comfort slipped into sorrow—a personal one. Six years ago, Margaret, her siblings, her father, and the first Lord Baltimore with Cecil had all been together—another most unhappy occasion. They had congregated in the village of Bredon for her mother's funeral.

Margaret tugged open the door to the drawing room. The men, intent on documents spread before them, ignored all. This seriousness of her three brothers—Fulke, Giles, and Edward—her father, and the second Lord Baltimore, Cecil Calvert worried her. They stood around the large walnut table. Their murmurs and questions mixed with the crackle of a fresh-laid fire.

The glowing flames enhanced the sun-colored limestone of their fireplace. Three of Margaret's sisters, Mary, Ann, and Jane, stood near the hearth, conversing as if waiting for some pronouncement from the men.

Her other three sisters resided in a French convent. Margaret doubted she'd ever see them again.

Dary must have been summoned to lay the fire. The sandy-haired lad pulled the brocaded tapestries across the multi-paned windows. The drapes, the room's oak panels running from floor to ceiling, and the warmth of the fire had not erased the evening's chill.

No one noticed Margaret enter the room. She unclasped her cloak and slid it from her shoulders.

Crissa, ever present, whisked it away. Margaret moved to the table to join her brothers.

What papers had captured their attention?

Everyone ignored her.

"Lord Baltimore, Father, what enchants everyone so this evening?"

The men raised their gaze, and her father straightened. She wanted to be let in closer, but as usual, her brothers would not step aside.

"My lady," Lord Calvert spoke, "the evening would not be complete without your presence. I say, Sir Richard, your house is full of charming women."

"I quite agree, Lord Calvert. And here you are at last, my dear." Richard Brent raised an eyebrow and smiled.

"Father, I am curious to see what causes such great interest."

"And so, you should be." Lord Calvert grinned. "We're studying a rather newly drawn map by Hendrik Hondius. You know—of Holland."

"I am surprised to learn a map of Holland engages you so."

"My apologies. He's a cartographer who resides in Holland. This map shows a section of the New World—the Colony of Virginia and the fertile lands to the north."

Richard motioned his sons to step aside and let him pass. The years had not stolen her father's inherent good looks even though the sharpness of his jaw and brow had softened. His eyebrows grew bushier and grayer with the passing of time, but he still stood straight and tall. He could issue commands without saying a word.

His three sons stepped aside to let him pass. Then the brothers crowded back to the table, filling the space Richard had just vacated. Her father took her elbow and escorted her nearer her sisters by the fireplace. He stopped, frowned, and pointed to Margaret's cheek. Her sisters watched.

Margaret tilted her head, and he made a wiping motion.

Mud. She brushed the fleck from her face.

The three sisters in turn averted their eyes and continued their conversation.

Richard said, "When darkness fell, I started to worry."

"You are kind to be concerned about me at my age, Father. I am sorry for any distress I may have caused, but I faced an unavoidable delay."

"My worry has nothing to do with your capabilities but more to do with the unpredictability of these times. I'm relieved to know you're home."

Margaret put her hand on her father's wrist. "This visit surprises me. Does not Cecil live in Ireland?"

"He and his wife are staying with her ailing father, Lord Arundel, at Wardour Castle."

"Still quite far."

"West of Salisbury. Manageable."

Margaret nodded. "I suspect Cecil has come here to propose some untenable situation, which occupies your thoughts, Father."

"He arrived only a few minutes before you. We've not had an opportunity to sort out his matters of concern. However, I can assure you there's nothing new we haven't already heard. But it's good of him to come, don't you think?" He paused. "I believe the occasion of his visit warrants all of us to be regaled with goblets of fine wine or even pale ale. Would you see to this please?"

Margaret glanced around for Dary. He knelt at the fireplace now, touching candle to flame so he could proceed to light more lamps. Soft footsteps behind her announced Crissa had returned.

"May I be of service to you, my lady?"

The girl seemed to sense when Margaret needed help. Margaret sent her off to tell Pursell to serve them the Chablis from Pontigny Abbey.

Her father had regained his former place, bending over the table.

This familiar irritable sense of exclusion more than annoyed her. Her cheeks warmed. She never knew how to contend with her anger when the men shut her out of discussions.

Anger—a shameful emotion.

Yet, she refused to be rude. Still, with God's hand, if tonight's assembly concerned her or her sisters, they *would* hear her voice.

Mary touched Margaret's arm. "Come sit."

Fatigue settled into her bones. Yet curiosity about what the men plotted kept her on her feet. Jane and Ann looked at her as if they expected some comment.

Unlike Mary and Margaret, these younger two, still in their early twenties, showed exuberance undiminished by a life of familiarity, customs, and disappointments. Ann's wide-blue eyes studied Margaret, waiting for something. Her cinnamon-blonde curls fell softly along her pale face and blushing cheeks.

She is a lovely creature.

"Margaret," Mary said, "what do you think of Ann's dress?" Mary touched one of the puffy satin sleeves tightened near the elbows with tiny dark-blue ribbons.

"You have finished it." Margaret pulled her lips in. She should have noticed, but to admire material indulgences of the day didn't often come into her mind. "Ann, the frock becomes you, as if *you* were made for *it*. The lightness of the blue matches your eyes."

Jane, larger boned, sturdily built, yet timid as a bird, leaned nearer. Her hazelnut hair caught golden light from the fire. She whispered, "We've been waiting to hear about your afternoon in Stratford."

Mary scowled and put her finger to her lips.

"Jane, in my bedroom chest I have some yardage of golden silk, which would create a stunning gown for you. You may have it." Margaret nodded toward the men. "Tell me what you know of the matter in this room."

The three sisters started whispering at once. Margaret discerned little from their murmurs. She held up her hands to quiet them and then nodded to Mary.

Mary, taller than the other two, pushed an errant dark brown curl behind her ear. Her wide, hazel eyes with long dark lashes flashed toward the men. "They discuss maps and something entailing colonization of the New World—again."

Margaret sighed. Her father's comment about "nothing new" ended her curiosity.

Pursell entered with numerous bottles of recently acquired French wine. Crissa followed, carrying a tray of engraved goblets. She set them on the wooden-inlaid table near the couches and high-back chairs surrounding the fireplace. Pursell filled each goblet, while Crissa served everyone.

Margaret slid into the crimson and copper brocaded chair by the hearth, sipped, and let the flames burn away the privation of pleasantries from this day.

"Gentlemen, let us take our ease." Her father motioned them toward the fireplace.

With drinks in hand, the men broke from their tight circle and joined the ladies, finding seats near the hearth. Lord Calvert held his wine goblet high and cleared his throat, preparing to make a toast.

"Here's to a world unexplored, the darkness of ignorance, and to the bold who dare bring us light."

Everyone, in good cheer, agreed and sipped.

"Cousin Cecil," Margaret gave him a smile to show no ill will. "Your toast reminisces of something written by our prolific late Stratford neighbor, William."

He laughed, then held his wine toward her. "They call me a learned man, but you've caught me assembling and twisting pieces of Shakespeare's works for mine own use."

Margaret considered Cousin Cecil's appearance rather mundane in that he borrowed the style of all the prominent men. He, like the other men and women of title, selected their dashing attire to impress. She suppressed a smile. Her brothers and father did no less. There must be some law requiring men and women of means to flaunt their status by the lavish costumes they elected to wear.

Cecil had wisely shunned the high-collared ruff of his father's generation in favor of the cutwork display of the current flat-linen collar. His mossy-green silk doublet, embroidered with scrolls of golden-brown and pink-rose threads, emphasized his slashed sleeves, which in turn showed his ivory silk shirt beneath.

This did make him appear powerful and intelligent. As a barrister of The Honorable Society of Grey's Inn, he embodied the concept of integrity.

Regardless, this visit could not be dismissed as social. Her distant cousin always came with a plan. Margaret fingered her goblet and guessed as to what disruptive words he would present to her father. Of course, Cecil would claim his proposal to consist of pure logic.

She could pick her younger brother Giles's spirited voice from the several conversations saying, "What a ghastly experience when I sailed with your father from Newfoundland to Jamestown a little over what? Ten years ago, at least. Not only did we battle the elements, scrounged for food and shelter, but clearly, as Catholics, were not in the least welcomed. However, for the fun of it, I would do so again."

"Quite a time." Cecil chuckled. "Father rued his Newfoundland debacle along with the travesty of showing up in the Virginia Colony. He complained about it for years to follow." Cecil nodded toward the large round table. "Remember the area I showed you—on the map north of the Virginia Colony. It holds a great deal of promise and hasn't been colonized."

And here he presents the reason for his visit—again. Bored, Margaret stared into the fire and sipped.

"Lord Baltimore," Edward spoke in his deliberate, slow manner, "you must worry about the danger in all this sailing back and forth across the Atlantic. Everyone on your father's sailing ships experienced quite a scare the year the *Dove* sailed off and separated from the *Ark*. They all thought it doomed, and then years later the ship your stepmother—forgive me." He flushed and glanced at others' reactions. "I didn't mean to be insensitive."

Edward, tall, awkward, soft spoken, and hesitant to try anything new, believed anyone foolish enough to leave their homeland would encounter death.

Cecil appeared to have responded to this half-question many times. He didn't hesitate. "No apology necessary, Edward. Your concerns are just. Only a fool would say the sea imposes no risks. My stepmother and many good people died returning to our homeland because of unfortunate events. A storm and the rocks off the coast of Ireland would cause any experienced crew concern, but some speculate the captain may have suffered an incapacitating illness, bringing on poor judgement. We're talking of two ships here, but can you count how many ships have sailed the passage without harm?"

Fulke, the eldest and shortest brother, spoke. "Cecil, I know you have an urgent purpose for coming here tonight. Your carriage and horse stand unattended outside our door, you've arrived unannounced, and all the while your manners cause you to bide your time to play the social card."

"Fulke's right." Richard said. "Please, you may dispense with the formalities, Cecil, and get on with whatever concerns you."

Cecil surveyed the faces staring back at him. He leaned forward and fondled his clean-shaven chin.

After a brief hesitation, he said, "Your family may be under the scrutiny of the king. If you've a way to hear the latest news, and you already know these things, then I hope to God you're making plans. However, I suspect living so far away you haven't heard the terribleness of it all. Since King Charles dissolved Parliament, he's ruling uncontrolled."

Richard held his hand up for Cecil to stop talking. Her father stood. "Dary, stoke the fire once more, then you may retire after you ask Pip to attend Lord Baltimore's horse and carriage." Margaret understood her father's desire to keep whatever Cecil might say within the family. She nodded to Crissa, dismissing her for the evening.

"Will you be wanting more wine, your Lord?" Pursell removed the empty bottles.

"Thank you, Pursell. Please leave the other bottles on the table."

Richard made some superfluous comments until the door shut behind the butler, house boy, and the young maid. Margaret's brothers huddled in their own conversation.

Richard scowled. "The king's eye falls on my family because Catherine, Eleanor, and Elizabeth have become nuns, a clear statement about the family's distasteful view of the Church of England. My daughters must do what's in their hearts." He sighed. "The obvious is the obvious. My sons and my attendance at church seem no longer enough to placate the crown."

Giles nodded to his brothers. "You can wager our fines won't be enough to satisfy the crown either. The Brent estates are in danger—"

Their father scoffed. "I have protected my lands from the king's sequestration. Admington and Stoke have safely been signed over to relatives."

"Father," Fulke said, "your fourteen-year lease to protect Lark Stoke ended last year."

"Ah, time, time, time." Richard shrugged. "I have other lands the king can take for his damnable two thirds."

Lord Baltimore shifted in his chair, flexing his fingers. "There's more. Your name sake Richard and his writings—it pains me to say he'll no longer be fined, but next imprisoned."

Margaret watched Cecil start to say something else—instead he took a sip of wine.

He believes prison may not be the worst of what might happen to Richard.

Cecil glanced up at Margaret. After a moment, he set his goblet down, strode over, and took Margaret's hand. Holding it gently, he stared down at her, looked at her father and brothers, then cleared his throat, probably full of words he didn't want to say.

"Dear lady, some tell me they fear for your safety." He lowered his voice. "Rumors say since the Pope banned Mary Ward's institution, you've now taken up the call and are visiting Catholics in hiding."

Richard cocked his head. "What's this you say? Mary Ward?"

Margaret's blood chilled.

If he knew the whole of it, the mathematical and Latin lessons, the reading of the actual bible instead of prayer books sanctioned for women—gathering in the homes to sew and study.

"Margaret," Cecil said, "consider your family. If certain people hear of this all your lives will be in peril. Your family, nor I, would wish to see you swing from the gallows."

Chapter 3

The lady doth protest too much....
- William Shakespeare

"LORD CALVERT." MARGARET STOOD, withdrawing her hand from his. "Your kindness in watching over our family speaks well for your character. Yet does it not speak well for a gentleman who decides to do away with playing of cards, or for a lady who sets aside talks of fashion so they, in idle times, may go out and be of service to the poor?"

He raised an eyebrow. "Then you have found an admirable avocation, helping those less fortunate."

Cecil Calvert stepped closer to the fireplace as if to warm his hands.

Margaret found the room now verged on being stuffy. Cecil's change of mood had brought an unsettling inside her. He had not accepted this explanation. She needed to restore good cheer. Her evasive response had been the cause of this awkwardness.

"Tell us, Lord Calvert," Margaret touched his arm. "King Charles seems to have put his nose in hornets' nests, even when the non-Catholic hornets of Scotland shun any hint of things papal. I would think their being of the Protestant faith and detesting all things Catholic would please him."

Edward leaned toward Margaret. "I too am surprised. The king's eradicating all practices of the Catholic religion ought to keep him otherwise engaged rather than worry about how Protestants worship."

Margaret considered this for a moment, cupped one hand in the other, and then addressed Cecil. "This Scottish act of creating a National Covenant should tighten the king's noose around all their necks. Why has the king not sent his troops to Scotland?"

"Margaret," her father said, "you can't interpret the king's inaction as a charitable move toward religious tolerance. Not sending his troops to the North has nothing to do with leniency."

Fulke, Giles, and Edward, in a tight little cluster, muffled their comments, letting a few sniggers escape. Her sisters sat wide-eyed, listening. Mary patted the empty space next to her, indicating Margaret should sit.

Shaking her head, Margaret stepped away, set her jaw, and glared at her brothers.

Cecil must have noticed because he held up a finger. Their conversation died.

"Last year," Cecil said, "King Charles unwisely forced the Scots to accept bishops into their church governance. He should have stopped there. However, emboldened by their acquiescence, he decided to implement a new prayer book—

14

without forewarning them." He paused and a sly grin escaped. "A woman, when she read the prayer book that morning in St. Giles church in Edinburgh, stood up and flung her stool. Her fury started quite a riot. It's no wonder the Scots wish to enact a covenant demanding complete rejection of interference within their religious doctrines."

"Pfft." Margaret smirked. "I should fling a stool at the gentlemen in this household."

Cecil pulled back and stared down his nose at her.

"My brothers choose to keep all public knowledge private from their sisters. Perhaps they should consider ladies also desire to know of our king's intentions regarding recalcitrant neighbors. They forget whatever happens, especially war, casts burdens on us all."

'Tis often the women alone at home who are left to bear the weights resulting from their gentlemen's disagreements.

She seethed inside, feeling the fool.

Her father sighed. "It's not a secret, Margaret. The only reason no blood has been spilled is because King Charles no longer has funds to finance a war."

"I ask one more question then." Margaret nodded to her sisters and smoothed her skirt before sitting. "These past years, King Charles has been rather lenient in regard to those who embrace Catholicism, not unlike his father. By the heavens above, his queen is even Catholic. Whatever has changed this mood?"

Giles popped up. "Consarn it! He's angry because his realm lacks money."

"Well, what would you expect, Giles?" Fulke joined in. "His actions set everyone's innards in an uproar, too."

"That's because he has banned Parliament." Edward's voice drowned out the others. "With no Parliament, this king can do anything his royal posterior pleases."

"He certainly *must* do something," Giles said. "The masses believe he's betrayed them and demand he take action."

"Against the Scots or the Catholics?" Edward voice rose to match his brothers.

Fulke scowled. "We Catholics, naturally. It's the least expensive and simplest way to appease the citizens."

Margaret shook her head. "King Charles's unproductive reign, brought about by his abolition of Parliament and by instilling his own personal rule unsettles us all. Most worrisome, I agree. It stirs even his own ire."

Edward shrugged. "When history records this time, what will her words be?" He nodded to the men. "Perhaps the world will say it is good our great country experiences financial ruin because it hinders the cruelties of war."

Fulke scoffed. "Think again, brother. If attacked, the problems of insufficient funds prevent our defense."

"You watch," Giles said, "King Charles will reinstate Parliament, obtain the necessary funds, and then declare war on the Scots."

"Or he'll declare war," Fulke said, "without Parliament, by using whatever funds he can raise. Look at the taxes he's placed on the shipping ports."

"Please stop." Ann stood, her chin quivering. "Why do you all argue?"

The only sound in the room came from the crackle and pop of the fire.

Richard stared at his young daughter. Margaret suspected this might be one of the few times he bothered to actually see this intelligent and sensitive young woman. Then he caught Mary's eye.

"Would you be a dear and pour more wine?"

"Cecil," Fulke said, "your warning to us is duly noted, but I suspect you have a greater reason for riding here so late in the day."

"I pledged to the first Lord Baltimore I would keep a watchful eye over the fine family of Brent. Our prisons run full, the executioners stay busy, and tensions run high because their official spies report on those who act against the realm."

Uncomfortable with her own falseness, Margaret wanted him to get to the point. But she held her words.

Cecil strode about the room. "Richard, you and your family have to prepare for what lies ahead. Those who watch you, even if they tell lies, put you and your children at risk. Don't let complacency lead you to believe you can decide later." He stood eye to eye with her father. "The hourglass has run its course, dear friend."

Fulke and Edward exchanged looks. Margaret's sisters remained silent.

Her father set his goblet down. "If we've run out of time, then what might you suggest?"

Margaret knew. Lord Calvert's map told his story.

I shall not go to some foreign country to hide from our King.

"Ships sail every month or so to the New World. Maryland colonists enjoy freedoms, thanks to my father's dreams, and King James. The first Lord Baltimore strived to create a place free from religious persecution. All those who sail to the shores of Maryland, who transport adequate servants, will be granted land ownership, the right to help govern, and to worship in whatever manner they please."

Margaret shook her head. "Sir Cecil, this I cannot believe. Are you saying even a Catholic, might be granted—"

"There's more. For everyone in this family who goes and for every servant you take, you will be granted a generous portion of land." He looked over at Margaret and her sisters. "This means you all can be landowners."

All? Not just the eldest son?

Jane murmured something to Ann. Mary responded, but Margaret didn't understand their words.

Their cousin now addressed the men. "I've spoken of colonization before. You've listened politely, but your loyalties remain with your king and England. I understand, as do mine."

"Then you've no need to speak more of this." Edward said.

"But I do." Cecil narrowed his eyes.

Richard said, "You forgot something rather important, my friend."

Cecil hesitated.

"You must consider the king's act that restrains the popishly bred from going beyond the seas and the punishments for those who assist."

Giles looked up from the map. "Popish—the hell. King Charles can't even bring himself to say Catholic."

"Silly. Everyone but those of us who are says 'popish.'" Margaret now waited for her father to reprimand her, but he said nothing.

"A serious point, my friend. Dangerous times, indeed," said Cecil. "King

Charles's wrath increases and will come down on those who refuse to conform to the Church of England."

Fulke shut his eyes a moment before saying, "You're a kind gentleman, sir. But if you pursue this, you will certainly lose everything you and your father have acquired. Even your mentioning this to us puts you in jeopardy."

"Every second of every day puts us all in jeopardy. Today and the weeks forward, your family may suffer destruction beyond your imagination." He took several paces then stopped and studied each of the men. "Please, friends, decide to take my offer. It takes time and special negotiations to arrange a safe passage for you. Remember, a most disagreeable mood has overtaken England concerning passengers who refuse to take the oath of allegiance and acknowledge the king's supremacy. We need to be clever so as not to be entrapped."

A tap on the door stopped the conversation. Mary glanced at her father, then rose, and opened it.

Pursell stood waiting to be acknowledged.

"Yes?" said Richard.

"Sir, supper will be served within the hour, and also there's a man at the back door. He's asked to speak with you."

"Cecil, good friend, will you join us in a late supper?"

"It's past time for me to be on my way to Ilmington, and I admit to a midday indulgence of an unusually large dinner. Please consider what we've discussed, and we'll talk again—say shortly after the next Sabbath? I'll send word where we may engage in a private meeting."

"Pursell," Richard said, "have Dary see Lord Calvert's carriage and horse are brought forth."

Lord Calvert strode to the table and arranged a few papers. Then he placed with great care what must have been his cherished map on top. He slid the stack into a burgundy, embossed leather folio. He gathered his cape and hat and in good cheer, bowed his farewell.

They called goodbyes and wished safe travels to their cousin as he strode out the door to wait for his carriage.

Her father squinted at Pursell. "Tell me, what brings this fellow to our door at this hour?"

"He says his name is John Coates, sir. It seems a young girl saw Lady Margaret talking with his son earlier this afternoon. His son has gone missing, and the sheriff found a dead man."

Chapter 4

God is thy law, thou mine.
- John Milton

RICHARD SCOWLED, TAKING MARGARET by the elbow. "What do you know about this Coates boy's disappearance?"

"Heavens Father, any number of events could befall him." She shrugged and muttered, "Maybe a snake struck him dead."

Richard glared at her a moment, then moved on, making his way through the shadowy passage to the back staircase. Margaret followed him down winding stairs to the large stone-floor kitchen.

"If you saw the boy, you need to tell his father all you know."

They skirted around the square table with the marble top. Something, smelling of onions and brown gravy simmered in a kettle over the fireplace. When they entered the area with the long wooden table three servants stood. Her father nodded to Thomas Gedd to open the back door.

John Coates stood outside, his cap in his hand.

"Coates, please step inside." Richard motioned toward the table.

"Kind of you, Lord Brent, but I must find my boy. His mum and I feel sick with worry."

"Margaret, what can you tell John Coates?"

She told him what she knew. Though tall, this man appeared meek. The town's women said the sharp tongue of this man's wife could terrorize a rabid dog, causing it to turn tail and run.

When Margaret ended her story about Ellie and the snake, Coates pursed his lips.

"Would you mind, sir, if I looked in your outbuildings? Someone killed a man from Stratford. They wacked him over the head up in the woods near that little chapel. Stole his belongings. Peter may be hiding, afeared someone might do the same to him."

Dear God—did someone murder William Keith?

"Take your time, Coates. Gedd, take a lantern and give assist. We wish you well."

He mumbled about having supper at such a late hour. With her heart racing, Margaret let him usher her up the darkened stairs.

* * *

Midmorning several days later, Margaret set her book of Milton's poetry aside as Giles and Fulke ambled across the verdant lawn. She appreciated this

18

quiet time to read, sitting here in the sugary air under their vine-covered arbor. Brothers indulging sisters in conversation amused her. They probably came to speak about their father's private meeting with the second Lord Baltimore.

Nonsense.

They would not enlighten her about any such discussions unless she asked directly.

"Good morning, Margaret." Fulke touched his finger to the cover of her book, then scoffed.

"Milton writes well." She tilted her chin up to meet his eyes.

He took the book and thumbed through it.

"Only if you can stomach his views on religion. However, you have selected a pleasant place to do your reading." He didn't return her book but sat next to her.

She watched an ant struggle to transport a translucent wing, probably torn from some nearby dead dragonfly. Margaret couldn't see its little mound of soil called home. Consigning herself to the nature of survival, she looked up at her oldest brother.

"Milton's Catholic grandfather," Margaret felt obliged to explain, "disinherited Milton's Protestant father. I fear the son, this poet, may find himself locked in the king's tower because of his outspoken eccentricity. He has written his meanings, which verge on rebelliousness, under a much too thin cloak." She studied her brother's expression, but he gazed off into the meadow as if not listening. Margaret deliberately cleared her throat. "I find wisdom in understanding how others contemplate decisions with which I disagree. You might find this useful, Fulke."

Giles snorted and slid down on the bench across from them. Fulke gave Giles the side eye.

Margaret folded her hands in her lap.

Giles scuffed his foot. "Guess I need to be the one. Have you given thought to what our cousin asked of us when he visited our home?"

She bristled.

Our family's world would change because of Lord Baltimore.

"I see no reason for me to leave England."

The brothers glanced at each other, telling Margaret she must have been a topic of some unpleasant discussion.

"May I have my book? I shall leave now."

Fulke stopped on a page in her book, as if studying it. "The man who came to the backdoor the night Cousin Cecil—"

Margaret stood, causing her brothers to stand.

"John Coates." Giles said, "He seemed to know much about what you do when you make your visits," he smirked, saying, "to *assist* the poor."

Her spine stiffened. She stared at each of them.

Fulke motioned to where she had sat. "You tell us. We shouldn't have to take what a stranger says as a truth."

"I am sure this is no one's business but my own."

Fulke looked at Giles, then rubbed his jaw. "What you're doing is our business, because others know your secret."

She continued to stand, holding stone still except for the pounding of her heart. *Could they hear it?*

"Margaret," Fulke said, "the Coates man, desperate to find his son, talked to Keith's son whose father had been bludgeoned to death the evening Peter Coates went missing. Young Keith, beside himself with grief, also worried over the disappearance of his father's donkey, and wondered if you had crowned his father. He said his father, earlier in an ill mood, had ridden off on the donkey. He announced he'd 'teach that spinster a good lesson.' Young Keith told Coates he thought the spinster might be you because you had called on his mother and other women earlier that day in Stratford."

"William Keith." She sighed.

"Cecil fears you shall be accused." Giles frowned. "Another problem. Whoever clobbered William Keith must have stolen his donkey. Without the donkey to transport their wares, the Keith family has no livelihood."

"Pfft. Tell Cecil I have no connection to this. I wished the man no ill will." Margaret took her book. "I'm surprised the donkey has not returned home by now. He is a sweet, clever little animal."

Fulke touched her arm. "I don't know the man, but if the donkey hasn't returned by now, it's crippled, confined, or dead. You haven't answered our question."

"No matter, Fulke. She verifies what they say about her by not saying anything. Where does that put us?"

"In the middle of nowhere. Our dear sisters' devotion to women's ecclesiastical and educational studies has put our household in danger. Now we'll all be under scrutiny." Fulke paced a few steps away, then came back. "Latin and mathematics—Father argued with Mother. He didn't want you participating in our lessons from Father Clark when we were young."

Margaret shrugged.

Fulke squinted. "He worried your lessons would somehow become a problem, and now they have. Where in the Lord's name did you learn Latin?"

"Why would you bother?" Giles screwed up his face. "It's difficult enough for us. Fulke and I refuse to believe you find these studies of any great interest. If you're bored with sewing and practicing your music, you could learn the art of painting or busy yourself with games."

Margaret examined a spotted caterpillar making its way across a leaf, and in a soft voice said, "Perhaps you could understand if you had been denied the opportunity to learn from your tutors or, when older, denied attending your private schools. Father even refused Mary and me enrollment in one of Strafford's Dame schools."

"Dame schools." Giles scowled. "Not much more than care homes for children. You learned to read and write. That's quite sufficient."

Fulke held up his hand to quiet Giles. "Even though father rejects Lord Baltimore's offer, Margaret, you need to know what Cecil proposes."

"If father regards any proposition offered by our cousin as unworthy, then it is of no interest to me." She turned to leave. This conversation tired her.

"Don't be so sure, dear sister." Fulke raised his voice. "Knowing you as I do, this might be something much more enticing to you than painting or elevating the religious and academic education of other women."

Giles face brightened, the sunlight catching his blue eyes. "Cecil's on a mission to populate his province of Maryland. I've seen its fertile lands, and he's right about it being perfect for crops. Those who venture there will achieve wealth beyond belief."

"Wealth, as in the Jamestown disappointment?" She scoffed.

"Wealth from furs, crops, and large holdings of land." Giles said.

Margaret sat and shook her head. She shuddered to think of the carpenters, blacksmiths, saws, nails, lumber, and livestock, carrying the burdens needed to tame wild, forested land. Then a worse image came to her. One of starving villagers, staring at desolate furrows of dirt ridges holding dried up sprouts of wheat.

She sighed. "Your mind fills too quickly with the dreams of others, Giles. Even Fulke will agree with me on this. Think of the plight that befell Jamestown, and you experienced it with your own misery, if only for a few days. Now you are ready to tag along, chasing after Cecil Calvert's grand scheme."

"Settlers of Jamestown erred by not planting bearable crops. Those first comers, lured by promises of gold and silver, only found raw land and wild game. They were fools. Nothing existed except forest, streams, and the ocean—certainly not riches of valuable metals. Even if they had found any, they couldn't eat the metals or even use it to purchase bread. Dupes, all of them."

Fulke sat next to her. "Maryland provides a different experience. In the township of St. Mary's, one probably can purchase goods from merchants. Settlers have been living, worshiping, and working there for several years. Listen. Lord Baltimore's father devised a grand vision, and King James and now King Charles have sanctioned it. What astonishes me is since George Calvert's passing, King Charles continues to honor their agreement. The first Lord Baltimore's plan now rests in the hands of Cecil."

"More like, it rests on his head." Margaret smirked.

Giles grinned at Margaret. "Imagine the pressure Cousin Cecil endures to make his father's grand design work. No small wonder he's eager to populate his new country with men of substantial means who will be competent leaders, landowners, and wealthy enough to pay the passages of others."

Margaret held her lips tight and listened. When her brothers finished, she said, "Cecil spoke of this when he visited. Land, religious freedom, the hardships of the Atlantic crossing. Nothing new or of interest for me. Go on—scurry off and play in your New World. I will enjoy my comforts here in England."

"Clear enough but listen." Fulke said, "If we go as a family and take our servants, we'll be given patents for large tracts of land—ours to own. Protestants and Catholics will each have their churches, and no matter what the religion, all can be a part of the politics of this province."

"Clear enough is right." Margaret huffed. "I now understand why you will haggle us until the last tomorrow. You need the family's support of increased numbers of people to build your own expansive estates. Again, I am not interested. Your talk bores me."

She smoothed her skirt, stood, and clutched her book to her breast. Fulke rose and faced her.

"We may not be as stimulating as your book of Protestant poetry, but you must care about not bringing our family to harm with your behaviors." He stared into her eyes. "Lord Baltimore knows this. He worries about your safety. He needs educated families of substantial means to help him populate his Maryland." Fulke gave her shoulder the gentlest of touch. "Cecil said he will arrange transportation if we each pay the passages of at least five men servants during our first year. Then he will grant us large acreages of land, enough to grow sizable fields of crops."

Giles stood too. "It's called the headright system. These men work for us until they've repaid the price of their passage. The size of our land is based on the number of people we bring."

Her eldest brother then took her hand. "He specifically mentioned if you, Margaret, decided to settle there, you would receive a generous parcel of land in or around St. Mary's next to ours. If you or our other sisters decide to cross and settle there and each take at least five men servants during the first year, patents will be granted in *your* names. Margaret, you may worship as you please there, but more profound, you, even as a woman, will be permitted to own land."

Her heart quickened. She let the meaning of these words soak through her skin and into her soul.

Owning large tracts of soil beneath my feet—being a landowner would bring authority to my voice as it has for men. Na. They jest. This would never be.

Chapter 5

I did not know the ample bread 'twas so unlike the crumb....
- Emily Dickinson

MARGARET FOUND THE STABLE comforting. The softness of fresh straw on the floor, the animals munching their oats, and hay in their wooden feed troughs tickled the air with the scent of mowed fields and the sounds of slobbery contentment.

"You must promise to follow my instructions exactly," Margaret said to the houseboy.

Dary chewed his lip.

Margaret frowned. "There's no shame in your returning without making this agreement with young Keith. In fact, I expect you to do so if he does not consent. If that happens, I will be furious if you don't refuse him."

The houseboy glanced over at Pip who had almost finished grooming Sprite. Little Sprite stretched his neck forward for more vigorous brushing behind his ear. This young donkey seemed a gentle soul, eager to please. Dary squinted back at Margaret and rubbed his arm.

"Dary, you are worried because you are unclear as to what I ask. Go on. Tell me what it is I want you to do."

He shuffled his feet, took a deep breath, then answered, "I am to take Sprite to Stratford to the son of William Keith. He lives with his mother and four siblings in the third wooden house on the road behind the smithy."

Margaret nodded approval.

"I am to tell him I want to sell him the donkey to replace the one stolen from his deceased father. When he says he can't afford it, I tell him he can." Dary grinned, as if pleased with his memory. He scratched the side of his nose and continued. "Young Keith is to make his sign on the bottom of this paper if he agrees."

"And what agreement is he to make?"

"What it says here." Dary unfolded the paper. With a distinct voice sounding full of pride, he read, "For purchase of one donkey named Sprite of the Brent estate..." He glanced at Margaret. She nodded. He continued, "Young Keith gives as payment his father's leather whip, or if it is not available then something of equal value, along with his good word to never flay nor harm the donkey for as long as he owns said donkey."

"What if he does not agree?"

"If he does not trade his father's whip or anything of like kind and do also give his word, then I am to bring the paper and donkey back."

"You read well, young Dary. You are the right person to be selected for this mission." The boy's future held more than being a houseboy. "If you obtain the whip and his word, what are you to tell young Keith before he puts his mark on this paper?"

"With the making of his mark on the paper this agreement becomes binding. If any of the Brents hear of his mistreatment of this donkey, it will mean young Keith has broken the agreement. The donkey will be confiscated and returned to the Brents."

"Your mother must be quite proud of you."

Pip led the saddled blue roan over to them. After Dary mounted the large horse, Pip handed him the rope that dangled from Sprite's halter.

"Dary, understand what is happening here, and Pip, please continue to listen. This information will serve you well as you grow older." She checked to be certain they attended to her words. "Never take away a person's dignity. William Keith's death leaves his family with no income. His son knows no way to support the family except by following in his father's trade. Yet he cannot transport goods to market unless he has a donkey. Even though someone stole his father's donkey, if anyone tried to give young Keith one, he would reject it. They are a proud, hard-working family. They would be humiliated if anyone considered them to be poor."

They both kept their eyes fastened on her. She smiled at them.

"If you give a near stranger something they will think you pity them, or they will start to expect others to take care of them, or they won't find much worth in the item. However, if they must give up something they value, like money, a prized leather whip, or promise some oath for what you're offering them, then the object increases in value. Unfortunately, Dary, young Keith does not have to keep this oath I ask of him. We cannot enforce it. This must be our secret. Swear to me you will not tell him."

"I swear." Dary grinned and nodded.

"Off with you, then. If all goes well, leave the halter and rope with young Keith. We shall see you one way or another before nightfall. Safe travels."

Margaret watched the lad plod down the lane past the flowering honeysuckle to the main road.

"Where's Dary going with the new donkey?" Fulke had come up behind her.

"To right a wrong, help mend ill ways, and feed five children."

"Father expects us all in the drawing room, thus I don't have time to figure out this word puzzle. Yet, I am curious. Will we ever see our donkey again?"

"I find it difficult to say." Margaret grinned and looked away.

"Margaret, Margaret, you're such a conundrum. I never know what to expect from you."

"Thank you for the compliment."

Fulke stopped. "Tell me about the donkey, please. If you're giving it away—it isn't yours to give."

"If Dary does not return with Sprite, then consider the deed being in the interest of the Brent family." She began to pick the straw off the bottom of her petticoat.

"You better hurry and not keep father waiting." Fulke strode away, shaking his head.

* * *

Margaret tagged a little behind Fulke, continuing to brush straw off her skirt, and plucking at her sleeves for more errant blades. She saw no reason to rush and would incur her father's wrath soon enough. Margaret adored Fulke for his caring ways, but she knew he would not keep this little endeavor private. She strolled past the garden well and ducked under the low willow tree. Fulke stood at the entrance waiting.

He held the door for her and nodded down the hallway toward the parlor.

"I see no carriage nearby. Our cousin must not be joining us today." Her stomach knotted. No visitors meant her father must have summoned them for something serious.

Please, Dear Lord, our absent brothers and sisters—stay them from harm.

She and Fulke entered the parlor. Margaret's sisters sat near the cold hearth. Her two other brothers stood by the windows, talking with her father. He left Edward and Giles and came to greet her.

"Hello, Margaret. Where is Dary? Someone said they saw him in the stables with you and Pip. When I sent Gedd to fetch him, he reported Dary was nowhere around."

"He should be back by nightfall, Father." She needed to praise Pip for his quiet discretion. "I sent him on an errand."

Fulke interrupted, "With your new donkey, Father. I fear my dear sister is giving away your livestock."

Margaret bowed her head. Every part of her heated with anger, but she stood as cold as a statue waiting for the admonition. Her brothers and sisters stopped their chatting. She could hear her father's heavy breathing. One of her sister's skirts whispered a slight rustle.

Richard cleared his throat. "Margaret, why is it whenever we need to consider something important, you stir the pot with some outrageous doings of yours? Now you've sent Dary off on one of your eccentric missions—riding my new donkey."

"He is not riding him, Father. Dary is riding the roan and leading the donkey." Margaret sighed.

Giles snapped around and glared at her. "Why the slippery hell is he riding my horse?"

"Because Gingo is too much for him." Margaret stared back. "He would be on the ground in minutes."

Murmurs and sniggers started up.

"Oh stop, Giles. Be a little charitable. Your roan will be fine."

Her father signaled everyone to be quiet. "Margaret, what is it you've sent Dary off to do?"

She told them how William Keith beat his donkey with his whip. How the family now had no way to support themselves with their father and donkey both gone. She mentioned the contract she drew up for William Keith's son. If he agreed, then he would make his mark. With the donkey, he could support his mother and his siblings and take his rightful place as head of their family.

When she finished, Fulke said, "Margaret told me these actions furthered the interests of the Brent family."

"How could this be of any interest," her father asked, "except for the Keith family?"

"William Keith would not have been in the woods waiting for me if he had not been so irate about my meeting with his wife. He was angry with me, and I fear he was not keeping quiet about why. If young Keith accepts my terms for the donkey and can start earning a living, he may feel kindlier toward us."

"If we become his benefactor, she believes he'll not talk about the Lady Brent." Fulke cocked his head and studied her.

"No matter." Richard squeezed Fulke's shoulder. "She's bargained with something that is not hers to sell. If Dary does not return with the donkey, then you must repay me."

Margaret smirked. "Father, you really don't expect me to pay you for an animal like Sprite."

"Sprite?"

"Your donkey."

"Donkey—livestock—next you'll be naming the damnable chickens."

Her sisters giggled. Jane and Ann had already named the hens and rooster.

Richard knocked on the wooden table nearest him, shushing them.

"If the donkey is not returned, then consider Gingo to be your payment."

Margaret caught her breath. She had raised Gingo as a colt. She could never give him up.

Before she could utter her protest, she caught the softening of her father's face, which put a twinkle in his eyes.

"Next time, please remember this encounter before you give away someone's property."

"I shall. Thank you, Father." She managed a conciliatory grin.

"My daughter, we all have taken you too lightly." He then addressed the rest of the family. "I asked you to meet this afternoon because, even though we have peace and quiet here on our estates, we can't ignore the strife and chaos overtaking England."

Margaret raised a finger for acknowledgement. "When Cecil Calvert visited us, we discussed this at length. Even after a private meeting with him, you clearly decided to ignore his warnings. Why should we not follow your example?"

"Each moment becomes more dangerous. Montague, with his publications and his intimate counsel with our king, incenses not only commoners but also nobility." Richard continued, "I fear Montague's influence grows each day since he's become the Bishop of Norwich."

"Wait, Father." Fulke stepped nearer. "What would you have to say about William Laud? As The Archbishop of Canterbury, he espouses the most contentious of all theocracies. I hear people arguing about Laudianism. Now the strife over promoting free will as opposed to Calvinism's predestination upsets all the Protestants."

"What in God's name," Margaret announced with her hands on her hips, "does this have to do with us?"

Giles ignored her, saying, "There's civil unrest in the ale houses and on the docks—or wherever I go. Three days ago, two fishwives, yelling about free will and predestation, engaged in a tussle and one chucked the other into the River Severn."

"What do you expect, Fulke?" Edward joined the conversation. "An autocrat like William Laud as the Church of England's highest authority can't expect submission when he stuffs his radical Laudianism views down the gullets of Puritans and Calvinists."

Margaret gave an audible huff. "Edward, he has banned Calvinism. So, it no longer exists." Her remark stopped their arguing. This bickering made her tired. "Father, why should we care if the Protestants fight among themselves? This Protestant infighting, how can it be such a serious force of contention that it sends Catholics fleeing across the sea?"

"William Laud insists on celebrating the High-Church style, which mimics the reason for the Scots rebelling against King Charles. Many English citizens, especially the Puritans, are furious at Laud's embracing anything that appears to be ceremonial and borrowed from Catholicism. Their hatred of Laud only intensifies their associated hatred of us as each hour passes."

Edward drew his finger across his neck. "The archbishop needs to sleep with one eye open." Her brothers chuckled and added their ideas to Edward's plots of treachery.

A sharp rap on the table again quieted the siblings. Richard paused until he had everyone's attention.

"Sadly, as the second Lord Baltimore said on his last visit, 'our hourglass is running out.' Be assured, each of you, when we retire for the night, we shall know who will make the voyage to help settle the Province of Maryland, and who will take their chances and remain behind in our beloved England. We'll take our supper here and not leave this room until I have recorded each of your choices."

Oh, Dear Lord, some of us will sail far across that treacherous sea never to be seen again. Please let your countenance shine on us in this hour of indecision.

Young Jane brushed down her ruffled sleeves and stood. While smoothing her skirt over her substantial frame, she said, "Father, please tell, what decision will you choose for me?"

Margaret reached for Jane's hand. She would need to explain this life-changing situation to the naïve young woman.

Dear young Jane, we must never let others take over our choices.

Chapter 6

O Captain! My Captain! our fearful trip is done,
The ship has weathered every rack, the prize we sought has won....
- Walt Whitman

THEIR FATHER RANG THE bell for the butler. He glanced around the room and strode to the door to intercept Pursell.

Mary leaned close to Margaret and murmured, "What do you think about us spending countless days crowded in some sweat-smelly ship and tossed around in turbulent waves? I know I shall be plenty tired of eating stinking, uncooked fish. We will probably be expected to catch and prepare the poor slippery things, too."

Lowering her head, letting these unpleasant images soak in, she didn't doubt the accuracy of her sister's voyage assessment. Margaret would prefer the plague to fishing.

Mary examined everything with a critical eye—always questioned the underlying nature of a problem—unlike Jane who relied on others to tell her what she needed to know.

Their brothers were huddled in a conference near the bookcases.

"Look at Fulke," Mary continued. "He reminds me of a pompous raven—dark, always fluffing his ragged feathers, and commanding attention to whatever he croaks about."

Mary's perceptions amuse me.

Clearly, Fulke did dominate the ongoing animated discussion, with Giles interrupting.

"What do you think we should do?" Ann spoke. Ann, a hesitant, fair young woman, would explore and question, backtrack, and then full of doubt present her answer.

"Let's wait and see what's offered." Margaret stopped talking to hear what her father was saying to Pursell, who now stood in the doorway.

"If young Dary hasn't returned by dusk, send someone to light the lamps. Also, tell the cook we'll be having a light supper at seven o'clock here in the parlor. In the meantime, bring us tankards of that exceptionally fine pale ale William discovered in Gloucester."

Fulke strode to the round walnut table. "Let's sit over here and sort out our future. Is this agreeable with you, Father?" Unlike Fulke, Mary's labeling of the men didn't seem to extend to her father, and Margaret didn't see a need for him to have one. A determined man with a once rugged face now turned rumpled, Richard always took the practical path. However, today, he appeared exhausted.

The ridges and valleys in his face sagged. He no longer had his wife by his side to keep his spirits bolstered.

Our parents have created a strong family, but father knows within some near future morrow it will be ripped apart.

At this her thoughts, unbidden, turned to John Donne's "The Good-Morrow." The poet of love wrote of sea travel to other worlds, and maps, and one world— she sighed. Still, she had no idea what choices her sisters would select. With their love for their father, if he did not go, no one cared to leave him.

Cockles and berries, Margaret would never leave him.

With some mumbling and shuffling the men found their places at the large round table. Giles beckoned to the sisters. "Ladies, you're to join us. Come sit next to me, Margaret."

His invitation to sit next to him surprised her. Giles never gave anything much thought except what would serve his immediate need. She did as he bid. Lean, thin faced, hair dark, but not as black as Fulke's, he stood almost as tall as Edward. People remembered Giles less for his striking features than for his winsome personality, overly effervescent. The ladies all had eyes for his charm.

Fulke, as did Margaret, thought about everything from all angles. Then he would come to some conclusion. Edward, the tall, angular, and blond, would listen to everyone, then would let the worst possible of outcomes guide his decisions. Giles made it difficult to take him seriously with his unpredictable actions.

When the ladies selected where they wanted to sit and seemed settled, Richard gathered his writing tray of quills, inkwell, and paper. He placed them on the table, sat, cleared his throat, and dipped his quill into the inkwell.

With quill poised, he said, "Once we decide who is going and who isn't, we must list personal items for each traveler to take to the New World. Thankfully, Cecil has given me a general accounting of what voyagers will need after landing across the sea. You, my children, because of being indulged in every convenience of your desire, will quickly learn the value of common objects in which you've never given thought. Now then, who will help settle the Province of Maryland, and who will be staying?"

Cocking her head, Mary said, "Besides soap and candles, what common objects, Father?"

"Your axe will become one of your most valued possessions."

After his remark, the parlor held no sound except what Margaret could hear through the open windows. A bird trilled for its mate, or maybe for the joy of the afternoon. A hint of fragrance from the honeysuckle recalled the sound and images of bees seeking their sweet nectar. A lamb bleated, probably for its mother, over on the far hillside.

Her father waited, cleared his throat again, and finally set the quill down.

In turn, everyone except her and Fulke cast their glazes to the tabletop. Some shifted in their chairs. Margaret held still, watching them.

"Fine." Fulke scanned the faces of the family and settled on his father's. "Father, it seems you need to lead us. Are you going or staying?"

Richard shook his head. "I answer last. I don't want to influence anyone's decision."

"Then I'll start." Fulke drummed his fingers on the table, slapped it, and stood. He marched to the window and stared out. "I love this place. Those graceful weeping willows, the verdant hills where our sheep graze, the stream where I caught my first fish—to leave this, to never see it again—"

Richard picked up his quill. "So, it sounds like Fulke stays."

"I haven't made up my mind. England flows through my soul, but from what I know about the Province of Maryland, we have an opportunity for not only prosperity, but to experience a great adventure. Lord Baltimore's vision of what life could be, of the harmony between people, religion, and politics..."

"And you've never seen a native up close." Giles grinned. "The Indians we encountered in Virginia—I swear you could never imagine."

"Father," Jane said, "I've heard natives eat people, so I don't care to meet any." With her chin up, she tucked a long brown curl behind an ear. Her brothers took little pain to hide their chuckles.

"You've no need to worry little sister." Edward ruffled the top of Jane's head. She swatted at his hand, smoothing her hair back into place. He added, "They'd never eat anything as pretty as you."

Richard sighed and made a notation. "One undecided. Edward, what about you?"

"And one not going." Jane crossed her arms. "I'm sure you heard me, Father. I just told you. I'm not going because I don't care to be eaten by some savage."

Richard set his quill down. "Jane, I don't expect any of you girls to go unless you're under the protection of your brothers. As of yet, none have agreed to make the crossing. Let's see what Edward says."

"What?" Margaret felt a wave of heat. She needed no protection.

"We haven't heard from Edward yet. Go on, Edward."

Must everything I do be anchored down by my father or brothers? She sat back and crossed her arms like Jane.

"No, no—not one bit of interest in seeing new worlds." Edward motioned for his father to write down his response. "Jane, no need to fear being eaten, but the crossing could cause everyone to get sick and drown, and once we get there, we would all starve. Many of them did just that when they landed in Jamestown. I prefer my comfortable bed and my food prepared by a cook, not me cooking alone over some fire in the wilds of the woods with bears breathing down my neck."

"Father," Ann said, "I agree with Edward. I suspect those who go, man or woman, will be required to do the work our servants now do. I cannot see myself with axe chopping wood, not because I think I'm too precious for this work, but because I really have no strength or mind for such matters."

"Yet, Ann," Mary said, "your quiet fortitude and unwavering determination would be useful for any new settlement. I suspect you could hire someone to do the more laborious tasks."

Margaret nodded in agreement. "Since a toddler, you have followed the servants on their heels, studying whatever they do. You tend a vegetable garden better than any of us; your cleverness in the kitchen brings many delights to our meals; and look at the lovely dresses you design and sew. All these are skills any settler would be well to have."

"To tell the truth," Ann glanced around before continuing, "the passage across the ocean terrifies me, and I have no temperance for tending to strangers who are ill. Everything about this adventure unsettles me. Mayhaps, if we knew of kind hearts who lived over there and would keep our company, then my lack of willingness would change."

Richard regarded her for a moment. "I suppose our distant cousin, Leonard Calvert would not be enough in the way of compassionate company to encourage your making the trip."

"Have any of you met the governor?" When no one responded, Ann crossed her arms. "I am certain any governor, relative or not, would be far too busy to keep me company."

Richard mumbled something as he made a mark next to Ann's name.

Fulke left the window and reclaimed his place at the table. "Edward, you heard Cecil. Settlers have been in Maryland for four years now. They've built churches, mills, homes and maybe a few stores. Trade ships along with settlers sail in and out all the time. It's not like you'll be unprotected out in the woods."

"Not going. Final word from me." Edward sat back and crossed his arms too.

Margaret uncrossed her arms and leaned forward. "Fulke, when you disturbed my reading a while back, you said Cecil vowed to give anyone, including me, large tracts of land. Is this the truth?"

"Except for one point. Those who agree to go and desire Cecil's offered land patents must also pay the passages for at least five men. Only then will they receive a patent for a tract of land large enough to grow a reputable crop of tobacco."

"He made a similar offer to the settlers four years ago, did he not?" Margaret waited for his response.

"He did. That offer may have been more generous, but still—"

"Father, mark me down as a voyager. If I receive the same offer Lord Baltimore made to his first settlers, I shall be quite willing to leave England for the gain of being a landowner."

Richard shoved his chair back and stood, glaring at her. "You heard what I told your sister. None of you will be making this voyage unless accompanied by your brothers."

Margaret set her jaw, sat back, and once again crossed her arms.

"You're too old to be insolent." Richard pulled his chair back up to the table. "It's a matter of safety."

Her insides roiled. She should have expected this. Margaret jumped up and leaned her palms heavily on the table. "By God's name, if Cecil Calvert accepts the rights of women to own land and to work it, then your stubborn ways are of the past. I need no brother to keep me safe. Edward will attest to my straight shot. My aim brings home more pigeons and ducks than the rest of you." Her glance swept around the table. "Only a fool would attempt to cause me grief."

With a knock on the door, Pursell entered with Crissa. She set tankards at each place, and he poured the ale. Before leaving, Pursell said, "I understand young Dary is helping Pip brush down the roan. When he finishes, he'll be up to light the lamps. Your supper will be brought in shortly. Will that be all, Sir?"

Chapter 7

...they [are] not called to live in [a monastery] which they can devote themselves only to themselves; but [these women must be self-governed without interference and dressed in ordinary clothes]... prepare themselves to undertake any labour whatever in the [educational] instruction of virgins and young girls.
- Mary Ward (1585-1645)

THE DONKEY BUSINESS, CECIL'S vow of abundant land, her conflict with her father... what unease.

Margaret stared at the ornate ceiling, savoring the robustness of the crisp ale. She filled her mouth again, allowing the sweetness to soften the sharp points of their conversations. She held the liquid there, shut her eyes, and cleared her mind from sibling chatter.

"My turn." Giles exuberant voice intruded into her moment. "You all can guess what my answer is. Ah yes—the sea calls to me—along with the fertile lands of Maryland. I can't wait to squish her rich soil between my fingers and toes. You've never seen anything like it. Rugged and beautiful, the forests and wildlife and resources abound. The next time you see me I'll be one of the wealthiest and most respected men you know."

"Father, mark me going with Margaret." Mary's voice came strong, clear, and determined as if it settled any doubt he may have had about women, land ownership, and sailing into dangerous territories.

Margaret sat straighter, catching Mary's gaze, and her sister returned a nod.

Richard sighed, put his quill down, and took a long sip of ale. The silence of the room surrounded them. Somewhere, far off, a dog barked. Someone knocked on the parlor door.

"Enter," Richard grumbled.

Dary stuck his head in, assessed the situation, trotted directly over to Margaret and handed her the signed contract. He then began his task of lighting the lamps for the evening.

Margaret looked at William Keith's son's mark and showed it to her father. "We've extinguished one small flame amid a roaring bonfire."

"It sounds like we could have traded a chicken for this inconsequential result. Instead, I've sacrificed one good donkey." He exchanged his tankard for the quill and stared at Fulke. He even nodded. "Who else?"

Fulke studied Mary and Margaret, then glanced at Giles. "You may mark me as going, Father."

Ever the dutiful son, agreeing to help manage the gentleman's unruly

32

daughters.

"Because of some faint gnawing within me, Fulke." Margaret said, "I believe you care not to be a part of this adventure. You agree with father and are going only to be the guardian of two headstrong women."

"It makes no matter why I go, just that I am."

Richard penned in his ledger. "We've finished the most difficult part, now we start a list of what you'll need for your Maryland adventure. All of us along with our voyagers will need to discern what items we have in abundance here and what will need to be purchased. Next week Fulke and Giles will take the wagon into the city and procure the remainder of essential goods."

Edward furrowed his brow. "Father, what about you?"

"I've no intentions of going. My heart and mind embrace England, and at my age I don't care to change. Ann and Jane, you'll stay here and help me run the houses. Edward, I'm pleased you'll be staying too, as will your absent brothers. Now let's stretch our legs before we eat and then start the list of provisions for the voyage and setting up homesteads."

Giles grabbed Margaret's arm. "I hear there are many, many men compared to women in Maryland, six to one, I believe. So even at your age you'll be able to find a husband."

Mary pinched Giles's ear. "Rude, you're nothing but rude."

He jerked away. "Stop it! I'm not a little kid anymore."

"Then stop acting like one." She flounced away, glancing at him over her shoulder with her jaw set.

"I get it." He called to her back. "You're angry because I didn't say you could catch a man." He followed her and turned her toward him. "Seriously, Mary, you're quite striking with your shining brown hair, knowledge, and a face to treat the eye. Carving out a life in this new world, men need healthy and sturdy women. Both of you undoubtedly will be married before next year."

"We do not want to be married. Ever!" Mary hissed low at him.

Giles looked from Mary to Margaret and back again. "What is this? What am I not understanding? Doesn't every woman desire a kind and prosperous husband? Doesn't every woman yearn to cradle her own babes in her arms and coo to them and watch each child grow into a respected citizen?"

Like a murder of crows watching a squabble in the midst of their flock, the siblings closed in and around. Mary's pale face blushed crimson. She jutted out her chin and locked eyes with Giles. He stood, mouth open, shoulders hunched, and palms turned out.

Margaret put her arm around Mary. "Leave her alone, Giles. You have no right to information about this personal matter."

"But why would you not want a husband?" He rubbed his chin and glanced over at his father. "This is unnatural. The bible says—Father, what do you say about this?"

Their father looked up from one of his ledgers. Setting his quill down, he walked over to Margaret. "Are you telling me all these years it's been your desire to discourage your suitors? Did you actually send them away?"

"They will tell you I treated them kindly."

Edward and Fulke moved in closer.

"And you, Mary, do your suitors face this same fate?"

"We see no benefit to marriage." Mary glanced at her other sisters, then studied the carpet.

Dary, having finished lighting the lamps, crept to the door with his eyes lowered. Margaret watched the young boy slip out of the room unnoticed by others.

Giles, Fulke, and Edward stood silently, their mouths agape.

Richard waved his hand toward Ann and Jane. "What about the two of you? Is it your grand design to be spinsters also?"

Jane looked at Ann, then nodded her head. Ann said, "I haven't decided, but for now I, too, have taken the vow of chastity."

Their father roared, "A what? A vow of chastity? You aren't cloistered like your other sisters. I understand their vows, but yours... In your lessons, your prayer book, our Holy Father would not expect this of you. Where did you come by such nonsense?" He spun around and faced Margaret. "You're the one. You've indoctrinated them into this—this silliness."

Edward cleared his throat and, locking his arms behind his back, face flushing, he glanced furtively at his brothers.

Margaret hated making her father angry and knew she would have a headache before the evening ended. A tightness started at the back of her neck, near its base, and crept up into her temples. His high standing would allow, maybe even expect, him to be callous, direct, and even stingy if his nature demanded. Instead, her father's associates and friends admired him for his kindness and altruism. As a lord, he led by example. He probably was unaware of his daughters obediently following him no matter where his path took them.

Until tonight.

She now stared at him and pondered how much more she should say. She had already stated these men had no right to interfere in such an intimate womanly matter. She drew in a deep breath and studied each of them. Giles and Fulke appeared as ill at ease as Edward.

However, her father's dark eyes bore into her from underneath his heavy unruly grey brows, silently demanding an explanation.

Margaret had no choice. Addressing only her father, she said, "If one elects to embrace the vow of chastity, it is one's own private commitment. There is no reason or need to share this knowledge with others. Since Giles has embarrassed Mary with no regard for her dignity, it is appropriate for me to set this matter to rest."

Her sisters glanced everywhere except at Margaret.

Trapped little squirrels with nowhere to hide their acorns.

She continued. "What we women decide to do in this regard bothers no one and must not be questioned."

"Bothers no one?" Her father then bellowed, "Bothers no one!"

Her brothers each stepped back. They too didn't seem to know where to look.

"Father, this vow harms no one, and no one does this without deep contemplation. Our vows are made freely, and we must periodically renew them without coercion."

Richard glanced at his sons. Their dazed faces sagged in great defeat. "I am astounded to know you daughters care so little for me or my sons you now shun all men. What have I done to create such hatred?"

A shock of disbelief swept through Margaret. She had never imagined this action of pure love to be taken as hatred. She searched for words. She had to heal this injury she'd inflicted, repair their misconception.

"Father—I—we—all of us have great love for you and for each of our brothers." Margaret glanced at her sisters.

They nodded and murmured agreement. Like a bird without a song, or a harpsichord with no music, Margaret didn't know quite what to say. She never wanted to hurt her father, nor her brothers. When she found her linen square, she dabbed her neck and willed her throat to let the right words flow out.

Mary took her father's hand and held it to her cheek. "Margaret speaks the truth, Father. We love each of you with every breath in our soul."

Now Margaret had no choice but to fully explain.

"We have chosen a singular life not devoted to ourselves or family, but to Divine Love. We've prepared ourselves to instruct young virgins and women in their own salvation, putting their education before our own desires. We set about to arm these women so they can be defenders of the faith, and we supply them with the knowledge they need to survive. You all know the hardships women encounter living under the oppressive laws of our country. They can be judged harshly and have no voice, except for the opinions and words of their husbands or eldest sons. We, your daughters, have no quarrel with marriage. However, if we marry, then we lose what little voice we might gain and are obligated to divide our devotion between God and our husbands. This distracts us from our work, Divine Love, and our eternal salvation."

Again, the room held only silence.

Then Richard spoke. "Margaret, Mary, life in the new settlements will be difficult enough even with the strength endowed in men. Forests must be cleared, roads created, fences built, and structures to live in and to serve the community. Your studies and handiwork, embroidery and sewing, haven't begun to prepare you for the physical work ahead. Fulke and Giles will manage your land and much of this labor, but still you will be faced with difficulties only solved by men. A reconsideration of your vows must be examined."

Our brothers will manage our land? Never.

Chapter 8
July 1638

If we are true to ourselves, we cannot be false to anyone.
- William Shakespeare

MARY, THE TWO BROTHERS, and Margaret had bumped and jostled along this road since before sunup, all the time sitting in the heat on hardwood planks. Margaret wouldn't have minded the journey if they could have ridden in father's carriage. Good Lord—this trip challenged her tolerance.

Mary leaned close, about to whisper something when the wheels of Richard Brent's rough-hewn wagon, pulled by a pair of sturdy white horses, plunged in and out of a deep rut.

Both women caught hold of their seat boards. The two brothers in front, driving the team, paid the jolt no attention.

"Heavens, Margaret, our teeth will fall out." Mary snatched the pale blue bonnet from the dirty floor. She dusted it off but instead of placing it back on her lap she positioned it on her head. "I hate these clothes. It's obvious why they are called sad colors. "I'm being squeezed quite to death. Crissa needs to gain some weight." She tugged at the borrowed, ill-fitting, rusty-brown bodice worn over a flax-blue and gray petticoat. "Puritan women go about so serious, looking drab and unhappy. No wonder they hate our Catholic Church ceremonies. Sad, indeed."

"It is not sad, but *s-a-a-d*. It does not mean sad looking colors." Margaret patted her white linen coif, to be sure it remained secure on her head. "It pertains more to seriousness, and you, dear sister, could lose a pinch here and there and give this lovely day its due by not complaining so." Margaret grinned at her. "You don't even come close to looking like a Puritan, but I agree with Father. We dare not stand out in town. Catholics who purchase large volumes of merchandise would certainly prompt officials to stop and make arrests."

Mary shrugged. "Father said the city would be swarming with people this time of year. No one will pay us any mind."

"Yet if someone discovered us preparing for our over-the-sea adventure, we could lose our heads." Margaret fumbled for her hidden rosary around her neck, assuring herself it kept its place under the fabric.

Mary's gaze rested on Margaret's hand, then swept over her sister's attire. "Tut-tut. Your collar and the stomacher with that dress—maybe ten years ago, dear Margaret."

Margaret had sorted through some of her mother's clothing for this trip. When she touched the fine lace of the high-neck ruff, she decided it was too out-dated. Yet in her mother's apparel she found worn-looking fabrics in subtle colors and a less ruffled collar. She couldn't resist pinning a triangle embroidered placket behind the lower opening of her doublet—she had never worn a stomacher before. However, no Puritan woman ever wore embroidery. The choice had been made, and her sister's assessment correct, but still, Mary need not be so grumpy.

"The souring of your sweet nature, young sister, is certain to exhaust us all." A painful lump grew in her throat.

I also find it near impossible to keep a happy smile when my insides churn from not knowing what lies before us. My heart will not believe we shall live the rest of our lives and never see again our dear father or our brothers and sisters once we sail from the shores of England. Yet, this will be true.

Mary sat straighter. "We do make a pathetic sight. However, I'm beginning to believe we may never arrive in Gloucester."

Giles glanced over his shoulder. "We're almost there. However, Father told you two to stay home."

"Not for a pound and a pence, Giles." Mary said, "You would make a mess of it all. I'd be a fool to trust any brother to tend to my shopping." She glanced at Margaret. "I wouldn't mind their selections of our heavy skillets and pots, all those tools—the axes and other this-and-that of stuff and things they said we must have—but whatever would these brothers do about our woolens?"

"Worse yet," Margaret said, "their choice of linens and homespun no matter how adept our sewing skills, I shudder at the sorry sight we'd make of our maids and men servants' clothes."

"And pins." Mary flicked Giles's hair. "You two have no idea the importance of pins. How many would you buy? A mere thousand and all of one kind, I'm sure." She scoffed. "Wouldn't last us four months. Especially if Margaret continues wearing fancy out-of-fashion clothes."

"I had enough of mother's starchy, pinned collar, but I need pins for my hair."

"And different ones for our hats," Mary straightened her bonnet.

"And certainly, for the pinafores for our maids," Margaret said.

"And they will need pins to hold them in place." Mary grinned at Margaret. "I know something else we must have pins for."

Margaret grinned back, knowing her sister too well.

Mary whispered, "Pins for our underpinnings."

Giles jutted his jaw out, ignoring the sisters.

Fulke said, "Gloucester has one of the finest of pin-pulling facilities."

Giles turned to Mary. "I shall have you understand I am known for an excellent sense of style. Selection of suitable cloths would not be an issue."

"Young brother," Fulke said, "your head grows bigger than your mouth." He snapped the reins. The plodding team pointed their ears backwards and stepped out. "Your style speaks to others as… rather fussy."

"And your unkind comment stings." Giles flipped Fulke's words away with the back of his hand.

"Sometimes words of truth do that, good brother." Fulke glanced back at Margaret. "I live with a deep sting from the veracity of a certain sister's recent sharp words."

He referred to Margaret's remark about his dutiful decision to go to the New

World and watch over his sisters. He had no desire for a Maryland adventure.

If Margaret had been Fulke, she would have stood her ground.

A thing is easy to say when it can never be tested. Poor obedient Fulke. He saw no choice but to make the dreaded crossing.

To Mary and Margaret's delight they had found several maid servants eager to make the ocean voyage. These maids had no family. Knowing their lives would be secure with full employment and their passages paid for, the maids talked of going to Maryland like it would be a lovely lark. The abundance of strong, eligible men may have enhanced their expectations.

Once in the New World, the Brents would provide for their employees' basic needs of decent shelter, food, and clothing until his or her debt of passage had been repaid.

When freed from their servitude, the Brents would see to it they had what they needed to start their new lives. This was the law, the headright system. *A fair and just law.*

Finding men to make the voyage was difficult. She and Mary needed five men, or they couldn't receive any large tracks of land.

'Tis a shame Dary isn't of age.

Margaret had spent over a fortnight convincing her father to give his permission to ask Thomas Gedd and their new man, John Robinson. After two weeks her father consented.

These servants agreed to go, filling her with gratitude along with a tinge of guilt. Father depended on his men's service—he valued their steadfastness as well as their common sense. The difficulties and emotions tied up with securing these two men left her flustered. Yet, she and Mary needed three more.

Giles and Fulke, always out and about and in and out of ale houses, seemed to have no problems discovering men who wanted work or an adventure.

Unfortunately, most decent, hardworking men she and Mary knew had families. They wouldn't leave their wives or children and wouldn't risk the danger of an ocean crossing.

Where could they stir up three more? Mary suggested she and Margaret frequent taverns like their brothers.

'Twas not an easy task to find willing adventurers. Leaving all that's known and loved hurts.

Lord Baltimore had scoured the countryside for aristocratic voyagers—like the Brent family. He needed passengers who had considerable means, those who could afford to pay the sailing fares of their employees, and in turn help populate Maryland.

Heavens. Giles said only a few hundred people inhabited the territory of Maryland.

The wagon trended southwest, down gentle slopes. Hills rose in the northwest cloaked in summer hues of misty greens. In a passing field, a colt pranced over and nuzzled his mother's ear, as if to tell secrets.

Margaret leaned in nearer Mary. "You had started to whisper something."

Mary glanced at her brothers. "I fear Father's mind may be missing some cogs."

"Why would you ever?" Margaret sat upright.

"Shhh." Again, Mary regarded her brothers. Fulke and Giles continued some silly dispute, so she beckoned her sister to lean close. "We're purchasing materials and goods needed in the New World, yet look at this wagon. It's full of every last thing we had carefully sorted and stored in the barn to take to Maryland. Why, in the name of our Mother, are we dragging all our belongings to Gloucester?"

"Dear sister, maybe they need an airing out," Margaret murmured.

"You are not the least amusing." Mary brushed a fly away and straightened her bonnet again. She put her hand up to her mouth, whispering, "Look back there. I see no room at all for our new purchases. Fulke or Giles didn't even stop this nonsense." She tut-tutted. "I'm truly worried about Father."

"Fretting doesn't become you." Margaret kept her voice low. "Father received a letter of instructions from Lord Baltimore. Yet with this bumping about it isn't easy to discuss such matters. Accept Father knows what needs to be done."

"It's such a puzzlement." Mary tucked a lock of hair behind her bonnet and looked over at the hills. "It makes no sense." Then she locked onto Margaret's eyes. "If I felt certain Father still had his wits, I could accept this. However, his decision for us to go to Gloucester rather than Worcester affirms my original thoughts. We could have been to Worcester by now. I heard Edward say Gloucester has only a few broadweavers left in the city whereas in the past they had well over a hundred looms. He said the weavers' company is in chaos, and there may be no more clothiers. Besides, I am past ready to stop all this bouncing and jerking and swatting at flies."

"We'll be resting the horses shortly. I could use a walk around too." Margaret patted Mary's hand. "Our father's mind is clear. He's only watching after our health. Last year Gloucester had another invasion of nasty plague, but now it seems Worcester's turn to suffer."

"Both these places harbor dreadful illnesses. I'm certain the foul air they breathe is to blame. Thank the heavens we can enjoy the abounding purity found in pastures and hills of our countryside. We shall all be better off if we only take small little breaths while here."

Fulke looked over his shoulder, then pulled the team off to the side of the road. "Horsemen approaching. How many, Giles?"

"Four. Keep calm, ladies. Lots of people are moving into the city or coming to purchase or trade. Nothing to cause undue fuss. We'll handle this. I'm sure they'll just pass by. No problem here. Right, Fulke?"

Fulke turned in his seat and watched the horsemen approach. "They don't seem to be in a hurry. A good sign and they wear large hats."

Mary touched Margaret's hand. "Why would slowness and hats stop us from worrying?"

Fulke took a deep breath. "They're not interested in catching up to us, and the hats tell us they are not vagabonds. These men dress like nobility. So, speak little. We'll wait here until they pass and then a bit longer until the dust settles."

Vibrations of hooves clopping on the hard packed road told Margaret the riding party approached. She and Mary kept their backs straight and eyes lowered.

"Good day, m'lords." Giles doffed his floppy hat and nodded. Fulke climbed down from the wagon and stood with his cap in hand. Both had worn linen shirts with simple high-waist jerkins. With the breeches they'd selected, the brothers took on the appearance of country farmers.

"Good day," said one of the men. "Off to spend some time in the big city?"

"We are." Fulke nodded to them. "But only a few hours to replenish supplies. Must get back and tend to stock."

The horsemen wore slashed-sleeved doublets made from rich-colored satin, loose breeches, tight hose, and fine leather boots with large cuffs, identifying them as aristocracy.

Giles climbed down, saying, "We've never eaten at the New Inn. After shopping, we plan to treat our ladies to a small meal there. And you gentlemen?"

Margaret cringed. The New Inn catered only to gentry. She noticed a slight flicker of knowledge pass between the men's eyes.

Fulke stepped a foot forward and squinted back at Giles. "More likely we'll settle for having some supper at an alehouse."

One of the men who sported the popular Van Dyke beard spoke. "We're on our way to a meeting in Bristol—have a long journey ahead, so good day to you all. Safe travels."

Her brothers responded in kind.

Margaret slid back into tranquility as the men took up their reins and prepared to leave. She looked forward to spending the night at the New Inn. Her father knew the proprietor, so their current attire wouldn't be an issue.

The four started to trot on past their wagon, but the one with the beard pulled his horse around to a halt. "I say there, you have a rather full wagon—with some valuable tools."

Giles glanced at Fulke and then Giles started to stammer. Fulke held up his hand to silence him. "We do. Some need repairing and sharpening. Some items we mean to sell to pay for our purchases of other supplies."

The cold whisper of the lie slid through Margaret. Would this be the first of many they would tell to keep their possessions and selves safe? She had promised God she'd not let falsehoods take purchase in her heart. Yet, here she sat at the mercy of other untruths.

All the horsemen had reined their horses around and now stared at the wagon's contents.

Margaret heard Mary's heart pounding, but no. It was her own.

"Gentlemen, ladies," the bearded horseman said with a soft, but commanding voice, "a word of caution. Gloucester is not the safe city of yesterday. Today it's full of immigrants, looking for ways to survive. Many come from Germany to escape their ongoing war. They all arrive at the city gates, hoping to make a living. Apprentices and craftsmen come to Gloucester searching for work. Yet others fill their pockets by taking advantage of unsuspecting newcomers. With these possessions of yours exposed—heed my words, be aware of the unscrupulous—the quacks and gypsies."

"Gentlemen, ladies..." With this, the four horsemen tipped their hats and galloped off in a cloud of dust.

Margaret shuddered. *We fool only ourselves.*

Chapter 9

...by temperament I am a vagabond and a tramp.
- William Faulkner

WHEN THE HORSEMEN DISAPPEARED over the hill, Fulke and Giles flung things around in the back of the wagon looking for anything they could use as a cover. They held up a bundle of silk. Margaret and Mary gasped and shook their heads. Exasperated, the brothers gave up and climbed back into their places behind the horses.

With resignation, obviously combined with new worry, the brothers settled into shared silence. Margaret, too, held the horsemen's words in her mind, yet she couldn't help marvel at the beauty of this land. Verdant farmland changed into individual homes scattered on small plots with chickens, a cow or goat, and family gardens. The stone walls of the city drew nearer. The open land along the road grew sparser as white-painted timbered and cream-colored stone homes clustered tightly together along the road.

"Ahead," Giles pointed. "Over there. That's the city gate we'll be going through."

Their team of horses snorted and plodded down the road. Fulke pointed to a small copse bordered with wild grasses. "Let's give the horses a rest under those trees."

"Inside the city," Giles said, "we should not stop until we get to Goodwin's place."

Mary frowned. "Goodwin?"

"Little sister," Giles said, "we need storage for all these things in this wagon. Lord Baltimore said Goodwin, the blacksmith, knows where storage has been arranged. Cecil Calvert wants our possessions kept near the waterways so they can be loaded onto a ship at a moment's notice."

"This seems such a muddle." Mary said. "The River Severn's flows at least some twenty-five miles from Gloucester before it gets down to the open sea."

"Mary," Margaret said, "this isn't some caper where we frolic about then return safely home. If you value our lives, then you must take what our brothers say with less contention and absolute seriousness."

Mary's cheeks flushed. Margaret wished she had spoken more gently. She disliked chastising her younger sister, but sometimes Mary's eagerness to set everything right stirred the pudding into a mess.

Fulke picked up the conversation. "Do you remember Father talking with Cecil about the Act to prohibit popish men, women, or children to go beyond the sea? Cecil's stories confirmed how dangerous these times are for Catholics. Still, he puts himself in a most precarious position when he recruits Catholic settlers for his Maryland. If the king's men discover his transporting of citizens out of the kingdom, he risks losing his title, his lands, all he owns, and even his head."

"Heavens." Mary's face paled. She clasped her hands together. "Why does he bother about a country so far away? I should think he'd have more sense."

Margaret would normally agree, but with the promise of a more just and equal place she could not help but embrace this uncertainty with an eagerness.

"Cecil's passion comes from the noble title of Lord Baltimore," Giles said. "I suspect Cecil is willing to give up all in the name of honor for his father's dream, the great Maryland experiment where men can live, worship, be free, and govern as they will."

Fulke shook his head. "Many have died in the name of honor. We four must *honor* all of Cecil's instructions, or we put him and ourselves in peril. Margaret, Mary, you must understand. Only those may board an oceangoing vessel if they pledge loyalty to the king *and* the Church of England."

"Fulke." Margaret shook her head. "This will not be a problem for us. The Magna Carta states clearly that any man may leave and return to this country without fear of harm."

"Beatle-headed, cow-chaser." Giles punched Fulke on the shoulder. "How would she know?"

"Quit smacking me around, brother, or I'll throw you from this wagon. She reads. She reads all the time. She reads everything. However, Margaret, the Magna Carta also states the person must swear allegiance, and this is our nasty problem."

Giles held up his hand to speak. "Problem? That's hardly the word to describe the evils of this act. The righteous assemblymen of Jamestown unceremoniously ushered the first Lord Baltimore and me, along with others, out of their colony in Virginia nine years ago. We could have died. All because we stood fast and refused to take their bloody required Oath of Allegiance and denounce the supremacy of the Pope's authority."

Fulke pulled to the side of the road, letting the horses feast on fresh growing grass. "We must trust Cecil. He'll arrange a way for us to board a ship and escape giving this pledge. The horses will rest here, eat, and drink before we enter the city. You may want a walk around yourselves."

"Fulke?" Margaret touched his shoulder. "I've been doing some figures in my head. We need to double the numbers of candles we purchase. We've made enough soap, and in Maryland, come spring we can make more. Yet, a shortage of candles worries me."

Mary smiled, announcing, "Please, dear brother, we can make do with little soap, but not candles. Oh, Dear Lord, do not let us be without candles."

Fulke called to Giles, "I don't recall seeing candles in the market last time. Do you?"

"They've moved into their own soap and candle shop over on Northgate Street. We'll pass it on the way to the New Inn this evening. If the shop is closed, you can buy what you need in the morning."

"I hate to see the markets disappear." Fulke said, "Seems many follow the London way of selling their wares from out of little shops nowadays." Fulke unhitched the horses in the shade and let them graze in the long, untamed grasses beside the roadway.

Margaret stepped onto the grass. "Probably because of gypsies and thieves. Our first order of business must be getting our wagon unloaded and these goods locked in storage."

Mary climbed down and offered Margaret a sugared lemon-gel square wrapped in a tiny, oiled paper.

Savoring the sweetness, Margaret watched a few children stride down the dusty road. Dogs with puppies followed them, yipping and barking. Others, mostly young boys, joined the procession. They chattered and shoved each other. Some skipped and whistled. They traveled in noisy little clusters of erratic forward movements. A few strode out alone, while some ran to catch up.

* * *

The Brent wagon entered the walls of the city, with a disparate pack of barefooted children and dogs darting along beside. The dirt road turned into a wide cobbled street and shortly they pulled to a stop. The horses were unable to go because a gathering crowd pressed in front of them, packing the street going past the Tolsey.

Giles shook his head and sighed. "Must be some big to do at the town hall. Nothing for us except to wait."

Margaret didn't see how children could be this excited over some governing body event at the Tolsey. She searched the crowd and the side streets as far as she could see for a solution to this quandary.

"I hear music," Mary pointed to the south. "It's coming from somewhere over there."

"It's St. Anne's Day," Margaret said, "but the music isn't coming from the cathedral. It certainly doesn't sound like any hymn. They must be having a parade."

"Young man?" Mary leaned over the side of the wagon and called to a ruddy cheeked, barefooted boy. He glanced up and whipped off his cap. The boy clearly saw it was a *Lady* who called to him.

"Ma'am?"

Mary unwrapped and handed him a small, licorice-root sweet. "Tell me why we have a crowd here?"

"Thank ye, Ma'am." He popped it in his mouth, then mumbled, "'Tis the weavers' company new officials." He jiggled around so, it appeared he needed to have a wee. "Ye be seeing the cake they carry to the new master's house. If I don't squeeze through to the front, I'll not get me piece of tiny cake." He hopped from one foot to the other glancing toward the street.

"By all means," Mary said, "squeeze on through. Off you run, now."

Mary looked at Margaret. They tittered, watching the boy scamper off.

Indeed, a parade with cake.

"Now we know why all the children were in such a hurry." Margaret caught a touch of the childlike excitement. "...me piece of tiny cake."

Sounds of cymbals, drums, and fifes echoed, mixed with clapping, dogs barking, and cheers. The music makers came around the corner far down the street, marching in high step adorned with colorful capes and hats. Margaret and Mary strained around their brothers to have a glimpse.

Giles popped up, shaking Fulke's arm, and yelled, "Look—just have a big look at what's coming down the way!"

He turned to his sisters and motioned for them to stand up to see.

Mary jumped up and grabbed Margaret's arm, tugging at her. All the while, the townspeople whistled and hooted. Mary made a soft cooing sound. The brothers grew still.

Margaret peered around Giles and gasped. The throng that had gathered in the roadway parted. Everyone stood silent, in awe. Nine men dressed in their finest boots, hose and breeches, dark-brocade doublets, and hats—each bedecked with a different colored feather—carried a cake unlike any Margaret had ever seen.

One man led, marching in front, with four men on each side, and a final man followed. The four men on each side cautiously carried the heavy, elaborately decorated cake. The first tier was a rectangular shape almost two yards long, a yard wide, and standing at least a foot high. The second and third tiers of the cake, not quite as long or wide or thick, were oval in form, with the third being the smallest.

This lovely piece of edible art had been frosted with a creamy-white, buttery frosting. The bakers had piped all the edges with florets, leaves, and tiny buds in soft pastel pinks, blues, and greens. Silver beaded garlands woven with delicate fresh flowers draped fancifully from one tier to the next, and were anchored to the cake with tiny, bright-colored silk ribbons. On the top of the cake a centerpiece of fresh-cut maroon, cream, and purple garden flowers nestled in lush green leaves.

Others in the weavers' guild, identified by their capes, marched behind the cake bearers. Women wearing pinafores and carrying woven baskets, handed out tiny cakes and tossed small apples to children as the procession passed on to the newly elected master's home.

Oh, for the tangy-juicy taste of oranges instead of the common apple. I'd even settle for a chunk of the Master Weaver's cake.

Hints of hunger pangs increased Margaret's desire. Richard Brent had once mentioned Gloucester carried on a thriving trade with Mediterranean countries, trading wheat and grains for citrus fruits and oils.

Maybe forty or fifty years ago...

Gloucester's exotic trading ended because Bristol and other English ports purchased or traded their goods for this shire's abundant crops of grain. She glanced around at the dispersing crowd, children running every which way. Dogs barked and puppies nipped at the boys' bare feet and ankles. One large boy swaggered away from the masses, calling to two gypsy girls. They giggled and ran up to him, with his handfuls of apples and tiny cakes. The three sauntered off down an alleyway.

"Mary." Margaret pointed toward the alley. "I believe I saw the Coates boy."

"Here? Could that be? He lives outside of Stratford."

"He does. Do you remember the evening I arrived home late? Cecil had come to visit us with his maps. His father came to our house searching for him."

After the streets cleared, Fulke snapped the reins, guiding the team on toward the River Severn and the docks. Margaret twisted around, hoping to catch a glimpse of the alleyway as their wagon passed. She couldn't see the three young people anywhere in the shadowed narrow passage. The Coates boy seemed to have a way of disappearing.

Chapter 10

So God created the great sea creatures and every living creature that moves....

\- Genesis 1:21

WHEN ONE OF THE large open markets came into view, Giles broke their silence. "Tomorrow when we buy our grains, peas, oatmeal, and all those other staples, we should check the quality of nails and barrel hoops here."

Fulke objected. "I'm sure Maryland has a smithy by now. We can make our own hoops out of copper. Let's just stick to Lord Baltimore's list."

Margaret searched her pouch. "Where's the paper about the food provisions?" She ignored the oily, decaying odors rising from the cobbles.

Her sister shrugged. "Giles had it yesterday."

Tugging at Giles's shirt, Margaret said, "Are you listening? Mary and I are the ones who made sure the beef in vinegar, along with the sheep meats, were packed in earthen pots. You might be surprised to know it took the kitchen maid a whole day to bake them. We have been so busy I can't remember what else we need for our shipboard provisions."

"I remember some of it," Mary said, "cheeses, bacon, spices, and naturally, fine wheat flour."

"I don't remember any. Giles, I hope you have that document."

"Live poultry," Mary said, "we must take live chickens—what's that awful smell."

"Lord Calvert listed more." Margaret leaned forward. "Please tell me you brought that list, Giles."

"Stop fussing." Giles said, "It's here somewhere."

They drove past the market. The air smelled heavy with the weighty, acrid smells of death.

Waving her handkerchief about, Mary sniffed and held her breath. "I told you this town is unhealthy. These horrid smells—and flies."

"Silly, dear sister." Margaret motioned toward the stalls of meat. "The smelly air won't make you sick. It is just waste and entrails of fish, slaughtered beef and pigs, and rotting vegetables and fruit."

She didn't mention the freshly strangled chickens hanging upside down, nor the animal excrement left for feet and horse-drawn wagons to crush.

How in heaven's name would they find time to purchase all the supplies on Cecil's lists before they make the long journey home tomorrow? Worse yet, where would the ship find room to store them?

"Hoot-hoot!" Giles nodded toward a small group of gaily dressed people.

46

"The horsemen spoke the truth. Don't let us become distracted, while others set to stealing what we own."

The team continued down the streets past ale houses, narrow shops, and a few small homes with gardens of magnificent deep-blue cornflowers, white gypsophila, multicolored sweet pea, and even a cluster of sunflowers, turning yellow faces to catch the rays of the late afternoon sun.

"Mary and I will definitely want to buy a variety of seeds. And I won't hear any grief about that." She and Mary would use flowers to craft sweet-smelling oils, lotions, and maybe put a wee bit in some of their soap.

Fulke slowed the horses, raised his hand, and pointed. "Over there."

He pulled the team into a space by a wooden sign nailed to an oak tree. The black painted letters spelled Smithy.

Goodwin's double shop doors opened wide onto the street. Next to the shop, tethered livestock stood in the shade of several hickory trees near a watering trough. Fulke and Giles hopped down and told their sisters they'd be only a few minutes.

Goodwin seemed focused on some red-hot metal he held with tongs and pounded flat.

Margaret enjoyed the stillness of the wagon not bouncing about. She soaked in the sights around her of the narrow shops with people bustling in and out, the sounds of greetings, hens clucking, and two irritated men arguing about prices. A black cat crept behind a barrel, stalking something near the tethered horse and donkey. A niggle in the back of her mind reminded her of some unfinished business.

It had something to do with the surprise of seeing the Coates boy. She could do nothing about him except to inform his father of his whereabouts.

Margaret put him out of her mind and returned to study the open doors of the windowless shops—some wooden, a few brick, and fewer made with wood and stone. She watched the people passing by and the brash vendors who strolled, pushing carts and hawking wares, interrupting any chance for quietness.

The image of the Coates boy stayed in her head. She looked over to where the tethered livestock munched mounds of hay.

The donkey—like the stolen donkey.

She slipped down from the wagon, clutched her skirts up from the dirt, and strode over to the animal. She gave the donkey a pat, inspecting its hind end. She swung around, and bumped into Mary, knocking her sister into a nervous horse.

The tethered horse nickered, sidestepped, and watched wide-eyed, whipping its tail side to side. Mary skittered away.

"Goodness, Mary. Sneaking up like that, you even gave me a fright."

Her sister tugged at her jacket and smoothed her skirt. "I never sneak. What has happened to that poor donkey? Would you look at those marks? It's been whipped unmercifully. Sinful."

Margaret glanced over to where her brothers stood, talking with Goodwin. The three seemed deep in discussion. She strode over. Mary followed.

Goodwin plunged the red-hot metal into a barrel of water, causing a sizzle. Steam erupted. After he pulled the metal out and set it on top of an overturned barrel, he pointed down the road toward the river. Fulke thanked him and started to leave when Goodwin held up a finger for them to wait. He stepped over to a shelf, lifted the lid off a tin box, and pulled out a large brass key. He handed it to Fulke.

"Sir." Margaret said to Goodwin. "Please tell me where the owner of that donkey is?"

"You're talking to him, m'lady." Goodwin put his hands on his hips.

Margaret glanced around to see if anyone had heard what he'd called her. No one paid any attention. She relaxed, he must address all women by m'lady, but then the boy at the parade who saw them hadn't believed their 'poor farmer' ruses either.

It's because I'm wearing the ancient, ruffled collar. The vanity of it all. For shame.

"Why do you ask?" Fulke glared at her.

"Because Goodwin's donkey was stolen from the Keith family over by Stratford." She faced Goodwin. "How did you come by it, sir?"

"Aw, when I saw the poor little beast all skinny and abused, I couldn't let he be treated tha way." Goodwin shifted his gaze to the shelves, then looked down at the burning coals in his forge.

She didn't want to embarrass this man more, but still she had to know. Margaret said, "Tell me about the person who had this donkey."

"A strapping ox of a fella, he was. He lumbered in a few days—naw, at least a week or so ago, wanting me to refurbish his cutlass. 'Fix this cutlass for me, will ya?' he said." Goodwin studied Margaret before continuing his story. "He had naw manners. Me, I said, 'Why, what canna be wrong with it?' The lad whipped it up and wacked tha rope hanging over there and said, tha's what be wrong, you old goat. I cain't cut nuthin with it.' Don't know where he got it, but tha cutlass was dented and dull as a board. I tell him, 'Gie me that donkey and I'll sharpen it for ye.' Tha kid's a tough one. He poked me with the point of the battered cutlass—in the chest, right here." Goodwin patted his heart.

"And when you sharpened it, he gave you the donkey?" Margaret wanted him to hurry and tell her where to find the boy.

"Didn't happen tha way. He, 'na,' and be stubborn. Said the donkey be worth way more. For a while bit he whined and fussed for me to give him one of my flintlocks. Said I could then have his donkey."

"Was he a tall young man with dirty-yellow hair?" Margaret glanced back at the gentle animal.

"Every bit much. His cutlass looked like he ha' found from some rubbish heap, all bent and nicked. Pretty much worthless if he want ta use it in a fuffle and me old flintlock ha' a mind to misfired often as not. But he din't care. Now the little donkey gets shelter and food, and I get a fine wee donkey."

Fulke tapped Margaret on her arm, attempting to escort her to the wagon. Margaret had one more question before she'd cooperate.

"Do you know where he is—where the boy lives?" She expected him to say he didn't.

"Sure do. He hangs around with some rough and tumbles down by tha dock.

They fixed up a rickety ol' ship—say they be sailing off to tha New World. Mind ye, as much as I wish to leave all this here to the thieve'n scalawags tha have taken over this city, and as much as I wish to start anew across the ocean, nary a fool would climb on board such an ill put-together crate of floating timber."

Fulke took Margaret's arm. "The sun will be setting in a few hours, and we must finish what we came to do before we go to the inn."

The brothers bid the blacksmith a good day and hurried the sisters back to the wagon. Their team of horses picked their way through the crowded streets.

"I'll feel better about our horses once we unload all of this." Fulke reined them to a halt on the waterfront next to a squat, brick building with no windows. The brothers slid off the wagon and positioned the rig close to the door.

Giles nodded. "The empty wagon will make for a quicker trip home. We won't have to rest them so much."

Fulke unlocked the bolted door and slid it open, revealing a large unlit space with a dirt floor. "Good. There'll be room for tomorrow's purchases, too."

Then the brothers climbed down and set to unloading the wagon, while Margaret sat and scanned the seaside dock for a worthless "crate of floating timber."

Chapter 11

We hang the petty thieves and appoint the great ones to public office.
- Aesop

MARY OPENED HER POUCH and produced a piece of sesame honey brittle. She offered it to Margaret, saying, "It a relief to not worry about our things being stolen."

"Well, cockles and berries, Mary. What else is in your bag? Did you only bring sweets?"

Her sister grinned. "I guessed this journey would be exhausting, so I came duly prepared. Here's some sassafras sweets brought over from the New World, if you would prefer." She popped the sesame honey brittle in her mouth.

Margaret slid down off the wagon, leaving her brothers to unload and store their possessions and Mary to suck happily on her comforting little candies.

Her sister said, "I am reassured the settlers find ways to trade with England—sassafras."

Margaret glanced back. "Trading across the ocean does bode well for our future—quite comforting to be able to keep in steady contact with our homeland. However, I do hope we deal in more than those tiny sweets."

She strolled over to the waterfront and watched the docked ships, listened to the gulls' plaintive cries, and enjoyed the sound of water sloshing against the pilings.

A group of tough-talking ruffians sauntered and swaggered down the gangplank of an old pinnace tied up at the end of the pier. They jostled each other about. One hefty lad took a misstep and nearly toppled into the river. All of them doubled over in laughter, increasing their penchant for nonsense.

Elderly fellows, she counted five in number, squatted around a fire built near one of the wooden warehouses not far from where her brothers labored. The men looked up to see what caused the ruckus on the pier. Their clothes appeared to have been fine once but now were shabby. One man held up a piece of string dangling a few dead fish, maybe a grayling with a couple bream. Margaret would leave fish identification to Mary.

A weary-looking man plunged his knife into a dead fish throat, slit it from stem to stern, then tugged out the entrails, tossing them aside. Another man skewered two gutted fish on a long stick, preparing to cook them. The men's lined faces told stories of hardships and exhaustion as they went about their tasks and swatted at flies. They didn't look English born. Margaret guessed they'd traveled across the country, maybe from as far away as Germany.

Lithe and trim sailors from a good-sized brig, probably a merchant ship, trotted down a wooden gangplank, discussing which alehouse they should visit.

A troupe of gypsies danced, sang, and tapped tambourines, which caused the sailors to pause. A magnificent red rooster strutted between them, eyeing everything in his path, especially the toddling-waddling seagulls.

Margaret watched the young girls and wondered what it must feel like to bend and twist and twirl. Obviously, gypsy girls didn't wear whalebone stays. Their backs must be quite strong.

What an exhilarating day full of so many strange and unusual happenings.

She stared out across the wide river, watching the gulls dive and dip for fish. Having spent most of her life on their father's different estates doing what was expected as a woman, Margaret could only imagine the thrill of sailing to a mysterious New World—a world not new—but so different she couldn't even guess what she should expect... or what might be expected of her. She decided the most exciting part of all came from not being in the least fearful of this grand adventure.

The excitement of the land beyond the ocean—Goodwin—Goodwin said he wanted to go.

If he agreed to her terms and consented, she could have three of the five men acquired to gain title to her land. The thought made her impatient. However, she'd have to wait until her brothers finished unloading the wagon. She would see to it they return to his shop. She would offer him passage for his service. He appeared to be a brave, decent, and good-hearted man.

The sailors skirted around the gypsies. One of the sailors hopped and side-stepped over the underfoot rooster. The tambourine music, the dancing, and the singing stopped.

An old hag shouted, "Why ye kick my bird?" She grabbed the sailor's arm.

He doffed his cap and sputtered something inaudible. His companions shoved up around him, assuring the old woman the rooster had not been harmed. The rest of the gypsies gathered around and started defending the rooster and the old hag.

A young girl in a green and orange skirt, dangling with spangles, and wearing a yellow kerchief tied around her dark curly locks, worked her dainty fingers into one of the sailor's purse that hung from his waist. Two other gypsy children seemed to be fussing around the third inattentive sailor.

"You—children!" Margaret yelled out, "Stop right now! Give up those thieving ways."

A tremendous crashing and the hollering of men behind her muffled Margaret's yelling. She swirled around to see tongues of fire licking up the front of the old wooden building where the fish-cooking men had sat. Wisps of black smoke gathered into billows. The ruffians and the immigrants, oblivious to all, exchanged curses and fisting blows.

Vendors and store owners dashed with buckets to fill with water. Merchants and sailors formed a brigade. Town officials and a sheriff appeared from somewhere, shouting commands to which no one listened. A nearby chapel bell started a furious tolling.

Fulke yelled to Margaret, saying, "If the fire reaches this building, the roof will burn and all of our belongings—"

He didn't finish but ran to join Giles and the bucket brigade. Mary wasn't on the wagon.

Gypsies have kidnapped her—what a silly thought.

Breathing deeply and shutting her mind to the events around her, she hurried toward the wagon. She found her sister, not hiding, but standing behind it next to the storage building.

"What are you doing?"

"Fulke tossed me the key and asked me to lock up. Keep the key will you. It will get sticky from the sweets in my pouch." She pressed the key into Margaret's hand.

Margaret shoved it into her bag. "Did you see what caused the fire?"

"Those awful boys kicked up a fight with those men. The tall, mean-looking one cracked a brick over that old man's head, the one sprawled on the cobbles. He's bleeding. I want to help but with those fists flying, they would knock me cold. The short kid grabbed a crate and slung it at the white-bearded man. Both landed smack in the fire. Then it all got mixed up with more cussing and slugging and sparks flying all over. An old man snatched the burning crate out of the fire and tossed it. It flew apart and landed against the building."

The sisters tied the horses and ran to join the bucket brigade with the townspeople, their brothers, and the sea goers. Even the gypsies joined. No one wanted the fire to spread.

Margaret shouted to Mary and pointed toward the clockmaker's shop. Peter Coates strolled around the corner whistling. He stopped and looked at the sodden mess, then dashed over and shouted to the ruffians. He threw his hands in the air, left them still scuffling with the men, grabbed a bucket, and joined the brigade.

His mates, even though covered in soot and water, shouted obscenities at the older men. A skinny kid kicked one man bloody who had sunk to the ground. Moments later, after the fire had been extinguished, Peter tossed his bucket aside and strode over to them, hollering something. He grabbed the skinny kid and threw him against a wall.

The city officials and sheriff rounded up the local townspeople, including the ruffians, gypsies, and immigrants to sort out who'd done what.

Fulke shook his head, and he and Giles, covered in soot and soaking wet like the others, untied the team. He motioned for his sisters to take their places in the wagon, and he climbed up, shifting around in his wet uncomfortable clothes. Fulke snapped the reins. The horses moved back a bit, then forward into a tight turn ready to plod up the cobbles to the New Inn.

Evidently, believing the old men and the witnesses, the sheriff and the good men of the city roped all the ruffians together in a line. A doctor came and pronounced the bloody man dead. Others loaded him onto a cart. The sheriff motioned for his men to take the bound kids up the street to jail. The gypsies jeered and shook their fingers at them. Peter Coates, finding himself tied up with the others, protested so obnoxiously the lonely rooster started crowing. The bird's great distress could be heard over the murmurs and shouts of the crowd.

"Stop, please!" Margaret grabbed Fulke's arm. He ignored her. She jerked his arm and yelled again. He pulled the wagon to a halt.

"Sister, I'm dead tired, and we two are a bloody mess. You ladies don't look much better. Let's have no more nonsense. We're going to the inn."

Margaret scoffed and leaped off the wagon. She marched over to the bound arsonists and murderers and stated to the sheriff he had made a mistake. He stared at her, then continued on up the road.

No one respects women.

"Mary, come here." Margaret detested yelling, even though her internal fuming encouraged even more unspeakable feelings. "Hurry yourself now, come quickly."

Mary obeyed. Giles and Fulke pulled the team to the side of the road, and Fulke handed Giles the reins. Grumbling, he followed his sisters.

The sheriff, ignoring Margaret, strode at the head of the line. He slowed when Margaret caught up with him. Walking backwards in front of him, with her muddy petticoats held clear of the cobbles, she insisted he listen to her. He motioned for her to step aside.

"You must stop and hear me out, sir." Her hair tangled freely in front of her eyes. She brushed it back. "One of your captives came on site after the fire started. I have another witness."

He pushed around past her.

"Will you listen? Please."

The sheriff continued marching his prisoners on up the road.

"Sir," Fulke moved along side of the sheriff. "Do you hear my sister talking to you? I'm Fulke Brent, son of Richard Brent. This is the Lady Margaret Brent and our sister Lady Mary."

"You're dressed like a common farmer." The sheriff paused and looked him up and down. "Brent, you say. What are you doing here?"

"We needed some tools repaired and planned to purchase some imported merchandise. In these times if you're suspected of being peerage, the merchants and craftsmen believe their services and wares have higher values."

"And what may I do to assist you, sir?"

Margaret bristled. "First, you may address your questions about me to me when I stand right in front of you."

Fulke, touched her arm and the twitch above his eyes pleaded for her to be compliant.

"Sir." She took a deep breath. "I do apologize. We've traveled all day and now this."

She spread her hand toward the devastated building and then to her unkempt brother and sister.

"Young Peter Coates, the tall blond youth bound up in the middle of your rope, was nowhere around when the fighting and fire started. My sister saw the ruffians who started it all, and Peter Coates was not one of them. I, myself, saw him coming around the corner by the clockmaker's shop. He stopped the one who kicked the man that died, then picked up a bucket and joined the brigade. If you would be kind enough to release him to my brothers, we will escort him back to Stratford and his parents."

She didn't dare look at Fulke. If the sheriff released Peter Coates into their care, she might as well have cast her siblings into a dark pool of eels. Fulke and Giles would detest taking Peter to the New Inn and be furious at having to drag him along while they made their morning purchases. Her brothers had planned to again secure all their new purchases in the storage building before they set out. They wouldn't arrive home until the middle of the night. Mary's tolerance for wagon bouncing and Peter's nonsense would make Fulke want to push everyone's head into the nearest slop bucket.

Margaret shuddered at the thought. Yet how could she keep her mouth shut over such an injustice?

The sheriff stared at Margaret, then studied each of the Brents from under his bushy brows. He worked his jaw back and forth and a few moments later called to the nearby assemblymen. They gathered around him—heads lowered in consultation.

When the councilmen straightened and went on about their business, the sheriff ordered his men to untie Peter Coates. He admonished the boy to remain under the guardianship of the Brents. Then the sheriff proceeded on his way with his less fortunate prisoners.

"Why ye do that?" Peter, jaw set, glared at Margaret. "Ye don' care a whit for me."

"You have a better mind than I imagined, young Peter. You are most correct. I have not the least bit of affection toward you. You killed William Keith, stole his donkey, and you have let your mum worry sick over your disappearance. Regardless, you did nothing to start the fight and the fire, nor should you hang for a man you did not kill, only for the man you did kill. You carry a rogue's heart, with no remorse, but it is wrong to convict you of something you did not do." Margaret pointed to their wagon. "Come on, then, sit up in front with my brothers. Tomorrow you are going home."

"I didn't kill no one. I found me a donkey running free, and the bloody hell if I be going with the likes of you. But then I do thank ye kindly for my freedom, ye ole spinster hag."

Peter Coates swung around and bounded away from the wagon, sprinting on down and along the harbor. Margaret watched him leap onto the pier and swagger off toward a rickety old pinnace, the same ship the other ruffians had disembarked from a while ago.

Margaret sighed and climbed up onto the wooden bench next to her sister.

Fulke snapped the reins. "Margaret." The horses jolted, then fell into step. "Your impulsive judgement makes the case of you and Mary living on your own a most specious argument. We'll see what father has to say."

Chapter 12
Mid-October 1638

It is easy to be brave from a safe distance.
- Aesop

A PINPRICK OF LIGHT punctured the inky-black night. Margaret stifled her inclination to point this bit of brightness out to her siblings. In darkness she suspected they had been lolled into dreams from the steady undulation of Cecil Calvert's fine carriage wheels. Mary had rested her head on Margaret's shoulder. The waxing sliver of the crescent moon kept Margaret company.

With one hand she pulled her woolen cloak tighter and smoothed the blankets over her lap. All Hallows Eve always brought bone-chilling cold, and tonight heralded its nearness with crisp-cutting air. The festival, celebrating the first day of winter, was only a few weeks away. This freezing temperature would paint their cheeks and noses red.

She wondered how their coachman and the horse could keep to the road with nothing to guide them through the thickness of this night. Perhaps the coachman's eyes and the horse's memory knew well the feel and habits of this journey. The hoof beats of all the horses thrummed in rhythm. Margaret could catch an occasional sound of chatter from maidservants in the carriage with Thomas Gedd and John Robinson. Fulke and Giles's menservants followed in the other carriages.

After their exhausting trip to Gloucester, Fulke, indeed, had spoken with their father. Several days of heated discourse ensued but Margaret's arguments prevailed. She and Mary looked forward to having their own home. They would not live under their brothers' care.

Landowners in Maryland and our property will be called Sisters Freehold.

Margaret grinned out into the endless velvety back. Giles, when he talked about sailing across the ocean, said one would cast their gaze on endless water. He said on a calm, clear night the darkness of the world would wrap a voyager in a floor and ceiling made of sparkling stars.

My mind cannot imagine such expanse.

For days, there would be no land, no birds, no trees, only endless waves roiling off to places unknown.

Heavens, it must be nearly midnight. She recounted the carriage stops—ten times this journey—to change horses. She knew they traveled close to two hours between each stop. Cousin Cecil had planned everything meticulously, arranging for fresh horses from trusted and discreet farmers.

Horses.

Her throat tightened. *Gingo.* Even Lord Baltimore insisted they leave the stallion in England—for his safety and health, he said. The tossing at sea would excite him—not be good for him. Horses often didn't fare well during the crossing. Pip promised to watch over Gingo and see he was exercised properly. Margaret feared her father would eventually sell him. She squeezed her eyes shut, shutting out the memories of the sweaty smell of his neck and the coarse feel of his mane between her fingers.

And Father, dear father.

With a lump in her throat, stiffness settled into her bones. Margaret searched for her pinpoint of light, looking for some type of anchor for her wandering mind. Her tired eyes no longer focused because now she saw two lights. The carriage swayed and rolled on along a hilltop. She rubbed and blinked and looked again. Where she had seen one, then two—now a handful of lights flickered below in the distance.

"Fulke, Giles, Mary, I believe we near a village." Her breath quickened. She desperately wanted a walk around. Her siblings stirred and stretched. Giles and Fulke, who had ridden facing the sisters, twisted around to see where she pointed.

"Any guess as to the hour?" Fulke pulled out his pocket watch. "It's bloody dark and cold. I can't see a flaming thing."

"You and your gadgets, Fulke." Mary yawned. "Even if you could see, I doubt if it would tell the correct time."

"It must be near midnight." Margaret wondered why the town seemed awake. The waste of so many candles burning must cost a whole counting house of money.

The carriage jittered and rolled steadily forward and the flickering lights disappeared, along with Margaret's hopes for a good stretch away from the confined coach. The horse nickered, and the coachman clicked his tongue. She could tell by the shift of weight they were climbing a hill. Cresting the hilltop, they headed down again toward the brightness of moving lights and of a wide awake village.

Drawing nearer, they found the town asleep in darkness, while the dancing lights, reflecting off the dark water, illuminated a bustle of activity on a dock. They had arrived at a seaport.

The horses brought them dockside where candled lanterns hung, spilling their light on stacks of barrels and other cargo. A tidy ship secured fast, bobbed in the water with masts and sails greater than a pinnace. Yet this ship was not as magnificent as Lord Baltimore's *Ark*, which sailed from the Isle of Wight. Seamen shouted orders and hustled to and fro, loading crates, grain sacks, pigs, cows, oxen, chickens, and goats into the belly of the vessel. The cows snorted steam and plodded up the gangplank. Barrels stood stacked in a row, waiting to be rolled onto the ship and stowed.

Other wagons of travelers had arrived. A few passengers stood on the dock close to their belongings, waiting silently, while three gulls argued over entrails of a dead fish.

Lord Baltimore's carriages pulled nearer and stopped. Each coachman climbed down and held doors open. When their coachman opened the door, he offered Margaret his arm. She grabbed Mary's hand and gave it a quick squeeze, then stepped down onto the worn, wooden dock, looking around.

Giles stood next to Margaret and slapped his leg. "Well, here we are. Let our great adventure begin."

A stout, happy looking man, wearing a dark woolen cape over a deep-blue coat with a stiff standing collar strode toward the brothers and sisters. Gold buttons peeked out from under the warm cape with a linen bow securing his white starched ruff. He bowed ever so slightly.

"Well, here you are. I am Quartermaster Simon." He unknowing had echoed Giles's sentiments. "The captain's duties require him to remain on board. He apologizes for not greeting you himself."

Fulke extended his hand. "We are pleased to be placed in your care for the passage."

The quartermaster shook hands. "Lord Baltimore will be delighted to learn the Brent family has arrived and in good spirits. Let's get you tucked safely aboard. 'Tis cold and late. Surely, you'll want a good night's sleep after your long journey."

Several young seamen gathered the Brent's travel bundles and whisked them away. The servants unloaded their possessions from the carriages and stood in a cluster behind the Brent siblings.

"Come on, then." Escorting them to the ship, the quartermaster slipped his arm securely through Margaret's, all the while patting her gloved hand. Margaret stiffened and felt flushed. She hadn't expected such intimacy from a stranger. However, her impulse to withdraw her arm seemed petty as the quartermaster was undoubtedly showing supreme respect for Lord Baltimore's passengers.

The jolly man called to the boatswain, telling him to hold back loading the ship until all the other passengers had boarded. Then he guided Margaret up the gangplank. Her sister and brothers followed. Their men and women employees tagged along behind. Margaret glanced back to see others from the wagons fall in line behind the Brent's entourage. It appeared to her this ship's passenger list would consist mostly of indentured servants.

"You'll find our little beauty, the *Charity*, a most seaworthy vessel." He continued as he and Margaret stepped onto the wooden deck. "Look over there." He stopped at the railing and pointed behind the *Charity*. "See her pinnace bobbing next to the dock? That's the *Swan*. Sweet wee ship, she is, and she'll be tagging along with her big sister, *Charity*, the whole trip. They serve us well."

Giles took position on the other side of the quartermaster. "Sir, are we in the port of Plymouth?"

"You are. 'Tis less of a hassle than the Isle of Wight." He winked.

The other travelers with their bundles crowded the ship's deck, until one of the seamen called for them to follow. He led the servants down below to hammocks or bunks in steerage.

Then the quartermaster leaned over the railing and yelled, "John Short, get those barrels on board as quickly as you can. We've no time to waste. Dallying around brings us nothing but trouble." He muttered to Fulke and Giles, "By sunup, maybe before, the authorities will arrive. They come to inspect for compliance with the royal orders and take the fidelity oath from all who travel the seas. 'Tis high time we be sailing off."

The quartermaster excused himself, but a sailor hollered at him and pointed to a moving light on the hill. Quartermaster Simon, red-faced, dashed around, barking orders. A cacophony of shouts filled the air. The sailors clambered over the ship hoisting sails. John Short helped shove the last barrel up the plank. His team wrestled it below.

Quartermaster Simon bellowed to all, "Look—six riders now with torches coming. Get those ropes untied—pull the anchor—"

Margaret placed her hand on Fulke's. "Where's Goodwin? Cecil said he would meet us here, but I see him not, or the donkey, nor his cow."

Giles must have heard, because he ran along the ship gangway, scanning the dock. He yelled back, "I don't see any sign of him, Fulke."

Quartermaster Simon called, "Hoist that gangplank—Now!"

The *Charity's* sails snapped smartly in the breeze. Margaret's cheeks burned from the sharpness of the freezing air. Searching for Goodwin, she steadied herself when the ship moved. The deck shifted, tilted sideways, straightened, and glided away from the dock as the royal guard galloped onto the wharf, waving and yelling.

"Oh no, please." Margaret ran to the grinning quartermaster and grabbed his arm. "We must wait for Blacksmith Goodwin. We cannot leave without him."

"Goodwin?"

"He's a blacksmith from Gloucester. He has a donkey and a cow."

"The man with the donkey and cow. M'lady, he arrived well before the sun went down. I suspect he's having a quiet, wee nap below in his hammock by now."

The dock, the workers, and lights grew smaller as the guardsmen scrambled off their horses and sent shots flying toward the *Charity*.

Chapter 13

It is not in the stars to hold our destiny but in ourselves.
- William Shakespeare

WEEKS LATER, MARY HELD a swaying one-candle lantern above Margaret's cot. "Wake up. Hurry. You must not miss this."

The rest of the tiny cabin she and Mary shared with a discreet gray rat remained in darkness. Mary yanked the blanket covering her sister.

"There is nothing to miss in the middle of the night. Now, leave my quilt be. It is shivering cold."

"Don't be so delicate. Up with you. The sun will rise soon. Come greet the New World. Come, I shall get you a biscuit and cider. Hurry now—dress and meet me topside."

Margaret climbed the roiling steps to the deck, grasping anything to stay upright. Her younger sister sat starboard on a rough-hewn storage chest under a glowing lantern. This position would afford them a clear view of land appearing on the right in front of the *Charity*.

Leather tankards stood where Margaret had been used to seeing the usual cider pot and mugs. Next to the drink sat a small wood tray of tiny biscuits. The sun below the horizon grew brighter, dissolving the gloomy predawn light.

A cabin boy came and snuffed out the lantern as an icy breeze flipped Mary's auburn locks across her freckled face.

"You said cider." Margaret grimaced. "You give me beer."

"All cider is gone, and the water grows more rank each hour. We daren't use it."

Margaret agreed. She had heard terrible tales about sickness on ships. Few young children survived the passage.

On the first night of their journey, a sailor full of appalling stories told them a dreadful tale of a passage. He said it had taken place several years earlier on another ship. A woman started birthing one morning. By nightfall, everyone knew the process was much too difficult for her and would cause the death of the young mother along with the unborn child. They debated how best to end the poor woman's agony. While they argued, two men tossed her and the unborn babe into the ocean.

So far, their voyage had proceeded without such horrors. She settled on the high, long box and selected one of the biscuits. She scoffed at the rock-like tidbit, flipping it back into the tray with the others.

"My dear sister, travel and time has been at work with these little rocks." Margaret clutched the edge of the box as the ship rolled and tossed. Her sister grabbed the tray of sliding biscuits.

"Not much else is left except wrinkled apples. I'm ready for some of Missus Brookes' hot-apple biscuits. Please don't let our Maryland accommodations be this scant."

Margaret sighed. "Until we move into our home, I suspect we will have to make do."

The queasiness she'd felt the first night on the rolling ocean came back. She worried about Cecil Calvert's agreement. If anyone protested about the sisters' land and home, Cecil would be far across the ocean.

"I dislike this foul weather on land. At sea it is even more disagreeable." Margaret unfolded the medallion quilt from her Grandmother Reed and tucked it around her. "I understand this grand plan Lord Baltimore inherited from his father has bloomed into something quite unexpected. According to the letter Giles received from his governor friend Leonard Calvert, Cecil has designated land for sixty manors for those bringing five servants."

"Heavens, we may each end up with a manor." Mary grinned and nibbled on one of the biscuits, causing Margaret to think of their little, hungry gray roommate.

I worry for naught. Of course, we will have a fine home.

"I have doubts about the number. However, when I wavered about making this journey, Cousin Cecil promised us a fine temporary home until we secured our own manor. Considering the rawness of this tossing and rolling environment, I suspect once on solid land we shall become comfortable. Now where is this New World you so rudely insisted I awake to see?"

Tops of dark waves sparkled with the early light of dawn, and damp breezes encircled the women.

"We're farther out than I thought." Mary pointed to the west. "There under the line of clouds. We've seen little clouds like those over small islands we passed. You have to admit the length of those clouds tell us we're approaching an impressive landmass."

"I could have slept for another half a day and not missed anything." Margaret spent a moment to appreciate the smoothness of the stitched leather tankard in her fingers. "November. Such a chilly month to travel over water. Puritans talk how winters may be quite harsh in this New World."

"I can well do without perishing cold."

"If the New World lies under those clouds, then why have we not seen birds?"

A hesitation, then Mary said, "Most birds do not fly this far out to sea."

"You are saying the ship is still hours away from land." Margaret glared at Mary. "Well, no matter. I am up now."

Whingeing about it would not make this ship sail any faster. Margaret sighed and fluffed-up her foul mood. She would not fault Mary for being over exuberant. Her sister had always embraced new experiences with high-spirited expectations. Heavens above, Mary would not have come on this interminable voyage if she had not held such enthusiasm for life.

The brightness of the dawning day didn't seem to move them any closer to land. Clouds along the western horizon threaded along the ocean surface to boil up in lumps then dissipate into soft strands of lamb's wool, settling over ultramarine blue water.

"Look." Mary stood and tugged at Margaret's arm. "We're no longer going due west. We've changed course." Her sister broke out in a huge grin. "I suspect the *Charity* has decided to travel alongside the continent."

The smallest of events, significant or not, could bring great joy to her younger sister. Margaret stood to see.

"Mary, are you aware two of our maids are named Elizabeth and two are named Mary? How will we ever keep them straight?"

"We could call them each by their given names like we do the men. Yet it does sound rather brusk."

Margaret sighed and sat. "On a thought, let us call them Missus with their given names. This seems more respectful."

Giles came up the steps and joined them.

Smiling, Mary offered him a biscuit. He took it and seemed pleased.

Not being privy to Cousin Cecil's correspondence and Fulke so private about everything, Margaret might pry information from her younger brother.

"Tell me, how bustling do you believe St. Mary's City to be? I will be dismayed if we find half the shops and people we saw in Gloucester—so crowded with all the immigrants." She sat back on the bench, then chuckled. "Oh dear, what am I saying? We are the immigrants."

Giles wore his maroon woolen cape and seemed not the least bothered by the chill of the air.

He helped himself to another biscuit. "I am told the first Lord Baltimore's ship, the *Ark*, carried about two hundred passengers to St. Mary's four years ago. There may be as many as four hundred there now. But it's not uncommon for new arrivals to be overcome with fever and die."

"Heed the water and food we consume on shore," Mary said. "It must be fouled. I don't know what we shall do if it is the air we have to breath."

"Nonsense, Mary. The book Cecil gave us extolls the qualities of most agreeable air." Margaret bit her bottom lip. "Giles, your information about the numbers of people puts us in a sticky mess."

He grinned. "Don't fret. All of us have strong constitutions. Most who die are the young, the old, and the weakened indentured."

"I'm not worried about illness, Giles, but the land and houses."

Mary offered him a tankard. "If the *Ark* brought two hundred people, and now there are four hundred, and Cecil has land for only sixty manors—there won't be any left for us. We shall be left to the weather's mercy in our willow-made hut."

He cocked his head and studied them. "Mary, he's set aside land for sixty manors. I haven't a hint why you're so worried. Lord Baltimore made you a promise. Certainly, he wrote to his brother that you two should have a fine home and sufficient land in the town proper and around the township until they can verify your bringing five men servants over. Leonard Calvert will treat you well."

He chewed a biscuit, drank his beer, and gazed out to sea.

Margaret waited, but he said no more. Finally, she spoke. "He may have promised, but even if there be but two hundred residents in St. Mary's, and he planned for sixty manors, it seems the math comes up a wee short for any homes for newcomers, Giles, and we are the newcomers."

"How many people lived on father's land?" Giles smirked. "If each gentleman paid passage, say for nine people—his family and five headright-indentured, will there be manor land left for the fine Brent family? I'd say any gentleman would have a pick of about forty." Giles grinned wide and popped another biscuit completely into his mouth.

After he had chewed sufficiently, Mary said, "Please, tell more about the town, the markets, and shops. Also, if natives gave up their land willingly, as you say, for the making of St. Mary's, I fear they may take it back."

Margaret stared in awe at her brother. "I am more interested in how you manage to down those biscuits without breaking your teeth."

He ignored her. "The Piscataway tribe of the Yaocomaco village natives gave their land in trade to Calvert's men. They're actually a rather friendly sort. Still, Leonard and Cecil had a fort built around the town proper because the Susquehannock continually threatened the Piscataway. A smart move, that fort, because Wannas, the tayac of the Piscataway, mistrusted us."

"You said they are friendly." Margaret shook her head. "Now we must fear them and hide behind the walls of some fort." She did not trust the wisdom of her younger brother, and this conversation didn't help.

"Don't worry about Wannas. He's dead. We're talking about when Leonard Calvert first arrived in 1634."

"Tayac—you said he was a tayac?" Mary waited for his clarification.

"Head Chief."

"If our people killed him," Margaret said, "then they shall be vengeful. I've heard stories about how the Indian's skin their captives alive and burn them. Have these St. Mary's natives killed any English yet?"

"The English didn't kill him. His younger brother did because he was worried Wannas would kill the English. Kittamaquund, the brother, is the current tayac. His men call him wise because he knows the English will help protect them from the Susquehannock."

"Heavens, Giles." Margaret clasped her rosary. "We are about to make our homes with a murdering lot who kill their own kin."

"Hardly. Leonard insists they enjoy peace and respect the English. Shy, but quite friendly. The tales you've heard about the scalping, skinning, and stake burning came from the Virginia natives and the Jamestown settlers."

Margaret did not feel as confident about this matter as her brother. "Tell us about the homes Cecil has built."

"He commissioned a large frame home for Leonard, because the Governor of Maryland needs to conduct business from his home. He holds general assemblies and provincial courts there. I do hope they've built an ordinary by now." He grinned. "I look forward to evenings with ale and good conversation." He shook his head. "I must say it will be a joy to be where the floor doesn't roll all the blasted time."

They didn't appear to have moved much closer to any landmass. But then distances at sea were deceiving. The last island they approached took forever for them to reach. Margaret had hoped the island would have a Catholic Church. How many days ago had that been? How many days had they been at sea? She'd lost track.

"Tell me, will they have a church? Cecil kept saying Catholics in Maryland could worship without fear." Being so near to Maryland made her jittery.

He stared out to sea. "I know personally that St. Mary's has two Catholic Priests, and several more by now."

"Two and more—heavens." Mary clasped Margaret's hand.

"This year they built a small brick church."

Coming to this new place had been the right choice. At least two priests, a lovely church, and everyone welcoming them within their faith.

Peaceful prayers in public...

"I must ask," Giles said, "what brings you two up on deck so early this morning?"

"We planned to be the first to see the Province of Maryland." Mary giggled and glanced at Margaret. "I came up before dawn and watched them drop the lead line."

Margaret tilted her head and waited.

"It helps the captain know where they are. If it's dark or foggy, they drop a weighted line down with the end covered in tallow and bee's wax. When they pull it up, they can see if it's sandy or whatever might be below."

"I see." Margaret said, "If it is sandy then they know we are close to land."

Mary flushed and gave a shrug. "I presume."

Giles knitted his brow. "And why do you think you'll see Maryland today?"

Mary turned and studied him without speaking. Her brow pinched.

"Those clouds," Margaret pointed, saying, "on the horizon—Mary said—"

"Dear ladies, those clouds cover Nova Scotia. We'll be docking for fresh water and supplies. We've days to go before we get to Maryland."

Mary's mouth opened, then shut. She jutted her chin out, looking away.

He touched his sister's shoulder. "We are all tired of being trapped on this dank and dreary vessel. I understand you want off, but what made you think we would arrive today?"

After a pause, Mary, cheeks burning red, mumbled, "The quartermaster said we'd see land today. I do so need to be on land, and it's been so long. Naturally, I thought—"

"When we dock to replenish the water and supplies, you'll be able to go on shore for a short time. The captain could have gone the way of the *Ark* and *Dove*, a longer way to the West Indies, but we would be sailing many more weeks. This way is quicker. The West Indies islands have a large importation of Irish, many of whom are criminals, and also the interesting West Africans. This creates a climate of unrest and distrust. You would not be leaving the ship if we docked there. Say a blessing that the captain sailed this route."

PART TWO

ST. MARY'S CITY PROVINCE OF MARYLAND

Chapter 14
November 22, 1638

Within the character of the citizens lies the welfare of the nation.
- Cicero

ENDLESS DAYS LATER, WHEN the quartermaster announced the *Charity* and *Swan* would turn into the Chesapeake Bay, all on board cheered. Morning became afternoon when the two ships left the bay and sailed up a wide river, then in time rounded a corner, and glided up another river.

A small but authoritative chirping came from a treetop. Then rich flute-like whistles from a neighboring tree echoed, along with a series of low chirps. After which, silence took hold except for the murmur of shipmates and a steady slosh of the deep water flowing against the *Charity's* hull. The ship continued up the St. George River. Everyone on deck stood in the quietness, watching, and waiting. Another treetop call invited a chorus of similar sounds.

"See—there." Mary pointed to the trees. "Way up—on the highest branch of the tallest tree?"

Margaret caught a glimpse of the music maker, a blackbird. It flew from tree to tree. This appeared to be unlike any blackbird she had seen before. He displayed a flash of bright orange, a black and orange bird.

"I am surprised these birds winter this far north." Mary searched the other trees.

"I do not see any others."

"They must be stragglers." Mary said. "The rest of the flock have flown off to enjoy a holiday."

The bird disappeared. Mary grabbed Margaret's wrist and shook it.

"Did you see its colors? Orange and black—the colors of Lord Baltimore—a most fitting welcome to this lovely place."

The river flowed wide and deep and, according to the captain, allowed any ship of any size and breadth passage without concern. The huge trees along the high banks reached to the heavens, and shrubbery stood apart leaving breathing space between—not like entangled undergrowth messes found in England. Everything appeared permanent and solid. Margaret saw no swamps or marshes, just gentle banks jutting from the river with an occasional sandy strip of beach washed up from the salty St. George River.

Four or five leagues to go until they would arrive at St. Mary's, according to the captain when they had entered the St. George. She searched the tops of the hickory, oak, and other trees along the river for Mary's Baltimore bird, one cloaked in the colors of the English Lord of this land.

Everything, including the chilliness of the winter air around them, felt fresh and strange, yet ancient and untouched. Her wonder at being in this strange place, knowing she'd be here for the rest of her life, made it difficult to breathe.

A movement on the deck caught her attention. Two members of the ship's crew stood by one of the cannons, a small one.

One ceremoniously leaned over and lit the fuse—

"Holy Mother, help us." Margaret gripped her sister with one hand and her rosary with the other.

The silence exploded.

She stumbled backwards, pulling Mary with her.

"We are being attacked!" Margaret shouted to Giles. "What to do—?"

The two brothers broke out in guffaws. Mary and Margaret darted looks at each other and stepped smartly away from them, clutching their woolen cloaks close.

"We're almost there, silly women." Giles laughed. "All ships announce their arrival by firing shots from their ordnance."

Margaret regained her original position next to the railing, standing upright and still. She allowed an ill mood to overtake her.

This cannon shot will be the first of many unpleasant reasons for our brothers to ridicule us.

"Brothers." Mary smirked. "You jest about our lack of knowledge, but still when we approached Nova Scotia, no shots were fired."

Fulke answered. "Our pinnace, the *Swan*, went before."

Giles studied the banks of the shore. "They saw us coming. No need to notify with cannons."

Such an unpleasant blast of noise would send the colorful birds and other little creatures into hiding for months. Yet Margaret saw movement on the high banks between the brush and trees. She didn't get a clear look, but it had crouched, then lurched.

She had seen fur. She was sure of it—like some large animal—no. The cannon would have frightened it away. She glanced to see if Giles had seen anything, but he stood with head bent in conference with Fulke.

The *Charity* rounded a point of land and seconds later the dock, with a gathering of villagers, came into view. They cheered and waved from the high slopes of the bank as well as the sandy shore.

Like a new colt about to be born, or as if one prepared to open a birthday gift, Margaret's anticipation grew beyond containment. She lifted her hand, waving back to the exuberant faces on shore—her foul mood bubbled away into grins of new possibilities.

The ship glided up to the dock. Seamen and dock workers leapt and scurried around to attend the sails and secure the ship. The *Swan* followed—an obedient shadow.

"We made it—we crossed the ocean." Mary actually chortled. She said more, but Margaret's mind screened out the words and focused on the welcoming of the waving strangers who would soon be her friends, neighbors, and fellow townspeople. She picked out the priest—not one, but two. And who was that handsome, tall fellow on the dock with sleepy eyes, wavy dark hair, and looking quite splendid, dressed in his finest? His chin even had an endearing slight cleft.

He appeared outstanding by comparison to the nervous man who stood next to him, displaying a tight smile—a smile he protected like it might end up broken. He held the hand of a young boy who mirrored the older man in dress and rigid manner. A pretty young woman stood next to him—probably his wife. Deep inside Margaret felt a churning.

Dear Mother above, how will I ever have the wisdom to remember who each of these people are and their names?

Sailors lowered the gangplank and the ship's captain welcomed the tall, elegantly dressed man on board. When he doffed his feathered hat, Margaret caught her breath. The man with lace cuffs, gilded hat band, and silken hose had to be her cousin, Governor Leonard Calvert, Lord Baltimore's brother. Fulke extended his hand as did Giles. The three talked for a moment, then the Governor's attention drew to included Mary and Margaret.

"The Ladies Brent, I trust you made this long, treacherous voyage with minimum discomfort. You both appear refreshed and well."

Margaret extended her hand, and he took it to his lip for the ceremonial kiss. He did the same with Mary.

"Thank you, sir." Margaret said, "I fear your kind words about our appearance are far from actuality. We did manage well, and the captain and the quartermaster, as did the ship's crew, kindly saw our needs were met. I do ask a favor, sir, if you wouldn't object."

"I am at your service." He gave a slight bow.

"Governor, if you do not mind, we would wish you to dispense with such formalities. Please call us by our forenames, Mary and Margaret. After all, if you remember, we once played together as children, and we have a relation—a great-grandparent in common, I believe."

"Well and good, then. Mary and Margaret, it 'tis." He smiled at her brothers. "My cook has prepared a late-day repast for us. I've invited a few of my associates to join us. However, if your trip was too arduous, we could plan to socialize another time."

"Speaking for my brother and sisters," Giles said, "You may be assured—we would take delight in meeting our new neighbors and would receive with pleasure any meal not prepared on any blasted ship."

Leonard chuckled. "Well put, Giles. The four of you will spend the night as my guests. Meanwhile, I'll see to it the servants are shown to your new house. My maids will provide them with dinner. Your people can take care of storing your possessions and preparing your home for occupancy tomorrow. Your livestock will need tending also."

House? Home? Margaret bristled, but maybe he had misspoken.

"Thoughtful of you, Leonard." Fulke waved for his sisters to pass in front to descend the gangway.

Margaret sensed she had something akin to frogs leaping around in her stomach. She found it difficult to concentrate. Dinner with the governor and associates, a new home she hadn't seen, and strange people waiting to meet her... It appeared everyone on the dock and hillside watched her every move.

The young boy, whose father clutched his hand, raised his other and gave a small wave.

Margaret swallowed, managed a tiny smile, and waved back. Then everyone on the dock followed with a nod or wave in welcoming them.

She carefully stepped onto the narrow gangway and cautiously moved down the steep slope. When she stepped onto the dock, its solidity took her aback. She took another careful, unusually high step. Of course, the dock held firm, unlike the constant rolling and listing she had experienced this last month.

Mary's gait, too, appeared unsure. They might as well still be on the high sea for they had lost their sense of stability. Margaret had not thought much about it during their brief island stop, but this would be more than a short time ashore. This would be their home. What if their legs and feet would forever expect the world to pitch and roll? Margaret held Mary's hand, and they exchanged worried glances.

Her brothers disembarked with Governor Calvert following.

Before Leonard Calvert could usher them any farther, both priests scurried over and introduced themselves.

Father Andrew White motioned for Father Philip Fisher to acknowledge the villagers and asked all to bow their heads in prayer. Margaret bowed hers—her heart thumping.

Lord Baltimore's promises were true. They could pray out in public on this glorious day.

Leonard cleared his throat several times. Margaret glanced at him. He strode toward Father White, his palm raised as if to halt what would come next.

But Father White hadn't seen him, and in his strong voice carried on.

"Oh, most heavenly father," he began the invocation, "we rejoice in this hour with humble gratitude for your numerous blessings not only for this pristine winter day wrapped in sunshine but for carrying safely to our shores these devout servants of yours. Grant these brothers and sisters peace and plenty and surround them with the goodness of your love as they continue their journey forward in their new life as our friends and our neighbors. We ask in thy name, Jesus Christ our Lord. Amen."

A soft chorus echoed, "Amen."

The nervous, tight-lipped man frowned, then strode over and mumbled something to Leonard Calvert. Margaret couldn't hear but something had stirred the pleasantness out of the day.

Calvert, now the one with tight lips, waved him away, and strode over to the two priests, interrupting their conversation with Giles and Fulke.

"Pardon me, but I must ask for a personal word with Father White and Father Fisher."

One thing of value Margaret had learned growing up was when men had no regard for the women around, the women gained quiet moments to evaluate the actions of those men.

Calvert and the two fathers stepped a few paces away, and anyone could tell the conversation did not end pleasantly. They stared at each other for a moment, then worked smiles on their faces, and greeted the Brents. Father White bid them a farewell and said he looked forward to visiting with them later. Father Phillip Fisher followed, *as any obedient shadow would.*

"Mister Lewger," Leonard said to the nervous man inclined to mumble in Calvert's ear. "These are the Brents from Gloucester—Fulke, Giles, and the Ladies Margaret and Mary. Mister Lewger has been appointed by my brother as secretary to the council and is a most valuable assemblyman."

Secretary Lewger, a round man of short but healthy stature, removed his hat that covered his shiny blonde locks, and bowed. "Lord Baltimore speaks highly of your father. Welcome to St. Mary's Township." He beckoned to the woman and boy, who had waved to her. "Ann, John, please step over to greet the Brents. My dear wife Ann, and my son John. He's become quite a worker now that he's ten."

The diminutive, quiet woman with sky blue eyes and light brown hair walked next to a clean-scrubbed boy, sporting locks like his father's, nodded, but said nothing.

Margaret leaned over toward young John, "When did you come to St. Mary's City?"

"Last year, ma'am." He looked up at his father, then added, "My father's a friend of Lord Baltimore. He brought important papers from him for our Governor."

"Ahem." Lewger glared at his son, The boy hunched up, wrapped his arms around his middle, and studied the ground.

If Lewger in fact had just intimidated his son, Margaret refused to let it stand. "Tell me, young John, do you like being here in St. Mary's City?"

He glanced back at his father, then nodded.

"If I may ask," Margaret continued, "what preferences occupy your time here in Maryland?"

"Fishing, trapping, and whittling." He stole a glance at his father, who stared back at the boy. "I find pleasure in my studies, too."

A pleasant, rugged-looking man stepped up next to the Lewger family. Removing his hat, he held out his hand toward Fulke and Giles. "Gentlemen, what an honor to meet you at last. I am Robert Clarke, surveyor. We are privileged to have the Brent brothers as part of our community. I have surveyed your land patent—a bully piece of land you have." He chuckled. "I suspect you'll keep me busy over the years, bringing more people to St. Mary's City."

"Undoubtedly so," Leonard said. "Robert does fine work. It's unfortunate the Brents cannot meet our good friend Captain Cornwallis." Leonard nodded to her brothers. "He is one of our councilmen, but he's off to England on business. No matter, you'll meet him in a few weeks when he returns." Leonard nodded and waved farewell to those crowded on the dock. "We shall walk up this path to my carriage on the cliff."

Chapter 15

What lies behind you and what lies before you, pales compared to what lies within you.

- Ralph Waldo Emerson

MORE SHIP PASSENGERS BEGAN to disembark. The indentured servants had spent most of the crossing down in steerage. The seamen would clear the ship of all travelers, then start the arduous process of unloading the *Charity's* cargo. Next, they would stow the large volumes of goods stacked on the dock to be taken to England. The dockworkers and the sailors would roll the barrels of tobacco and other merchandise up the gangplank along with carrying crates filled with trade goods and finally the livestock would be boarded.

"Leonard," Giles said, "we would like to have our belongings fetched that are stowed in our cabins on the *Charity*."

"My men will bring them to the house." He directed the Brents along the narrow sandy beach. "I decided it fitting to harness up the horses today because of your exhausting voyage. However, we do engage in much walking about." Leonard's face softened once he had departed from the group who visited on the dock. "Over there we have a wider trail, but when ships arrive, we leave it open for the wagons."

Leonard held his arm out for Margaret. She turned from watching the sailors and stared at him. His long nose complemented a linear face—along with the creased chin and a small mustache. His heavy lidded, greenish eyes gave him a perpetual agreeable appearance. Leonard seemed to be a true, though earnest, gentle man. It would be impolite not to oblige him. Margaret smiled and placed her wrist loosely through the crook of his elbow.

He seemed to take command in an unspoken way. She approved.

"Cousin Leonard," Margaret said, "Please do not think me bold, but I perceived some uncomfortable business between you and the two priests. Has our arrival stirred up some consternation?"

"Uncomfortable?" He stopped and studied her. She wondered what he might see in her face.

With her arm still looped through his, she lowered her eyes. "I don't mean to be intrusive into private matters, but if it has to do with my sister, brothers and—"

"Uncomfortable. I dare say." He sighed. "Your words only hint at the seriousness of the situation... a most grave matter. However, dear lady, your family has nothing to do with this *uncomfortable* matter." He gazed off across the river, then said, "Delicate negotiations will be the only tool to keep us all from suffering in the end."

"My new homeland," Margaret said, "will serve me best if I have an understanding of the people who inhabit it. I fear it will take me a long while to learn what incites each person's passion. However, through the four years you have been governor, you undoubtedly know who has the good of the public in their hearts, and who works only for selfish gains."

"The pain of it is, Margaret, I see many townsmen embracing the need for self-advancement over all else." Calvert patted Margaret's wrist and then continued up the winding dirt path. "My brother Cecil sent over a list of rules with Sir Lewger this last year... Well, no matter. We have much to tell each other. Let's not spoil our welcoming with, as you said, *uncomfortableness*." And there was that smile again, a smile requiring much work to convince.

Margaret surveyed the small groups gathered down by the dock where the ship's cargo was being unloaded. Oxen, harnessed to empty wagons and carts, stood waiting as men sorted, selected, and packed items accordingly. A large "B" labeled their goods.

Two men began to load a cart with items marked with the "B". Margaret glanced at Leonard. He had sent his people down to help transfer the Brent belongings to their new homes. When she caught sight of Goodwin's donkey in front of his cow coming down the ramp, an unidentified feeling swept over her. *A sign?* The donkey, who had been through the most troubling of times during its wee life, had survived and had arrived safely in this new place where he would be cared for and appreciated.

Fulke, Giles, and Mary chatted about the differences between England and Maryland and compared the land, air, and even the rivers Severn and Avalon to the St. George. Exhaustion from the crossing had not quelled their spirits. The path folded back on itself. Margaret looked out over the dock, the ships below, and the river as they neared the top of the embankment.

Some of the townspeople had departed the upper bank. Those who remained greeted Governor Calvert and the Brents with nods and smiles, and words such as, "Welcome home. Welcome to St. Mary's City."

Welcome home. Yes, this is home, but here stand strangers... not those who know me or whom I love.

Her frogs started leaping around again. She had nowhere to go to quiet them.

Leonard waited for Margaret's siblings to catch up, then they all walked over to the giant trees lining the bank where his horses and carriage waited. Once seated, Leonard's coachman called to the horses. They moved along the riverbank under a canopy of walnut, ash, chestnut, and oak, not toward what appeared to be a decrepit, wooden palisade sporting cannons.

Leonard leaned forward and said, "I've asked my coachman to drive past your home."

"Home, who's home?" Margaret glanced over to Mary. Heat rose.

He talks of only one home.

"Ladies, you no longer live in your sweet Gloucester with no need for a fort."

Fort? That pathetic fort would protect no one.

Margaret couldn't bring herself to insult her host with degrading remarks about the city's ramshackle security, but still she had to speak her mind.

"Your tastes for England belie the sour truth, my cousin." Margaret fought to control her voice. "Would it be for forts in England, Catholics might keep their heads a bit longer. Did Lord Baltimore not mention, to persuade my sister and I to make this voyage, he promised all the rights of the first settlers, and upon arriving said Mary and I should have as fine a home as available."

"Margaret, you do not know what this country holds. The physical labor necessary to survive—"

"We expect no less than Cecil promised." She glared at him. "We will not be living with our dear brothers, even for a night. We, if necessary, shall sleep under the stars."

His shoulders slumped.

Fulke patted him on the back. "We've fought this battle, Leonard. You should see our scars."

"Your promise will be fulfilled. Let's drive south to see Giles and Fulke's home, then back toward the fort to show the ladies where they'll live until they bring their fifth man over."

"We shall meet our agreement for the land patents before the end of next year."

Less than a mile later, Mary pointed, "Oh my—Look at this lovely white manor."

But Margaret ignored Mary and kept her sight fastened to where she had seen movement behind a cluster of trees. She kept searching for what had looked like a sinewy and hairy figure. *There.* She saw it crouching, silently watching them like a cat ready to pounce on a rat. Her skin raised in tiny bumps. This must be what she saw from the ship.

Keeping her gaze on the human-like animal, she leaned over ready to tell Leonard.

"Gentlemen." Leonard's voice made her jump. "Do you find this home to your liking? The design follows the hall and parlor houses of Virginia and the southern provinces. You'll find a free-standing kitchen off the back door and another room in the rear. Naturally, you may add on as you wish."

Maybe her eyes had played tricks on her. The creature had vanished.

Calvert's horses trotted up the lane, stopping at the two storied, white-framed house. Two fireplaces constructed at opposite ends of the long house had been lit. Chimney smoke rose out, up, and wove around itself on this cold but quiet afternoon.

Everyone exclaimed and chittered. When Mary asked if they could go in, Leonard said he didn't want to bother the servants preparing the home for the next morning's occupancy.

Margaret decided this would be one of Lord Baltimore's proposed sixty manors.

Leonard's coachman drove them back to the shabby remains of the fort and past a row of thatched wooden cottages to a smaller manor where Margaret and Mary would live. It looked of similar build as Fulke and Giles's, but not washed in white and no second floor, just a loft. Margaret worried if this lot had room enough for some livestock, gardens, and an outbuilding or two. Their fireplaces had not been lit.

"Some of my people will assist your men and maids in readying the house for your occupancy tomorrow." His voice carried worry, wrapped in resignation.

When they came to Leonard's home, everyone agreed none would lack for English comfort here. However, Margaret knew it didn't compare.

"We require sufficient space for our court and assembly gathering." His home, less impressive, had a slight resemblance to Fulke and Giles's. "I have been fiddling with plans to construct a larger structure outside the walls of the fort that will contain guest rooms for visiting assemblymen as well as a meeting hall. You met John Lewger and his family at the dock. As soon as the Lewger's home is finished—a mile north of here, the provincial court and general assembly will be meeting there."

Leonard Calvert approached his door. A tall servant opened it and showed them into a long, high ceiling room. The many diamond-paned glass windows let the low evening sunlight play on carved, dark walnut furniture, including a table-top which fashionably displayed a multicolored carpet. Fragrant burning hard-wood in the fireplace, with sounds of soft grumbles and snaps, cast a welcoming glow, replacing the golden light of the disappearing sun.

One of Leonard's maids removed their cloaks.

"Since the two priests, a few of my assemblymen, and some wives will be joining us this evening, I suspect you'll want a few minutes to yourselves before dinner."

Margaret inhaled the rich smell of polished wood, warm spices coming from the back of the house, and the abundant beeswax candles. Her greatest pleasure came from not being jounced around in the cramped, musky quarters she had shared with a small gray rat.

For now, she soaked in the welcoming enormous space with four untilting walls.

Leonard motioned toward an elderly woman wearing an apron. "Missus Davis will show you to your rooms, and you'll be notified when our guests have arrived, in about an hour." Then he excused himself.

She and Mary, with their brothers, followed Missus Davis up the stairs. They walked through a low-ceiling room and passed two doors. Missus Davis opened another door and smiled at Margaret. Even though the ceiling was low, the bed seemed huge after her bunk on the ship. She sank down on the periwinkle-blue covering, enjoying its softness. The heaviness of the day overtook her, and she curled up, closing her eyes... for just a moment

A tap on the door woke her.

My angels above—

"Please enter." Margaret stood, smoothing her dress, and set her mind back into this new strange world.

Mary peeked around the door. She slipped in, closing it behind her. "Aren't you surprised at the grandness of our rooms way over here in this wilderness? Goodness, sister, you've been sleeping. You haven't yet changed for dinner. Show me where Missus Davis put your bundle. We're bound to be late. We must not have that."

Before Margaret could respond, Mary glanced around, rushed over by the window, picked up the travel bundle, and put it on the bed.

Margaret sorted through her belongings, pulled out an emerald-green skirt and matching bodice to replace the gray woolen ones she had worn over her petticoat. She dropped them on the bed and hunted for her hairbrush.

Her younger sister full of exhausting exuberance said, "Missus Davis filled our washbasins with hot water but yours is certain to be tepid by now." Mary carefully spread out Margaret's skirt on the bed, then she turned around fluffing out her own skirt. "I do hope my gown doesn't look like it's spent a month on some musty ship."

"Dark rose flatters your complexion. You're lovely as always." Margaret splashed the cool water on her face and then patted it dry.

"Margaret, for heaven's sake. Missus Davis will be here any moment." Mary held the green skirt up for her.

Changing quickly, Margaret grabbed her brush, praying her uncooperative red hair would behave. All the while, Mary chided her for being pokey and chattered about who might attend the dinner and what exciting things they might learn.

This incessant babble did nothing to quiet Margaret's leaping frogs.

Another rap on the door, and Mary rushed over to open it. "This must be Missus Davis—are you ready?"

"Peasley here, to escort the Gentlemen and Ladies Brent to the hall." A lean, tall, balding servant with dark eyes, dressed in dark apparel with white sleeves and collar, bowed slightly. Their brothers stood behind him with bemused looks.

Chapter 16

The greatness of character is dependent on personality.
- James Fenimore Cooper

MARGARET SUPPOSED THEY MADE quite a procession marching down the steep staircase following Peasley. He led them to the great hall where a handful of guests stood around the governor in discussion.

Peasley stopped the Brents at the door and announced, "Ladies and Gentlemen, arriving on our shores today from Gloucester, England, I present the gentlemen Fulke Brent, Giles Brent, and their sisters, the Ladies Margaret and Mary Brent."

Silence filled the immense room where abundant candles in wall brackets cast golden light. Mary flushed as everyone turned toward them. Margaret felt certain she must be blushing too. The two of them seldom courted or enjoyed singular attention. Everyone clapped.

Leonard stepped forward and raised his hand. "These fine voyagers made the long, arduous journey mindful and dedicated to our Lord Proprietor's purpose. As Catholics, Lord Baltimore put before us this great task of being one with our Protestant brothers. We gentlemen, with our friends and neighbors, understand the value of legislating together, refining our laws and policies not only for the prosperity of Maryland, but for the good of her citizens regardless of our own religious beliefs. We, under the Common Law of England, shall worship as we like but remain united as equals in governing this land."

"Here, here," a chorus of male voices rang out. The women smiled.

Leonard waved his hand to bring them all closer. "Please come now and introduce yourselves before Missus Davis calls us into the dining hall for our repast."

The mellow tones of a calf-skin bow being drawn across the strings of a gamba caused Margaret to ignore the gathering and study the origin of the music. In the corner farthest from the glow of the fireplace a man, eyes closed, seemed lost in the sweet sounds coming from his viola. A harpsichord, unused, stood beside him.

Someone said something to her.

"Forgive me, please." Margaret recognized her as the wife of the man and mother of the boy at the dock. "I didn't mean to ignore you, but I don't know what I expected. I had not anticipated lovely music. I didn't intend to be rude."

The petite, pretty woman in a rose and cream taffeta gown said, "That's Henry. He finished his four years and no longer serves the governor as an indentured. Yet he enjoys playing for an audience along with the little extra income, probably because he and his wife expect their first baby soon."

"A well-played musical instrument is an asset to any community." Margaret said. "Who plays the harpsicord?"

"No one I know of... I've never heard a sound from it."

"I met you on the dock with your son and husband, Missus Lewger, is it?"

"My, what a memory. Please call me Ann. I hope you and your sister will see your way to pay me visit after you have settled. Our manor lands and home lie north of St. Mary's Fort near the mill across Mill Creek. Our men have taken weeks in the building of our home. There's still much to do, but it is ready to receive visitors."

The woman's welcoming words surprised Margaret. Building large homes in England took much longer than weeks, and the distances between their England estates made visits to neighbors an infrequent occurrence.

"It is delightful to be so welcomed."

"And welcomed you are," Ann said. "Soon our home will be host to all the assemblymen. You may understand with so few ladies here in Maryland how I much desire your company."

"Leonard, or rather Governor Calvert, said everyone walks most places. We Brents will need to learn the land and learn who lives where, I fear." Margaret hadn't passed any shops or businesses within the fort of St. Mary's City. "I am pleased to know this community has a mill. Are there markets?"

"Our city is a cluster of houses within the fort and then outlying homes, farms, and manor lands up and down St. George River. Captain Cornwallis received permission from the Lord Proprietor to build the mill. The trading ships sailing up the St. George become our markets. I believe it was your thoughtful brothers who made sure we have a smithy. We soon hope to have an ordinary." She glanced around at a woman waiting behind her, then leaned in and said in a soft voice, "You must meet the captain when he returns."

Margaret hid her own curiosity behind a practiced smile about Ann's whispering.

Touching Margaret's sleeve, Ann stepped aside and nodded to the serious-faced woman waiting to speak to Margaret. Even the woman's dress, a gray frock, looked solemn. Then the memories of Margaret's mother's death flooded back when she noticed the woman's black armband.

Ann motioned to the woman to come forward, and said, "Lady Brent, have you met Missus Hawley?"

"Please, call me Margaret—and my sister—" Margaret looked around and saw Mary engaged in a discussion with an elegant woman and one of the priests. "My sister Mary appears occupied right now. Have you met her?"

Peasley had entered the room carrying a tray of ornate wine goblets and made his way around to each guest. Ann Lewger accepted hers and excused herself, saying she wanted to meet Mary. Margaret took one, but Missus Hawley refused.

"Missus Hawley," Margaret said, "It saddens me to see you wear the black band of mourning, and it brings to mind my dear mother. I hope my mentioning it does not cause you pain."

The woman closed her eyes, took a deep breath, and then looked up at

Margaret and smiled. "I'm sorry about your mother. Death usually inflicts long-lasting wounds."

She dabbed her cheeks with a small piece of lace cloth and looked away.

"How awful of me." Margaret didn't know how to fix this. "I fear whenever I open my mouth, my thoughts spill out."

"You needn't apologize." Missus Hawley swallowed hard and seemed back in control. "I should never have come. The governor asked if I might, he said he wanted me to meet you and your sister. His close association with my husband, the three of them, the captain, my Mister Hawley, and Governor Calvert—" She turned away again.

Margaret stood silent. Her lack of understanding left her helpless to console.

"You see," Missus Hawley said, "the three of them, they were the heart of Lord Baltimore's council. But... it's too soon. I should keep to my home. One just should not die alone."

Without thinking, Margaret said, "My Heavens, what happened? Was Mister Hawley ill?"

"Not at all. Well, no one knows." She heaved a sigh, shaking her head. "Last July they found him. Maybe, well, some say it might have been an accident."

Desperate to manage a more acceptable conversation, Margaret said, "Tell me, Missus Hawley, I am curious to know who the handsome couple over by the musician with the viola is? The gentleman seems completely lost in whatever the lady tells him."

"Hmm, yes. Thomas Greene and his insipid wife, Ann. They were married the year they arrived on the banks of St. George, and everyone says their wedding was the first Christian wedding in Maryland. I would not bet my bonnet on that. One should consider she had been married prior to arriving, but I don't know to whom. Cox, somebody, and I believe she's the sister of the surgeon, Doctor Gerard, over in St. Clemmons. They all sailed together in 1634 on the *Ark*. I suspect there's a scandal hiding somewhere. You'll have to excuse them. Even though they have two little boys, they still act like newlyweds. Pfft, it's been four years."

This woman was like a rooster, knowing all the activities in the barnyard, keeping a beady eye on the flock. The wise decision for Margaret would be to quiet her tongue. Yet there stood Mary, conversing with a stylish woman—someone quite intriguing.

"Who might the elegant lady engaged with my sister be?"

"She's something else. Her husband is always running back and forth to England or somewhere. Sometimes she goes with him, but he's been known to give her charge of all his business matters and to look after their servants. I swear, they must have at least twenty, and he trusts her enough to leave her in charge of it all. Can't imagine any sane man leaving such a fortune in the hands of a woman. No matter. That will end soon. Captain Cornwallis has employed a man with a family to oversee his estate." Missus Hawley glanced back at Mister Greene and his wife. "I suspect because he's a gentleman, Mister Greene tolerates her husband, but he certainly doesn't much care for him. I know, because he and my husband had many dealings together."

"Your husband and who? Mister Greene?" Margaret wanted to leave—go to her room. This conversation had become confusing and seemed of ill purpose.

"Oh no, my husband and Captain Cornwallis. My—when the captain enters the room, we all lose our wits. A captain of all, I say, with a tall great stance, quite sturdy but not barrel-like, and his deep-set eyes see everything. Your red hair reminds me of cinnamon and flames, but his hair seems more the softness of a robin's breast."

"I see." Margaret didn't see at all.

"Mister Greene knows Lord Baltimore values Captain Cornwallis. Considering his wealth, everyone values the captain. But I know Mister Greene doesn't much like his ways." She jutted out her jaw. "My husband told me so, and my husband knew what went on between these men. He knew a lot, my Mister Hawley. And he and Mister Cornwallis worked together quite closely. They shipped things, planned things, and didn't always agree with Governor Calvert. At least not to his face. They thought it all a waste of their time."

"Pardon? What wasted their time?" Margaret hated when her curiosity rushed ahead of good manners.

Missus Hawley glanced around. "You know," she whispered, "that horrid Kent Island problem."

Chapter 17

The man who has no other existence than that which he partakes in common with all around him, will never have any other than the existence of mediocrity.

- James Fenimore Cooper

LEONARD CALLED OUT. "LADIES, gentlemen, I've been informed the dining hall awaits us." He led them from the meeting hall across the narrow entrance way and through the open doorway.

A fireplace at the far end of the enormous dining hall roared with warmth. Numerous beeswax candles burned in their wall brackets, groups of candles flickered in candelabras set along the table, and more shed their light from the hanging chandelier in the middle of the room. The center of the table held all manner of breads next to freshly churned butter. Platters of various and unusual colored steaming vegetables sat on either side of the mound of baked goods.

Leonard escorted Margaret and Mary to the table where they were to sit, one on each side of him. Their brothers would sit next to their sisters.

Margaret enjoyed seeing him place men with the women in between. This would lead to interesting conversations.

When they all sat, Leonard leaned close to Margaret's ear and whispered, "I've waited an eternity for this evening—for you to actually set foot in Maryland."

"I am quite pleased to be here, Leonard. You must thank your brother for making all this possible." She knew her enjoyment showed on her face.

Then Margaret noticed Mary staring at them. Mary tilted her head, set her jaw, and narrowed her eyes. If Mary had some sort of a problem, Margaret certainly couldn't ask her about it leaning across Leonard. Mary would have to sort it out herself. Margaret studied the other guests.

Father White stood to say grace, then the servants entered. They first carried soup to be ladled into wooden bowls set next to pewter plates. Margaret dipped her spoon in to taste and recognized it as asparagus. She had missed flavorful meals—her mouth watered. She enjoyed another taste. A stout woman, grinning ear to ear, came into the room holding a large platter with spicy cooked meats—venison, mutton, turkey, and fish.

"My dear Missus Hawley," Gentleman Greene's eyes followed the trays of meat while he spoke, "Am I to understand you'll soon be returning to England?" He now looked for the answer in her face.

"There's no reason for me to stay, Mister Greene. With my Mister Hawley gone to his eternal home, I'm left with nothing but worry and creditors. I'll be in a better position to settle his affairs once I'm back on the soil of our dear homeland."

The kitchen staff brought in more dishes and removed others, filling the tankards with light ale. The Brent brothers lifted the dark mood of the conversation by jesting about how fitting the cake in Gloucester would be for this meal. They each took great pains to describe its every detail.

Leonard relaxed. His eyes sparkled in the candlelight as he listened to the elaborate cake story.

"Please permit me a question." Margaret spoke up during a conversation pause and between bites. "Today I thought I saw some sort of furry beast lurking behind trees, watching us. Leonard, do you have any idea what I might have seen?"

Mary's eyes opened wide. "Are we now to worry about being eaten?"

"You didn't imagine it." Leonard tore off a piece of bread and looked at the brothers. Then he said, "It is a rather common occurrence, especially when a ship arrives. Fulke, Giles, any guesses?"

"The curiosity of the Wild Indian is ever present." Giles winked at Margaret. "I'm sure you saw one or more of the tribesmen. They like to know who arrives and who leaves."

"But, Giles, what I saw was quite hairy—not like a human except in stance."

"Furs and feathers," Leonard said. "In winter, beaver fur makes warm cloaks for the natives."

Margaret glanced around at everyone else. No one but her sister seemed concerned. "I should think it a worry to have them lurking about, spying."

"We're all God's creatures, Lady Brent." Father Fisher said, "Their ways keep them safe. They must be alert and ever watch for enemies."

"They regard us as their enemies?" Mary stopped eating.

"They receive us in friendship." Father Fisher said. "If allowed, Father White would live among the savages. He's learning their language, but unless he spends more time with them, his efforts are slowed."

"Fascinating. You communicate with them." Mary cocked her head. Margaret knew what her inquisitive younger sister would ask next. "Is their language difficult to learn?"

Father Fisher answered, "Ah, with practice, and careful hearing, no. However, it is full of soft guttural sounds we don't use in our language."

Her older brother spoke up. "Whatever would they have to say of importance?"

"Fulke," Leonard said, "do not underestimate these gentle people. They welcomed us and almost gave us this land because these humble people saw it necessary to remove themselves to a more protected area nearer their kin. By the time we arrived, many had already left. They fear the Susquehannock tribe's frequent invasions."

Eleanor Hawley smiled sweetly, leaned over, and touched Fulke's hand. "They even steal the Yaocomaco women. So terrifying."

Fulke flinched and slid his hand from under hers. Margaret suspected he feigned the need to take a drink.

"What do you find about these natives," Mary said, "that engages you in conversation with them, Father White?"

The priest continued to eat. Mary flushed and looked down. Margaret started to say something subtle to the rude priest, but Missus Hawley interrupted.

"My dear Lady Brent," Eleanor Hawley said, "Father White has acquired a slight hearing loss. His affliction probably comes from a bout with malaria, lingering still after all these years. You do know, everyone gets sick here until they are seasoned." In her loudest voice, she said, "Andrew—Andrew White, I say. We have something to ask of you—Father White!"

Everyone, including the priest startled. He stopped chewing and gave Missus Hawley his attention.

"Lady Mary Bent has asked why you're interested in the Indians. What brings you to bother with them?"

"Oh, well." He looked around and cleared his throat. "We have much to learn from our indigenous forest friends. They've taught us many utilitarian lessons." Father White tore off a chunk of venison. "Look around tomorrow. You'll see their artful craft in thatched huts still standing in this village. Yes, if not for these Piscataway Indians, many of us would have passed to the other side. Their large confederacy of tribes, led by the great tayac, extends from the western shores of the Chesapeake to the Potomac River."

No one said anything. He pulled off a smaller piece of the moist, dark meat, and chewed thoughtfully.

"Yes, yes, they know how to best prepare roots and corn for the table, and they show us how and what to hunt for nourishment. Naturally, considering the labor in crushing corn, great appreciation goes to Captain Cornwallis for St. Mary's mill."

"I can only imagine," Mary said, "the hours it would take to crush such hard kernels by hand."

"As we did before the mill and as our natives must do. You see, tonight we enjoy wild turkey as well as venison. When one understands their language, one can teach them to read the Good Book, and then they can become God's children."

Leonard leaned in and said, "Father White has been writing down Catholic Catechism lessons in the Piscataway dialect."

In a loud voice, Father Fisher said, "Please tell everyone how you became endeared to Tayac Kittamaquund and the Piscataway."

"Well, then." Father White wiped his fingers. "They know healing roots and herbs that quell pain or lower fever. However, they did not have the bark from a certain tree that grows in South America and the West Indies. I encountered a Spanish Jesuit there, and after a few hours of verbal exchange he told me this bark to be the best when treating ague. Certainly, going to a new country one must be well prepared for any illness. Upon his advice, I purchased a goodly sized parcel. That was in 1634. After we arrived here, the tayac, Kittamaquund, became ill with chills, fevers, and sweats. No matter what we did, he maintained a sickly lemon pallor. I've seen this before in people who live in England's marsh lands. None of the Piscataway healing herbs cooled him or gave him comfort. I prepared strong hot beverages from my new bark and insisted he drink them. Blessed be to Our Lord who saw fit to rid his body of the wretched fever and spare his life."

"Within the coming months Tayac Kittamaquund and his wife will be baptized." Father Fisher held up his finger and said, "The rest of this tribe of creatures shall not find their real salvation until they are all taught the value of the Good Word. Once they learn, then they too will be baptized as any good Christian."

Mister Greene laughed, "Our priests should teach that indomitable creature Claiborne the Good Word. He shall be the undoing of us all."

Leonard cleared his throat, setting his lips into a hard line.

The two priests exchanged glances. Father White, with a kindly smile, said, "We may tame the savage, but we hold no hope for that Protestant."

"Tell us about your crossing, Lady Mary." Leonard picked up his ale and gave her his crafted smile. "The first time over, we all found the sea quite endless."

Before Mary could respond, Giles interrupted. "Who is this Claiborne fellow?"

Leonard waived his hand dismissively. "We should not discuss bad history tonight. Just know, Claiborne refuses to acknowledge that what was once part of Virginia has now been officially declared a part of Maryland." Leonard set his jaw and glared at the townspeople around the table.

Margaret asked, "Does this Mister Claiborne then believe he has a rightful claim to St. Mary's City?"

Any corrosive acts of contention over borders chilled her. Often this type of strife turned into war. She noticed Giles and Fulke had stopped eating, and they too waited for the answer.

"No, not St. Mary's City. Not at all." Leonard shifted in his place and glanced in turn at Mister Greene, and then the two priests. He cleared his throat and said, "If you must. Mister Claiborne had established his holdings on Kent Island years ago when it belonged to Virginia. However, an appeal to the king's Privy Council five years ago denied his request and all lands within Maryland's province remain in the possession of Lord Baltimore's original grant." Leonard clapped his hands. "Here now. Let's see what delectables have been prepared for the evenings end."

Around the table, men interjected their own versions of the Claiborne story, drowning out each other's words. Margaret sat in silence as voices grew louder, listening as her brothers asked questions.

"Please," Leonard spoke softly to Margaret and Mary, "do not let this talk alarm you. As with all communities, some things are disagreeable, but we have much to offer. Did you know we use tobacco for our currency?"

"I did hear," Mary said, "but I paid no heed. I thought it idle chatter."

"What if one has no crops, such as ourselves?" Margaret's leaping stomach frogs returned. The idea of being in poverty horrified her.

Leonard gave a genuine smile, and said, "We make allowances for those who first arrive. We extend credit to everyone until after the first season's harvest."

Margaret considered this, then said, "Often credit substitutes for the less pleasant concept of debt. I suspect you have many who owe debts that are never paid." She paused, then said, "I believe this might cause many to await some form of restitution while others await punishment."

Chapter 18
February 2, 1639

Make sure you're right then go ahead.
- Davey Crocket

"I SO WISH FOR spring." Mary, coughing, moved her chair closer to the hearth. She had fallen ill these last few weeks. "We should have arrived during warmer weather."

Their maid, Missus Taylor, handed Mary a blanket and stoked up the fire. Margaret looked up from her book and shifted a bit on the hardwood chair, which gave little comfort. When Missus Taylor finished with the fireplace, Margaret smiled—nodding gratitude, then setting her Bible down, rubbed her hands together. Her fingers tingled with numbness.

"I certainly hope our new home will not be this drafty." Margaret fingered through pages to find her place. "No wonder so many fall sick."

Mary picked up her needle, inspecting her sewing. "Father used to keep our lumber a whole year before the servants could build with it. He said the wood needed to dry. If not, it would shrink and leave gaps big enough for vermin to enter."

"Let us keep our woolens in good repair and have our men build twice as many fireplaces."

Mary chuckled.

"You are more agreeable today, Mary. You must be over your fever."

"Why do so many people, especially children, die this first year? It is your turn to endure the first-year sickness, and you too can be *seasoned*."

"I pray the illness spares me. We have missed enough churchgoing."

Mary started to speak, then went back to her sewing.

"Your thoughts spill out, but your words hold back." Margaret cocked her head.

"I am nettled to no end." Mary scowled. "We should not have to share our church with the Protestant faith. These people favor England's Parliament and breed a growing dislike for our king."

Sounds of deep voices with heavy footsteps on crushed oyster shells brought Margaret to the window. Fulke and Giles trotted up their pathway.

"Our brothers have left the meeting at the governor's house." She set her Bible aside and opened the door. "Hurry, now, do not let the heat out."

They stepped through the doorway, removed their hats, shook off their capes, and stomped mud from their shoes.

Before Margaret could protest, Mary interrupted. "Missus Brooks will fix us some hot cider."

One of the maids rushed over to tidy up the floor, but Giles stood there, wearing an unusual grin.

"Obviously, Giles," Margaret said, "you have come to share news."

He glanced around, still smiling, and said, "Events have called me to go to Kent Island tomorrow. We're glad to see you recovering, Mary."

Margaret pulled out the bench and indicated for them to sit at the table, which would allow the maid to clean up the muddy mess.

"When shall we expect to see you again?"

"I plan to return for a couple of days to attend Assembly next month. Leonard will want me to report."

The maid waited with a rag and brush in her hand.

Margaret stared at him. "Your assignment then is good news."

He strode to the table, his face full of expectations. "Why wouldn't it be?"

Fulke's sullen eyes told a different story.

"Oh, you know," Mary waved her hand in the air, and said, "mayhaps the whisperings concerning the Kent Island problem might cause us to worry."

A maid placed leather tankards on the table while Missus Brooks took fresh-baked oat biscuits from the oven and put them on a serving board.

Margaret sighed. Whatever folly this might be, Giles would tell all, but not until savoring the moments of everyone's attention resting on himself. Yet Fulke's concern for this adventure justified hers.

Standing behind his chair, Giles puffed up his chest, and said, "It seems the Susquehannock Indians have invaded and killed a trader on the island. Leonard is quite worried the natives and Claiborne's people will conspire against us here in St. Mary's City. So, for now, you may call me Captain Giles Brent."

"This sounds dangerous." Margaret paused then poured cider into everyone's tankard.

He grinned wider.

"Rather cavalier, younger brother." Fulke picked up his tankard. "You've never led men into battle before, and you're not one whit cautious. I'm surprised Cousin Leonard doesn't see disaster in the making."

"Hoot-hoot, you timid elder. 'Tis a wise captain who uses words before swords."

"Words? You've no sense at all." Mary sat. "How can you use words when you don't even know their language?"

Fulke laughed, punched Giles in the arm, then took a long swig of the hot cider.

"I am searching, but I cannot find anything amusing in this conversation." Margaret scowled at Fulke.

"You are both—so frustrating." Mary stifled a cough.

Giles scowled but Fulke helped himself to a warm biscuit.

Examining the biscuit before sinking his teeth into it, Fulke said, "It seems there is no wheat here in Maryland, except what we brought. However, no one fills our stomachs with such tasty food as your Missus Brookes. Back to the issue of the Susquehannock. Leonard says they mostly threaten the settlers on Kent

Island."

"Yet they killed a trader." Mary set her lips.

"They did." Giles said, "He probably provoked them. From what I hear they come to steal Yaocomaco women."

"You reassure us not." Mary slapped both hands down on the table, staring at him. "What's to keep them from coming here? Everyone talks about *the problem with Kent Island*. It must be more than the Susquehannock, yet no one defines the problem. Here we sit, waiting for these wild natives to come murder us. The only protection we have is Giles's incompetence."

"We're safe enough here," Fulke said, "but there is more to worry about with that island. The inhabitants think the island should not belong to Maryland. Long before the first adventurers came to Maryland, Kent Island, like Maryland, belonged to Virginia. A handful of Virginians petitioned to King Charles, protesting Lord Baltimore's entitlement to the island. The settlers had established a fur-trading business, built a stockade, church, mill, trading post, grew crops and orchards. They simply will not acknowledge Leonard Calvert as their Governor."

"How can we believe a jot of what you're saying, Fulke?" Mary's voice grew louder. "Cecil and his father must have set clear boundaries for Maryland years ago. Even the first Lord Baltimore must have held claim to all his territory before he died. Everyone had to have known the extent of Maryland's province."

Fulke tented his fingers, nodded at Giles, and waited.

Stroking his new beard, Giles shook his head. "Nothing new here, and it all goes back to the early 1630s and one man, William Claiborne."

This sibling conversation would certainly give Margaret a headache.

"You announced," Mary said, "that Leonard sends you because of threats from the Indians, not some crazy man."

"Do you care to know the whole of it or not, sister?" Giles's good humor had flown.

Silence filled the room. Fulke picked up his tankard, drained it, and nodded approvingly to Mary. She answered him with a stone-solid face.

Margaret motioned to the maid to refill his tankard.

Giles, in a softer tone, started his story again. "The feud with Claiborne runs deep and long. Several years ago, and probably still, Claiborne had been involved in illegal trading. This places our Governor, England, Maryland, and even Virginia in an indefensible situation. We cannot tolerate this, or we will be at war. Leonard and Captain Cornwallis have gone to the island several times—armed—"

Margaret interrupted. "Why have we not heard of this?"

"Because it happened several years before we arrived." Giles said, "The first time they confiscated Claiborne's merchant ship, *Longtail,* and refused to return it because of his illegal trading. Claiborne returned with an armed ship, the *Cockatrice*, to retrieve his *Longtail*."

"I fear our cousin Leonard," Fulke said, "still harbors deep anger for the blood they shed."

"However," Giles said, "their efforts were unsuccessful. Last April Leonard, with Captain Cornwallis and others, invaded the island in the early dawn. Claiborne wasn't there, but Leonard, after capturing the settlers, proclaimed he would give amnesty to all who vowed their loyalty to the province."

"Pfft," Mary shook her head. "If I were them, I would have none of it."

Margaret set her tankard down, folded her hands, and studied Mary.

"Think of it." Mary shook her head. "They settled on Virginia land. Then some patent or edict from England comes years later, saying they now live on Maryland soil and have to change their ways. The sheriff doesn't have room to lock them all up. If they did not vow loyalty, what would Leonard do? Hang them?"

"Leonard's lucky you didn't give them advice, little sister." Giles said, "Most of the settlers did vow fidelity to Governor Calvert and Maryland."

"Except for a few like Claiborne," Fulke said, "who will never be loyal. Leonard believes Claiborne will goad the Susquehannock Indians into attacking St. Mary's City."

"I do question Leonard's judgement." Margaret had been silent long enough. "He has unearned faith in his friends' loyalties, and now I wonder about how he selects his appointees. Giles could be slaughtered."

Fulke, in a quiet voice, said, "Margaret, I agree. I too am fearful our cousin may place blind trust in the wrong men."

"You're jealous, brother," Giles said, "because Leonard appointed me captain."

Fulke waved his hand at nothing. "I talk not about you, Giles. I've heard disagreeable stories about men whom Leonard values as his closest council. One of Leonard's officials encouraged his men to participate in an early morning invasion of Kent Island by telling them the plunder would be well worth their time. If Leonard knew this, he'd have the man flogged."

If he's talking about Missus Hawley's husband, maybe she's right in denying his death an accident.

Sighing, Giles nodded. "I also heard that Cornwallis thought invading Kent Island a waste of his valuable time. We must be watchful in selecting confidantes."

"Leonard brought several Kent men to court. Strange results." Fulke said, "After the raid Leonard arrested Thomas Smith, Edward Beckler, along with John Butler, Claiborne's brother-in-law. When Smith pleaded Benefit of Clergy, Leonard refused the plea, saying he could not accept a plea made after the judgment had been declared and never in the case of piracy. They voted eighteen to one. Leonard had Beckler and Smith hanged."

"Not strange at all, I'd say. Leonard had great dislike for Thomas Smith." Giles said, "Smith took part in the killing of Leonard's men during the *Longtail* and *Cockatrice* conflict."

"Smith pleaded Benefit of Clergy." Margaret raised an eyebrow. "So, this man could read and write?" *Had Thomas Smith been a nobleman?* "Yet I too don't understand why you say it is strange to hang two treasonous men."

"They had been burgesses. He ordered them to be hanged, but Leonard had the sheriff release Butler. He claimed Butler had a more agreeable disposition and took the man to live in his home."

Margaret and Mary stared at him.

"Evidently, Leonard thought Butler could be swayed into becoming a loyal commander of Kent Island."

"When did you say this happened?" Margaret asked.

"Short of a year ago." Fulke said.

Giles laughed and shook his head. "Guess that didn't work out so well. Now I'm captain."

"Leonard has no eye for deceit or a person's capability." Mary whispered to Margaret.

Margaret shrugged. "Nothing keeps these people or the natives from sailing up our St. George."

"Maybe some good might be had in all this." Fulke grinned at his younger brother. "Let me set my trust in you, dear brother, to do something most important. Since there are none to be found around St. Mary's City, please bring back two suitable and preferably lovely Kent Island women who might agree to become our wives."

Chapter 19
Early April 1639

Sooner or later we all discover that the important moments in life are not the advertised ones....
- Susan B. Anthony

MARGARET TOOK A MOMENT to breathe in the fresh smell of spring grasses and to enjoy the pink geraniums, dotting the nearby land. She knelt in their garden and squeezed a small lump of warm, damp earth between her fingers. Earth's promises had appeared because of her devoted attention to the tending of this soil.

Her father and sisters would be appalled if they knew what manual labor now engaged Margaret and Mary as daily demands. Plunging fingers into the soil to plant tobacco seeds and then diligently sorting and tossing away all the unwanted weeds filled Margaret with an unexplained closeness to this new country. Seeing tiny delicate tips of green appear on the ends of curved white stems washed a satisfying wave of triumph over her.

She had caught herself checking the dark soil every day—sometimes twice or maybe more. Then a few days ago, finally emerging from the depths of darkness up into the sunlight, these miniature leaves had slowly opened to bask in the morning's warmth.

The garden comforted her—in a spiritual way. She would have never thought to plant a garden weeks ago in the middle of winter and look at what came of it. These tiny tobacco leaves would grow large and become their security in the coming months. Margaret filled with great hope for their future.

Such a strange new world.

Mary decided to organize the maid servants in soap making this morning. She selected a place outside and a little beyond the kitchen door for what would now be an annual task. The maids chattered with no lack of opinions on what might be the better way to do whatever needed to be done. This life in their new world required much labor.

From sunup to sundown, Margaret scrubbed, dug, sorted, inspected, lugged buckets of grain or water, repaired clothing, monitored food preparation, took inventories, and tended to their livestock, leaving only bits of time here and there to study her Bible. True, they had the maids to help, but the amount of work required all their efforts.

Margaret resigned herself to the commotion. They would be up to their elbows in soap making for most of the day and exhausted by nightfall. For over the last five months Mary and Margaret had saved all their wood ash from their winter fires. This morning Mary told Missus Lawne to scoop the ash into the leaching barrel. Then she instructed the maid on how to pour collected rainwater over the ash to leach out the lye until an egg would float just under the surface.

The sisters had carefully saved the fat trimmings from butchered meat and duck grease all winter along. The bear Giles had killed yielded the densest fat of all the animals. They spared their rendered pork fat from this activity because they preferred to use it in their cooking.

Mary insisted bear meat was unpleasantly strong, but Margaret rather liked it, especially with the seasonings their cook, Missus Brookes, used. The fat hung nearby stuffed in a rawhide bag. One of the maids, Missus Taylor, took it down and scooped the lard-like substance into a huge cast-iron pot.

Missus Guesse stirred the pot as lard and grease melted over the fire.

"Missus Guesse," Mary called out, "mind your petticoat and sleeves and don't get too close to the fire. Tuck them up, please."

When the lye was ready it would be added to the hot mixture.

"Good morning, Lady Brent." An indentured women from Jacob Cole's place approached. She glanced around, then moved closer to the garden fence. Over her arm she carried a basket of cuttings and other items. She waited, eyes darting around, then cast downward.

Margaret stood, brushing soil from her hands and long gardening apron. "You have selected a pleasant morning for a walk about, Carrie Wells."

The young maid servant, like most of the others, went barefooted in the warmer weather—not wanting to wear out her good shoes. Seeing these workers with no shoes reminded Margaret of the street urchins running all over London. The sisters had agreed their servants would not work barefooted unless they preferred. Regardless, their servants would wear shoes whenever they left the Brent's property.

"My intentions did not bring me here for a walk, my lady. I have some little bundles of dried mint and sunflower and sassafras for Lady Mary's soap making, and for you I have some Indian pumpkin bread, and I flavored it with a touch of cinnamon brought from the West Indies. I sweetened the whole loaf with spoonsful of honey."

Margaret unwrapped the warm bread from the cloth and smelled it. "My, you have a way with preparing food."

Indian meal with pumpkin when turned into bread appealed to no one in either texture or taste, but this loaf would cause even the king to drool.

"We will enjoy this with our dinner and have pleasant smelling soap at the end of this day. I suspect Missus Brookes, our cook, will want to know how you prepared this."

Margaret beckoned to Mary. Mary held up a finger. She seemed to be in the thick of a discussion with one of the maids.

"Lady Margaret, I actually came to ask a favor of you, and I hope I'm not being too bold as I'm often said to be."

The young woman's face, tanned and freckled, had a worn look, not from age but maybe troubles beyond her ability to repair. Margaret waited for her to say more.

"I understand you and the governor—well, I hear you—people say you visit and talk and are the closest of—but—oh shame on me. I do not mean disrespect." Tears verged on spilling down her cheeks. "This is not what I wanted to say."

Heavens, Leonard and I have caused the townspeople to whisper. They speculate about our friendship. This shall never do.

Her throat burned dry while the Wells girl's eyes filled with moisture.

The young woman wiped at her eyes with a corner of her pinafore. "When I become upset, everything comes out twisted, and it sounds terrible."

Curious now, Margaret nodded her head and said, "Go on then, tell me what you want to say."

"I'm in a horrible fix, and I don't know what to do, and I would never dare to face the governor myself. Might I ask a small favor of you?"

The young woman flushed and lowered her head so as not to meet Margaret's eyes.

"What sort of trouble bothers you, Carrie Wells?"

"Master Cole will not keep his word, and he only wants me to stay—be his wife." Pain covered her face and she said, "I am with child, and my time is up, and my dear Tom works on Kent Island, and I don't know how we can ever be together because Master Cole refuses to honor his agreement, and he's a horrid man, and I would die first if I were forced to be his wife. I promise I shall throw myself into the river and be done with all this rotten, horrid, life and leave my love waiting and wondering what happened to me."

She covered her eyes with both hands. Margaret, ignoring the buzzing of flies and the damp heat of the morning sun, worked to untangle the girl's words in her mind.

"If the river doesn't take me, then I shall have my baby alone and will have to live with Master Cole, and I shall never see my dear Tom again." With that, she burst into tears.

"You do not look like you are about to have a baby. Why do you say your time is up?"

"Master Cole brought me here four years ago. He said after I had worked for him for four years, I wouldn't owe him a tad more, and now he says I can't leave, and so I might as well marry him. Lady Brent. I worked hard from early morning until after dark every day, and my time is up. Even the devil would say this isn't right." She sniffed and looked away.

Margaret set her jaw. "Heaven help us if other masters here in Maryland treat their servants in this manner."

"There's nothing I can do." She bit her lip. "I thought maybe the next time you talked with Governor Calvert you might say something on my behalf, and I pray my request is not one of cheekiness."

"Mary." Margaret called sharply across to the soap making group. "Would you please come here?"

When Mary finished saying something, she trotted over to the garden. "Hello, Carrie. Are you not feeling well—your face seems flushed?"

"So, you are acquainted with Carrie Wells?" Margaret studied her sister, slipped the basket from Carrie, and moved it into Mary's hands. "She brought these for us and herbs to scent your soap."

"Sometimes on Sundays after church Carrie walks with me in the woods and shows me barks, roots, and herbs that heal." She glanced at the basket. "Why, these are lovely." She glanced at the young woman, then put her hand on Carrie's arm. "Are you still having trouble with Jacob Cole?"

"Jacob Cole is about to have troubles with her. Has Giles returned from Kent for Assembly today? Will both our brothers be at the meeting?" Margaret's frogs roiled inside her.

How dare these men take advantage of their servants?

"I saw him and Fulke along with some other men heading to Lewger's home earlier."

"Come, Carrie Wells. We shall also attend Assembly."

"But—Margaret," Mary grabbed her arm. "Certainly, women would not be allowed—"

Margaret shrugged Mary away, snatched Carrie Wells by her hand, and stomped off down the path.

"Sister," Mary called after her, "you must take off that filthy apron. You're covered in soil."

Margaret jerked it untied and slung it. "There is a difference between God's soil and men's dirt. Carrie Wells and I are about to sort this very thing out with all those fine gentlemen of Assembly."

"Oh goodness." Carrie pulled back and stopped. "You really mean to go there. We mustn't go into the Assembly. We daren't."

"Why not? Who has told you we are not allowed? Come along now." Margaret tromped up the road—holding the young woman's hand tightly and insisting Carrie Wells keep up. "Indeed. Not one person has told us we cannot."

Chapter 20

Women are wiser than men because they know less and understand more.
- James Thurber

WHEN THEY ARRIVED AT Secretary Lewger's mansion, Margaret marched up to the big wood door and gave it a sounding rap. Carrie Wells stood beside her, making little whimpering sounds.

"Shush, Carrie Wells. You must be strong in front of these men. Now hold your head high, shoulders back, and do not dare even look to cry."

When Margaret raised her knuckles to knock again, Carrie touched her hand gently and said, "We should just leave. I'll find a way to live with—"

"My dear child, you do not understand. You must never let someone take from you what is rightfully yours. That is no way to live your life, and it will encourage others to do the same."

The huge wooden door creaked open. Peasley stood before them, in severe black and white attire with a face that would match the Grim Reaper's.

Leonard's man, Peasley, now guards Lewger's Assembly entrance.

"Lady Brent, Carrie Wells, you knocked at the wrong door. To visit with Lady Lewger, you must go to the smaller entry on the side of the house. I shall show you."

"You need not bother Peasley." Margaret stared into his dark hooded eyes. "I have come to lay a matter in front of Assembly. I know the way."

"I see. However, you cannot interrupt—"

"I can, Peasley." She yanked Carrie beside her as she swished past the imposing servant and strode on toward the shut inner door of the great Assembly Hall. Margaret's head started to throb.

A fever, I must have a fever. Ridiculous, I just haven't thought through what to say. No matter, Carrie Wells must have what is entitled to her.

Margaret jerked open the heavy door, pulling Carrie after her, and ignoring Peasley's protest. She marched into the hall. Leonard, Mister Lewger, and the assemblymen took up business at the far end of the long room. Leonard sat behind a huge, carved walnut table with John Lewger beside him. Burgesses and gentlemen engaged in a discussion that evoked some sort of dissention. Some stood and others sat at tables. Their voices shared a conversational tone punctuated with bursts of disagreement. Giles and Fulke blended in with these gentlemen. No one had noticed Margaret or the maid.

"Gentlemen." Leonard slapped the tabletop, bringing the men to attention. "We must choose someone this morning. We cannot be without a working ferry to transport us to Lord Baltimore's estate, and we have no way to move his cattle across the river to West St. Mary's. Please submit your suggestions for this position."

"Lord Governor." Margaret, with Carrie at her side, strode forward.

Leonard's attention shifted squarely to Margaret. His face paled. He set his paper aside. The men stopped talking and followed his gaze.

Margaret started to push her way through the cluster of men. However, they politely bowed and parted to make room for the women, glancing uncomfortably at each other. All the seated burgesses stood out of traditional respect for any women who entered a room.

Leonard rose, but before he could speak, Margaret's voice rang out.

"Gentlemen, I stand before you to protest a grave injustice imposed on Carrie Wells."

"Lady Brent," Leonard, standing to his full height, let his voice sound over hers. "Carrie Wells, as an indentured, cannot bring an action at Common Law. Your business here at Assembly, I'm obligated to say, is inappropriate."

She heard a mutual mutter of agreement among the gathered men, making her little frogs-in-the-stomach leap about quite wildly. Margaret refused to acknowledge or even look at her brothers.

"However, sir, you and your assemblymen gather today to create and uphold the laws of this beautiful and great Maryland. Your commission requires the assurance of religious freedom, political equality, and also attention to the administration for the welfare of our Proprietor's citizens." Margaret continued in a softer voice, "My Lord, Carrie Wells, ten days ago, fulfilled her indenture contract. Her master refuses to submit the documents that will certify her freedom."

Margaret knew this matter should be brought before the Provincial Court. She also knew these men often blurred the governing lines between Assembly and the court, so she gave it no real concern.

Leonard stared long at Margaret, then shifted his attention to Carrie. "Carrie Wells, do you have the papers that define your contract with Jacob Cole?"

Carrie glanced up at Margaret, then back at Leonard, trembling, said, "I do—did—but now I don't. He snatched them from me when I showed him I had finished my four years of labor."

"So, Jacob Cole has your papers."

Carrie shook her head. "He did, but he doesn't have them either. He tossed them into his burning fireplace, and my freedom turned to ashes before my very face, and the fire was too hot for me to save them."

Leonard sighed, leaned toward John Lewger and said something Margaret couldn't hear. Lewger looked in one of his ledgers and replied. Leonard nodded and said, "You didn't come over on the *Ark*. Which passage brought you?"

"A gentleman arranged for me to come on a small ship to be Master Cole's indentured servant and it carried Master Cole and another woman servant and mostly a lot of cargo and not many people, actually only several boys, and they wanted to become freemen after their indentures too."

The Governor appeared tired. "Carrie Wells, tell us the name of the ship that brought you to our shores."

"I don't know, but someone told me I arrived on April 2nd, and one of your assemblymen wrote it on my paper, right up at the top next to where someone had written my name. I know because he told me what it said, and he read the whole paper to me, and it said April 2, 1635, and my indenture was to last for four years, and he asked me to make my mark."

John Lewger picked up another ledger and began to thumb through it.

"I worked hard and long hours, from early morning until after dark for Master Cole, but he won't let me go because he says he needs me to stay, and now he says I have to be his wife." She chewed her bottom lip. Her neck and face developed a raspberry rash.

Lewger tapped the Governor and pointed to an entry in the book.

Margaret could not stand silent any longer. "I suspect Jacob Cole gained property for transporting Carrie Wells and those boys. Therefore, he not only must release her but fulfill his headright obligation."

Some of the assemblymen coughed, and Margaret heard some shuffling and whispering behind her. Her brothers probably contrived different ways to murder her. She glanced at them, tilting her chin up and narrowing her eyes.

"Mister Lewger's records show you tell the truth, Carrie Wells. Jacob Cole has not registered your release. Sometimes landowners forget to file their papers."

"Your honor," Margaret kept her voice soft and even. "As Carrie Wells stated a few minutes ago, Jacob Cole has no intentions of filing anything. His intentions are most dishonorable as his only intentions are to keep Carrie Wells as his wife."

These men's ears go deaf when a woman speaks, including our esteemed Governor.

"Sheriff Baldridge please step forward." Leonard Calvert said.

The assemblymen began the shuffling and murmuring again.

"Silence." The Governor gave a rap with his knuckles on the table, causing Carrie Wells to jump.

The room settled into quiet.

"In the name of justice, we must hear Jacob Cole's account. Our conservator will write a summons for Sheriff Baldridge to deliver, ordering Jacob Cole to appear before the court."

John Lewger took a strip of paper and penned the summons.

Margaret used this time to boldly study each man's appearance, assessing any thoughts belied by their eyes. Her brothers scowled at her. Let them. She didn't give a whit.

When finished, John Lewger stamped the summons with an official seal and handed it to James Baldridge. The sheriff promptly left the assembly room.

Margaret faced Leonard Calvert and said, "If this action goes unpunished, talk of it will spread throughout St. Mary's City. Your servants will harbor distrust and suspicion against not only their masters, but of you gentlemen who stand here in council. Those of the headright system along with the indentured have a right to expect their contracts be honored. Your ears do recall the second Lord Baltimore's promise to those who inhabit Maryland. Those who become freemen will dwell in an equalized society. You may not take that away from them. Gentlemen, for all our sakes, please do not ignore this injustice."

Chapter 21

...it should be remembered that men always prize that most which is least enjoyed.
- James Fenimore Cooper

AFTER THE DAY OF soap making and assembly speaking, Margaret settled down for a bowl of grouse, sweet potato, and root vegetable stew. Before she savored the first taste, she heard men's voices—coming up the path to their front door—arguing.

Mary set Carrie's loaf of Indian pumpkin bread on the table with a lump of fresh-churned butter. She whispered, "I wish we could ignore whoever may be coming to visit. I'm exhausted."

"It sounds like our brothers." Margaret looked out the window, then opened the door, waiting for them to enter. "I suspect you've come to give me a tongue lashing."

"Mary," Fulke nodded, as he stepped through the doorway. "Are we interrupting your supper?"

"Join us." Mary jumped to her feet and ladled soup into two more bowls before the men could protest.

Fulke held his hand up, saying, "We haven't stopped by for a pleasant chat. We're here to help Margaret understand the inappropriateness of her actions today."

"What I cannot fathom," Giles said, "is why you thought it permissible to just appear like that—without even an invitation."

Margaret looked up at the ceiling and silently prayed for her brothers to stop assuming attitudes more appropriately shown by the rear end of donkeys. No one wanted to hear their gentlemanly nonsense, most of all her.

Mary glared at them and plunked the two wooden bowls of stew with spoons down on the table.

Fulke paced across the room and came back to face her. "Margaret, you are dear to me, but your appearance in assembly transcended all levels of protocol and dignity."

"As for what happened today—" Giles ran his fingers along his newly grown Van Dyke beard. He seemed to hunt for the right words. "You—you never would have engaged in such disrespectful acts in England. Why do you have the notion it's acceptable to do so here?"

He sniffed, smelling the stew, sat, and dipped his spoon in, taking a taste. Then he broke off a piece of Carrie's bread, smeared it in butter, and took a bite.

"I plan to exercise my rights. Mary and I must be seen and known as landowners." Margaret picked up her spoon, and said, "Fulke, sit and join your brother. We two women gave up much in England to come here in return for experiencing freedom to worship as we desire and becoming landholders. Think about the political and social tenor of Maryland. It requires much from those who have brought the common people of England here to work." She sighed, then said, "We must govern with foresight."

"I never cared much for Indian pumpkin bread, but this is delicious." Giles tore off another chunk of the bread.

Fulke sat and stared at the stew. Margaret could almost hear his thoughts.

"Brothers, this new land, this Maryland, cannot exist if we do not have adequate people to work the land."

"Why do you bother to tell us what we know?" Fulke picked up his spoon and sipped.

"You've got to taste this bread, Fulke." Giles handed him a piece.

"Because" Margaret said, "none of you seem to have given any thought to what is happening. More and more of the servants who came over on the *Ark* four years ago have worked their time." Margaret waited to see if they understood the implications.

Giles put his wrists on the table and leaned in toward Margaret. "You first say we need adequate servants to work the land. Then you argue in Assembly about this woman who claims she's completed her headright contract and should be free. Next you conclude too many servants entitled to be freemen will become a problem. You're talking in circles."

"I understand what she's saying," Mary said. "There are many more servants than the gentlemen who paid their passage. Soon more servants will be freemen than those of us who brought them over. They shall own lands and start businesses like Goodwin will do because you, dear Giles, insisted on building a smithy for him. When he becomes a freeman—he'll become the town's blacksmith. Then we shall be short another servant to work our crops."

"Consarn it, Margaret!" Giles shook his head. "This can't be right. Why would you then have the audacity to storm into Assembly, demanding that girl be released from her servitude?"

"Because—"

Fulke interrupted Margaret, saying, "She told you why, brother. She did the right thing. Maryland cannot afford to have servants rising up against their masters because their masters refuse to release them when their indentured time is up."

The sisters exchanged glances, then Mary said, "There's more. Jacob Cole demands Carrie be his wife. The man she loves, and whose child she carries, lives on Kent Island."

Watching a dark mood descend over her eldest brother, Margaret wondered why this disturbed Fulke so.

Giles finished his stew, pushed his bowl away and said, "Simple solution. We must bring more men over to work the tobacco fields. Margaret, you still have two or three more coming sometime this summer."

"I shall receive my land patent around August. It is that grand piece of land south of yours, next to the river. Let us hope we do not have to wait for the men to arrive. We must receive the patent before we can start building or planting, and tobacco sprouts must be transplanted soon."

Mary added, "Robinson, Gedd, and Goodwin should start clearing and girdling our trees too. They have plans to build our manor along with the smaller structures but not until Leonard gives his approval."

Fulke had barely tasted his stew, but he had eaten all the bread Giles had given him. He stood. "Blast it all. Maryland not only needs more men to work the field, but it needs more women. Women, please dear Lord, unlike the two of you."

"I have never heard you be so discourteous." Mary set her jaw and stared.

"Maryland provokes my ill manners." He paced the kitchen floor as he talked. "We need women who are willing to marry. There are no wives to be had."

Mary flushed and looked at Margaret for her to say something reassuring. Margaret's first impulse was to lash out and defend their religious choice. Instead, she held her tongue. It would do no good, serve no purpose, and convince no one of the righteousness in their decision.

"Take heart, brother," Giles said, "maybe the next ship will bring some pretty ladies for us."

Hesitant to speak, but then doing so, Margaret said, "Fulke, if it's not beneath your standards, Mary and I would release any of our four maids from their servitude, any of which I am certain would agree to marry you."

Fulke shook his head. "None are well born. These types of marriages only bring strife."

Mary leaned over to him. "Sweet brother, our city has a couple of widows. Have you thought about courting them?"

"Like the Widow Hawley?" He glowered at her. "I would never choose her to be your sister-in-law—let alone live with that woman."

His brother laughed and said, "Patience, Fulke. There's still hope."

"Giles, didn't you listen to what our sisters said about the indentures becoming freemen? These young kids of four years ago are about to become freemen of age—looking for wives. They already outnumber their masters, who also want wives. I'm too old for all this waiting around. I need a loving wife who will bear me children."

"Hold fast." Giles said, "See what the next ship brings. Imagine some golden-haired beauty with a winsome smile strolling down the gangplank. Think of her pretty little shoes, stepping daintily onto our Maryland's soil. When she looks around the gathered crowd to find a husband and sees your handsome face, she will swoon into your arms. A ship from England will arrive any day now."

"Good." Fulke strode to the door.

Then he swung around and pointed his finger at Margaret.

"Why Father thought I needed protect you, Margaret, I have no idea. It's not you who needs protection. Anyone you judge to be on the wrong side of right— they need protection. I shall leave on the next ship back to England."

Chapter 22

Men, their rights and nothing more; Women, their rights and nothing less.
- Susan B. Anthony

A FEW MORNINGS LATER a frantic tapping on the door interrupted Margaret's early morning prayers. Today's devotions required her contrition for embarrassing her brothers and supplication to bless and protect Giles's endeavor on Kent Island. She crossed herself, rose from her bedside, and blew out the small candle. She waited until the tiny, dark wisp of smoke, rising towards the heavens, disappeared.

The tapping persisted, accompanied by a call. "Lady Margaret. Lady Margaret."

"My goodness," Mary called as she hurried to the door. "Who has gnats in her hair?" She pulled open the door to find Carrie Wells, all flushed and out of breath, waving a bit of paper.

"Oh, Lady Mary, I must see Lady Margaret right this minute."

"I am here." The girl's appearance befuddled Margaret. Carrie seemed to be wearing her Sunday dress with shoes. "You've been running—I hardly believe you should exert yourself as such in your condition. It must be well over a mile from Cole's place, and the weather is quite warm."

"You have to read this." She shoved the paper in Margaret's face. "The sheriff read it to me, and we must hurry. Aren't you scared to death?"

Mary leaned over Margaret's arm and gasped. "Carrie, you've been summoned to court."

"I am shivering chills in terror, Lady Brent. Why do they want me to come to that Assembly again? What are they going to do to me?"

"Carrie, warm your heart and banish your fears. These fine gentlemen of the courts have agreed to listen to what you have to say. A good thing, this." Margaret handed the paper back to Carrie, grinning. "The Provincial Court has given Carrie Wells permission to invite the Lady Brent to speak for her. Or at least Governor Calvert has invited me. I doubt if the council approves."

"Oh, Lady Brent, I cannot stop my terrors. Master Cole left earlier this morning to appear in front of the court. He stomped and grumbled in such a foul mood I hid from him, and came out after he had left, and then I heard the sheriff calling my name. What do they expect from me?" Her bottom lip quivered.

Margaret glanced back at Mary, saying, "With a room of men judging, it is difficult to say what will happen." Then again, Leonard might just join her brothers and give her a tongue lashing. "However, now we have an invitation. Let us hurry and set these gentlemen's minds right."

They tramped up the dusty path to the Lewger's manor. This time when they rapped on the front door, Peasley opened it. Giving a slight bow, he escorted them to the Assembly Hall without a word.

Everything felt different. The hall seemed colder and larger, the room longer, and the carved walnut table overpowering. Burgesses were not in attendance, only stern gentlemen of the court.

Margaret whispered to Carrie, "Hold your head high and walk with your back straight. Look Governor Calvert in the eye when you speak to him."

They entered the room and strode to the middle where they stood facing the governor. All the men respectfully stood—again.

Carrie had followed Margaret's instructions and now imitated her actions. Margaret relaxed a smidgen.

Governor Calvert nodded, and said, "Carrie Wells, Lady Brent, and Jacob Cole please move forward."

John Lewger wrote something in his ledger.

Margaret and Carrie obeyed and stood directly in front of the Governor's table. Jacob Cole, sitting at one of the back tables, scowling, marched up and stood in front of John Lewger. This put the trembling girl, Carrie, between Margaret and him.

The Governor looked at all the men standing and sighed.

"The council and participants may sit. Carrie Wells," Leonard Calvert said in a fatherly tone, "a few days ago you rudely appeared before this august house and made claims against your master. Indentures are forbidden to bring action to Common Law. However, Lady Brent believes your assignment void, and you no longer are bound by the indentured mandates. Jacob Cole, your master, disagrees. Tell us again why you believe you should be granted your freedom."

"I told you, she's got no papers to prove otherwise." Jacob Cole, a stout man of mid-age with leathery skin wiped his runny nose with a piece of rag.

"You must hold your tongue until I call on you to speak, Jacob Cole."

Margaret nudged Carrie. The girl looked at her with wide eyes, then back at the Governor.

"Go on," Margaret said. "Tell your story again. This time it will be recorded."

"I—I came over on a freighter, or a merchant ship—a small one full of more things than people, and it carried our little group of English here four years ago first two days of April, not long after everyone else had come over on the big ship they called the *Ark*."

She stopped and looked down at the floor, but Margaret touched her arm and nodded for her to continue. She glanced at Margaret with a pleading look.

Margaret set her jaw and this time nodded toward the governor.

Carrie stood straighter and stared directly at Leonard Calvert's face. "The gentleman—" Her voice cracked, and she stopped. She started again and it sounded steady. "The gentleman who paid my passage had sold my services to Master Jacob Cole. The gentleman gave me a paper with writing on it and had put my name at the top written in black ink and how long I had to be indentured. When I got off the ship, an Assemblyman wrote the date of my arrival, April 2, 1635, right next to my name, and then the Assemblyman told me my service would end on

April 2, 1639."

The Governor waited until John Lewger stopped writing, then said, "Jacob Cole, our records show Carrie Wells did, in fact, arrive on April 2, 1635. Why have you not submitted her papers of release and afforded the rights due her?"

Jacob Cole shifted in place and then said, "She not have her papers. How am I to know this?"

"Because you, sir, burned—"

Margaret grabbed Carries arm and warned her to shush.

"Carrie Wells," the Governor said, "tell us why you do not have your papers."

Again, Margaret leaned into Carrie's ear and said, "Tell them again, for the record."

"I—when I—I told Master Cole my time working for him was up, and then he called me a liar. I ran and got my document and showed it to him, and he snatched it from me, and then he threw it in the fire. He burned it to ashes." She stared again at the floor, shaking.

"Jacob Cole, what have you to say about this?" The Governor said, after Lewger indicated he had finished writing.

The farmer shook his head and shifted in place again. "It were not like that, sir. This girl not earned her four years of work a t'all. She's one of those lazy ones. Sleeps late and goes to bed early, not tend the chickens properly, not keep my house clean. She whines all the time. I not get her to do the simplest of tasks like even fix me meals. When she did, if she ever did, it all tasted like sawdust. I think she tried to poison me. I work my fields and tend to my livestock. I have to do her work too. I need victuals. I not have time for meal making and food keeping. I'm near close to starving to death from her neglect."

Leonard cocked his head, glanced at Margaret, and then looked at Lewger who nodded he had finished documenting this conversation.

"Carrie Wells, how do you plan to counter these accusations?"

Carrie looked at Margaret, her face showed obvious panic. The girl clearly had not understood the governor's question.

"May I speak, your lord?" Margaret stepped forward.

"You may."

"Master Jacob Cole claims Carrie Wells is too lazy to cook or do her work. He says Carrie Wells cannot prepare a decent meal. My brothers, my sister, and I have tasted food Carrie Wells has prepared, and I am sure they will attest to the excellence of her cooking abilities. Carrie Wells has expert knowledge of the best wild Maryland herbs for use as medicines and in seasonings. I have been told the wild herbs she uses in her cooking creates a table of sustenance to be envied. You can clearly see by Master Jacob Cole's ample girth; he does not want from missing meals."

Muffled sniggers covered by coughs made not smiling difficult for Margaret.

Leonard raised his hand for silence.

"Clearly," Margaret said, "Jacob Cole has not told the truth about Carrie Wells's cooking. If he hasn't told the truth about this, then we can assume the rest of what Jacob Cole has declared about Carrie Wells as being lazy may also being untrue. He has not told the truth because it's more than his wanting her to remain his servant. Carrie Wells told my sister and me, just before the two of us came and stood here the last time, Jacob Cole's refusal to grant her freedom came from his own personal need."

"What would that be?"

"He intends to keep her as his wife."

The council and men broke into discussions.

Leonard Calvert shouted, "Silence!"

His voice echoing throughout the hall, preceded absolute quiet.

"Master Jacob Cole recognizes a crucial problem." Margaret looked at each man in turn. "Maryland sorely lacks marriageable women. We see many young men who have reached the end of their indentures and now look to marry. They most assuredly will be disappointed in their quest. As the master of an indentured woman, Jacob Cole has found a solution for himself. Yet, it discounts *jura personarum*, the rights of the person, including between master and servant. I ask the gentlemen of this court, has Carrie Wells no rights? Does she not have the right to refuse a proposal of marriage?"

The voices of the men erupted with a cacophony of opinions. Leonard again wielded his voice and raised his hands to quiet the assembly.

"If," Margaret gestured toward the councilmen saying, "as men, your answer falls in the negative arising out of your own frustration to find a suitable wife, then I ask you another question. What will become of our Lord Baltimore's grand dream of political equality, freedom of worship, and other civil liberties when the world hears about Maryland's masters of indentured servants entrapping their workers? More important, you must ask yourselves what is to become of your beloved Maryland?"

Chapter 23

Make everything as simple as possible, but not simpler.
- Albert Einstein

WHEN MARGARET AND CARRIE Wells, whispering excitedly, burst though the Assembly Hall door, they nearly knocked Peasley to the floor. He recovered his balance and bowed with a guilty smile. Seeing him, they quieted as he escorted them to the main doorway.

When he opened the front door, he bowed again, saying, "You have drawn an approving crowd, it appears."

Sunlight streamed in, temporarily blinding Margaret, but she could hear murmurs coming from a group of people beyond the gate of Lewger's mansion. Shielding her eyes, she stepped out, and cheers erupted. Befuddled, she looked back and studied Peasley.

He shrugged, then said, "They all seemed curious as to what the court would decide about Carrie Wells."

"Peasley, they already know the court decided in her favor. How can this be?"

Margaret stayed her place in the doorway, with Carrie standing next to her. The citizens in the road continued to cheer and shout questions. Margaret tilted her head, waiting for Leonard's servant's response.

He clearly seemed embarrassed and most reluctant to answer.

"Peasley—you dear man—you eavesdropped outside the door."

Even his balding head turned crimson. Then he paled. "If the Governor knew—"

Margaret laid a hand on his wrist. "He shall not hear a word of this."

"Lady Margaret," Carried squealed, "there's your sister and Master Cole's other servants and look, there's the Widow Hawley."

"And all of our women servants," Margaret said, "have come here along with some of our friends. Carrie, I am exhausted. You and I shall go home now."

Margaret took Carrie's elbow and together they walked toward the cheering, clapping crowd.

"Please hang on tight to your document. Do not let anyone burn this one. Did you understand Jacob Cole must give you your due? You will need to bundle your belongings and find passage to the ferry that will take you to Kent Island—Wait. Here is another thought, I shall ask my brother Giles to take you to the island on his pinnace. He is returning to Kent this afternoon. Hurry now, gather your things, and meet him there. You must know where it is—tied to his dock."

A blast from a cannon shook the land. At once everyone covered their ears, looking toward the river.

Heavens, a war has started!

Someone yelled, "A ship—let's go meet the ship!"

Of course, a ship's cannon announced its arrival.

The crowd forgot about the indentured servant Carrie Wells's triumph in court. They dashed to the banks of the St. George to see which ship would be sailing into port. Mary ran up to Margaret and Carrie, grinning.

"I do believe our Good Lord smiled down on the two of you today. Carrie, I'm so happy for you."

"Carrie," Margaret said, "do you wish to come with us to watch the ship dock? I am certain my brothers won't leave until they see who disembarks and what news from England they might have."

"Thank you, m'lady, but I'm too excited, and I am off to gather my things, and I want to be with my sweet Tom, and I'll be forever grateful to you and your kindness, and if we have a baby girl, I'll ask Tom if we can name her Margaret."

Carrie curtsied. Then the girl tore off down the road, clutching her precious document bearing Lord Baltimore's great seal.

Mary and Margaret strolled over to join the group scurrying along the road so they could stand high on the bank, overlooking the St. George.

"Do you remember the day we arrived?" Mary stared out toward the bend in the river. "There. I see the sails."

Shielding her eyes, Margaret watched the sails come nearer, then the bow of the ship came into view around the bend. "Only months ago—still, it seemed dreamlike and exhausting. I felt a total stranger in an even stranger land."

"Maybe our new men will be on this ship."

Margaret shrugged. "Governor Calvert thought they might get passage by late summer. English unrest escalates every day, making the boarding of ships most difficult for Catholics. I hope they leave soon."

"The Virginia Governor told Captain Cornwallis some news about how Scotland's assembly signed a National Covenant. They have refused the king to make any changes to their religion." Mary chewed the inside of her lip. "England has been waiting for a reason to go to war with Scotland. Do you believe King Charles will invade?"

Widow Hawley approached. "You had a fine day in court, Lady Margaret, showing those oppressive men a thing or two. If anyone cares, I am all packed and will be returning home on this ship tomorrow. Thank heavens I planned ahead for whatever opportunity presents, and now it has arrived. I have found it a pleasure to have known both of you, but I can say I am not sorry to leave. Certainly not after how my Mister Hawley died. He received no thank you for his part in settling this wild land. There I was, standing with his values, until the end. I have nary been given even as much as a fare-thee-well."

An appropriate and kind response to the woman did not come to mind. Margaret simply said, "The two of us wish you good health and safe travels."

"Your Governor Calvert and even your Gentlemen Brent, heed my word, may give their life for this country, and no one will care a whit. My Mister Hawley, a fine councilman to your Governor, worked day and night for the good of Maryland. I'll never believe his death an accident. You watch out for your men if you know what's best."

Margaret had to stop this conversation. "When you arrive on English shores, if we wrote some words to our father would you ask a messenger to carry it to Gloucester?"

"No need for that, my dear sister." Fulke had appeared behind her. "I'll deliver it myself."

"Fulke, no. Please no. I do so wish..." Margaret lowered her gaze, her dry throat unable to get words to come forth.

Evidently, the gentlemen of the court had been dismissed on the occasion of the ship's arrival. She heard Giles and Leonard talking as they strode up to the group under the towering pine and walnut trees along the bank. Leonard smiled at her and made his way through the growing crowd to stand by her side.

Mary took Fulke's hand and pressed it to her cheek. "Won't you please reconsider? England is so far away, and this country needs strong, smart men such as you."

He looked at Mary, kissed the top of her head, then addressed Margaret. "You knew from the beginning my heart wasn't in this voyage. You guessed I only came over out of my love and sense of duty to our father. Today you have proven what I knew. Dear sister, no one needs to care for you. You have a strong mind such as any man I know. And, my God in Heaven—you fight for the rights of individuals."

Then he held her at arm's length, staring into her eyes, and a laugh emerged from deep in his belly. It erupted to echo in Margaret's ears, and she grinned.

"Latin." Giles came up to her, shaking his head. "What crowing flapdragon will come next?"

"I wish you did not have to return to Kent Island." She held his eyes with her smile.

"My absence won't be a long one." he said.

"Today in the court," Mary said softly to Fulke, "I so wish I could have witnessed what happened."

Leonard, next to Margaret, looked into her face and said, "*jura personarum, jura personarum.* Indeed, my lady? I suspect this won't be the last time you will grace my court."

Chapter 24

Not everything that is faced can be changed, but nothing can be changed until it is faced.

- James A. Baldwin

SOME OF THE GROUP stayed high on the bank. Margaret watched the two priests stride down the path to greet the ship. Many of the indentured passengers on these ships did not embrace the Catholic faith. Most worshiped simply as Puritans or at least, Protestants. She wondered if the priests would openly defy Lord Baltimore's decree and pray as they had when the *Charity* came into port.

"Pardon my leave, ladies and gentlemen. I need to welcome the captain of this vessel." Leonard hurried down the path toward the dock. Margaret watched as he intercepted the priests and spoke to them. They in turn nodded, stepped aside, and waited obediently.

She sighed. Their worshiping in public would not be tolerated. According to Leonard, Lord Baltimore feared a physical clash between the Catholics, Protestants, and Puritans here in St. Mary's City if Catholics continued to be bold in regard to their religion. Indentured Protestants and Puritans far outnumbered the Catholic gentry.

"Look behind those brambles." Mary indicated the direction with a slight nod of her head.

A slender man with ebony black hair, tied and hanging down to his waist, crouched to watch the dock below. He wore a feather cape with deer hide trousers. Beside him a small child dressed in a too large smock of painted deer hide leaned against him, watching the ship.

"Those are our neighbors, the Yaocomaco people of the Piscataway tribe," Giles said.

More natives crept up along the high banks of the river and watched. Their clothing, skin, and hair blended with the unpredictable patterns of sunlit browns mixed with black shadows.

"No wonder I did not see them clearly when we arrived." Margaret found these invisible people more interesting than the docking ship.

"Maybe we will receive a packet from father and our siblings." Mary's attention had turned to England. "Honestly, sometimes I'm terribly homesick, and I wish we were there."

Shaking her head, Margaret said, "You would be wiser to wish they were here, Mary. I am quite anxious to know about the current events happening in England. Certainly, King Charles will invade Scotland if they keep defying him."

"I agree, sister," Giles said. "Those tenacious Scots stand firm, no matter their cause. A war with them would be expensive, long, and not wise."

"Would you also agree many decisions of late have not been wise?" Margaret's attention went back to the natives hidden in between the trees. "We are all fortunate to be here and not worried about being locked away in some prison."

"Lord Baltimore has more to lose than we do." Fulke shielded his eyes from the sun and watched the passengers disembark. "His actions seem blatant. He ignored the king's proclamations by providing us passage. Men have lost their heads for less."

"And now, you will make that long trip home, Fulke." Mary took his hand. "I hate the thought of your leaving."

"Look, brother." Giles pointed. "Those men disembarking are Gloucester men."

"I say, quite right. Let's go greet them. Mary, Margaret, your indentured servants will most certainly come on the next ship."

"Giles," Margaret called, "before you leave, I told Carrie Wells you would carry her to Kent Island. Please do not leave without her."

He waved acknowledgement, and she watched her brothers hurry off, only to stop and greet Councilor Lewger. He joined them on their descent down the path to the dock.

"Mary, Margaret, how wonderful the sound of a ship's arrival brings us together."

Ann Lewger and her handsome young son strolled up.

"Heavens, John, you've grown another foot." Margaret smiled at the lanky boy. "What are you now, eleven?"

"Almost, Lady Brent. My birthday comes in June. My father said we could have a party."

His mother grinned. "We would enjoy having you both and your brothers attend."

"Oh, please do." Young John glanced up at his mother. "We'll be having music, games, cake, and noisemakers, won't we, Mother? I have not had a party since we left England."

"Well, young John," Mary said, "We have not attended a birthday party since we left England either. What a splendid event. Here, have a piece of lemon candy with me."

While they talked, Margaret noticed a rugged ox of a man with permanent windblown red hair standing a few feet away, watching them. She thought to ignore him, but he stayed close by, waiting. He obviously wanted to say something.

"Is there something troubling you, sir?

He bowed to Margaret.

"Are you the Lady Brent?"

"I am one of two." Margaret smiled.

Holding his cap in his hand, he shifted positions for a few seconds, then said, "I don't care for tussles one whit. I say nothing when they steal my chickens. They grabbed my pig, and when I asked for her to be returned, they laughed. Now they've offed with my goat. That there goat gave my little boy his milk and us cheese. I cannot stand stuck and do nothing anymore."

Confused, Margaret stared up at him.

"Everyone says to talk to you about the whole of this. You saw to it the court gave the Wells girl her due." He flushed as red as his hair. "Would you help me get back what's mine?"

Good Heavens—why would this brute of a man come to me?

"What makes you think I can be of help in this matter? I have no power to make someone give back your livestock, and I dare not loan you my man servants because I cannot afford to have them injured. None of them would win a fisting tussle." Margaret sorted through what else she might do and came to an empty conclusion. "Sir, you need attend to your own business as everyone here in Maryland must do."

The farmer lowered his head in understanding, and with his hat in his hand, and his head down, he scuffed off in the direction he had come.

"Margaret." Mary scowled at her.

"His concern is no concern for a lady." Margaret nodded to Ann. "Would you not agree?"

Ann Lewger and young John didn't speak. They watched the man leave.

"I am at a loss to understand you." Mary scowled. "You have never let an injustice pass. Why now? Clearly the man has been bullied and abused? What about his wife and child?"

"You saw him. Fulke and Giles would agree with me. He is a horse of a man. With his brawn and build he can certainly stand up for what is his. Why should he come to a woman for help?"

Mary shook her head. "I never thought you as cruel."

"How could that be cruel?" Margaret said, "The size of the man should scare any thief off. He has got something wrong in the head."

Mary took Margaret's hand. "Dear sister, you are so wise and yet so ignorant, and now wrong. The man may be large, but that doesn't matter. What matters is what he holds in his heart. I think he must be a kind man who does not understand why these things are happening to him. He said he didn't like tussles. He's not a fighter. He probably doesn't read or write and has no idea how to address the fine gentlemen of the court. If this happened to a young girl, you would drag her into the court by her pinafore straps before she could think."

Margaret watched the man retreat. She glanced at her sibling. The Lewgers just stared at her. Mary always seemed to see things others didn't.

"Cockles and berries." Margaret picked up her skirts and stomped off down the road. When she caught up to the man, she said, "Sir, if we go to court, I shall need information. Did you take care to give your goat a special mark?"

Chapter 25
Mid-April 1639

The strong do what they have to do....
- Thucydides

THREE MAIDS, MISSUS TAYLOR, Missus Guesse, and Missus Lawne formed and dipped candles outside the kitchen, while Missus Brookes prepared something cooked with basil, onions, and pepper on the other side of the door. Mary and Margaret knelt in the west hall, sorting through the trunk that stored fabrics.

"I understand you represented John Morton well in court."

Margaret stopped and gave Mary a sideways look. "Poking into other's business seems to be Maryland's key entertainment."

Holding up folded velvet cloth, Mary examined it and put it aside.

"Margaret, I believe we should purchase damask from one of the trading ships. Damask would be more like the governor's exquisite draperies. It would be suitable all year round."

"Except one never knows when the right ship will arrive—one selling what we want."

Missus Taylor came through the kitchen door. "If you please, my ladies. John Morton and his wife sent these tulips to thank you and to brighten the ladies Brent's morning. He says he still waits to know if the sheriff has caught the scoundrels who stole from him. Also, Governor Calvert's houseboy asked me to give this to Lady Margaret."

Margaret stood and accepted the small, folded ivory-colored paper sealed with wax, while Mary put the bright yellow flowers in a bowl of water. Missus Taylor left to continue the candle making. Staring at the note, Margaret traced a fingertip over Leonard's orange-red beeswax seal. Then she broke it, too curious for further delay. She read the note silently.

Heavens. All I wanted was a simple answer. Now I do not know what to expect or say.

She stared at the paper for a few more seconds, then refolded it, and slipped it into the little pocket she kept secured to her petticoat. Her mind too full of thoughts about the note, she ignored Mary's stare and left her sister's unasked questions go unanswered. The open trunk of fabrics offered her the opportunity to dismiss the troubling note for the present.

"Maybe we should use this." Margaret knelt and picked up thick yards of material. "Brocade would do well to cover our new windows." She unfolded a length of it and held it up.

"Whatever might suit you. I seem to have no right to know what goes on in your mind so I have no counter to anything you may suggest."

Margaret cast a slanted regard toward her sister. Mary jutted her jaw forward in petulance. There would be no teasing her sister out of this mood today. Margaret unfolded more of the brocade, studying it.

"Mary, see the tiny birds tucked in among the different leaves and flowers. I should think you would find delight to have this cover the windows in your new bedroom."

In turn Mary ignored her, ruffled through the trunk, and muttered something. Then she promptly stood and stormed out the door to where the maids melted the wax and made candles.

Margaret slipped the packet from Leonard out and reread the message. She sat back on her heels and wondered how to prepare her words. The upcoming situation might become awkward because of a sense of something she didn't understand. Perhaps Mary might.

"Mary?" Margaret strode into the kitchen and called outside to her. "I desire your counsel if you would be so kind."

The maids stopped and looked up, probably hoping to catch a bit of gossip.

Mary left them, entered the house, and waited.

Holding up the note, she placed it into Mary's hand.

Her sister studied Margaret's face, then carefully unfolded the paper and read. When she had finished, she toyed with it for a moment, then handed it back.

Margaret took a seat on the bench in the kitchen, saying, "I do not know what to make of this. I asked him a simple question, but instead of answering, he insists on meeting me under the marked tree on Giles's property boundary."

"You are quite aware," Mary said, "for garden and wall entertainment everyone seeks out knowledge of what everyone else does. They have no intentions to keep their minds on their own doings. If Lady Ann Greene's maidservants do not have the laundry started by noon on Monday, 'tis as scandalous as if one of them had stabbed the harbormaster and hidden his body behind the church altar. News and any credible-sounding blather flies as far north as Kent Island as well as south to Virginia. I pray you are not seriously thinking of meeting with Leonard like this, to have yourself a cozy little picnic under the trees."

"I have an honest reason for being with him. The location of where I keep my good intention should not be a bother to anyone."

"Nonsense. Leonard may as well be trading you chicken feathers for goose down. He could have written the answer to our question but instead he sent this note of contrivance. He has calculated a clever way to spend some time with you, alone in the grass."

"Mary!" Margaret covered her lips with her fingers and shot a glance at Missus Brooke. The cook nodded, excused herself to join the other maids outside.

"I speak what I know." Mary set her face until hard lines appeared on her forehead.

Silence followed. Margaret could hold back no longer.

"I asked you for counsel, dear sister—instead your foul mood creates hurtful folly in your mind."

Her younger sister's scorching insinuations had cut deep into Margaret. She seethed with anger underneath supreme embarrassment. Margaret scooped up her skirts, strode out of the kitchen, and up the stairs to her room. She would meet Leonard, and she would hold her head high on her way to meet him as she walked past their neighbors.

However, anger toward her sister made something inside her crumble. She and Mary rarely argued—but this from Mary—she couldn't understand. Margaret sat thinking on the edge of her bed.

A tap sounded at her door, then Mary entered. Mary slipped over and sat next to Margaret, taking her hand. "I have upset you. But unlike you, I can't help but listen to the maids when they discuss what they hear." She positioned her face so Margaret couldn't ignore her.

"Your relationship with Leonard has caused many to gossip."

"Oh, fluff." Margaret smoothed her petticoats and stood. "They have not one thing to converse about. Leonard and I, as cousins, find solace and comfort in our discussions. We have no intentions of serving up anything improper."

"*You* may not, dear sister. However, I assure you Leonard's plans differ from yours. His plans include more than cousinly chats." Mary rose and stood next to her. "How will you handle him when he becomes brave enough to ask you to marry?"

Margaret's mouth opened. She could not move or breathe. Once, as a young girl, her bindings had been too tightly secured by her maid. On a hot afternoon she had fainted from standing too quickly. Before she passed out, all the sounds around her silenced, darkness closed in, and light-headedness overtook her. She closed her eyes, willing this sensation to go away.

"Oh, my dear older and quite silly sister."

Mary's words sounded miles away—like tiny whispers in Margaret's ear.

She continued her chatter. "By now you must know how smitten he is. From the very first day he couldn't keep his eyes or hands off you. He's quite in love. His heart belongs to you."

This must not be true.

Mary shook her head. "Seriously, you are the only one in St. Mary's City who does not see."

"I will not have it." Margaret unpinned her hair, picked up her brush, and several times drew it hard through her red, unruly hair.

Her younger sister held silent, but her face drew pale.

"Mary—you've lost color. Tell me. Something other than these rumors troubles you." Margaret touched her sister's shoulder. "I'm so sorry, dear. We must not be at odds with each other."

A flicker of prescience appeared in Mary's eyes, but she held her tongue.

"If something else bothers you, please do not keep it hidden," Margaret set her brush down. This was a strange new behavior and it worried her.

Mary took Margaret's hands in hers and locked onto her eyes.

"We have taken on something much larger than this land. You and I have no way to extricate ourselves from something soon to be laid bare before us. My dearest sister, I fear if you do not disentangle yourself from Governor Calvert's ardor, then we both shall be eternally lost."

"Goodness, Mary. Your seriousness distresses me, along with your speaking in riddles. I see no reason why my friendship with Leonard should cause you angst or any worry about some eternal damnation."

After a deep sigh, Mary let loose of Margaret's hands and said, "Since we've arrived, certain men have let their desires be known to me. This has nothing to do with love or even affection. When I hunt for mushrooms or roots in the woods alone, I often need to fear for my safety. I have of late taken to carrying a pin—a very long, sharp one."

Margaret had no notion of this. She bowed her head and listened.

"Remember Fulke's frustration at not finding a suitable wife? All of these men feel the same. Living here without a helpmate makes life unbearably difficult. Since indentures are not allowed to marry this might not be an issue, but as more and more become freemen, their desires and desperation for a wife become obvious."

"Are you saying Leonard is like these brutish men you speak of? I dare say not."

"You would never think to call Fulke or Giles brutish. So, in some ways, yes. Leonard must want a wife as much as any other man. Of this I am certain. Yet one only needs to watch him in your presence to clearly understand he not only has respect but deep adoration for you."

Mary touched Margaret's hair, emphasizing her affection. "If you find yourself wanting to marry Leonard, then I, too, am lost. I fear I will not have the strength to go alone to Father White to give my vow of chastity."

Shaking her head, Margaret walked to the opened window for time to sort out her words.

"We agreed to ask Leonard about you and I moving into our new home prior to our fifth man's arrival. You must be as concerned as I am that our new men may not arrive on these shores for a few more months. We must move now even if we have not fulfilled our contract for the land patent. I have to replant our tobacco seedling on our new property and tend to them daily, or we will not have an income. Then there is the corn crop and gardens to be planted. If not, our food will be in short supply this next winter. Certainly, Leonard would not want that."

"Then my counsel to you, dear sister, is to stay public, out in the open for all to see. Allay any gossipy notions about your relationship. Do not be tempted to dally in the forest. More still, prepare your speech to our governor so when you break his heart you haven't cut the bonds of his friendship. Our most valuable possession in this new land is his power."

Margaret patted her sister's arm. "Mary, Mary. You must not give another worry about me being romantically entangled with any man. *Couverture*, my sister. Do not ever forget couverture. If either of us should foolishly fall in love and marry, you know what happens. Our husbands control our property, and we will have given up our voices."

Chapter 26

If you want a happy life tie it to a goal, not a person.
- Albert Einstein

THE NEXT AFTERNOON MARGARET headed towards the smithy Giles insisted on having built. She strolled along a worn path leading down through the hollow and then up the gentle hill to the tall walnut tree that marked the corner of Giles's land. She glanced back at the fort proper, its small cannon, all the thatched huts, and its manors.

Leonard Calvert, with those sleepy-looking eyes and a hint of expectation in his grin stood in the shade, watching her. He embodied the fine, handsome young gentleman any woman's heart would desire.

She acknowledged him with her sweetest smile.

"My Lady Margaret." He swept his feathered hat from his head, bowed, and kissed her hand. Then he held his palm up to her, saying, "Now that I have rid my head of that ingrained greeting you so detest, I, with no less respect, shall call you the dearest name in my heart." He grinned. "Margaret, you are lovely this afternoon."

She knew not how to stop a blush. She turned slightly away, letting her hair fall loose around the side of her face.

"You always flatter me, my cousin. I have looked forward to today. I believe we shall find our conversing somewhere other than the courts a more pleasant occasion." She gave him an earnest look before saying, "Yet, I am confused as to why you asked to meet. I thought you would take pen to paper and simply answer my question. Instead, you have gone to the bother of preparing a picnic."

"No writing required. Only a fool would entertain doubt that you would have a fifth man coming to our shores. Knowing you, many more will follow."

"Leonard, you have not answered me. The time comes upon us to move my tobacco plants and replant them in their permanent rows or they will die. Mary and I will soon need to set our corn crop as well as our vegetable garden. If we wait until August or September when our fifth man arrives, we shall be in need for food this winter, not to mention the devastation of our finances. I need your affirmation."

"My affirmation? Dear lady, you may start building your new home today if you like. Your trivial request didn't deserve a response. Do you not understand that my brother and I will give you whatever you want?"

"Mary and I would never presume—"

"Since we've settled that little nonsense, let's take a walk about." He carried a willow basket covered with white linen napkins.

113

"Would not you prefer to sit here?" Margaret held back. "Under the shade of this fine tree seems a splendid place to picnic. We can enjoy the view of the river flowing below, listen to the birds—admire the forest."

He shook his head, smiled, and offered his elbow. She sighed, slipped her arm through his, and thought of the senseless ways men argued.

With an easy laugh, he said, "Let me tell you some things you should know about this land." He pointed back to the way she had come—to the wide depression below the hill. From here she could see down to the path that she had followed up the hill. Below, tall grasses and scrubby little trees and bushes spread out and away from the river that flowed to the west. This hollow lazily followed the contour of the northern part of the hill on which they now stood, wrapping east toward the south.

"The area down there floods during heavy spring rains. The water then flows to the east, over where the forest starts and empties into a small stream. Now look back at the St. George River. Marsh grasses and reeds fill the lowland where it meets the river. Marshes have value, and so does the more solid lowland. If we have a dry growing season and you've planted some crops in these lowlands, they'll probably bring a decent yield. Yet our weather is unpredictable, leaving our crops to its mercy. If it's a wet season, the lowlands will be flooded and crops ruined. However, if you've planted the uplands in a dry season, even with irrigating, you'll struggle to create a good yield."

Studying the landscape with new eyes, Margaret understood. "Clever. You're suggesting we plant both low and high lands and be willing to sacrifice one of the crops depending on the harshness of weather." She watched the soft look of pleasure spread across his face.

"Another important issue about the lowlands, m'lady," he said with a twinkle in his eyes. "You, Mary, and your brother won't want to spend much time around them during the late spring and summer months. That's when little pools of water and mud accumulate down there. The mosquitoes thrive, and if you're anywhere near they will sting face and skin raw."

She had no affection for flying, biting insects. "This advice about our new country has much value, dear cousin. Next, you will tell me how not to be swept away in the St. George or be eaten by bears."

Leonard chuckled and continued to stride out, heading south from town along the high banks of the river. Their route took them further from the fort and the prying eyes of their neighbors. Margaret glanced about to see who might watch.

He stopped and pointed down at the river. "I never tire of seeing this beautiful body of water. We're fortunate the depths allow the largest of ships to sail here. Giles has a dock, but the Brent ladies may want their own for shipping tobacco. When we get there, I'll show you the perfect place—a place where you won't have to climb down steep cliffs. At the bottom is a narrow, but short, strip of sandy beach." He took her hand. "Over there in the forest, pigs roam free. Most landowners mark their sows and hogs and turn them loose. It's easier than trying to contain the little beasts, and the forest provides an abundance of food."

Giles's large, white manor, now in view, stood empty except for the few servants he'd not taken to Kent Island. They stayed behind to tend to his crops and care for livestock.

"If I may ask," Margaret said, "I have been wondering how Giles is doing on Kent Island. He said he would be gone but for a few months. From what I have heard, Kent Island sounds quite dangerous. Mary and I worry about him."

Leonard's face relaxed. "He's accomplishing what others before him have not, negotiating peace. You should see these Susquehannock warriors—tall, muscular, fearsome beings. However, I am disliking every thought I've had about that island. It's not because of the Susquehannock invaders. Ever since we first landed here, that damnable island has been a harbor for illegal trading and incitement of bad behaviors."

"Then my brother must be quite busy in whatever he is doing. Should I worry about his safety?"

"He's clever and watchful." Leonard shook his head. "I would be pleased to keep Giles there for the long term. He has a way of convincing renegade Indians to behave, yet I value him closer to me. My brother should have left that indomitable island to Claiborne and the whole of Virginia."

"Since Fulke sailed for England and Giles left for Kent Island, Mary and I find our conversations full of worrisome exchanges. We miss our brothers. Giles's hovering over us is quite annoying, but his return will ease us into more sunny discourses."

"If only I could pin my attitude on something that simple." He drew quiet.

She detected a change in his mood—an instant of furrowing brow. She wasn't sure what she had seen, but his happy spark had changed to one of contemplation.

Margaret stopped walking. "Whatever could be a bother to you?"

He burst into a loud laugh. "I couldn't even begin to say. What I took for granted has become a nightmare with no solution. Maryland, Kent Island, the priests, and the Puritans will be the death of me, for sure."

Margaret, mouth agape, had no idea what she should say next.

He studied her, then took her hand and said, "Come, let's make pleasant use of this sunny afternoon and enjoy a picnic on your new land. No matter that I cannot officially grant you the ceremony of your land patent at this time." He laughed again. "Maryland's ceremonies and procedures, unlike dear England's, have become most whimsical."

"Whimsical? Leonard, whimsical? You jest."

"It's a jumble among Jesuits who believe they have a right to acquire land from the Indians, though my brother proprietor disagrees, and says all of Maryland belongs to him unless he bestows it. Then he angers the good priestly men by providing generous farms for future Anglican ministers. You've heard of the Jesuits—those who inhabit St. Inigoes Neck to the south of your new land. We are forbidden to give them their land patents, but they are good men. We've come up with an arrangement of sorts, which we shall not disclose to my brother. Now the Jesuits may work and live on their lands. They've earned the right, paid enough headrights to be entitled, but their dispute with my brother continues. I don't understand his animosity. These Jesuits and priests seem to be the only ones here who actually pay their taxes."

"Cecil Calvert—not being fair. This makes no sense."

"I swear ill humor in England causes our troubles. Hostilities increase against all suspected Catholics. Traitors, assassins, and pretenders lurk every-where along with the king's men. No one trusts anyone. That's why Cecil cannot allow these Jesuits to embarrass him with their boldness or ownership of large parcels of land holdings. What happens here is heard about back there. Cecil sent us his good friend John Lewger to present to our body politic a long list of Cecil's mandates and to be my secretary. Ideally, the provincial court and the people's assembly govern in tandem, but his new laws caused the two political bodies to erupt into a stew of madness. No matter what my brother in England says or what we do here in Maryland, by the time communications arrive on either shore, protocols, mandates, and ideas have become bungled."

"Leonard, I had no idea." Margaret had mistaken Leonard's role in Maryland to be one of delightful paternity over his grateful settlers.

"The good Lord Baltimore's long list of thou shalt and thou shalt nots—what a bother. My head still hurts after all these months. John Lewger and I served up Cecil's list of laws, only to have them stir up ire and be thrown back in our faces with resentment."

"If this is so, your brother has created undue hostilities toward the both of you."

"With cleverness and acts of humility, we did bring the gentlemen together to rewrite many of Cecil's laws—laws more fitting for our needs. Cecil shocked us in return. He actually agreed for the most part. John Lewger is a good and loyal man, even though some say unbearably rigid—a polite way to say stuffy."

"Heavens. What type of reception did Cecil expect from declaring new laws?" She thought Cecil a man who would know his own mind and hold steady. "Change is not agreeable to most people, and you now paint him as rather fickle."

"Cecil decided he'd been too generous with his land patents. If he kept farms smaller, then more crops would be planted, bringing in more income. Gentleman Lewger and I did our best to support my brother, causing the rest of the assembly to erupt into outrage."

Margaret said. "This all comes from Cecil's new laws."

"Sad to say, it does. Most of the indentures here are Protestants. It galls me to seek privacy in our worship, whereas Puritans of every ilk can exhibit their devotion unrestricted. Maryland's tolerance of religious differences has become quite one-sided. How does one be Catholic but not act Catholic?"

He offered her his arm once more, and they walked in silence.

She needed to change this dark conversation. "Listening to the songs of all these birds, I must agree with my sister. They sound as if they constantly converse with each other. Mary believes birds argue, agree, praise, instruct, and confide in each other the same as we do. Do you think this could be?"

He cocked his head to listen, then said, "Your sister amuses me. I would en-joy being in the community of those little socializing birds. I'm ashamed to admit I almost pity myself for my loneliness."

She gave him her skeptical look, an eyebrow slightly raised.

"Be damned. Here I am the most powerful man in Maryland, and I suspect I am one of the unhappiest."

"This cannot be. You surround yourself with gentlemen and ladies who show much respect for your efforts, as well as do many Protestants and those of the newly made freemen."

Leonard continued on without comment.

His unhappiness bothered her more than she would have thought, but there was little she could do about it except maybe get Leonard to discuss what troubled him.

"As the esteemed governor of this land, there is naught you can do about the communication between here and England. There is naught you can do about your brother's change in policies." She paused to be sure he still listened. Satisfied, she continued. "The Kent Island problem seems to be under control now. You, and heaven knows we, are used to this usual skirmish between Protestant and Catholic—but at least here in Maryland we will not be losing our heads. Pray tell me, what else makes you so unhappy?"

Chapter 27

LEONARD STARED OFF IN the distance, then looked at her out of the corner of his eye.

She waited for his answer.

He led her toward a large oak tree several yards away. "You're wrong about Kent Island. We constantly remind the inhabitants in the strongest of manner they owe their allegiance to Maryland, not Virginia. I also fear you're wrong about the Protestant issue. Less than a year ago one of the servants, along with a freeman, wrote up a petition to take to the governor of Virginia, saying the servant suffered daily abuse at our Jesuit manor on St. Inigoes. The Jesuit, Lewis, had called Protestant ministers and their books *instruments of the devil*, and the servant and freeman claimed the Pope to be the antichrist. I was away, but Captain Cornwallis stepped in and took control. In court, John Lewger claimed the guilty party to be Lewis, the overseer of the Jesuit Manor. Protestant books the servant used to goad the overseer would not have been illegal in England. Right or wrong, the turmoil over religion grows here as it does in England. England once more is on the doorstep of war, and the Protestants in Maryland and Virginia are well stirred up over this."

Leonard motioned to a large patch of tangled grasses shaded by an oak tree.

She gazed down on the deep flowing river, reflecting the blue sky above. Then she glanced around and across the open grassy meadow dotted with every imaginable color found in the earliest of spring wildflowers.

"What a lovely place for a picnic, Leonard." She picked a tiny, purple daisy and stroked it.

"Here marks the boundary between Giles's land and yours. We shall have our picnic on your land."

She helped him spread the cloth and set out the bundles of food Missus Davis had asked the cook to prepare for them. The largest contained a roasted bird. Margaret unwrapped a mound of soft cheese and placed it next to the shelled walnuts, a wooden box of wild berries, and slices of melon.

Leonard handed her one of two bronze cups and a flask of ale to share. He indicated she should help herself to the roasted meat. After pulling off a tiny juicy leg with thigh, she pinched off a piece and tasted.

"This has no resemblance to chicken." She dabbed her mouth with one of the napkins. "I do not recognize this pleasing flavor."

"Quail," he said. "A brown and white quail—you must know of the bob-white. This is one of my favorites."

She nodded approval, then said, "I still marvel at the thought of the sky darkened by cranes. They blacked out the sun when they flew earlier this spring. I have never seen so many birds together in my whole life."

While they ate, Leonard talked of her neighbors. "Over there to the east of your property is Clarke's Freehold. Father Fisher paid for the man's passage, but after working his lands and in his missions, he's now a freeman. Have you met Robert Clarke yet?"

"I shall be pleased to do so. Oh wait, he introduced himself to my brothers the day the *Charity* docked."

"He surveyed this land for you. You have already met your neighbor to the south."

"I hope it is someone agreeable." She grinned at him.

"He's an assemblyman. The gentleman Thomas Greene and his wife Ann live on Greene's Freehold."

"We do know them. Mary and I shall be right at home with our Sisters Freehold between the Greene's and the Clarke's Freeholds. After we eat, may we have a walk about so you can show where to put our dock and also maybe suggest the location for our house?"

"Your house…" He put the flask down, wiped his hands, and stared deep into her eyes. "Margaret, I cannot keep still about my feelings any longer."

His eyebrows raised a touch, his mouth not quite shut, the hopeful look on his face made what he was about to say obvious. Margaret pulled her gaze away, wiped her hand, and glanced out over the river. When she turned back, he still stared at her.

"I have not one soul I may confide in as you and I have done today. Except for when I'm in your company, Margaret, I am always on stage. To be otherwise would declare me weak." He studied her. "I've never felt this way before—never had the desire to be close."

Mary had been right. Margaret's frogs danced. She knew what he would ask—she didn't want to hear. The chirping and songs of birds filled her ears—flies and insects buzzed around their food. With her hands clasping and unclasping, she stared at the river rushing between its wide banks—wide and deep—full of amazing creatures.

He kept telling her to listen to him. Then he touched her chin and lifted it up until she looked into his eyes.

"Please, dear lady. If you're worried about Mary, there is no need. Everyday men tell me how desirable she is. Until then, she should live with us. I've never trusted anyone until you came, and I know we will have a sweet life. Together we will make my father's grand Maryland adventure what he had hoped. You must be my wife."

Thoughts jumbled in her mind. Her lips dry, her throat closed tight, and the air within didn't stir. Her words became incoherent as they worked their way up and out, sounding like a small, tortured animal. Even she couldn't understand the sounds, so she pulled away and started to stand.

He grabbed her hand, saying noises that sounded like words.

"Margaret. Please." He tugged on her hand.

She crumpled next to him. She wanted to go but could not leave. Words evaporated. Yet they had always been her best defense. She struggled to breathe and closed her eyes.

He pulled her close and held her.

Leonard's strong arms supported her in a cocoon of safety. He sent her emotions into chaos. His firm but gentle touch, his warmth, soft words, and the faint perfume of barberry soap, filled her with a needed sense of security.

Everything in this new land came from struggling. The simplest of tasks required extreme effort. Margaret now toiled in the garden on hands and knees. Dirt imbedded in her chipped fingernails—like a servant. She and Mary labored from sunup to sundown. This land required muscle and sweat even from women. Whatever the sisters needed, or whatever they wanted, she and Mary had to figure out how to make it or learn how to do it. Alone, they held all the responsibility if they were to succeed.

Margaret's resistance faded in exchange for her confusion entangled with his nearness. Leaning into his chest and feeling his heart pounding, she silently prayed for the moment to never end.

His disturbing words comforted—yet in a way terrified her. An unsettling, a fear, a wisp of something wrong shivered into her mind.

She must flee.

Beautiful Maryland, you exhaust me.

"Leonard, I—" She leaned away.

"Say yes, or my heart will break."

"As mine does." She was shaking her head again, and again.

He held her face still, then placed a finger over her lips and said, "Please do not turn me down. I want children. Think of what we could offer them. This has to be, not just for me but for Maryland, for us all. I need you as my wife—my confidant. You must not tell me otherwise because I cannot bear to hear. Dear one, I am beside myself with loneliness and for want of you."

His face now within inches of hers—his low, soft voice carried the warmth of his breath to her lips. An ache, deep within, started to grow warm and heavy, slowly changing into an unfamiliar yearning. Trembling, she knew at some level she must end this—now—this moment or never.

What to do? Poor Leonard.

A buzzing started in her ears, the frogs began bounding around inside her stomach, and the chattering of the birds grew uncomfortably loud up in the trees. Her head, her mind, the confusion of it all kept Margaret from forming words. Nothing agreed. Everything fought at odds. She forced herself to push away, gently removed his large hands from her face, swallowed hard, and shushed him with her finger across his lips.

"My dear Governor." she whispered. Then finding her voice, said, "Leonard, you and I have something special, but my love for you must be the same as for a treasured brother. Our walks, our talks, our sharing of private matters belong only to you and me. This gives our troubled lives a sweetness unlike I have ever known. Please understand my sister and I have reasons to never wed, and these reasons should not matter to anyone other than ourselves. Yet I will give you one you will understand, *couverture*. Mary and I desire to be recognized in our own right, not as wives of our husbands. We have no desire to relinquish our property or the ability to speak for ourselves. I shall not have my voice denied."

Leonard's chest slumped, his head shaking.

"I desperately hope you choose not to destroy this preciousness you and I have together because I am declining your most gracious offer with my own breaking heart."

Margaret couldn't bear to watch his agony and whatever else he seemed to be wrestling within his being. She spoke the truth. She valued their time they shared. She did love him, unlike a brother—but he must believe as a brother—a brother and a sister.

"You've become as dear to me as any of my brothers, even dearer in many ways because you treat me as an equal. Leonard, you are lonely. Fulke's loneliness drove him back to England."

England, dear England and our family...

She paused. She now knew what to say.

"I offer you a thought. When you next go to England, pay a visit to my younger sister, Ann. I will write an introduction to her about you. She is a lovely young lady in every way. She might agree to take your hand in marriage and return here to Maryland. The two of you would be so right together. She is intelligent, capable, quite fetching, and would be a kind and wonderful wife and mother."

He stared out toward the St. George, not saying anything.

"Please think about this, Leonard. If the two of you did marry, then you and I would truly be sister and brother."

Chapter 28
Late May 1639

It is better to know some of the questions, rather than all the answers.
- James Thurber

AFTERNOON CLOUDS GATHERED AND rumbled, while the sisters prepared to move into their grand new home, Sisters Freehold. Giles's men, along with their own, had worked from sunup to sundown for weeks building fireplaces, constructing thresholds and walls, raising the roof, and laying beautiful floor planking. Mary and Margaret had discussed the placements of the windows. The men cut out holes, installed casings, sills, and window glass, and then their fine oak doors. Some of the men erected fences, then built the servants quarters, the chicken coop, and their barn. Yesterday, they moved their livestock to Sisters Freehold. The outside kitchen and tobacco drying shed would be built later.

Pillows of white and gray hung on the horizon, but the azure sky overhead sang out spring. Rains had come down in short bursts the last two days, cooling the hot afternoons. Margaret rushed over to where Robinson worked.

In the process of packing, Margaret had set aside an old wobbly table. Today she had Robinson saw its legs down a foot or so. He built sides around the upside-down table and then secured it to a two-runner sledge he'd finished constructing.

"Robinson, have you finished the sledge? We will have to make several trips, and I certainly do not want to be pulling it in a storm. Besides, Stephens and Goodwin should have some of the rows ready for planting by now."

"You're displeased I'm not working fast enough." Robinson continued hammering on a nail.

"I make no such implication, Robinson." This man hunted for personal affronts. "I only impart information. This storm may be a problem for us."

She and Mary calculated what percentage of their acreage they could plant with only six men. No matter how they planned, their tobacco fields would be small until they convinced more men to come from England.

Along with the tobacco planting and care, the men would need to attend to everyday repairs and maintenance tasks and care for a sizable corn crop. Lord Baltimore required landowners to plant enough corn to ensure food for everyone living on the manor lands—two acres per person.

"Governor Calvert has sent a man with a horse and cart for the household items. The wagon should be here any minute now. Please help load the cart before we set off with the sledge." She glanced up at the clouds.

Robinson grunted and stood, indicating with his hand she could now load the sledge.

Margaret knelt in the dirt and carefully dug up each tobacco plant, leaving lots of soil around the root. She placed them carefully in the tray on the sledge. Forty minutes later she'd squeezed in a final one.

She counted the plants, then looked at the remaining ones, and calculated how many trips the sledge would have to make. Margaret decided to walk this first time with Robinson as he pulled the sledge to their home. Even though she had given Goodwin and Stephens careful instructions, she wanted to be sure they placed these young tobacco shoots correctly in the soil.

Sisters Freehold's livelihood leaned heavily on producing a good first year crop. Brushing the damp earth from her hands, she stretched her back, and looked around. The big ox of a man whom she'd helped a few weeks ago in court strode up the road.

"Lady Brent." He waved. "A moment if you will."

Margaret liked this man. John Morton, a freeman, a Protestant, and a man who could not read nor write. He had worked hard and borrowed heavily from friends and family in a rare gamble to pay his family's passage to Maryland. He mentioned he'd always been a dreamer. Even when small, he wanted nothing more on this earth but to die as a landowner. God must have smiled on this huge person—even as a Protestant. His baby boy seemed healthy. Few children ever survived the crossing or their first year.

Of course, God would take care of him. Gentle John's heart had grown as big as a house.

"Good morning to you, John. I trust your wife and son do well."

"Indeed. I've brought you gifts from a grateful goat and chickens now home where they belong. My sweet Bess made you cheese, and here's a basket of eggs for you."

"Heavens. I never thought about recompense for my persuasion of the court's council."

"When those ruffians pay their penalty to me, I'll be bringing a hundred pounds of tobacco to you." He set his jaw, looked down at her face, and then said, "Unless you find it an insult, then I'll give you half what I got. I don't mean to be stingy. Maybe I should give you all except what it cost me to replace the pig they butchered and et. I don't deserve more."

"What silliness, John. You deserve all they awarded."

"I pay you, for sure. My friends talk about you. About how you help anyone who stands mute when we have no hanker'n to give our say in court." He held out the cheese and eggs. "I never dreamed I could become an old man without debts, all thanks to your strong talk to make the council believe."

"There does come pride in being a landowner."

"I now have means to provide for my family. I no longer suffer debt notice due other men." His grin covered his face making his eyes crinkle.

"Your wife must be pleased with you, John. You are a fine man."

"And you are a good woman, Lady Brent. If ever I can be of service—" He nodded, placed his cap on his head, and whistled a jaunty tune as he strode off toward his home.

Being compensated for representing others in court—goodness be.

Robinson came around the corner of their house.

"They are almost finished loading the cart, and it will be on the way as soon as your sister's ready." He checked the sledge.

He picked up the two handles of the sledge and started walking down the path to the road as if it were full of goose down, not heavy, damp soil with plants. Margaret scurried to catch up.

"I have wanted to discuss something with you, Robinson," she said, "and this seems as good a time as any."

He remained silent.

"Our new neighbor, Gentleman Greene, has been asking about your carpentry skills. He stopped by our new manor and admired the fine chairs and table you have made for us, also that lovely chest you carved for our linens."

Robinson continued his pace. "I'm a barber by trade."

She nodded. "Greene asked me if he could contract with you to build a cabinet for his kitchen."

Margaret studied Robinson, watching for a reaction. His expression did not change.

She sighed. "Well?"

He shrugged and kept walking.

"Is there a reason you do not desire to work for him on this project?'

Robinson looked up at the clouds, then without missing a step, said, "My debt is to you and your sister. If I take on his work, then I'm not fulfilling my obligation to the two of you. I am anxious to become a freeman as soon as possible. I take no pleasure in extending my time as an indentured servant to you because I detest working at anyone's whim."

"I see." She had seen his flare of temper when he had to bow to authority. His words today did not surprise her.

Margaret fell into the rhythm as they walked side by side. The trees cast deep shadows with bright sunlight playing tag between the roiling clouds. Here and there a daisy poked its white petals through the greens of the woodland floor. Small gray birds chittered high above and somewhere off in the far tree tops another one trilled. Margaret gave Robinson's dilemma some thought.

"Robinson, Virginia has laws that no indenture can work on Sunday, as we do here."

"I've heard."

"They also have a law that indentures may not work on Saturdays either."

Heat washed over her, even though clouds filled the sky. The wrongness of her need to have him use his talent for her had never been a thought. She drew her lips into a hard line. He'd seemed eager to create their fine dining table. Then, naturally, they needed chairs, and cupboards, and then furniture for their living area to take to their new manor. She and Mary had kept him busy beyond the five-day week.

Dear Father, please guide me to be charitable and erase my greed. I've deprived this man of his due.

He stopped walking and looked at her, then said, "It appears you or Maryland has no concern for this law."

Margaret studied his face. "I should have seen that you enjoyed your Saturdays with no tasks. I am not sure if it is a law here or if St. Mary's chooses to ignore it. What you have created for our home speaks well for your carpentry skills. I shall see to it your Saturdays will be your own from now on. You will encounter no objections if you decide to use your talent for extra income. Mary will agree as long as it does not interfere with your work as an indentured."

Margaret's father had assured her they would not need to bring much furniture with them because Lord Calvert had expounded on the quality of fine woods in the new world. They came with only some chests and boxes and a few other objects. At the time she hadn't known Robinson to be so adept at woodworking and creating fine furniture. However, considering his surly demeanor, she would welcome him gone from their household.

Robinson gave a quiet snort. A few minutes later he said, "Tell the gentleman I'll stop by Saturday late afternoon and consider what he has in mind."

Margaret smiled because Thomas Greene would be pleased. Robinson enjoyed carpentry and would earn an income, and he might pay off his servitude early.

Heavens and stars, what am I doing? Sisters Freehold will be short field workers as it is.

Chapter 29

Either define the moment or the moment will define you.
- Walt Whitman

WHEN MARGARET AND ROBINSON arrived, Stephens and Goodwin stopped peeling bark and ran over to the sledge.

"Suspect ye'll be making a few more trips with tha contraption." Goodwin crouched and picked up a clod of dirt with a small plant clinging to it. "Better be planting these babies afore they dry up."

He motioned to Robinson to pull the sledge closer to the fence line. Stephens helped Robinson and Goodwin unload the tiny tobacco plants while Margaret inspected her men's creation of mounded dirt rows around the bark-stripped trees. Girdling these trees would cause them to die, saving trouble and time by not having to cut them down. Tree roots must not compete with young tobacco plants for nutrients and water.

She knelt and began to place the plants into the prepared ground.

"Lady Brent," Stephens said, "Those storm clouds are building. Should we put the plants somewhere safe until it passes over?"

The clouds bunched and roiled then seemed to spread out, changing from sooty clumps to lumpy, gray milk. "A little water will not hurt. Besides, we have nowhere to store them. Robinson, you must hurry. Take Stephens with you to help load the sledge."

After they left, Goodwin carried clusters of the tiny greenery over to Margaret as she created holes for their roots.

"M'lady," Goodwin placed the shoots beside her and said, "remember tha lad you asked for at my smithy in Gloucester? He been here and there, stealin' chickens and hogs from people."

"Here?" Margaret looked around.

"Not here at m'ladies' manor. But around these parts, they've been. They grab and flee to their rickety ship. Tha tie tha ol' thing up to one of tha private docks up and down tha St. George. I thought ye should know."

"Goodwin, let it be known Mary and I are excellent shooters. We will scare away any young hoodlums."

Goodwin shook his head, picked up more plants and started placing each one carefully in the mounded soil.

Margaret wasn't sure if he disagreed with her shooting abilities or if he shook his head because of the boys' behaviors.

"Please place them three feet apart, Goodwin."

"One more thing you ta know, m'lady." He tamped the soil gently around each

126

shoot but didn't speak while he worked.

She untangled two of the plants, waiting for him to say more.

"These lads, tha be seen with tha merchant Puritan."

"A merchant Puritan. And who might that be?"

"From Virginia. Captain Ingle." Goodwin said. "Do you know who he be?"

"Should I?" She didn't remember the name, but outside of the local indentured servants and the ones who recently gained their freeman status, she didn't know many Protestants.

"Naw, it be nuttin', I suppose." He looked up and nodded toward the path.

The sound of horses snorting caused her to stand. Leonard's wagon approached with two men and with Mary sitting up front with the sisters' household belongings piled high in the back. Margaret brushed the soil from her hands and waved to them as they came down the lane. Goodwin finished putting the last little plant in the ground.

Large drops of rain splatted on the dirt.

"Goodwin, we need to get the furnishing into the house before this rain lets loose."

Their maids, who had been wandering down the path, now came rushing to help as the rain became steadier. Thomas Gedd hurried across the field where he had been building fences.

Mary called out, "I fear Robinson and Stephens will end up soaked. We must hurry." Leonard's men untied the rope securing the sisters' belongings, and everyone hauled what they could into their new home. Mary directed where things should be placed until Margaret told her to shush. Hail pelted down in the whipping winds.

"Just bring it all inside as quickly as you can. Mary, we will move it around as needed later." The hail gave way to a torrent of rain.

Mary called to one of the maids, "Elizabeth Guesse, please get a rag and wipe the water off the furniture."

When they had finished unloading everything, the governor's men bid them well, and directed the team of horses on the path toward home. The horses, with heads low against the deluge of weather, plodded on a path that had turned into a mess of mud.

Robinson and Stephens came slipping and sliding up the path with another load of tobacco plants on the sledge. Margaret ran out to help but stopped and motioned for them to leave the sledge where it was.

"Unstrap the tray and bring those plants into the house—get out of the storm."

Sheets of rain spilled down on her. The wind whipped Margaret's skirts about, and her hair flew around her face. Mary yelled for her to come.

Margaret ignored her. She had to check the tobacco sprouts. Her heart fell like a stone.

The delicate shoots had been pummeled. The soil had washed from around them. What she and Goodwin had planted a few hours ago could not be saved. She stared at the tiny, tender white roots churning in ice and drowning in muddy puddles—along with their dreams.

Chapter 30

The winds there are variable; from the South comes heat, gusts, and thunder; from the North, or Northwest, cold-weather, and winter, frost and snow; from the East and Southeast, raine.
– Cornwallis & Hawley. *A Relation of Maryland*

WIND-DRIVEN RAIN HOWLED and pelted Sisters Freehold all night and for most of the following day. Late on the second day, golden rays of sunlight poked through charcoal-colored clouds but only for brief moments prior to the sun settling for the night. Then the storm resumed.

While the storm had rumbled and moaned outside on moving day, the servants scurried about helping Mary and Margaret. They arranged the furniture inside the main house as well as the servants' quarters.

Missus Brookes finally found a moment to slip into their indoor kitchen where she made a simple clam-vegetable stew for their dinner. Someone had lit the candles, and the servants sat around the kitchen fireplace. Everyone seemed to have a story about their part in this move and bemoaned about work still waiting. When they had finished eating, the servants bid Mary and Margaret a goodnight and dashed in the downpour from the main house to their own new living quarters a few yards away. All the while, Margaret had sat quietly beside Mary, listening to their tales and concerns.

As much as she mourned the loss of her tobacco plants, Margaret found admiration for these people who had left England and mustered the enormous initiative required to live here in Maryland.

The following morning the rain continued to cascade down in sheets. Clouds rumbled, echoing sounds of heavy furniture being moved. Tiny rivulets cut through the sodden pasture. After a restless sleep, Margaret joined Mary in the kitchen where the maids argued over proper places to stow the bundles, sacks, barrels, and baskets of food along with the cookware and eating implements.

Goodwin insisted on hanging hooks from the walls and the kitchen ceiling for cooking pots.

"Goodwin, we shall not want this many hooks here once we have the outside kitchen finished, and whatever you use must be strong and anchored securely." Margaret guessed some of their kettles weighed forty pounds.

Thank goodness for the strength and health of Missus Brookes.

Not to be outdone, Robinson decided he would build some shelves and a cupboard in the kitchen for storage of the eating and drinking implements. He measured and paced around the kitchen until Mary stopped him.

"If there are to be shelves, they must be out of the way, Robinson. Construct them over in that far back corner, and when you build the cupboard, please make it movable so we may place it in the new kitchen if we desire."

"Lady Brent, do you or do you not care to have these objects constructed? If so, then be off with your lectures. Give me credit for sound judgement."

"Robinson, I—"

He left to get his tools.

The servants kept dashing to the barn or an outbuilding to collect items of necessity. With the doors opening and closing, the two fireplaces could not keep the house from taking on a damp and chilled disposition.

Margaret, exasperated, spread her hands, indicating for Mary to look at the filthy, streaked plank floors. They would require heavy scouring and waxing to rid them of the caked mud and to regain their vigor.

There sat the tray of puny, water-soaked shoots. Someone had placed it in a dark corner of the indoor kitchen. Margaret turned away from the pitiful sight.

Fatigued and downhearted, she retired early to her room, ignoring supper and idle gossip. After her evening prayers, Margaret blew out the candle, and settled into bed, watching the shadows of the quiet night sky out her window. The expectations of two days ago had been washed away and drained, leaving her hollow. Those tiny dying tobacco plants had held their financial vision.

Delicate raps on her door interrupted her thoughts.

"I am awake, Mary." Margaret sat up and arranged pillows behind her. "Please enter."

Mary, illuminated by her candle, crept in and closed the door behind her.

"Come. Sit next to me." Margaret fluffed a pillow for Mary. "We need to discuss how our affairs have changed because of this storm."

"Heavens be calm." Mary said, "I tossed and turned all night. Thunder and lightning was not the half of it. I am fairly sick over the damage to our little plants."

"I too have not been given much sleep."

"And Robinson's attitude unravels my tolerance." Mary set her small candleholder on the rough-wood table and climbed up on the large bed.

"He is the second son of a rather well-off gentleman. Evidently, he elected not to pursue life in the military or the church."

"So many men are here because their older brothers will inherit the family estate." Mary fluffed the pillow and wiggled into comfort. "Their best hope to ever own land comes from being a servant here."

"Robinson resents being anyone's servant. More than that, Mary, when a servant becomes free, he also becomes an assemblyman. Robinson, as an equal in the governing body, will help enact laws concerning Maryland." Margaret considered her words. "The man is quite talented in several ways. He is known as a barber but look at the fine furniture he builds."

"Sister, you have talent—those delicate little sprouts—I have not the mind for gardens. They seemed strong and healthy until the rain."

"Our currency, Mary. You know how I detest being indebted to anyone."

"This whole adventure—" Mary's voice cracked. "Coming here to St. Mary's—it's hard. Harder than I expected but now what?"

Margaret found nothing to say, reflecting on the many times she and Mary had taken on work servants would have performed in England.

"Another concern," Mary said. "Catholics do not worship as freely the Protestants. They judge us and expect us to keep our religion to ourselves." She muttered to herself. "Those damnable Parliamentarian Protestants do as they please. And those sanctimonious Puritans!"

"Shush, Mary. Do not speak so."

"It is the truest thought in my mind right now."

"Yet, the least holy and unladylike."

Margaret held back even less charitable words. Lord Baltimore, in the center of Protestant England, could not allow Maryland to be known as a Catholic settlement.

Evidently, to accomplish this, he must treat us as the least-favored child.

"When I picnicked with Leonard, he did affirm what you say. If you and I are to get any sleep at all we must settle some larger issues."

"Nothing is larger than our being Catholic and pretending to not be Catholic in public."

"I argue for you to accept the enormity of our current financial troubles. This is the greater problem of the moment." Margaret smoothed out the thin blanket.

"Before we talk finances," Mary said, "I am all crickets about your picnic. Your near silence over the event causes me madness. If you insist in not confiding, I have no choice but to show vexation."

"I sent a letter to our sister Ann, asking her if our good governor might on occasion write to her."

"Ann?" Mary's mouth hung open.

"Enough about this. We must straighten out what to do about our finances."

"I keep wondering why our Good Lord has put us in this situation."

"Perchance, He wants to see whether we wring our hands and complain, or if we hike up our petticoats and make the best of it. He will make us a path to satisfaction and peace, but each of us must discover the way."

"Margaret." She snickered. "You discovered our way—I know you have some clever strategy."

"First, give thanks to John Morton. Word has spread of my representing him in court. I had not one thought of recompence until he insisted. When others follow it should help our finances. The next part will not be easy. We must do more household chores, as we need our maids to help tend our gardens, the corn crops, and livestock."

"Do not tell me our men will go on some lovely holiday."

"Since we have no tobacco crops, we shall have no currency." Margaret spoke firmly as to anchor her words into reality. "However, we can turn our indentured men's work into coinage if we rent them out to work the crops for others."

Mary clapped her hands. "Planters complain all the time they don't have enough men to tend their tobacco fields properly." She paused. "Yet their fields may be washed away too."

"If the plants had been established, they would have fared better through the storm. We shall set a standard price for hourly work charged to the landowner, and our men will, in turn, get credit from us to pay off their indentured debt."

"What if the men wish to work for their own pay on Saturdays or Sundays, like Robinson?" Mary said.

Margaret thought for a few minutes. "That we need to discourage. Working in the field is exhausting. We cannot have them worn out, slacking off during the week."

"Robinson said you approved him doing carpentry on weekends for Thomas Greene and his wife."

"I did, but woodworking taxes one's body and mind differently than plowing and weeding a field under the noonday sun."

Mary shook her head. "You have set precedence with Robinson. We'll be in the middle of arguments about this with the men."

Knowing the truth of Mary's words, Margaret said, "When they signed on to be indentured for their given period of time, they swore to us they would work diligently from morning to night regardless of the tasks asked of them. If these men spend themselves to exhaustion in another man's field on the weekends, how can they work assiduously the rest of the week? I swear to you, Mary, a few incidences of laziness and no one will want to hire them."

"We can't force them to rest, attend church, or find some pleasurable entertainment on their Saturdays and Sundays." Mary yawned, slid off the bed, took up her candle, and said, "I'll sleep much sounder tonight if you come up with that answer."

"Let us call them together tomorrow and have a talk. Our financial situation affects not just the two of us but also each of them."

Chapter 31
Fall 1639

...every day bettering itself, by increase of planters & plantations & large crops this year of corn & tobacco, the servants' time now expiring."
- Father Andrew White

MARY AND MARGARET'S PLANS made last spring had, in fact, secured their financial wellbeing. Today, Margaret, in the quietness of their home this sunny morning, stared at her ledger, and then back at dozens of her small, penned notes. She had finished entering last month's legal accounts received from farmers and landowners who had contracted with her to collect their overdue debts in Provincial Court.

She smiled, knowing the good men of Maryland were becoming accustomed to her brief, yet almost daily, appearance in front of the governor and his council.

The sisters' tactic of renting out their servants to work in other men's tobacco fields had also been profitable, bringing her even more satisfaction this morning with more ledger entries. The question of the men earning their own pay on weekends had been solved by allowing them to perform whatever services their talents allowed. Goodwin opened his smithy shop for a few hours each weekend and now talked about enlarging his shop. The servants had agreed, for the benefit of all, not to exhaust themselves in hard labor on the weekend.

Margaret, ignoring the buzzing of flies, rechecked her figures. Those pestering insects could drive anyone mad beyond reason. The house creaked, settling. She glanced around, feeling a tug of unexpected resentment as it wiggled through a crack in her disposition.

'Tis impossible to concentrate when everyone has run off to greet the merchant ship.

She, too, wanted to hear news of England, and know where the ship came from, and who was on it, and what merchandise there might be to buy, and if it carried any messages from home.

She scolded herself for staying at home with her ledgers. Margaret picked up one of the notes. Dipping her nib in ink, she drew her finger down the column under Thomas Gedd's name and marked, *St. Indigo's Neck, Jesuits, fifty hours*, and then penned the date. The next went under Goodwin's name. *St. Barbara's. Mary Troughton, twenty-eight hours,* and again the date. Goodwin spent some of his time helping her, and then he worked for the villagers at the smithy. She wouldn't record his weekend earnings. They belonged to him. Someone always needed metal work.

Her men worked hard. She reached for another note, but a crash, a horrific squeal, and some type of outside turbulence brought her to her feet.

Hens squawked frantically, making the rooster crow as if about to be strangled.

She lunged through the doorway. The noise escalated. A large, hairy, dirt-caked swine had plowed through the garden fence. The hens, who had been lazily hunting grasshoppers and flies among the vegetables all morning, now perched on the fence, fluffing their feathers, and scolding the clumsy fat animal. Standing tall on one of their porch eaves, the rooster continued his call of alarm.

"Shoo—go on—get out of here!" Margaret flapped her skirt and waved her hand at the beast. The pig snorted and ignored her and continued rooting around in the carrots and turnips. Margaret darted back to the gate and picked up a piece of broken wood. Swinging it, she stomped up to the animal, and gave it a whack on its ample backside.

"Out of my garden you—"

"M'lady, le'me help ye." Goodwin trotted down the path and leapt over the fence. He grabbed a piece of rope from the garden shed and tied it around the pig's neck. "Come on, you rogue, I be taking you home."

"Do you know where she belongs?"

"Tha' I do, m'lady. This spotted rascal belongs to a couple of freemen who live northwest of the woods close to John Morton's place."

"When I last called on John Morton and his wife, she seemed quite thin and pale. I worry."

"John says the wee babe growing within her leaves her no strength. Saw your sister down at the dock. She says you have news from England. Now, 'tis that not great for ye?"

He tugged the rope, and to Margaret's amazement, the pig looked up, shook its head, and with a grunt obediently followed. Whistling some Celtic tune, Goodwin strode up the path, disappearing into the woods.

Most of the garden damage had happened in the root vegetable section. After the first few storms a drought ensued and had left their garden rather puny. Margaret shook her head and replanted the few that might survive.

She picked up the broken gate, studied the sections, and tossed them aside. Robinson would need to build a new one.

Everyone understood why most pig owners let their animals loose in the forest. These animals seem impossible to confine, always escaping and running off. Besides, the forest provided abundant pig-type foods—acorns, nuts, mushrooms, and roots.

Of this she couldn't complain. Mischievous pigs running wild often brought her before the court or Assembly. A free roaming pig would have many landowners knocking on her door for help to end disputes over ownership of the pig and who should pay damages.

A gentle breeze from the St. George River brushed over her.

The grasses below her feet, brown and sparse for want of rain, should have been tangled into deep green. All the plants needed a good steady drizzle to soak the ground. Margaret paused before going inside to continue her accounting. She swept her gaze again over the St. George.

Such a magnificent river in every way, and it adds a bonus for their economy.

An approaching merchant ship attested to her observation. She had noticed this ship often at different docks.

Goodness, it has dropped anchor here.

She strolled over to the embankment, stood, and watched. The crew scuttled around on the deck, one climbed down into a small shallop and rowed to the dock. The captain sprinted along the gangplank, glanced up, waved his hat toward her, and strode confidently up the embankment. His short haircut, high brown boots, the tan leather jerkin over his linen shirt, and his hint of a swagger raised her internal guard. An arrogant Protestant approached.

She shivered. Some would call him a Roundhead, a supporter of Parliament. This man smelled of trouble.

Over-confident men, such as he, think they can control whatever the discussion.

"Good morning to the lady." He removed his hat again but did not make the slightest of bows. "I'm pleased to encounter you here as all others have run off to welcome the English ship."

"Not all have run off, my good man. You will find others nearby. I took my pleasure in waving to the ship as it passed. Excuse me but my work waits unfinished." Being alone with a strange man unsettled her. She hoped Goodwin would hasten his return. Her bones whispered to her he would not.

"Forgive me, but your work is what fetches me. I am the owner of the finest merchant ship in these waters. Take a look. She's a beauty, and you will agree the most handsome vessel in these waters. For years I've carried many a hogshead of tobacco, pipe staves, and a variety of luscious furs to the homeland in loyal service of the landowners here in St. Mary's. It is becoming the season for you must know of my presence and abilities to increase your wealth. You are the Lady Margaret Brent, I deduce."

She studied this intrusive man. Then she stared at his ship and the name emblazoned on her side, *Reformation*. Fine hairs on the back of her neck itched.

This pompous Parliamentarian has the gall to flaunt his dislike for our king and his ideology to the world.

She met his gaze and said, "I have yet to hear your name."

"Unbelievable." He stepped back, then said, "Richard Ingle, the merchant, the tradesman, the master of shipping and bartering stands here before you to do your bidding. I ship goods for all the great landholders in Virginia and Maryland. Your neighbors—everyone knows me."

"Evidently not everyone, Captain Ingle. I do not."

"Well then, let me correct my pronouncement to say all the prosperous and wise *gentlemen* landowners know me." He glowered at her.

"Why do you come to my dock this morning instead of joining the others at St. Mary's? You appear here for a reason other than to introduce yourself and display your ship for me to contemplate."

"Hoot-no. You presume incorrectly, Lady Brent. My intentions serve only to introduce myself." He cleared his throat and studied her buildings. "I've been told you've amassed quite a supply of tobacco. You don't grow crops of your own, still you have constructed many hogsheads for it to be shipped. Is it Robinson who builds those fine oak barrels for you?"

He will get few answers from me.

He glanced around at the outbuilding. "Lady Brent, if you don't grow your own crops, why would you need such a long drying shed?"

Margaret stared at him.

Shaking his head, he said, "If what my friends tell me is true, then I offer you the service of my bargaining talent as well as my fine ship. Ask anyone. I am the best person between these shores and England to sell your goods—on your behalf, of course. Whatever you allow me to deliver to buyers in England will bring us both a fine return for our efforts. My merchant trading services are superior to any."

"The *best* you claim. You seem quite sure. I believe prices will be lower this year because of the drought."

"I'm as sure as I am of your fine rooster who welcomes the rising sun. I am as sure as the salty water flowing in the St. George River. I can get top of market price even if demand wanes and supplies become plentiful. The prices, you'll find, have trended lower this year for tobacco trade. However, my bargaining will bring you the highest return of any. Ask Captain Cornwallis and even your good governor. He consigns me to transport such items as shoes, hose, cloth, and even pipe staves to England." He glanced over at her storage shed. "If you happen to have furs in there, London will pay us surprisingly well."

The word *us* unsettled her. A manner of business involving the two of them made the word *us* acceptable. Whatever they might have in their tobacco shed did not belong to any *us*. This man's presumptuous air left her little else to think about.

"I'm wagering by the look on your face you have plenty of furs. If so, I'm making a trip within the next month. Give me your answer if you will because I will need to plan room for them. I prefer to sail only when I have a full ship."

"Captain Ingle, I will take into consideration whatever offer you decide to make, but only when my sister and I are ready to send our products to market. Until then, since everyone here, except for the Ladies Brent, know you, I assume we shall experience no trouble quickly getting word to you. We shall wait on our decision until after you give us your best offer."

"Of course. Before I leave, do tell if the talk I hear is true, for it befuddles me. I understand you've been allowed a strong tongue and a powerful presence in court and Assembly. It has been said you have a reputation for representing anyone you believe to have been wronged."

"Judging from what you have told me today, I suspect, Captain Ingle, you bargain with anyone and then, no matter the outcome, believe you have been wronged?"

He laughed.

She wondered if he scoffed her, but his fleeting outburst of merriment had indeed been spontaneous. This had not been premeditated, as a mocking would be. Still, Margaret knew arrogant men only looked out for themselves. She must warn Mary.

Ingle shook his head. "What about you and your cleverness? I never believed anyone could have a fine crop of tobacco without planting a single seed in the ground. Your indentures' labor and the judicial system fill your shed." He chuckled again. "Until you summon me, and this I know to be true—you will, I bid a good afternoon. I'll leave you to your business, Lady Brent."

"To settle your mind, Captain Ingle, next year these same ladies whose land you now stand on will be planting crops and will reap a fine return. Keep in mind—if we do decide to send any of our current tobacco to England this year, I shall expect you to come to us with your very best offer—immediately, without waste of time. Know we shall not tolerate foolish dickering."

Margaret did not care for this man but then had no good reason for her evaluation. She should not sit in judgement. An oppressive weight of wrong smothered her, bringing a long ago, toddler memory to mind. Despite being told numerous times not to, she saw no reason not to play on her mother's down bed. When she fell face first in the softness, terrifying memories of not being able to breathe flooded back. Margaret must ask forgiveness. In her evening prayers she would promise to be a better soul.

A self-absorbed man could still be a good man.

Chapter 32

Gently they go, the beautiful, the tender, the kind. Quietly they go, the intelligent, the witty, the brave. I know. But I do not approve. And I am not resigned.

- Edna St. Vincent Millay

WATCHING THE MAN MAKE his way back down to her dock, she puzzled over a familiar-looking sailor who stood by to take him to his offensive ship. She knew this person. He had been an ox of a boy with long dirty hair. Now hair shorn short, he appeared as skinny of frame as could be. Without doubt, the life of a sailor had imparted the meaning of hard work to young Peter Coates.

Margaret returned to their home, thinking about Captain Ingle's comment about their drying shed. It contained only hogsheads of tobacco received as payments. Next year when they had their own leaves to hang, turn, and nurture the shed would be filled. She would have to deal with Ingle, but she hadn't wanted him to know their current need to ship as urgent. He would use their emergency for his own monetary gain.

She sat and recalculated her figures. Pleased, Margaret closed her ledger and took a palm-sized piece of rough paper and carefully penned the names and dates of those she had agreed to represent in court. She longed for Gingo. Her horse would make the miles to Gentleman Lewger's home a faster journey.

Gingo. The murder in the woods—Peter Coates sailing near Sisters Freehold.

Margaret shuddered and turned her thoughts to how many pounds of tobacco she and Mary should ship to England. They needed to make more room in the storage shed for the tobacco paid to them for their men servants' work and from the men and women she represented in court.

Lighthearted chatter of men and women's voices mingled with the clucking of hens and the singing of the birds. Mary and the servants were returning. Margaret rose and hurried to the door. Lady Greene and her maids strolled along with Mary's group.

Goodwin had caught up with them—no pig on a rope in sight. Pleasant, good cheer had crowded out all shadows left by Richard Ingle.

"Good day to you, Lady Greene." Margaret waved to their neighbor. "I do hope all your news from home brings you pleasure." Leonard and Ann's corresponding came to mind.

Lady Greene waved back, smiling, "It is, Lady Brent. I wish the same for you and yours."

Mary sprinted up their dusty path to Margaret and shoved a package into her hands. "'Tis the burgundy silk we asked for. I peeked—I couldn't wait."

Joy slipped from Margaret. Mary had promised. They contracted not to read the messages from England until together. A promise is a promise. She tightened her lips and strode back into the house, resenting being left out of the docking experience.

No matter how much Fulke or Ann or Jane or their father wrote, it seemed everyone would have a little different bit of news in their packets. Mary, when she left, had assured her they would share the letters together.

"Everyone," Mary called out to their men and maids, "if you have news to tell, let us talk together tonight before darkness falls. May all your packages contain happiness." She waved them on and sighed. "Margaret, I do wish Giles could be here with us. It seems wrong to open these without him."

Mary handed Margaret the folded packets from their family, still sealed in wax with their father's emblem. Margaret's throat closed, preventing any response to her sister.

Again, I have sinned. I judged falsely, ignoring the goodness inherent within my dear sister. No breach comes from her opening a parcel of fabric. Forgive me.

"I too wish our brother home with us." Margaret slipped into the chair by her writing table and sorted through the letters, looking at the different handwritings. She studied the one of her father's, then slipped it back into the stack.

Unwrapping the package of silk, Mary placed a few lengths of the yardage in front of Margaret. Both slid their fingers over the sheen of the rich-colored fibers.

"Giles certainly wouldn't wait for us," Mary said, "so we shan't wait for him. I have good news right out of Leonard's mouth. He has a replacement for Giles. Our brother will be coming home in a day, and the office of Treasurer for the county shall be bestowed on him."

"Fine news indeed. Today I have missed more than the ship's arrival."

"There's more. I suspect next time you will not stay home to work on boring numbers. Father White has invited us to attend the baptism of Tayac Kittamaquund's family. He wants to have it in the church, but—well—with Cecil telling Leonard we must not display our Catholicism publicly, this converting of a native might be seen as a flaunting of our faith. Cecil makes my skin feel all nettles and thistles, letting the Protestants worship any way they please."

"Cecil surprises me not." Margaret refolded the fabric. "Wedding licenses, recording of wills, probating estates, and even punishing immorality—he has taken these ecclesiastical matters away from the church. Pfft. England did not separate the church from these functions. Yet Cecil has handed them over to laymen."

"You can see why, though, can't you?" Mary said, "The more he takes from the churches and gives to the courts, the less the congregations will argue, and then hopefully people will become more tolerant of other religions."

"No matter now." Margaret picked up the packets. "Let us celebrate our communications from the other side of the ocean. Pick one and read aloud while I listen."

Missus Lawne rapped on the door frame and stepped into their hall.

"Please, may I have a word with you?" She seemed unduly shy, but her face blushed like the cock's comb.

"Come in." Margaret motioned her forward. "You must have interesting news from England. I pray it is not unpleasant."

"My thoughts be not about England this day, Lady Margaret. My heart nearly bursts with joy. Tomorrow James Courtney will be purchasing my remaining debt and make me a freewoman. We will then be wed."

Margaret and Mary quickly stood. Margaret clasped her hand to her rosary. She needed to close her mouth. Mary hugged Missus Lawne and squealed something about how happy the two of them were for her.

So, this would be the start of their servants leaving them one by one. Margaret's mind flashed back to her ledger. They would need to recruit more from England. She smiled at Missus Lawne as redemption for her lack of graciousness in hearing the woman's happy news.

"Missus Lawne, your news surprises me." She needed to say more. "James Courtney is a fine man and will be a good provider for you. I am so pleased to know you have found a companion."

Heavens. Three maid servants cannot handle making the candle and soap while tending the livestock, the gardens, cooking, spinning, mending, and keeping this large home clean. Whatever will we do?

She glanced at Mary, who reprimanded her with raised eyebrow.

"Naturally, Mary and I both wish you well. You have been a loyal and hard-working addition to our little family. What can we do but congratulate you on the end of your indenture?" She caught Mary's approving smile and decided she could do even better. "Once we have signed all the papers and have your status set in the permanent record, Mary and I shall throw a fine party honoring you and James Courtney."

When she left, Mary said, "Isn't this the most fun?" She burst out laughing, but then a shadow of some thought erased the joy from her face. In silence, she stared off into the distance.

"Mary?' Margaret touched her sister's arm. "Something troubles you. Certainly, it would not come from my committing us to have a party."

"We feel so happy right now, yet..." Quickly spreading out the letter packets on the table, Mary picked the one up with her father's handwriting. She handed it to Margaret, saying, "Think of how miserable the day will be when some merchant ship brings us news from home and none of our packets are written with father's pen."

The two had evidently shared the same silent worry. Margaret swallowed.

"We know," Margaret said, "that day of sadness will come. Grief slips into our souls and consumes us no matter how many ocean waves rise, crash, and spread away between us. You and I and our sisters spent time sitting by mother's bedside. We held her hand, listened to her wishes, and then saw to the arrangements of her funeral. None of this lessens our missing her. Still, in some small way it helped us to prepare ourselves for the inevitable. When God took her into His arms, He left us with our grief. We each had to rectify our own loss. You and I will not have the luxury to prepare for father's passing."

Fingering the little packets of notes, Mary said, "How can we survive being this far away and learn about his death from pen strokes on a piece of paper?"

"You have omitted what makes this all bearable." Margaret would not let

Mary know these fears had been hers since the night they left Plymouth on the *Charity*.

"Nothing would ever make being here acceptable when we should be there."

"Mary, we are where we should be. Neither of us regrets our decision to come to Maryland. You love this land as much as I do."

"Our experience of being with the first to settle here has been a magnificent adventure, but I dearly miss him… and our other siblings."

"Those visits of sorrow brought by death come on wings of sweet memories. That is all any of us have, no matter where we are when it comes. The merchant ship brought news from our family. Please stop dallying and let us revel in this happy occasion. Hurry. Select one and read it."

Mary held up their father's message penned *To the Ladies Margaret and Mary Brent* in bold, black ink. She waved it in front of Margaret and smiled before breaking his seal. She started reading it aloud.

"My dearest daughters, it saddens me to impart the dreadful news…."

Mary caught her breath and stared at the paper—then slowly crumpled the note in her hand as her palms covered her lips and her eyes filled.

Margaret worked the paper from Mary's fingers, smoothed it, and studied the disturbing words.

My dearest daughters, it saddens me to impart the dreadful news we received from the English Abby of Our Lady of Consolation in Cambrai. The convent informs us your sister Catherine, having been ill for some time, has passed on to her eternal rest.

Chapter 33
December 1639

The message of Christmas is that the visible material world is bound to the invisible spiritual world.
- Author Unknown

SILENT CRYSTALS OF SNOW floated against the darkening sky. Margaret, her heavy mood sinking, watched the ground become blanketed. She ignored the fireplace flame reflections in the window and stared beyond into the winter storm. As a child, she had sat for hours in her window seat with her books and enjoyed the sight of fall's russet and barren world being obscured by winter's first snow. She adored the freshness of everything— a shabbiness dressed in the purist of white, like a redemption bestowed by the heavens.

Thirteen months here in Maryland. Along with our lives, we have changed.

A little over a month ago, Mary and Margaret had struck a bargain with Captain Ingle. Now he sailed to England to do their trading. When he would return could not be certain. But when he did, he would bring news—news from their family and news of England and their king.

We are blessed because, unlike in England, Maryland will have Christmas Mass.

Mary joined her at the window. "This might be a problem for us. We could miss Christmas Mass if it becomes too deep."

"I wish we could predict the seriousness of this storm." Margaret sighed. "I cannot believe God would prevent us from going to church on this holiest of nights."

"We could wear snowshoes, but it is quite a distance, and we would be returning in the dark."

Missus Taylor entered from the kitchen passage, removed her cloak, shook it out, and hung it on a peg. Then she started to sort through baskets of fresh-cut greenery.

"You found us some lovely branches." Mary knelt beside her, separating the holly from the pine boughs.

"And we have a little bit of rosemary too. Here, give it a smell." Missus Taylor placed the sprig in Mary's hand. "And Missus Guesse gathered huge pinecones, beautiful and useful for starting a fire. She's helping the men with the yule log. Said she would be in to join us soon."

"Come help us decorate, Margaret. If we can't go to church, we can at least assist in making our home festive."

The front door opened, and Missus Guesse called out, "Ladies Brent, would you mind if we brought the yule log in through this way? It's so large—"

"If you must." Margaret scowled. The floor would be messed, and the cold would come in. "Hurry now. Do not let the heat out."

Their men struggled with an enormous, gnarled stump. After some quarreling, they figured out which way to turn it so it would fit through the doorframe. No one lacked for suggestions, including Mary. They heaved it over to the hearth and then rolled it into the fireplace right on top of the little logs still burning. Sparks flew everywhere amid billows of rising smoke, accompanied by an argument of crackling and hissing.

"There ye be." Goodwin brushed off his hands. "This one should bring you good tidings for many days." He tipped his woolen cap and with the other men shuffled off the way they had come, back into the fading afternoon sunlight. The men needed to hurry to their end-of-day chores, then feed the livestock.

Missus Guesse and Missus Brookes had followed the men in, then stayed to help. Missus Taylor cleaned the floor. Muddy tracks, shredded bits of wood, dried grasses, and little piles of sawdust had littered the polished waxed planks.

When finished, the women begin sorting out and hanging the greens.

"Have you heard," Missus Guesse, high on the ladder, said, "up north there's talk of ending Christmas celebrations in the years to come? All the men jabbered on about it when we hunted for the yule log. How dismal this time would be with no celebration."

Margaret, watching the snowfall, said, "Why ever would Puritans do such a thing?"

"The yule log has much to do with it." Mary, now standing on the ladder, worked candles into the holders over the boughs Missus Guesse had secured to the wall. "John Robinson told us we celebrate a silly pagan tradition copied from the Norsemen, and it is nothing but folly."

"Pfft. Banning Christmas. The Christ's birthday—over a piece of wood— hardly." Margaret scowled and turned away from the window. "We could never walk to church in all this snow. Tell me. Will those Puritans do nothing to celebrate our Christ's birth? As devout they claim to be, it hardly seems likely."

Tired of agonizing over the depth of the snow and missing the season's special mass, Margaret strode to her chair and sat, keeping company with her own ill temper. She knew she was not behaving well by sulking.

"Our man Pursell agrees with you." Mary pointed to where Missus Guesse could hang the next group of boughs. "They would have Christmas become a day of regular work."

All the women talked at once.

"Or perhaps they would sit and pray all day." Margaret interrupted them. "Each of you who are Protestant, you must know the Puritans, as other Protestants here and in the north, wish us of the Catholic faith to be gone, if not worse. We hope the three of you and our men harbor no ill will toward us. Those of us who are Catholic came to Maryland to live in peace with each of you who are Protestant. Since Mary and I cannot attend Mass, we will celebrate our Christ's birthday in our home as Catholics. We welcome you to join us if you wish, or you may celebrate in the privacy of your own quarters."

The amiable conversations started up again. Margaret tuned them out. The freshness of cut green boughs, mixed with the smells of Missus Brookes' figgy pudding, along with everyone's good cheer should have been enough to settle Margaret's ill mood.

I have never missed a single Christmas Mass in my entire life until this day.

This weather denied her the privilege of sitting in their freezing little church. She wouldn't be hearing words given them by God, words meant to chase away the dark with His light and to bring comfort. Since Catherine's death, she needed to hear the words meant to encourage His lambs to stand at the eternal gates, account for their behaviors, and pray for admittance. This night's weather deadened her feelings. She could not shake herself from her intolerable state of self-pity.

Too many without snowshoes had lost their lives, trudging even short distances, on foot through deep snow. Even with their snowshoes, the distance in this freezing weather would be a challenge for her and her sister.

Gingo, with little consideration, could carry me safely from home to church and back again. Gingo—I do miss him.

A lump settled in her throat.

His strong muscles, beautiful coat, long mane—the way he nickered when I approached.

"Mary," Margaret said, "We shall purchase horses."

An energetic rapping on their door startled her.

"Good Lord. Who has come to call in this weather?"

Missus Taylor opened the door. Giles stood and grinned at them. Snow flecked his brows and shrouded his shoulders. "Good evening, dear sisters. I've brought you a festive cake made by my cook. He says it's full of every Christmas fruit and nut you might imagine."

"I expected you to be at the church by now." Mary took it from him, examined it, and handed it to Missus Brookes. "Come in. I'll have one of our men secure your horse and see it fed, sheltered, and watered."

Giles stomped his feet. Missus Taylor took his cape and hat. He strode over to Margaret and pecked her on the cheek. "And you, dear sister, are you well? You look befuddled."

"You tend to instill me with all sorts of befuddlement, sweet brother. Tell us why you are not in church as you should be?"

"I doubt you would believe me if I said I prefer to spend the evening with you."

"You can appreciate the wisdom of your own doubt. However, I doubt your intelligence in planning to navigate this snowfall when it becomes even deeper."

"No fear of that. The sky is clearing. We shall only have to navigate the intolerable cold."

"Who? Is someone with you?" Mary asked.

Giles gave her a blank stare. Cocked his head and shrugged.

Margaret studied him. "You said, *we shall,* talking about the cold."

A knock at their door interrupted this conversation. Mary gave Giles her squinty eye. Missus Taylor opened the door.

Leonard Calvert stood there with his hat in one hand and a large leather pouch in his other.

"Leonard?" Margaret's heart in her throat, found she had no other words. He too should be at church. She hurried to the door and tilted her head, expecting an explanation.

"This is for your table." He held his parcel out to her, staring into her eyes. "May I come in?"

"You should be in church." She didn't move to take it, nor did she understand his being there.

Mary stepped between them, and sweetly said, "How kind of you, Leonard, to join us on this special evening."

Leonard pulled his gaze from Margaret and cleared his voice. "I have brought a seasoned roast of pork and spiced mutton for your table." He handed them to Mary.

"Leonard, heavens, no mind whatever brought you here, please come in." Margaret motioned to Missus Taylor to whisk away his cloak and hat.

Leonard took Margaret's hand and raised it to his lips for a brief, gentle kiss. Margaret ignored Mary's squint-eyed, tight-lipped censure but still felt the familiar heat whenever Leonard paid her undue attention. It spread up her neck, warming her cheeks.

"Lord Governor," Missus Taylor said, "One of the men will tend to your horse."

"Thank you, Missus Taylor. Tell your men more shall arrive on horseback within the hour. However, Captain Cornwallis told my messenger his family would not join us until somewhat later. Ladies, I assumed you would enjoy company on this special evening. We know you are without horses, and ladies should not be expected to slip and slide on top of snow for such distances." He glanced out the window, then flung his arm high, imitating their old acquaintance, William Shakespeare. "Ah-ha, as I expected. Look yon at lanterns casting gold upon the snowy mantle as more visitors draw near."

They all rushed to the windows. Margaret, full of unidentified emotions, could not find any words. She stared as magnificent horses appeared coming out from the darkening of the evening under gently falling snow.

"Quickly," Mary called to one of the maids, "gather the men to assist with the horses and have the maids prepare the kitchen and dining table for feasting."

Dashing over, Margaret flung the door wide to the freezing night. She stared out into the winter night at horses snorting little fluffs of clouds and trotting up the lane, carrying people with lanterns. Others with candles and lanterns snow-shoed behind. Voices, singing *Gloria, Gloria, in Excelsis Deo* echoed through the crisp, bone-chilling air.

Her own voice rose from her throat with a hint of excitement. "Please—go tell the servants they shall join us in feast too. This evening must be celebrated by all. Missus Taylor, ask Missus Brookes to cook us a large pot of wassail. Use the hard cider. Be sure every guest's cup remains full. Tell her to make as much as the kettle will hold so all may enjoy and celebrate this special night with us."

With snow flurries hitting her face, Margaret remained standing in the doorway.

No cold could possibly enter now with so much warmth arriving.

She greeted her neighbors, Thomas and Ann Greene, each with a young son on their horses, being held tight in front of the parents. The small boys, smiles like the large sliver of moon, swung little lanterns high. The beams of light chased away the darkness that had been hiding within Margaret. As they dismounted, the Lewgers with their son John, appeared on their three prancing horses—John, the younger, looking quite the gentleman.

"Hurry in out of the cold. Our men will care for your horses." Margaret and Mary accepted parcels of mincemeat pie, spice-sweetened apples, pulled vanilla cane candy, pumpkin breads, squash pudding, and other festive smelling dishes.

Mary handed the proffered food off to Missus Guesse and helped Missus Taylor remove hats and outerwear. Margaret continued to hold the door wide, waiting for two men, one waving aloft a long, slim, candle lantern, as they trudged up the path on their snowshoes.

"Blessings to you, Lady Brent. Even from here, your home welcomes us with smells of warm spices and fresh-cut boughs." The voice came from Father Fisher.

Father White carried his small ornate chest, which Margaret knew held sacred vestments, wine for the holy sacrifice, a little slab altar for the mass, and other holy objects.

He called out, "This evening, let us unite as citizens of Maryland. Dear Protestant and Catholic friends, for this night please set aside your troubled thoughts of our beloved England and her tragedies. Join us in the celebration of a most blessed Christmas Mass."

Margaret tingled with joy. Celebrating a Catholic Christmas Mass tonight in their home would bring Mary and her delight and great comfort.

Mary passed tiny hard candies to the children and to any adult who wished for one, assuring them a mug of wassail would soon follow. A welcoming fellowship grew with smiles and quiet chatter among their friends.

Margaret glanced around the room assessing the measure of other maids and men's dispositions about the evening's celebration. Robinson tended the horses, but she knew his temperament.

Missus Guesse, frowning, stoked up the fire, making sparks fly. Pursell said something to her. She shrugged. Missus Taylor set her jaw and continued to hang cloaks neatly.

Yet a Christmas Mass would not bestow good cheer amid the Protestant indentures, nor would any word of it to inhabitants of Maryland. A swelling began in her throat. Margaret cherished this fragile country. She swallowed hard, but the lump grew.

She walked over to Father White's chest of scared items, slid a finger over the carvings, then stared at him with tightened lips. When he saw her, Margaret held a firm hand on the top of the closed sacred chest and shook her head. There could be no Christmas Mass.

"Good Fathers," Margaret's voice cracked. She gave a little cough and continued, "Ladies, gentlemen, children, worthy maids and fine men, let our Christmas celebration this evening be a testimony to our own goodness from the joy we each find through Christ's love. How we spiritually acknowledge this must remain in our individual hearts, but tonight let us enjoy festivities of friendship, united as one, as true Marylanders."

Chapter 34
Early Spring 1640

Death leaves a heartache no one can heal; love leaves a memory no one can steal.

- Unknown

MISSUS TAYLOR, ON HANDS and knees, scrubbing, attempted to keep up with tracked-in mud. The ground had become a bog from melting snow and spring rains. Margaret, thankful for the precipitation, hoped it would continue into summer.

Last year's drought had brought hardships to more than those around St. Mary's City. The Catholic priests, aware of this, had constructed a sizable store-house in Mattapany to supply their missions. Father White spent much time there, and because of the drought, the priests had prepared bread to carry up-river to feed the various natives. The mission, less than ten miles to the east near the mouth of the Patuxent River, stood on land given the priests by the Indians.

"Come see." Mary pulled Margaret's hand. "Gedd helped me hang tapestry on the dining hall wall."

The dark, heavy material sewn with silver and gold threads told a story of long-ago England in more idyllic times. Her mother had given it to her, saying it belonged to her grandmother. It had been stored in one of their traveling trunks until today.

Margaret stared at it, memories slipping to places in her mind she had not visited for years. "This reminds me of the woods to the east of us. They say England used to have such grand forests."

"Covering this wall may help to seal out the winter cold that seeps in be-tween these planks."

"We should have thought of this last fall."

Someone rapped violently on their front door. Missus Taylor opened it, and Missus Lawne rushed in.

"There's a grave problem, Ladies Brent. I thought you should know."

"Is someone hurt?" Margaret's heart skipped a beat. Accidents frightened them all.

"John Morton, you helped him get his livestock back last year—his wife, Bess, has been in labor since yesterday. I'm going to offer my help. She's in serious trouble."

"I shall go too."

Poor Bess. These past months have been difficult for her.

"I've ridden my husband's horse, Lady Brent." Missus Lawne had tied her birthing parcel to the horse's sidesaddle. "The danger of childbirth here seems no better than in the fetid alleys of London."

"Go. I'll catch up." Margaret, heart pounding, called for her horse and within minutes she nudged it into a gallop toward John Morton's place.

Maryland has so few children and even fewer women. Too many die—

Morton's cabin stood just north and east of the woods. A few minutes later she slowed and dismounted. Missus Lawne had already dashed into the thatched roof and bark-sided hut. Margaret secured her animal and followed.

Big John sat on the floor with his young son between his legs. He used corn kernels to make pictures of horses and chickens for the lad.

"Your son will be tall like his dad." Margaret said as she looked around. Missus Lawne must be behind the closed door with John's wife.

Big John glanced toward the door. He looked at Margaret, shook his head, and rearranged the kernels into another shape.

"Guess here what this be, John." he said.

A low moan and women's voices came from the closed off room.

Young John popped his thumb and a finger in his mouth and said, "Me wan mama."

"Lookee here, son. Tell me what this animal be."

The boy pulled his wet fingers out and slammed it into the corn.

"Bunny rabut!" Then he kicked the kernels with his bare foot, popped the thumb back into his mouth, and snuggled down into his father's massive chest.

"Who else is with your wife and Missus Lawne?"

"Maddy, a neighbor. She's birthed three babes. One born dead, and one lived about a year, then it passed. Probably from swamp fever. She has a daughter the same age as John here. Maddy be a good, hardworking woman like my dear Bess," His eyes filled, and he choked sounds that did not become words.

Young John burrowed deeper into his father's embrace, making louder sucking sounds with his thumb.

More moans, women voices, something scraped on the floor. Something clinked and crashed. The women's voices sounded frantic and louder. Quietness— then the weakest little cry like a small kitten broke the silence.

John's eyes caught Margaret's. They both strained to hear what would happen next. The cry stopped, silence, then the women spoke softly. The door opened.

The neighbor woman stood in the doorway with a tiny bundle wrapped in a clean white cloth. She closed the door behind her. John leapt to his feet and stood, staring. Young John, thumb still in his mouth, clung to his father's britches.

"Here's your wee baby girl, Mister Morton." She held the baby, all wrinkled and blue, up for him to see. "I'll be taking her back to her mother to nurse, but I thought you might want a wee look. Missus Lawne will want to baptize the baby now, just in case. Tell me her name."

"Margaret, we decided on Margaret. My Bess—?"

"'Tis a worry there, sir." She cast her gaze away and disappeared back into the room. When the door closed, Margaret heard the two women discussing something that sounded urgent. Margaret worked to process it all. The baby's coloring—Missus Lawne must not expect it to live if she's baptizing it now instead of waiting for a priest. Protestant midwives were instructed to do so if they had doubt about the viability of the newborn. Then the remark about John's wife....

Dear Lord, one expects death to run wild in the dark, damp, and crowed back alleys of London but here, with sweet air and clear water, why does not life prevail?

Young John whimpered for his mama. His comforting thumb stuck far back in his toddler mouth caused drool to slide down his fist and arm and onto the planks. Now his blond curls were damp and stuck to his forehead and chubby cheeks.

"John," Margaret held out her hands and knelt, "come pray with me."

The door opened again, and Maddy, the neighbor, holding the baby, stood with tears streaming down her cheeks.

The poor baby has passed.

Big John's face, colored deep by the sun, grew taunt and icy white.

"Mama—me want mama." Young John's whimpering changed into wailing. "Mama—"

Everything that held Margaret together, her muscles, her strength, her courage gave way to emptiness. She had come to comfort John, but this—the loss of that sweet innocent soul.

Young John stopped wailing to catch his breath. A tiny cry came from the little wrapped bundle.

Young John let go of his father's britches and charged toward the door, but Missus Lawne, covered in blood, blocked his entrance.

The horror of it all. The neighbor's tears gave way for Bess, John's wife.

* * *

Missus Lawne and Margaret kept their silence after leaving John Morton's home. The two horses knew their way back to their barns and plodded on methodically without instruction. Margaret could not guess how long they had stayed to comfort John and to figure out what he should do with his two little ones. Maddy graciously offered to take the wee ones home with her.

None of them could think of anyone in St. Mary's who might be nursing. Carrie Wells might still be in Kent Island, but it took six to eight hours to get there. Maddy said maybe they could find a wet nurse closer in Virginia who would be willing to take the child. She would ask her husband if he knew since he traveled there to trade. In the meantime, she would soak rags in goat's milk and do the best she could to see the child was nourished.

John didn't want to let his son go, but he had crops and animals to tend. The child was too young to be by his side.

Missus Lawne sighed and said, "As God must know, I tried my best—I did. How wretched I feel, and there be nothing to do for it."

"Missus Lawne, I should call you Missus Courtney now. Everyone says you have expert skills in midwifery. Poor Bess must have been exhausted after laboring through the night and all day."

"It was the bleeding. I used all the betony and most of my other herbs and still the bleeding would not stop."

Margaret nodded. "The baby's coloring was not right. If she could nurse, it would certainly change to pink."

She didn't really believe nursing would change the baby's color, but she had to find hope somewhere. The frogs that lurched around whenever she felt distressed now took residence in her throat. She swallowed. They refused to move and would not be calmed.

"Lady Margaret, there will be no need for a wet nurse. Poor babe. By tomorrow we shall attend two funerals."

"How will Big John Morton manage without his Bess?"

Oh Maryland, with your beautiful land, clean air, fresh water, and bountiful gifts to nurture our bodies, you hide a murderous darkness that steals the life from too many of those who have come to partake of your offerings. Dear Lord, bless us and the sweet Morton family.

Chapter 35
Several Days Later

They haue no Lawes, but the Law of Nature and discretion....
- Cornwallis & Hawley, *A Relation of Maryland*

THE SPRING CONTINUED TO produce healthy tobacco plants for Mary and Margaret. Robinson, Goodwin, and the rest of their men had acquired the requisite tobacco green-stained thumbs from tending other planters' tobacco crops during the last growing season.

"A consequence," Mary said, strolling around the healthy growths, "of the damaging rain and ensuing drought that left us with no tobacco last year has given us men who know how to cultivate these plants under the most trying of conditions."

Nodding her head, Margaret walked beside Mary. Margaret had nothing to say. She wanted to erase the image of John Morton's face standing beside his wife's grave. The new lines and furrows told his devastation.

Two funerals, one grave—mother and daughter eternally together.

Young John, in his father's strong arms, had clung to his father's jerkin with his thumb buried in his mouth—clearly, he did not understand a whit of it. A handful of Protestants, free and indentured, attended this graveside service and stood with bowed heads listening to the Protestant words meant to comfort. John's neighbor, Maddy, sobbed silently with her little girl and a slender man standing beside her. Missus Lawne, standing next to her handsome new husband, James Courtney, had left John and Margaret's side to place her arm around Maddy's shoulders. Two women shared the tragedy of their little sisterhood.

Too many deaths, too many graves, too many broken dreams. How easy for England to blame lack of nourishment and disease for infant and mother's deaths, but Maryland's women and newborn fail equally. Even our own mother suffered such.

Margaret stopped among the tobacco plants. She shut her eyes.

Mary touched her arm. "I know you're distraught over the deaths in the Morton family, and I've held off telling you about the troubles in England. Do you wish me to hold back a bit longer?"

"Of course not. Please."

"Sometime after we arrived in Maryland, the General Assembly of the Scottish Kirk met at Greyfriars Church. I heard thousands attended and the resulting action in Edinburgh at that time declared to disallow episcopacy."

Margaret sighed. "Bishops have finally been abolished."

"This happened a few months after we arrived in Maryland. You can imagine how King Charles reacted."

"Yet that night in England with father and Lord Baltimore, one of our brothers claimed there would be no war because King Charles had abolished Parliament and therefore had no funds."

"True." Mary almost whispered the words, "but last month King Charles decided to call a new Parliament."

"After eleven years of personal rule? He must be desperate for money. Pfft, his taxes did not raise enough for him to fight the Scots, did they now?"

"What makes this our worry comes from wondering if Parliament will grant him the means to go to war. Maybe they will withhold funds in retaliation of his leniency toward Catholics."

"Worry, indeed." Margaret removed a few small broken twigs resting on tobacco plants. "Those hostilities do not stay across the ocean. Every new group of Protestants feels freer to flaunt their religion. I sense increasing aggression toward our priests and even us."

Mary walked in silence for a few moments, then said, "A few days ago, Ann Lewger told me something so disturbing I hesitate to invite the thought back by retelling." She took a deep breath. "That scoundrel Claiborne on Kent planned to start an armed march against us here in St. Mary's. He couldn't get enough men to follow him. Ann said that was the only reason we were not invaded and attacked."

"Most of the people on that island, except for Giles, are Protestants. I am surprised they did not."

"They claimed Claiborne acted only on his own authority not from someone official."

"An ocean does not protect us from England's troubles." Margaret gazed out across the field. "I see a person coming our way. We must set this conversation aside."

A woman's voice called out. "Mary, Margaret." Ann Greene waved from a distance and called, "Come with me to St. Mary's."

Mary looked at Margaret—her brow furrowed. "Did we miss a ship announcing its arrival in port today?"

Margaret sighed. Over the last few weeks, she had spent many afternoons at John Lewger's home, appearing before court and Assembly. The task of representing someone wronged had always invigorated her, but Bess Morton's funeral had depleted her energy. Today she craved privacy, quiet, and a chance to attend to the work on their property.

Most unusual of Ann Greene to be hurrying to St. Mary's—and to invite us.

She and Mary ambled over to greet Ann and to learn what aroused her excitement.

Mary dusted off her palms and apron. She tilted her head in anticipation.

"My Thomas sent a messenger from Assembly, saying if we hurried, we could meet the tayac of the Piscataway. He's at the Jesuit's Hall next to the church."

Margaret's dark mood needed this diversion. "Mary, go on, I will catch up. Let me tell Missus Brookes where we shall be." She untied her gardening apron and took Mary's.

Margaret had wanted to see this great man up close. Father White and

Leonard had told interesting stories about this gentle, intelligent man. Up until today, her only experience with the natives came from fleeting glimpses of the few who wandered between the trees, mostly hidden, to watch the ships dock.

The English traded goods for the land and the village, now St. Mary's City. These natives had moved to a safer location miles north, away from the raiding Susquehannock. According to Father White, these people created a village across the river from Virginia. Whenever Leonard thought it safe enough, Father White would go and teach these people English language, English customs, and catechism.

Margaret entered the kitchen, hung the aprons, and informed Missus Brookes they would not be home for several hours.

By the time it would take to corral and saddle their horses, she and Mary could walk halfway to St. Mary's. Of course, it was never ladylike to run, but Margaret knew she could out-stride most. She gathered up her petticoats and soon caught up to Ann and Mary.

Ann's nod acknowledged Margaret. "Thomas told me Chitomachen Kittamaquund rules over all the Piscataway people, hundreds of them." She continued, saying, "I saw him once, with his family, when we first arrived. I don't want you to be shocked, but these people wear very little in the way of clothing, and especially in the summer."

"Margaret and I saw a painting of some Indians before we left England, all barelegged and nothing but paint and feathers above the waist." Mary shuddered. Margaret refrained from commenting.

"Still, they are fascinating creatures. I hope we aren't too late." Ann stepped up her pace. "What surprised me most, and something I would never understand, is he has several wives. Can you imagine?"

"I should think," Mary said, "one woman with her fits of emotions would be enough for any man to take into his home."

"And I would say," Margaret said, "any woman who agreed to such a preposterous union lacks fortitude."

The three women passed the heavily thatched Indian house the priests had renovated and used as the first church in Maryland. They continued on beyond the small brick church Captain Cornwallis had built for the Catholics, although Cecil Calvert demanded it be shared with the Protestants. Adjoining it was a newly built mission, not quite finished, but where several horses stood tethered to the tall black walnut tree and others to a fence post.

Men's voices carried through the open doors and windows.

Chapter 36

Only a man's character is the real criterion of worth.
- Eleanor Roosevelt

ANN LED MARY AND Margaret through the doorway into the crowded hall. They found a place to stand next to one of the windows. No one noticed them as the attendees seemed to have their gazes riveted to the matter happening at the front of the room.

Father White stood before the gathering. He wore his traditional lace-edged surplice of white linen over his black cassock, and a red stole draped around his neck. He appeared to be listening attentively to a tall, muscular, and handsome man with the blackest hair Margaret had ever seen. This man wore a white deerskin, jerkin-like top open down the front, with no sleeves or collar. He wore britches of the same fine leather decorated with feathers and tiny white shells down the outside seams. Shells and feathers woven into bracelet-like bands adorned his upper arms.

Around his neck he wore a thin leather strap connected to the sides of some sort of breastplate made of two rows of small, white and brown striped cylinders. They were only partially visible through the front opening of his modified jerkin. After a few minutes, Margaret decided the breastplate had been made from porcupine quills. By this time her ears had adjusted to the firm, but hesitant, guttural voice addressing the audience.

"Father White tells my people—trade our furs—along with other grain to English far over big ocean may bring us better life. I, Tayac Kittamaquund, say, 'No' to peoples of St. Mary's and Father White—our treasures given from this Father," he held his hand toward Father White, saying, "these treasures bring more than from over the ocean—Father White teaches us to know our one true God. This knowing forever comes my only wish."

The hall erupted in cheers and applause. Everyone stood in their excitement to hear this savage denounce his former beliefs and accept the Holy Father.

Chills spread over Margaret in this crowded, stuffy, hot, and humid room.

Would Father White now baptize this native... here, for all to witness?

If so, she and Mary would witness a most momentous occasion. She held her breath as Father White motioned for everyone to be seated. Then cleared his throat and waited until the shuffling and murmuring settled.

"Tayac Kittamaquund, king of the Piscataway, you can see how we welcome your words of devotion concerning Our God. To the citizens of St. Mary's City, this honorable man standing before you has denounced much of his heritage to embrace our faith. Within a meeting of his chiefs, he declared his belief in the one true God and denounced his ancestors' tribal superstitions. Once, not long ago, these people foraged and hunted as savages, wearing scant clothing, and the king of the Piscataway boasted of many wives. Today you see Chitomachen Kittamaquund dressed most modestly, and he now has pledged himself to one wife."

Again, the audience shoved their benches and chairs back and stood, cheering, shouting, and clapping. All the while Tayac Kittamaquund stood tall, stoic, and expressionless, appearing as a most powerful leader of the many men of his numerous tribes in Maryland.

Margaret held her breath, waiting for Father Andrew White to begin the baptism sacrament.

"Father White," Tayac Kittamaquund said, "I hold your one true God as my God. I declare I will love and follow the teaching of his disciples. Please perform your sacred rite—I ask you to baptize me, so everyone knows I am one with Him."

The shuffling of feet stopped. Everyone seemed to be staring at Father Andrew White, waiting his words. Father White bowed his head in silence.

Someone coughed. Flies buzzed in and out of the muggy-overcrowded room. Margaret focused on the sounds of birds singing their songs in the tall walnut tree.

After a brief moment he looked at Chitomachen Kittamaquund, cleared his throat, and said, "The rite of baptism must be shared with those who know and love you. To execute this sacred ritual here in front of strangers would be an injustice to you and your family. You, my brother, have proven your readiness to give yourself to Christianity. Father Altman and I shall travel to your village on the fifth of July, in this year of our lord, 1640, to perform your ceremony of baptism for all your tribe and visitors to witness. I invite any in this room to make the journey to observe this grand occasion, for not only will we conduct the rite of baptism, but your young children shall be christened."

Another wave of loss swept over Margaret. She so wanted to see this unique event.

Father White led the group in prayer before they all departed to the various duties they had set aside for this gathering. However, Father White and Tayac Kittamaquund retired through another door to a more private room.

The crowd shuffled past the women. Animated voices retold what they had just witnessed with no lack of ideas for traveling north on June fifth.

"Good morning, ladies—Ann." Thomas Greene strode over to the window, took his wife's hand, and kissed it. "Dear, I felt sure you would enjoy this unusual occasion. Kittamaquund fascinates us all."

"Your thoughtfulness to include us will long be remembered." Ann stared into her husband's blue eyes.

Margaret saw Leonard working his way through the crowd. Giles trailed behind him. A small burn of irritation started inside because Giles should have been the one who invited them.

Leonard broke into a broad smile when he saw the ladies by the window. Giles sprinted up. "You received my message. Bully good business wouldn't you say?"

"We did not." Margaret scowled. "We would not be here if it hadn't been for the kindness of Thomas Greene and his good wife."

"Curious. I had asked my man to stop and tell you. I sent him on an errand to Mattapany. He promised he would take a few minutes to dock my sloop at your place to let you know."

Leonard stepped forward. "Lovely ladies Greene and the Brents." With his eyes crinkling full of delight, he took Margaret's hand and kissed it.

Ann Greene raised her eyebrow, letting her face flash the briefest of smiles. Mary gave Margaret her deadliest squint eye.

"No matter." Giles oblivious to the social interplay. "You all had the chance to see the Tayac. I believe this to be the grandest show I've attended since we arrived."

Everyone agreed, including Margaret. If he had sent his sailboat while she and Mary strolled through their fields, then she must strive to be more forgiving when Giles causes her such befuddlement.

"I had hoped we would witness his baptism." Margaret studied their faces and said, "Yet, Father White's wisdom to perform this sacred rite among the Tayac's family and people fills me with gratitude for such thoughtfulness."

"I had been told a while ago the baptism would happen in the village," Mary said. "Margaret, we should go."

No Protestant would be there to give Lord Baltimore grief about Catholic services.

Ann Greene grabbed Mary's arm. "There's nothing I want to see more. Thomas, what do you think? Could we take the boys?"

Leonard shook his head. "The village lies over forty miles to the north of St. Mary's. Are you dear ladies willing to sleep along the trail for several nights? Even if you took your sloops, it would not be an easy journey."

"I certainly can't expose our young boys to such an adventure." Ann's disappointment could be read in her resignation.

"Mary, I am not comfortable piloting our pinnace into unknown waters for such a distance. We cannot spare our men from tending crops and caring for the livestock." She and Mary had inherited the tending of Lord Baltimore's cattle, except for those grazing across the river in West St. Mary's. "I certainly would not go by horseback and sleep in the wilderness."

"Giles," Mary said, "Could you take us? May we go with you?"

He glanced at Leonard then looked down.

Something else was happening here. Margaret waited.

"Ladies," the muscles around Leonard's mouth tensed as he said, "I do wish you to see this baptism. Yet as your governor, I'm not sure if I shall be going because of safety concerns. We still worry about small bands of irascible Susquehannocks who meander near the Piscataway village. It is with trepidation I've allowed Father White to spend so much time there."

"Then Father White's invitation to this audience today stands for nothing." Margaret, chin up, stood with hands on her hips. She stared boldly into Leonard's eyes.

Mary elbowed her.

She ignored her sister and waited for the reply she demanded. John Lewger came over with his wife and son.

"Ladies, gentlemen, what a wonderful performance Father White arranged for us. Giles, I hope you'll accompany young John and me on the fifth. We'll be going by horseback instead of sailing."

And there it was.

"Of course." Giles's endearing smile accompanied his words. "Greene, will you be joining us?"

"Lord Calvert." Margaret interrupted. Her voice came out strong with a sharp demanding edge—like she might be addressing Assembly.

He gave her a whipped puppy-dog look that told her he knew what she would make of all of this.

"Are you forbidding Mary, Ann Greene, and me, along with any other lady who might want to go, from attending Tayac Kittamaquund's baptism? I cannot believe a baptism could be dangerous."

"Ladies, the enmity grows brasher between the Piscataway and the Susquehannock, putting us all in grave danger. Several different traders, true or not, have said the people who have settled New Sweden are now trading arms with the Susquehannock for beaver pelts. Tayac Kittamaquund tells us Susquehannock warriors prowl outside Piscataway villages. St. Mary's City has caused these warriors great anger. With unapologetic boldness, we have settled in the middle of the Susquehannock enemies' land and have bestowed the great power of our mighty religion on their nemeses."

Chapter 37
February 1641

Cautious, careful people always casting about to preserve their reputation... can never effect a reform.
- Susan B. Anthony

ON THIS FROZEN FEBRUARY afternoon, Mary and Margaret worked to ensure the Sisters Freehold maintained enough supplies to last for the remainder of the winter and into April. Margaret, in woolen wrap and sturdy shoes, set to her tasks.

With summer long behind them, Margaret knew not going to the baptism in the Piscataway village last July had been a good decision. Father White had baptized the tayac with the Christian name of Charles Kittamaquund and also his wife, naming her Mary. Then he baptized the senior councilman Mosorcoques as John.

Father White refused to baptize the quiet, dark-eyed, older daughter of Tayac Kittamaquund. She had not yet achieved womanhood. The Father claimed she first needed to be schooled in the English ways. The young—almost a woman—child would someday be the ruler of all the Piscataway Tribes after her father passed. If the people were to revere her as their Empress, Father White wanted her to be knowledgeable in reading, writing, and social customs, as well as knowing the words of the one true God.

However, Father White joyfully christened the tayac's infant daughter, giving her the Christian name of Ann and a tribal councilman's son he named Robert.

Father Altman from Kent Island and Mattapany attended, as did many notable men from St. Mary's. All of this took place in a chapel made for the special event in the traditional way from the bark of trees. Others lined up in front of the sacred font to be baptized when a strange illness overtook Father White and also Father Altman.

Upon hearing this, Margaret had wondered at first if the two priests had been poisoned. Their illness erupted so violently it required them to be brought immediately back to St. Mary's City. They spent the rest of the summer and into the fall convalescing in the mission near St. Mary's church. Her sister Mary couldn't believe they had been poisoned. She thought the men might have ingested something that didn't settle well, causing an imbalance of their bodies' humors.

Illness in Maryland strikes most capriciously.

The summer, long and hot, dragged on and the priests, feverish and unable to maintain any nutrients for long, did not improve. Everyone in St. Mary's, fearful and in a panic, exhausted their knowledge of herbs that might cure. Ann Greene sent for her physician brother, Dr. Gerard who lived in St. Clemmons Island on the Potomac River. He came immediately and proceeded with bloodletting then left packets of powders that he believed might help with the digestion.

Fall slipped in with cooler weather, and Father White seemed to make some progress, then he would falter back to being bedridden and feverish. Father Altman kept declining.

In November, Father Altman left this world for his eternal home.

Father White eventually gained some of his strength, and to the relief of all, he returned to his former labors.

A few months earlier, in October, Richard Ingle, captain of the ship *Reformation*, had again transported hogsheads of Mary and Margaret's tobacco to England. He contracted for a healthy profit that would benefit the three of them. This would require him to spend several months in England negotiating exchanges and prices.

Now Margaret found herself listening day and night for the sound of the *Reformation*'s cannon, announcing Ingle's return.

The chilling bursts of wind off the river sawed into her as she tromped about the mud-frozen cutting yard, surveying their stack of winter firewood. Next, she entered the small storage shed attached to their home to count the remaining bundles of candles and check their larder of dried meats, fruits, bins of apples and other vegetables. In the corner of the shed, barrels of cider and ale stood. One still remained unopened.

Missus Brookes must have taken pride in her orderly hanging of various herbs, onions, and garlic dangling from the overhead beam. When the ground thawed, Margaret would have the men dig a root cellar.

She scurried out to the barn where Mary counted what they had left of bags of corn and grain. Margaret squinted through the open door into the dusty gloom. They needed to be sure they had an adequate supply of corn for cooking and to feed their livestock, along with the fall's fresh-cut hay. February had started out harsh. March might be worse. One never knew.

Mary didn't mind the barn, but Margaret avoided it if she could. Their large barn back in England felt more welcoming than this structure made from pieces of rough-hewn wood. She stepped inside the warm, damp-smelling building and saw Mary in the far corner. Something slithered over her shoe. Margaret bounded aside with a shriek.

"Good Lord, Mary. A huge snake—" She gasped for air. "The monster must have been six-feet long—leave this place at once!" Margaret scooted back outside into the milky daylight.

Mary chortled. "You should praise the Good Lord for sending us such a treasure as Mister Wiggles."

"Clearly, you've lost your mind. Come at once before he strikes. Forget the grain."

"Dear sister, if it weren't for my Mister Wiggles, we'd have no grain. The mice and rats would have finished it off last November." Mary stepped outside the barn. "He does no harm to people, but how he does relish a meal of a fat rat. With all the warmth coming from our livestock, he has a pleasant home. Our horses avoid him with wide eyes like yours because they are incapable of understanding. You, sweet sister, are an intelligent being, so I expect you to be more charitable to our helpful friends."

The booming sound of a ship's ordinance made both of them jump as it reverberated through the countryside.

Clasping Mary's arm, Margaret said, "I suspect Captain Ingle has returned to St. Mary's with our goods."

Goodwin and Robinson scurried into the barn to hitch up the wagon. Margaret called to them, "Watch out for the snake."

Giggling, Mary grabbed Margaret's hand, and both dashed to the house. They needed to fetch their list of ordered goods from England.

When they returned the men stood at the wagon, blowing on their hands to warm them.

"Should we saddle our horses?" Mary asked. "We want enough space in the wagon for all of our new belongings."

Goodwin shook his head. "Thar's plenty room."

He helped them in, and Robinson snapped the reigns.

"If our new items overload the wagon," Margaret said, "a brisk walk home will do us good."

The Brent's wagon rolled up and joined the many others who waited, and those who stood on the banks to watch. Teams of horses and oxen, shifting their weight from hoof to hoof, snorted white puffs into the freezing air. They looked as impatient as Margaret felt. Her cold fingers stung. Rubbing her hands together, she tucked them under her cloak.

Everyone on the bank watched for the disembarkation of Captain Ingle and the unloading of their merchandise. When the crew began to carry the English purchases down the gangplank, the crowd broke into discussions about what they had ordered from England, and what they hoped to buy from Captain Ingle's store of merchandise.

Fortunately, a few years ago the Assembly had worked out a solution to prevent wagons from clogging up the path down to the ship. Yet, no matter how logical this plan seemed, it never happened without much grumbling and confusion. The captain's quartermaster had been appointed to call out the person's name for the goods being unloaded onto the dock. Only then would the owner of the wagon be allowed to descend and load the purchases.

Mary and Margaret exchanged glances, knowing this would be a long wait in the bitter cold afternoon. Margaret's toes tingled from the cold. She wiggled them and stamped her feet.

Giles's wagon rolled up. He hopped down, and they visited until the name of G. Brent was called. Margaret watched him and his man drive the wagon down to the dock.

Once his wagon had been loaded, and the quartermaster waved him to move on, Giles refused to move. Margaret could hear Giles arguing about something with Captain Ingle.

"What could be their disagreement?" Mary leaned in toward Margaret.

"With Giles," Margaret said, "anything. He needs to stop delaying the process."

Giles flung his hand in the air, turned, and climbed into his wagon. His man snapped the reins, and his horses lugged up the path to the top.

When he drove past Mary and Margaret he yelled, "Check your list and count everything twice. He's a beetle-headed swindler."

"Good heavens." Margaret looked around and saw everyone watching, as if Giles had cursed at them all. Giles ignored them, and his wagon rumbled on down the road toward his manor.

Chapter 38
February 1641

Awareness of ignorance is the beginning of wisdom.
- Socrates

TWO MORE WAGONS WERE called. When the Lewger's wagon finished loading and lumbered back up the path, the quartermaster called Mary and Margaret's wagon.

On the dock, the ship's crew had stacked parcels, furniture, and barrels marked *M &M Brent.* Margaret caught a glimpse of Peter Coates up on the deck, evidently hauling things out of the belly of the ship for others to unload. He had the hardened, sinewy look of a sailor who spent too many days at sea with scant food and unhealthy water.

As the men positioned each item in their wagon, Margaret called out the article, and Mary checked it off their list. When they had finished, several coveted items had not been included.

"Don't drive away yet, Robinson." Margaret called out, "Quartermaster, I need to speak to the captain, if you please."

Mary rechecked her list against what had been loaded into their wagon. "I made no mistake, Margaret. These items have not been included."

"Ladies Brent." Captain Ingle, smelling of smoke from the tobacco weed, scowled as he strode down the gangplank.

"Captain," Margaret said, "our contract said you would return with two upholstered chairs, preferably of the French fashion, three more parcels of quality writing paper, two more broad axes, twelve more lengths of wool, and you've shorted half our order of nails. Where is our compensation for the tobacco we gave you to purchase these items?"

"Lady Brent, I brokered you the best deal possible. Unfortunately, our tobacco prices have dropped in buying power, but you must have noticed what I did bring you is of the finest quality."

"Our contract has not been fulfilled, and your compensation to us must follow, Captain Ingle. We will not let you take advantage of us because we are women."

"Ladies Brent, compensation will not be forthcoming, and I am not taking advantage of you. Since you could not have heard the news yet, I shall be the first to tell. The Scottish army has taken up residence in Northern England. I suspect you have never heard anything so preposterous, but it is true." He smirked, clearly enjoying his tale. "The Scots did this after defeating our inept king over his foolish endeavor of a war at the River Tyne last April." He laughed, saying,

"We've all heard the jokes about that one. Prices for English goods have climbed high because now the Scots refuse to leave England. They won't leave until His Royal Majesty reimburses them for their expenses." He grew serious and stared at them, each in turn.

"This cannot be true." Mary's face paled.

"Your king has no funds and now is a desperate man." Ingle smirked, "He re-instated Parliament once again. We all should have a good laugh about this, don't you think? I'm sure you have heard he summoned a new Parliament back in April. He hoped they would grant him money to go to war with those damnable Scots. When they wouldn't, he promptly dissolved them again. Dissolved them, he did, within the same month." He broke into a grin, saying, "On again, off again, higgle-dy piggledy. His eleven years of personal rule without Parliament, I say, brought him and England not a pudding's worth of anything." He set his jaw and pointed a finger at Margaret's nose. "What I negotiated for you two needs to be valued. Another merchant would send you home with a half-empty wagon."

He turned and strode back up the gangplank.

The Scots reside in Northern England. Heavens!

"Oh Margaret, I fear if what he says is true, then England will soon be at war." Mary bit her bottom lip.

Checking the men in the wagon, Margaret said, "Did you hear?"

They nodded.

She asked them, "Have you known this about England?"

They shook their heads. She believed them. Had Ingle told Giles this? Probably not. She found herself shivering. Mary appeared chilled too. She needed to do something besides stand on this damp, freezing dock.

"Robinson and Goodwin, go on home and unload the wagon and take care of the team. Tell Missus Brookes Lady Mary and I will be home within the hour. We want to stop by and talk to our brother for a few minutes." She waved them off, and the two women walked briskly up the footpath.

Captain Ingle had not treated her brother nor her and Mary kindly.

"Mary, I wonder if Leonard has heard the news about England from Lord Baltimore. But then again, Captain Ingle might not be telling the truth."

Chapter 39
Early April 1641

Educating the mind without educating the heart is no education at all.
- Aristotle

INGLE'S NEWS TWO MONTHS ago about England, as true and unsettling as it was, didn't irritate Margaret as much as having to negotiate trades with him. Today her greater concern involved news of the increasing Indian raids of properties belonging to the priests.

Mary held open the chapel's door. Margaret, carrying several bags, entered. She waited for Mary to step in and latch the door. They removed their cloaks and took the Catholic's carved-walnut box from the storage closet. Margaret removed the lid and held her bags open while Mary nestled their votive candles into the box. Come early Sunday morning, when they and their friends attended worship, they would have new beeswax candles to light.

"This feels inadequate." Mary brushed a strand of hair away from her face.

"I find no inadequacy in our asking the heavenly saints to watch over and assist good men."

"But we should do more than light candles and pray for Father White, and the other missionaries, and De Sousa. The heathens who ransacked their mission and burned the warehouse—I don't understand why they do such things."

"The Susquehannock despise the priests because the Jesuits bestow care and food on the Piscataway and lesser tribes."

"But—De Sousa has quite dark skin." Mary said, "The Susquehannock would know he is not a Jesuit."

Margaret straightened. "This West Indies man must be one of their indentured."

Mary placed the last candle in the box, closed the lid, and secured the lock.

"He has been a freeman for years, according to Father Fisher. Mathias de Sousa hunts and trades with the natives, and the pinnace he sailed belonged to the mission. God must protect him." Mary gathered their cloaks and handed Margaret hers.

"We shall give thanks at evening prayers that none were harmed."

The two women secured their wraps, left the church, and closed the heavy door behind them. The sickly sun with chilly breezes off the river gave little warmth.

Young John Lewger came sprinting down the path. His face flushed. He stopped in front of them, taking a moment to catch his breath.

"My heavens, young John, what could be so urgent?" Margaret said.

"Are you well?" Mary studied him.

"I am quite well, thank you. My parents were driving passed the Governor's mansion when Governor Calvert came out of the house and asked if they had seen the Ladies Brent."

Margaret couldn't imagine why.

Something must be terribly wrong. I hope Giles hasn't had another argument.

"The governor said he had to speak with the two of you right away, and I told him if my mother and father had no objection, I would be honored to run and fetch you from the church. I saw you go in earlier."

Margaret smiled. "Then do accompany us to his home and tell us why our governor bids our presence."

"As honest and as sorry as I can be, he did not say a whit about why. I must meet with my parents, now." He waved goodbye.

Margaret watched him lope northward on the path to his parents' manor.

"I had believed Captain Ingle lied about the Scots residing in the North of England, and about King Charles reconvening Parliament. When Leonard confirmed the truth of it, I feared more bad news would follow. Maybe this is why he has summoned us."

"Perhaps not. Giles believes England has calmed because Parliament passed the Triennial Act." Mary held her sister's arm as they walked.

"Flap dragon."

"You disagree?"

"Obliging a king to call a fifty-day session of Parliament every three years means little."

The sisters strode up to the door of Leonard's home. Before they could knock, Peasley, in his usual stark black attire, opened it.

"Please enter, Ladies Brent. My Lord expects you." He worked to hide a slight grin.

Most unusual of Peasley to show mirth of any type, whether he be here at the Governor's Mansion or at Assembly.

When they entered and passed into the large gathering hall, there at the far end sat Leonard, rather stiffly, across from a young native girl, who stared silently at him.

He jumped up when he saw the sisters and motioned them to hurry. He took Margaret's hand and instead of his usual formal kiss, he pulled her over to the child. Mary followed.

"Ladies Brent, this is Tayac Kittamaquund's daughter, the Empress Kittamaquund."

The girl stood. From a distance she had appeared to be about seven years old but on closer inspection she had to be about nine or ten. She wore a narrow, light tan buckskin smock that matched her skin. Her hair hung in a long braid. Someone had adorned the braid with feathers and small white shells with a strand of rawhide. Her smock ended just above rawhide boots. Near her on the floor lay a leather parcel. She clutched a cape made of lush beaver pelts and wild turkey feathers. With chin held high and dark unreadable eyes, she studied the women.

Margaret acknowledged the child with a nod and tilted her head, waiting for

Leonard to explain.

"Your cloak is lovely." Mary said, "Would you hold it open for me to see?"

The girl, statue-like, watched Mary.

Mary pointed to the cape and held her hands up as if she were showing it.

The Empress smiled and held her cape up for each to see, then handed it to Mary to inspect further. Which Mary did.

"Empress?" Margaret glanced at Leonard.

"She will assume her father's duties in time. Father White bestowed the title."

"Tell us why you are entertaining this delicate child." Margaret, fascinated, kept her eyes on the cloak as Mary turned it over and stroked it.

Mary handed the cape back to the little Empress.

"You saw her father last year when he came to the mission with Father White. He's ill. If he dies, or when the child becomes of age, she will become ruler of all the Piscataway tribes. Tayac Kittamaquund wants his daughter to be schooled in our religion and fluent in our language and ways. He believes we can prepare her to be a better leader of her people if we educate her. His senior counselor brought her here. He left a few minutes ago."

No wonder Peasley found this amusing. Leonard, manager of cannons, guns, troops, and provinces, has no clue what to do with this child.

"Tayac Kittamaquund sent his daughter to live here in St. Mary's City—with me. He's asked Father White to baptize her and me to see she's educated and learns the social ways of the English."

Margaret and Mary glanced at each other, then at the girl, and both of them started to chuckle. The governor had himself in a fine fix. Leonard's face grew cherry red.

"Oh, stop your titters. You know I can't do this. I know nothing about children and certainly nothing about little girls."

Margaret's dormant frog woke and began leaping wildly in her stomach. Leonard had summoned Mary and her. He expected them to care for this child.

"Besides, there is nothing proper about a young girl living in this manor with a thirty-four-year-old bachelor. I, with Margaret, shall be her official guardians during her time here in St. Mary's. She will be instructed and reside at Sisters Freehold."

Both women spoke at once, but when Margaret saw the girl's eyes widen and her chin start to quiver, Margaret fell silent.

Let Mary have her say.

"Exactly what will be her length of time here? What does the Tayac expect us to teach? Does she even understand our language? If not, how can she learn? Our life is totally different than hers, Leonard. We don't live as savages. We sleep in beds, eat at tables, and say Grace before our meals—"

Leonard held his hands up—but Mary continued.

"She's not a baby, so if she doesn't know our language we have to start with the simplest of words before she can learn anything. We have gardens and crops and soap and candle making to tend to, and Margaret spends most of her days in Assembly or court, righting wrongs for others. When she does come home, she spends hours entering her work into account ledgers. This child's success or failure will be on my sorry shoulders. When will I ever find time to do baby things with a grown child?"

"Piscataway Empress not be baby." A steady young voice, sounding like tones from a tubular bell, rang through the hall. "I am to be ruler, leader of others. I learn well."

Mary and Margaret stood staring at the girl, their mouths agape.

The girl continued. "The great Tayac Kittamaquund if die, I lead his people. I come here with word *cape*. You say word *cloak*. Father White show us bear, fish, and people *open* mouths. My father show me flower *open*. You show me cape *open*." The girl, with back straight and chin jutted up, stepped over to Mary. "I not baby. I show how make soap from root. I plant food in garden beside you."

Mary stood transfixed. Margaret started to say something, but the child spoke once more.

"You accept me, I say Grace before we eat."

The governor's eyes sparkled, and a grin lit up his face.

Chapter 40
April-May 1641

Nothing in life is to be feared. It is only to be understood.
- Marie Curie

SETTLED IN THE GOVERNOR'S carriage with the young native girl between them and a woolen blanket spread across their laps, Margaret and Mary headed home. Leonard insisted on piling stacks of books, paper, and ink in the carriage. He even said he'd have his harpsichord delivered to Sisters Freehold the next day and would hire Freeman Henry to teach the Empress how to play.

"Mary, our lives have just changed—again."

"I do wonder what our mother and sisters would say if they knew we had accepted a native into our household to live with us. They would believe it of me, but not of you."

"With your huge repertoire of strange and unusual information I hope you possess knowledge of Piscataway culture."

Mary gave Margaret a sideways glance. "Not enough to help us."

"Piscataway not big strange. We like English not be unusual." The Empress smiled at them.

Margaret studied this young girl and decided her age was a conundrum. The girl's wisdom and logic impressed her as adult-like, even with her labored English.

"I am pleased to hear you say this." Mary smiled back. "Please tell us more."

"We grow corn, pumpkins, beans, and—no word to say." She made like she held a long round object.

"Squash?" Mary crinkled her brow, evidently enjoying this conversation.

"Sssuash."

"*Squ*-ash." Mary repeated.

"Squash. I fish, dig clams, build fire, cook. I make tis." She held out the hem of her smock." She looked at Mary and pointed to her cloak. "You make tat. Father bows head to Grace at eating time. We eat. We not big strange. We same strange."

* * *

Over the month Margaret and Mary sorted through and compared the Empress's *sameness* in their lives. When Father White baptized her, he mentioned seeing her as a child when the *Ark* and *Dove* first landed in Maryland seven years ago. He guessed her to be a little older than a toddler. His judgement must have been incorrect. The young Empress, now baptized with the Christian name of Mary, could remember the smallest of details when the English first arrived. She had a role in helping the women and girls prepare in welcoming the people from the *Ark*. Young Mary must be at least ten by now.

With her daily Bible readings, recitations, and written lessons, young Mary's English improved. Many of her skills seemed transferable. Instead of sewing with a bone needle, using threads of rawhide and tough leather, her Aunt Mary showed her how to stitch more delicate materials using fine metal needles with cotton thread.

The young Empress deftly caught fish and dug clams. However, her hunting skills, other than for roots, herbs, and berries, had been limited to traps and bow and arrows.

After much discussion about the Susquehannock and other warring tribes, and the fact the Empress someday might need to protect herself and her village, the sisters asked Giles to teach her how to hunt with a musket, using Giles's flintlock.

Even before the first part of May young Mary's heavy leather smock, now above her knees, pulled taut against her growing body. Besides, she needed cooler spring clothing. Mary called Margaret into the girl's room to help make pattern pieces from material for young Mary to finish sewing.

"I use metal needle make my petcoat."

Mary smiled. "Say it like this, 'I will use a metal needle to make my new petticoat.'"

The girl said it perfectly and grinned wide. Her dark eyes sparkled with delight.

Barefooted, the child tugged off her well-worn doe-skin tunic, grabbed a length of material, and climbed up on the stool that Mary had placed for this purpose. She stood naked and proud, clutching the piece of chintz with tiny forest animals in colorful block print stamped over the pale background. The trader said it came from India. Margaret had purchased this particular yardage from a merchant ship.

Margaret said, "You have selected cloth you like."

"For my new petcoat—pett-i-coat, please."

"If we used the chintz," Margaret said, "for your petticoat, then most of the animals would be hidden under your gown. If your petticoat is made from this," she held up a piece of white cotton, saying, "then you could make a gown out of your chintz to go over it."

"You also need a shift and pinafores." Mary selected some other colorful fabrics and held them out for the girl to examine. "But we need to start with showing you how to sew your plain, white cotton shift."

Young Mary, wide-eyed, nodded.

After measuring a pattern for her shift and petticoat, the women continued to drape soft linens and colorful fabrics over the youngster's body, cutting and pinning here and there.

Margaret's eyes met Mary's. This person standing before them, no longer hidden under thick leather, was not a child. Here stood a young budding woman about to bloom. They hadn't noticed her youthful, rounded face change into fine chiseled features. Her diminutive childish stature had become quite elongated.

* * *

By the end of May, the Empress had outgrown her new linen shift. Her petticoats even had to be let out. She needed a larger and longer wardrobe.

Margaret sorted through remnants of colored material with Mary, having young Mary set aside the ones that pleased her.

"Goodness," Mary stood. "At the rate you're growing, we shall have to have a new shipload of cloth delivered. I had thought we would start making you woolens to wear this winter, but we had better wait and see."

Young Mary giggled and held up some brocaded silk under her chin. The yellow fabric displayed leaves of several shades of greens with pink, blue, and orange flowers. Butterflies and birds outlined with gold thread hid among the leaves.

Mary and Margaret both grinned and shook their heads. Young Mary now stood a little taller than her Auntie Mary.

* * *

The knock on the door came as it did every Wednesday at two o'clock. Young Mary set her embroidery aside and sprinted to the door.

Henry, cap in hand, stepped in. He gave a slight bow to the Ladies Brent.

"You are most punctual, Henry." Margaret glanced up from her ledger. "Give me an assessment of our young student's progress."

"The best assessment I can offer comes from your own enjoyment of her practice sessions."

Margaret laughed. "I speak for myself, but I adore the sounds she extracts from that harpsicord. It takes me back to our dear old England. What about you Mary?"

Young Mary grinned and waited for her Auntie Mary to comment.

"What I hear is our young charge finds much pleasure with her practice. But then she is quick to learn most tasks set before her."

Henry, obviously pleased, waved his hand toward young Mary and the harpsicord. "We must waste not another moment of your lesson."

The two sat at the instrument while he demonstrated chords and runs, and she imitated.

Another quick rap on the door brought Margaret to her feet. "Who now?"

Missus Taylor rushed to open the door where Giles paced back and forth. He had brought two horses. He bowed his head and whispered, "Sisters, please step outside."

They did. Mary closed the door behind them and waited.

"The Tayac Kittamaquund has passed. Lord Governor and Father White asked if I would take Empress Mary to her village to be with her mother. The Empress must lead her tribe through this time of agony."

"Oh, Giles." Margaret touched his sleeve. "Her father died. You must not expect her to ignore her sorrow and lead her tribe—she is but a child." Yet she wasn't a child. Any day now she would become a woman. Margaret's surprise at her own reluctance to let the girl go left her at a loss for words.

Mary said, "I'm surprised Father White would allow this. He knows the depth of pain when a loved one dies."

"Sisters, she has prepared for this moment from the time she was born. She understands what she must do, and she knows how to do it."

"Cockles and berries, Giles, we cannot let this young woman ride off into the forest with you on some long journey. There's nothing proper about this, and in your ignorance, you've not even put a sidesaddle on that horse."

"Yours and Mary's ignorance—" He sighed. "Listen to me. You two have no say in this. Besides, Piscataway women do not ride sidesaddle—if they ride at all." Giles patted his thigh as he collected his words. "We're only riding to my dock where we'll leave the horses with my men and sail to her village. Father White will meet us there with his sloop. Then he will stay with her until a proper time when she can return to St. Mary's. I'm only the messenger and her travel companion."

Chapter 41
Summer 1641

Europe was created by history. America was created by philosophy.
- Margaret Thatcher

A FAMILIAR SENSATION OF dread bothered Margaret. She missed young Mary, but this was more—a dull ache filled her heart. It felt like she could not right some wrong, and it niggled at her as she walked their tobacco fields. Margaret wiped the sweat off the back of her neck and pulled her bonnet lower to shade her eyes from the intense muggy summer sun. Her men had diligently pinched off the top bud of each plant to insure it would leaf out to its fullest.

After she had hired out her men last year to other planters the men had acquired not only the indelible green tobacco stain on their thumbs, but immense knowledge needed for growing a fine crop. She fingered a broad leaf, turning it over to inspect the underside. Her random inspections uncovered a few grubs. Not unexpected. She picked them off and crushed them.

Their fields had been carefully weeded. She looked beyond to unplanted fields and the ache grew.

This fallow land brings my dismay.

Weeks ago, Leonard lamented about lands not yet planted and concern over low tobacco prices in England this year.

Margaret lifted her apron and skirts and stepped over rough mounds of damp earth to get to the lane. Swatting at flies, she headed home. She and Mary had the same problem as Leonard. If they couldn't transport more men to Maryland, what good was it for them to have acquired so much land?

John Robinson no longer worked for her. He bought his freeman status as she had predicted. Soon Goodwin and the others would no longer be indentured either.

Leonard's English connections and acquaintances reached much further than hers and Mary's, yet even he couldn't entice men to leave England. Everyone complained about the shortage of women, but the backbone of the economy would be undermined because of the absence of indentured men. Why wouldn't any of them take a chance and come to the province? What a shame—so much land and no one to work it.

She stopped at their cornfield and gave it a quick check. Young Mary had shown them how to mound up soil and plant corn, beans, and squash in each mound together—with a dead fish or such as fertilizer. When the corn grew, the beans would grow up and twine around the cornstalk, while the large squash leaves would cover the ground below the corn and beans, keeping the weeds out.

Mary stood in front of their home, waving to her, and pointing toward the river. Then her sister disappeared along the path that led down to the dock.

She rushed along toward the bank and saw Father White's sloop below tied to their wharf. As Margaret made her way down, he helped Mary Kittamaquund out of the sailing vessel. All the while Margaret could hear her sister chatting with the two of them.

The young girl had grown considerably this last month and looked as regal as any Empress of any tribe could look. She wore a sleeveless, doe-skin shift with leather moccasins. Her black hair, pulled back in one big braid, gleamed in the hot, humid, noonday sun.

Remembering her new English social graces, she thanked Father White for transporting her on the river back to the Brents.

"We worried about you." Margaret took hold of one of her hands. "We feared you might decide not to return to us. How difficult this must be for your mother and younger siblings."

The Empress stood, cast her gaze downward, then said, "I want Aunt Mary to teach me how to sew the woolens she talked about for the winter. You told me I need to know the amount of tobacco someone owes to me if I sell a cow, and I want more music lessons from Henry. I have many reading and writing lessons still to learn. Is it satisfactory I come back?"

Margaret tilted her head. "Do you not need to lead your people at this time?"

"My father's senior counselor, Mosorcoques, and I work together. The people know they have him."

"I can think of nothing more satisfactory than your being here at Sisters Freehold with us. You must tell us about your mother and family." Margaret called over to Father White. "Please come to the house and Missus Brookes will have something for us to eat."

How secure our future would be if our Empress could teach us how to grow tobacco as efficiently as she has with corn, beans, and squash. Unused land has no purpose.

Chapter 42
June 1642

Thy friendship makes us fresh.
- William Shakespeare

ONE YEAR LATER, MARGARET, as well as some other landholders, still had no solution for growing crops on their unused land. If they couldn't entice Englishmen to make the voyage, she didn't know what they could do. She disliked Leonard's idea to sell idle land to the Puritans in Virginia.

On her way to court, Margaret stopped in St. Mary's proper to assess the work on Calvert's new house. When they first arrived on the shores of Maryland, he had mentioned the need for a larger place, one with rooms to accommodate and feed the burgesses when they came for Assembly. These men had made do with whatever lodging they could find and with meals prepared and served at Calvert or Lewger's home.

The new Calvert house, started several weeks ago, appeared to be almost finished. A cluster of men sorted window frames outside the doorstep and matched them to their various cutouts in the walls. The west door stood ajar. She entered and found herself standing in a long passage leading to many rooms, with one large door to the immediate left and another large one to right. That one stood open.

Margaret walked into its spacious area, similar to Lewger's, with a fireplace, high ceiling, and openings for south-facing windows.

"You know I miss you." Leonard's voice came from an adjoining room to the east. When she spied him, his smile widened. He maneuvered around construction wood and tools and stood close—too close. Margaret stepped back.

"Forgive me." He bowed his head. "My exuberance, taking in the vision of you, quells all decorum."

"What do you hear from my younger sister, Ann? Is all well in England?"

"We write. Her lovely pen tells me of her life, her dreams, and asks about Maryland, you, Mary, and Giles. I know her naught, but she presents herself as charming as I find you."

"Will she come to Maryland?" Margaret knew this question to be far too bold. If he said Ann would come, then that meant he had asked her to marry him. She had no right to know until he came upon the time to tell her.

"She does not care to leave England." His eyes lost their twinkle and his grin disappeared. "England's troubles worry her, as does the rebellion in Ireland, but not so much as the long journey to Maryland and the leaving of your father. I pleaded for her to think about the arising dangers. Our king continues his aggravation toward Parliament, and soon a civil war will be upon them."

Margaret nodded at the truth of his words.

"This house of yours surprises me. I knew it would be grand, but the size of—"

"'Tis not mine, sweet lady. Nathanial Pope purchased this house and land. This magnificent place will lodge our legislators, be a place of meeting for our Assembly and Provincial Court. When not otherwise occupied, this room will be an ordinary for St. Mary's City. Our citizens will welcome a place to visit over beer and maybe share a good meal, while conducting a fair bargain for their goods."

"Nathanial Pope?"

"A perfect solution. The man isn't married, and he has nine men servants. He's industrious but will never rise above a farmer with his meager income. I must have someone consistent to care for this place, and someone who will see to it our burgesses have food, drink, and a comfortable roof over their heads for the night. An ordinary serves this purpose. I thought about the widow who lives to the east. Industrious widows run the local ordinarys wherever you go in Virginia. But with Assembly and Provincial Court meeting here, and the burgesses needing housing when they arrive, and with my frequent trips abroad and to Virginia, I think Nathaniel, with his men servants, will be the perfect proprietor of this business. When I offered him the opportunity, he seemed delighted."

Rumors had reached Margaret's ears earlier this year, but she had ignored them. "Leonard, I know my brother will be most happy to have an ale in your— Pope's—ordinary. He has longed for his favorite one in Gloucester. When do you expect this to be finished?"

"The men tell me I can hold our next meeting here. I shall look forward to seeing you in court. We all would be surprised if the esteemed Lady Brent did not have a case or two to bring before me."

Margaret shrugged, grinning. "Edward Parker has requested I represent him for the 300 pounds of tobacco John Medley owes him, and John Lewger has requested I represent him for his demands of 700 pounds of tobacco from Randal Revell." She glanced at him, then said, "There seems to be a matter of Mary Courtney not paying her bill to Robert Clarke until the house repairs are completed according to their contract. Let us hope the business of the court does not fill the day, because with three more weeks before we meet, I may have more." She paused, then said, "Leonard, this all troubles me, your selling this beautiful place to Nathanial Pope. My court cases indicate many citizens believe they are entitled to take advantage of others."

Chapter 43
August 1642

That they inform themselves what they can of the present state of the old Colony of Virginea, both for matter of government and Plantation as likewise what trades they drive both at home and abroad...

- Cecilius Calvert, Second Lord Baltimore

ON ANY AGREEABLE MORNING such as this, being one without wind, Margaret found solace in walking. Her outing had one purpose—to arrive at Calvert's new manor, or rather Pope's house, before midmorning, in order to conduct some unpleasant business in front of the court. Lies, deceptions, and plain incompetence had Margaret righting wrongs and penning her wages in account ledgers.

Taffy-white clouds stole heat from the summer sun, while the chittering of birds talked of nothing in the treetops. Lost in her surroundings, Margaret strode out at her usual determined pace.

"May I walk with you?"

Giles.

The furrow between his eyes caused her to say, "Your somber face does not reflect my happiness to see you, brother. Where have you been?"

"Kent Island."

"Synonymous with eternal injustices. Will not that place ever settle down?"

"Not as long as Claiborne tells the Susquehannock warriors the English are like the Spanish. They decided to invade some settlements in Mattapany. Robbed and set fires."

"Come, I detest tardiness. Walk faster." Curious to know more about her brother's activities, Margaret said, "When young Mary came home with Father White a few weeks ago, it set me to worry about you."

"Then she's safe."

"Giles, something more than Susquehannock invaders and Kent bothers you."

"Susquehannock are enough. Damnable Claiborne tells pig-horn lies about us Catholics, making them want to kill us all. Leonard's proclamation last year demanding Kent Islanders kill any Indian setting foot on the land hasn't helped."

Lord Baltimore should have left Kent Island to Virginia.

"Nary a whit." Margaret brushed a fly away. "As I understand, someone here in St. Mary's shot a native who Cornwallis had sent out to hunt game. It's a problem for all of us."

Giles picked up a large branch and hurled it off the path. "Margaret, our uncle, Richard Reed, and a couple of others—I borrowed a sizable amount from them to make this Maryland adventure happen. With the drought our first year here, and tobacco prices down, I only see one way to pay back my debt."

"I'm relieved to know your debts bother you." The minute she said it, she knew how unkind it sounded.

He looked at her, then off in the distance—his face set hard.

A wave of shame burned through her. True, he found ways to irritate her, but why would she never let anything pass? Every moment in his company she judged him. Margaret had cared for him as a baby and through his boyhood years. She had been but a child herself, just three years older.

She had chased after him, as he ran on toddler legs. She had kissed count-less tears away when he would fall and cry. He had acquired more scratches and scrapes than all the other siblings. Diverting him from curiosity that might lead him to harm—changing his attention into doable and safe activities required all her cleverness. If she failed in her attempt to distract him from something harmful, one of his famous tantrums would ensue. Whenever Giles unleashed a lung-emptying fit, the younger children often joined in, wailing with red, wet faces. He had been a beautiful child, but far too willing to attempt something out-landish. She sighed. It was time for her to let go of this need to mother him.

Now Giles obviously felt troubled. He wouldn't have mentioned his debt to his uncle if he had not desired her counsel.

She tugged his sleeve and stopped walking. "Forgive me. My thoughtless remark should have remained unsaid. You deserve not to be judged so harshly." She looked into his eyes and softly said, "Please give me an opportunity to demon-strate my care and interest in what you do."

He actually smiled at her. His face relaxed, and he put her arm through the bend in his elbow, patted her hand, and resumed their walking. "I find it impos-sible to please you, but one day you shall see. I am determined to succeed. I will make you proud."

She thought about him as she matched his pace. This man who had Leonard's confidence was the brother who would do whatever she asked without question, unlike Fulke. This handsome young man only wanted to make something grand of himself and not be judged wrongly by his older sister. Yet something wasn't right. She knew of no huge debts to Richard Reed.

"Giles, you contemplate a scheme."

He grinned. "Not the slightest inconsistency is allowed to pass when you and I are together."

"We will arrive at the Governor's manor in a few minutes. Unless you want to wait another day you better get on with telling me." She stood with hands on her hips.

"Your calling Kent Island the *Land of Eternal Injustices* is exactly what it is. Since I spend a good deal of time in Kent, keeping the peace, Leonard has granted me acreages of land on the island and a manor. Yet, if he grants it, he can also take it away—along with what I rightfully own here at St. Mary's."

"Cockles and berries, Giles." Margaret started walking again. "I am surprised you would even think this."

"Remember father signing over his estates to our relatives because he feared the king would confiscate his lands—recusants who don't embrace the Church of England must pay."

"You want to use Uncle Richard as an excuse to sign your lands over to me— but why? English recusant laws do not happen here. What worries you?"

"Eternal injustices, Margaret. I have to or I'll probably lose everything. Calvert has placed me in an impossible situation. I fear I am bound to anger our governor. His cautious actions frustrate me, and my need to pop in and do whatever must be done annoys him. I just need you to put everything in your name and pay whatever debts are incurred."

She started calculating figures in her mind.

"My land adjoins your land," he said. "This exquisite acreage is not unlike my holdings in Kent. I would sign over my lands, the manors, my livestock, and servants."

Margaret stared at Giles.

He is fearful and knows so much more about the workings of this province than I do.

They had arrived at the front entrance. Peasley greeted them in his usual demeanor and attire. Captain Cornwallis drove up in his carriage, and other men secured their horses next to the other two carriages under a large-leafed sassafras tree. The horse master appeared to lead each horse in turn to the new stable.

Giles stood erect, holding his hat in his hand. Yet, like a little boy he ever so slightly chewed at his bottom lip.

Captain Cornwallis strode up the path. His eyes glowered for some unknown purpose. As angry as he appeared, with his solemn face, he still tipped his hat to the Brents before disappearing inside.

"Giles," Margaret said, "I'll talk to Mary. The two of us share equally in this Maryland adventure. I should go inside and present my cases and be gone. My frequent appearance here may be what maddens Captain Cornwallis. Regardless, I need to finish and leave before the good gentlemen and the freemen of St. Mary's express their annoyance at having petticoats invade their court and Assembly."

Chapter 44
August 1642

Persons also are divided by the law into either natural persons, or artificial. Natural persons are such as the God of nature formed us: artificial are such as created and devised by human laws for the purposes of society and government, which are called corporations or bodies politic.
- Sir William Blackstone (Commentaries on English Law)

THE GENTLEMEN, ALL LOOKING grand in their finest clothing, many with feathered hats and capes, stood in small groups. They used these few minutes before Leonard started the day's proceedings to exchange information or just visit. One sturdy man of African descent caught Margaret's interest.

He must be De Sousa.

De Sousa had become one of the burgesses this year. Until today she had not seen him. He wore the baggy britches and puffy sleeves of a seaman. Someone had mentioned, besides the priests' ketches, he often sailed one of John Lewger's ketches and traded with the natives.

When Giles and Margaret had entered the room, Lewger greeted Margaret, then pulled Giles aside, asking about the latest Indian raids.

Margaret remained in the far back of the long meeting hall, near the heavy, wooden door, and hoped not to attract attention. This room appeared grander than Leonard's other meeting hall. He had included huge multiple-paned windows opened to fresh air. At the far end of the room, a magnificent fireplace covered half of the wall. English tapestries and paintings—some Dutch, some French, and some by painters she didn't recognize, held her attention.

Assembly burgesses attended today to learn more about the continuous Indian raids. Leonard, at a table in front of the fireplace, shuffled some papers and placed them on John Lewger's desk next to Lewger's ever-present ledger, ink well, and quills. Then Leonard moved back to the ornately carved table and studied a document. His table had three chairs, one for him, and two for his council, Captain Cornwallis and Giles.

The burgesses, all gentlemen, and freemen, had chairs arranged for them next to tables running down each side of Lewger and Calvert's stations. The men's chairs stayed empty as they continued to socialize.

Margaret suspected many of the men probably saw no use for her presence. She had worn her soft gray and white gown with a large, flat-white collar and wide, lace cuffs over a pale petticoat of the lightest violet hue—subdued colors. She couldn't do much about her fox-colored hair except tie it back and pin the white coif on top. She stood perfectly still, affording herself a glimpse into the world of men who made and enforced the laws of their country.

Captain Cornwallis and several other Catholics stood within a few feet of her.

"All this baptism nonsense of these tribes needs to stop." Captain Cornwallis's voice increased in volume. Margaret glanced around. Evidently, others paid no attention. He had directed his comment to Thomas Greene and Father Fisher.

The nature of this conversation intrigued Margaret, considering not long ago young Mary Kittamaquund had been baptized. She feigned a study of the room, looking beyond the men, but their topic had captured her ears.

Father Fisher said, "Nonsense? 'Tis our mission."

"It's not perceived as such, Father," Cornwallis said, "Some have labeled baptism of these natives a dangerous act. They fear, once baptized, these naturals will take up arms against Protestants."

"Who says such a thing?" Greene said, "Some jealous Protestant, I bet my best cow on it." Thomas Greene lowered his voice. "I suspect they'll also worry about all the lands Indians have given priests."

"Humph." Cornwallis said, "Lest you forget—only Lord Baltimore has the right to distribute land."

Another man whom Margaret did not know had joined the group. He shook his head. "My bet Francis Gray stirs up this trouble about Indian baptisms. Remember the mess he and Seagrave caused in '34 with the Jesuit Mission overseer? He's a conniver."

Greene whispered, "Some would say perhaps the less our good English Lord knows about what goes on over here the better his humor. He should be thankful. I hear Jesuits pay more in taxes than anyone."

Cornwallis's own ill humor seemed to grow even darker after Greene's remark.

Father Fisher said, "William Lewis, that poor overseer at St. Inigoes. Those schemers would have sent that petition clear to the Virginia Assembly. Yet it does gall me that Lewis suffered the penalties and not those two disrupters. They antagonized Lewis with their loud reading of those insulting passages."

Captain Cornwallis glowered at Father Fisher. "The court under English law served justice. Reading their Protestant book is not a crime in England. Lewger, Calvert, and I had no choice but to rule as we did."

Greene shifted his stance and glanced around the room, probably worried if Protestant burgesses had overheard. Lord Baltimore and Leonard continually lectured the Maryland Catholics about keeping silent in public on religious issues.

Father Fisher, in his quiet way, mumbled, "Our mission seeks to bring these lambs into our fold. Baptism could never be called an instrument of harm."

Thomas Greene coughed once, looked around, then said in a loud voice, "Captain Cornwallis, did you settle your issue with Hardige?"

"I fear, my good man, Hardige and I shall continue to be at odds until one of us drops dead. The man has become most annoying with his whining—not paying what he owes. He's about to drive me mad."

"He's obviously a very fine tailor, Captain." Greene said. "Your cape and doublet fit you well."

"They should, considering what that robber charged me. I furnish him my cloth. He used half of it, then refuses to return the unused portion to me."

Margaret watched Leonard square his papers. Then the governor stood tall and studied the room before he made his announcement.

"Gentlemen and freemen of Maryland, the Provincial Court will now convene. Burgesses, please be seated. Council, take your places." The men parted to take their seats at the tables, some with promises to get together for more discussion over a tankard of ale.

Margaret hated this moment when she was left standing alone in the back. Leonard looked up and saw her. Her stomach's frogs fluttered. She fretted about him forgetting where he was and giving her one of his endearing smiles. If he did, she swore she would turn and leave. As always, and to her relief, he maintained his demeanor as governor.

"Lady Brent, step forward to tell us what business you have with us today."

She walked toward his table in the front of the long hall. All the men stood. Their social graces stayed with them even when they should be sitting until called up by the governor. She would give anything if there were some way she could avoid these men standing when she passed. She knew her cheeks flushed.

"Everyone except the Lady Brent may be seated."

The governor then waited until the shuffling and scrunching of feet and chairs had quieted, and all were where they should be.

"How many cases will you bring before us today? I see no witnesses or plaintiffs."

"Five. Action of debt—two of these are from February and March Court Assembly. This should take little of your time."

"Are the plaintiffs and defendants present?"

"The plaintiffs are. I am for four of the cases and Sir Thomas Greene for one. The defendants have been summoned and may appear at any time."

"Then proceed. Who do we hear first?"

"The Gentleman Walter Broadhurst on March 27 had been warned to court on April 5th on penalty of judgment. He did not appear in April. He owes 155 pounds of tobacco to Mary Brent and me for payment of debt."

Leonard leaned over to Lewger. "Since Gentleman Broadhurst did not appear in April, he forfeited his right of repeal. Send the sheriff to collect and deliver payment due to the Ladies Brent. Proceed with your next one, Lady Brent."

"The next three are accounts due to my sister and me. These men have been notified but are not here today to dispute our claim. William Hawkins, 400 pounds of tobacco due on account. Joseph Eldo, 250 pounds due on account. Thomas Allen, 100 pounds due upon account."

"Thomas Allen?" Leonard leaned over and asked something of Lewger. Lewger shrugged. "Lady Brent, when did you notify Thomas Allen to attend?"

"He has owed this debt since last summer. I sent one of my men two weeks ago to tell him I would be appearing in court today to demand payment of debt."

"Does anyone present know if Thomas Allen still resides in St. Mary's City?"

Many shifted in their chairs and glanced at their associates. For a minute, no one spoke.

"Lord Governor," Captain Cornwallis held his finger up, then stood, and said,

"It has been my understanding that Thomas Allen no longer lives here. I do not know if he has moved or if he has died."

Leonard looked around the room at the seated men one more time. Again, everyone remained quiet. Captain Cornwallis sat.

"Sheriff Baldwin, you are to summon Joseph Eldo and William Hawkins to court next November as per notice written by our secretary. Also, go to the last known lodging of Thomas Allen, and see if he is there or if anyone knows where he is and report back to Secretary Lewger."

The sheriff waited until Lewger had written out the summons, then took them and sat back at his table, waiting any further instructions.

"Lady Brent, please continue."

"If you please, Lord Governor, I represent Gentleman Thomas Greene today."

Leonard nodded at Thomas and said, "Gentleman Greene, please present yourself."

Thomas Greene pushed back his chair, rose, and strode to the front next to Margaret.

"Lord Governor," Margaret said, "council of the court, and good Assemblymen, my sister and I paid passage for John Robinson, a carpenter and barber by trade. He arrived in Maryland on the ship *Charity* with the rest of us in 1638. He committed to being our four-year indentured servant or until his work equaled the cost of his passage. John Robinson, the second son from a noteworthy family in England, intent on becoming a freeman, worked hard. As a barber, carpenter, and self-taught planter, he worked weekends for others to pay off his headright, which he did a year ago."

"Last summer, as a freeman, he agreed to labor in Gentleman Greene's tobacco fields and drying shed for a total of twelve weeks for a fee. A fortnight and three days prior to the end of his contract of work with Gentleman Greene, John Robinson stopped tending to the tobacco and did not reappear to execute his assigned tasks of the next seventeen days. He clearly owes repayment for his absent seventeen days. On February 1st of this year, John Robinson denied his debt."

"On February 6th of this year, Gentleman Greene and I appeared here to prosecute. Sheriff Baldwin had notified John Robinson to attend and answer the charges under penalty of judgment. John Robinson became obstinate and expressed contempt for authority. He refused to come to court whereupon in *contumacie* the court found the plaintiff's proof and ruled for the plaintiff, Thomas Greene, that he should recover two barrels and one bushel of corn and 585 pounds of tobacco. Gentleman Greene stands ready to answer any of your questions."

Leonard Calvert looked at John Lewger and then the Assembly. Freeman Robert Clarke stood and asked to be recognized. Calvert agreed.

"I'm a neighbor of the Ladies Brent, and I've watched John Robinson over the years. He is indeed a hard worker, but he has a foul temper when it comes to authority. He's never going to admit his fault or pay up unless made to do so. I vote to send the sheriff to collect what's due Gentleman Greene."

"Hear, hear!" The Assembly shouted.

Leonard looked at the council. When they nodded agreement, he leaned down to Lewger and said, "Let the record show Robinson forfeited his right to protest his debt. Sheriff Baldwin will collect from him and deliver 585 pounds of tobacco, two barrels and one bushel of corn to Gentleman Greene. Let it be known the province awards two additional barrels of Robinson's corn for court charges and sheriff's fees."

Margaret nodded at Leonard, saying, "Thank you, Lord Governor and to the fine men of this Assembly." She glanced at Giles, his lips tight and brow furrowed.

Unless I remain, I shall never know the truth of the real state of affairs befuddling Giles.

"Lord Governor." She had caught him, as well as herself, by surprise. He stopped his conference with Lewger and looked at her. She searched for an excuse.

"Distances are far and times not accurate and since you have not yet ruled on the cases presented concerning Eldo, Hawkins, and Allen, I will sit quietly at the last table to wait their possible appearance. If they do not come by the end of the session, you then could summons their November appearance."

Leonard stared at her. He studied the faces of the baffled men, then nodded agreement.

She forced herself to stand tall, hoping not to give hint at the unprecedented behavior she had just displayed.

Thomas Greene leaned over and quietly thanked her, then strode to his place at the tables. She marched past the men before they could stand and found an empty chair in the back. She sat and wondered about the action taken against John Robinson. *Contumacie*—obstinate and rebellious—this court had probably unleashed something unforeseen and troublesome.

Chapter 45

We have great hopes of a plentiful harvest of souls, if laborers are not wanting, that know the language and enjoy good health.
- Father Brock

AFTER MARGARET SAT, LEONARD announced, "The Council recognizes Burgess Robert Vaughan of Kent Island. Please stand and state your purpose."

"Your Lordship, in the July meeting I proposed a change of organization to our courts. I would like to revisit it for your renewed consideration."

"Unless you have additional matter to add to your previous argument, the issue is settled."

"Sir, in respect to what has happened between Parliament and the king of England, if we established two houses, giving the lower house the right to veto the council, we might avoid future difficulties."

"Mister Vaughan, Lord Baltimore has given no authority to grant the burgesses control of the legislature of Maryland. As before, your request is denied."

"One more item, if you please. The unrest in England between king and Parliament might be avoided here if you, unlike our king, called Assembly to meet annually, rather than wait for issues to arise. Parliament voted in the Triennial Act for such purposes. I move we put this to a vote."

"Again, Mister Vaughan, the burgesses have no authority to control the legislature or to convene Assembly. This request is denied."

Calvert's jaw set. He glanced around the room. Then he noticed Giles with a finger in the air, sitting next to Captain Cornwallis, a seat away.

"Commander Brent."

"Your Lordship." Giles turned to face the burgesses. "I have an item to bring before this Assembly, not requiring a vote. First, all trade in the north Chesapeake has essentially been halted this summer because of the Indian raids. The Susquehannock continue to terrorize Indian villages and English settlements along the bay. Most recently they attacked Mattapany. I wish to remind Assembly of several imperative instructions from his Lordship's proclamation earlier this summer. No one is to give the natives shot or powder. If you travel any distance, carry a loaded gun. If you are a head of the household, then provide each of your men with firearms. Don't forget, if you see danger, every fifteen minutes fire three shots. Anyone hearing the warning signal should return three shots." Giles nodded at the governor.

Interesting what they forget to tell those outside this hall. They must think as a woman I have no need to arm my men.

This caused the mischievous frogs that usually frolicked in her stomach to quietly light a tiny fire. She expected them to fan the sparks into one hot flame before the end of the Assembly.

"Does anyone have anything to add?" Leonard waited.

A hand raised from somewhere near the middle of the room. Margaret didn't recognize the man.

"The burgess from Patuxent is recognized to speak. Please state your name for the record."

"Burgess Thomas Harris of Sow's Creek, your Lordship. I move we march on the Indians."

Someone seconded the motion.

Wait? They just moved to march against the 'Indians'—which Indians—when?

Before Leonard could speak, there came a resounding, "Nay."

Margaret felt her face scrunch in confusion. What games were these men playing? Then she carefully studied the men who made the loudest objections. They seemed to be the ones who Leonard had refused to give the lower house veto privileges. Robert Vaughan wore a satisfied retaliatory smirk.

She compelled herself not to stand and scold them for such a farce.

"As your governor, I am the only one who can declare an act of war." Leonard leaned forward with both his palms on the table, his voice loud and strong. He surveyed the room, sighed, then said. "However, if we decide to march on any entity, we must know what surety each of you will contribute."

John Lewger stood. "Lord Governor, a levy of twenty pounds of tobacco per person appears reasonable. I so move."

The room erupted in controversy. Tight knots of men mumbled and argued among others seated at their table.

Someone shouted about the validity of Lord Baltimore's document that proposed to give sole power and control to the governor.

Leonard Calvert called out, "Order. Order. Come to order." He slammed his palm on the table getting most of the burgesses' attention.

A few continued to raise their voices at each other.

"We need to do something about the trade in the north Chesapeake."

"Something must be done about those marauders."

Margaret folded her hands in her lap and looked down at the floor.

This morning spent in Assembly had not been a waste of Margaret's time. Even though she felt pleased with herself for staying, this drama disturbed her.

At most, I have learned the young men who work desperately to hold Maryland together may be the ones who tear her apart.

Chapter 46

I declare to you that woman must not depend upon the protection of man,
but must be taught to protect herself....
- Susan B. Anthony

LEAVING COURT, MARGARET ARRIVED home early afternoon out of breath. She called out to Mary. "We have urgent decisions to make."

Mary studied her sister's face.

Walking home, Margaret had pondered the meaning of what she had witnessed. The awful truth came to her. There would have to be renovations to Sisters Freehold. She envisioned the materials and labor required to ensure their safety.

Mary sat and looked expectantly at Margaret.

"Fiddlesticks," Margaret shook her head. "I am quite uncomfortable with these frilly cuffs. Let me change first."

In her room, she unpinned her collar and cuffs, and tied a plain white scarf in the place of her stiff collar. She joined Mary at the table. Mary had poured cider into their tankards, set two blue China plates from Holland, and a board of biscuits and meats covered with a piece of linen before them.

"Ham, biscuits, and cider," Margaret said. "I had no thought of eating until this minute."

"My curiosity won't wait a whit longer." Mary set the jug on the table. "Today has set everyone off in intolerable moods."

"Giles has asked us to do for him what our relatives did for father and his estates. Placing his property in our name may be the most sensible action he has taken."

"You jest." Mary held a biscuit halfway to her lips—her eyes widened.

"Keep in mind our brother's impetuousness while I tell you what I heard and suspect."

Her sister twisted her mouth aside, waiting.

"As usual, I arrived at court early and planned to depart in the greatest haste possible. I have in the past attributed my presence in Assembly to be the origin of these men's fidgety and grumpy behaviors. As of late, their ill tempers have begun to spread scowls across all their faces. I am not about to stop representing those who need me in court, or my own cases. Yet, if having a woman in their chambers upsets their sensibilities to such an extent, I best rush in, do what I must, then leave."

Mary squinted over her tankard at Margaret.

"I stayed and listened to the proceedings for most of this morning. I, dear Mary, am not the cause for the darkness of these men's moods."

"Then please tell, what causes these gentlemen's displeasing behaviors?"

"All the way home I puzzled. What might it be—making these men's emotions swing wildly from one fervent cause to another with no boundaries? The most temperate of men, and they are but few, like Gentleman Greene and Lewger, have wives and families. I believe the majority of Maryland men have no need to control their zealousness. When they return home after a day of arduous work, negotiating, or Assembly, they give no thought to the safety or care of any wife or child."

Mary kept her silence.

"Dear sister, if a person answers to no one but themselves, they are free to risk all they have for what they believe is a righteous cause or what will gain them esteem. Cornwallis, a family man, arrived in a foul mood this morning. Unlike the others, he's frustrated over the actions of our priests. Not only have they acquired what Protestants see as expansive Catholic lands but, as in England, Maryland Protestants also fear retaliation from Catholics. Since the Jesuits have baptized numerous Piscataway and Patuxent tribes, these Protestants believe natives who are now Catholic may take up arms against them."

"Ridiculous. Most natives don't have arms."

"The Dutch now sell arms and ammunition to the Indians." Margaret's stomach churned. Was this from her hunger or from what the Dutch were doing?

"Tell me about our brother's plan for his estates."

Her sister, like Giles, lacked patience.

"A year ago, July, the Susquehannock attacked Mattapany. Calvert issued a proclamation saying if any set foot on Kent Island, they were to be shot. Giles, as commander, has the responsibility to see this happen. Then a few months ago the Susquehannocks threatened to raid and burn Indian and English settlements along the Patuxent River. You know Giles. If someone angers him, or if turmoil happens, he takes sides and acts without thought."

"If Leonard thought Giles did something illegal—"

"Precisely. If he and Leonard tangle over some edict or course of action, Leonard has the power of the courts behind him. He would not hesitate to punish Giles." Margaret took a piece of ham and savored the salty taste along with Missus Brookes' buttery biscuit.

"If Giles signs his possessions over to us then he better have a good excuse. If not, your handsome governor will be bitter toward you."

"Giles does have plans to pay off debts to his uncles in England. There is his excuse. Mary, this morning's events disturbed me. Some of the burgesses attempted to remove the power of veto from the governor. Leonard wouldn't let it stand."

"Protestant burgesses, I wager." Mary waited for Margaret to affirm.

"Like Parliament in England. They work to diminish the power of our king." Margaret finished her biscuit, swept the crumbs into her palm, and placed them on her plate. "Here is the most disturbing news of all. Leonard issued a proclamation a few weeks ago to all men who are landholders."

"He issues proclamations all the time." Mary shrugged.

"And Giles keeps us informed, but he has been gone. This time no one bothered to tell us. Even though you and I are landholders, the men forget. We could be in grave danger, and we would not be forewarned."

Ticking off on her fingers and smirking, Mary said, "The Dutch, who hate us because of trade deals and our religion, have armed the natives. The Catholics can't engage in Catholic rites, or we might offend those who hate us. The Protestants plot against our governor. The natives raid villages. Giles fears he may lose his temper and hence all his estates."

"Worst of all," Margaret interrupted, "the country is overrun with irrational angry young men with no wives to settle them."

Mary huffed. "Thank heavens for Leonard's proclamations."

"Your thoughts will change when I tell you and our servants what Leonard has declared." Margaret stood. "We have dallied too long. Living alongside the St. George River increases our danger. This waterway invites Susquehannock marauders to storm property and take what they want—or worse. We shall build a fort around our buildings." She strode to the back door. "Missus Taylor, Missus Brookes, please call the men from the fields. You women, stop your work. All must come to the house and not tarry."

Chapter 47
September 1642

Alone we can do little; together we can do so much.
- Helen Keller

TWO WEEKS LATER MARGARET stood in the quiet predawn at the large opening in the unfinished stockade being erected around their home and buildings. She studied the edges of the forest. A mosquito's high-pitched whine by her ear broke the quiet. She waved it away and continued to scan the rest of the countryside.

Soon their fortress would be completed. She and Mary had polled the men about their number of firearms and weapons. Sisters Freehold would purchase more flintlocks, gunpowder, and lead shot. Each man might do best with several of their own black-powder flasks. Perhaps she could procure some flintlock pistols too.

Margaret couldn't imagine they would be attacked but, considering what she knew and not knowing what she didn't know, this action felt necessary. She and Mary must be sure they had provisions for a dozen people—food, water, candles, and blankets—at least enough to last several days.

The light of dawn began to filter through the trees, keeping most of the Brents' land hidden in shadow. Mary's voice startled her.

"Where did our young charge go?"

Margaret shook her head, sighed, and leaned with her back against one of the large upright logs.

Mary, fully dressed, moved up next to her. She bent and slapped at her ankle. "I heard the door open and close, and now you're here. Young Mary is nowhere in the house and it's barely dawn."

Studying the paths and the line of cut tree stumps along the riverbank, then back to the forest's edge, Margaret said, "I woke when I heard her go out the door. I did not want to wake you. There is a mosquito on your cheek."

Mary brushed it away.

"I did not see where she went." Margaret said, "Do you plan to look for her?"

"There's no use. Cutting down the trees and building this fortress has frightened her." Mary scanned the perimeter. "Her tribe moved from here because of the Susquehannock." Her voice caught a little. "We should not blame her if she leaves."

"Maybe she does need to be alone for a while. We should respect that."

"I fear it is something more. Yesterday, young Mary decided to carry all the eggs in her gardening apron rather than use the basket. Of course, they slipped out and broke. She fell into a terrible state of despair. I have no idea what has overcome this child. I thought maybe a hunt for mushrooms in the wood might calm her, but she tripped over a fallen log, skinned her knee, and tore the elbow out of her gown. Later I found her sitting by the hearth, angry, and ripping out all her lovely embroidery stitches. I thought it best to send her out to get some fresh air—a walk along the river. Clearly something more pressing disturbs her. I wonder if she has decided to go back to her tribe."

"Perhaps." The thought gave Margaret a sinking feeling in her stomach.

"Yet she would have told us—wouldn't she?"

Margaret looked out at the sunlight illuminating patches of leaves on the tops of forest trees.

"Fall will be here soon." She studied Mary. "I suspect she will return to her home before winter anyway. Leonard asked us to teach her. We did it. We have prepared the Empress Mary Kittamaquund in English ways." These next words hurt to say. "Now she needs to lead her Piscataway Nation."

"I don't want her to go, Margaret. Let's talk to Leonard and—"

Margaret put her arm around Mary. "I am surprised at you."

Mary's chestnut hair hung forward, covering the freckles on her nose. "I've never been around such a charming, clever girl who improves everything around her. Forgive my selfishness."

"Perhaps she will divide her time between here and her village. She knows we shall always welcome her." Margaret squinted, then pointed. "Look, there. She has been in the forest."

Young Mary strode across the field carrying a basket and wearing one of her cotton petticoats over her shift.

"She comes half naked." Fear gripped Margaret, knowing the cruelties inflicted on young girls by brutish men.

They rushed down the path. When they grew closer Margaret could see the petticoat clinging to young Mary's legs—soaked and bloody.

Good Heavens, what has happened to this girl?

"We worried about you." Mary sprinted over to the girl and stopped. "Why are you wet—and blood? Margaret, she's hurt."

Young Mary shook her head while Margaret took her arm and checked her over.

"Please, Auntie Margaret, show me where I must stay."

"Stay?" Mary repeated.

"Did someone hurt you?" Margaret would not let go of her arm.

"I must have a place away from others to stay for a few days." Young Mary clutched the basket to her as if the safety of her life depended on it.

Margaret looked into the girl's dark eyes and saw something she didn't understand. "Tell me. Why is your petticoat wet and bloody?"

"I washed it in the stream." Then young Mary held up a fist full of absorbent, shredded cedar bark from her intricately woven handmade basket.

Margaret tilted her head. She should understand—but—young Mary grinned.

"You must put me in a private place. Today I am a woman."

Mary stood frozen.

Margaret's mind raced in scattered directions. She calmed herself. "Young Mary, you will stay in the house with us. I believe if you were home, you would stay where only women stay for the next few days. We shall not let any men come into our house until your time has passed. Mary, walk with her. Missus Brookes will fill the tub with warm water so young Mary may bathe properly."

Margaret strode to the back of the house carrying a weight of enormous responsibilities that were not hers yesterday. She and her sister would talk privately later. When she reached the doorway, she saw Missus Brookes carrying a bucket of water up from the well. She called to her and then whispered her instructions.

Margaret found Missus Taylor in the henhouse. "Our young Empress has become a woman today. I fear her bedding is soiled. You and Missus Guesse, as soon as you can, remove and launder the canvas covering the mattress. Young Mary's shift and petticoat will need laundering too. Have the men burn the stuffing from the mattress once you've taken it outside. Then when the laundry is dry, the two of you need to insert fresh straw."

After seeing everyone busy with their new assignments, Margaret left them and strolled through the garden to think while checking the pumpkins.

Mary joined her. "We have new worries now."

"We do."

"Giles will be back sometime this week to take her hunting."

"I heard." Margaret glanced out over the river. "We must send a message to him. Do you know of anyone going to Kent today?"

"I can ask at St. Inigoes. One of their priests may. They sail back and forth all the time."

"Give me a minute to write him a note. Young Mary will not be hunting this week. You should ride—have a horse saddled." Another thought niggled at her. She might as well say it. "Mary, we can no longer have Giles alone with young Mary."

"I know. I see how he gazes at her."

"In the future when they go hunting, you go with them. If not, I shall."

Margaret left to write the note. When she returned, she handed it to Mary, who quickly rode south down the pathway to St. Inigoes. As Margaret watched, she heard someone coming from the dock.

One of her men, Franc Stowre, strode toward her, a sturdy man with thin brown windswept hair, rough skin, and a protruding chin that portrayed him as perpetually determined. Margaret had hired him out to an estate over by the Patuxent River.

"Stowre, I am surprised to see you."

"Aw, Lady Brent. Sad news I bring. Gentleman Charinton has been murdered by those truculent Susquehannocks. Those damnable warriors stormed his estate, stole everything they could. I heard they killed others. They didn't burn his tobacco shed, so maybe my wages won't be lost."

"Who else in St. Mary's knows?"

"Your brother arrived about the same time as I did. We've been in Assembly. He asked me to tell what I saw, and Commander Brent urged Assembly to organize a march against the Susquehannocks. About time, I say."

"Good Lord. We do not have a militia."

"Governor Calvert has put out a call for one hundred men and asked Captain Cornwallis to request another one hundred from Virginia. They all started arguing about funding this attack. I've never seen Captain Cornwallis and the governor so angry with each other. The captain even stormed out saying he'd not be a part of the council anymore. I decided it best I leave. Those Susquehannocks are fierce. Lady Brent, you have a courageous brother."

Chapter 48
Mid-September 1642

It is forbidden to kill; therefore all murderers are punished unless they kill in large numbers and to the sound of trumpets.
- Voltaire

TWO WEEKS LATER MARGARET found young Mary wearing the doeskin smock she had been making the last few days. Her English clothes were folded and placed neatly at the foot of her bed. This young woman, with chiseled features and eyes that matched her shiny black hair, possessed an air of dignity and grace.

Young Mary, standing regal, stared at Margaret. "I must go to my people. Where is Auntie Mary?"

"She is collecting herbs from the garden. I dislike the thought of you traveling by yourself on foot."

"This must be. Lord Governor has forbidden Father White to go to Piscataway, and Commander Giles has gone to fight the Susquehannocks. I fear for our people and our village."

Margaret didn't want to forbid the girl from doing as she desired, but for her to leave now—

"Auntie Margaret, I can see in your face you do not wish me to go." Her face clouded. "I see you have built a fort. You have armed your men. You prepare for attack from the Susquehannock. I too must consult with Mosorcoques, my father's senior counselor. We must secure our old fort around Piscataway. My people may need provisions. I will now say my goodbye to Auntie Mary."

"Wait—there must be another way." Margaret's words failed her. She couldn't let this child—woman leave by herself.

Young Mary gave Margaret a flimsy smile and shook her head. She picked up the flintlock and powder flask Giles had given her and walked out the door.

The gun—Leonard's proclamation declared it illegal for anyone to give a gun to a native. *Oh horrors! If anyone sees her with that flintlock she shall be shot.*

Margaret charged after her and found her in the garden talking with Mary and Goodwin. She took a deep breath and collected her words before she joined them.

"Goodwin, how pleasant to see you." Margaret missed the man since he worked fulltime at his smithy.

"Dropped by to see if ye ladies needed anything. Of late I have an apprentice, and he be taking over my projects. In a fortnight he be moving to Virginia where a new wife waits for him to open his own smithy."

Mary smiled sweetly at him and then took young Mary's hand. "Goodwin doesn't want young Mary to make the trip home by herself. I say we loan them our pinnace."

A flood of comfort filled Margaret. She knew no one kinder than this ruddy-faced man. "Young Mary, would you be agreeable to Goodwin taking you to your village in our pinnace?"

The Piscataway Empress grinned.

"Lady Mary," Goodwin said, "after we have left would ye be so kind to tell Lady Margaret what I told thee?" Goodwin waved and led young Mary down to the dock.

Mary and Margaret waved back and watched until the pinnace had rounded point on the river at St. Inigoes neck.

"Goodwin came to tell us bad news." Mary started walking back up to the house.

"About—"

"Our brother."

"No," came out softly. A denial. A refusal. A demand for whatever came next not to be.

Giles has been murdered by Susquehannock.

Mary stopped and took Margaret's hand. "He's not hurt. Walk with me while I'll tell you the worst of it."

Goodwin told Mary the Governor exempted himself from paying any surety toward the march on the Susquehannock, infuriating Captain Cornwallis, who then refused to lead the attack. The captain even left his position on the council.

"Leonard put Giles in charge—our brother who knows nothing about military strategies but is too proud not to accept such a position."

"If Leonard appointed him, Giles would have no choice but to serve." Margaret plucked a weed from her hem.

"However, dear sister, Giles is the one who riled everyone up about attacking these savages, and Lewger at great personal expense supplied most everything, including two boats. Even Cornwallis, as mad as he was, still threw in powder and lead."

"If this happened over a week ago, I heard some of it from Francis Stowre."

"Evidently, when Giles arrived at Kent, and even after several days, he couldn't persuade any men to volunteer. Meantime the other volunteers on the ships had eaten most of the food. Giles had no choice but to sail home. Leonard, furious at Giles's failure, ordered him arrested."

Margaret gasped, then took a moment to consider. "Our governor will have our irresponsible brother stand trial."

"Since we have no jail, he has been bound to stay at his home, according to Goodwin."

* * *

Within the hour, both Mary and Margaret stood at Giles's door. Instead of one of his men answering it, Giles appeared—the corners of his mouth drawn tight.

"Good afternoon," Margaret pushed through. "Besides squandering Mister Lewger's supplies and failing to corral volunteers, you have stirred much mud into our governor's stew."

He hunched up his shoulders and waved them into his parlor. His men always kept the house spotless. The large room, though sparse of furnishings, provided comfortable seating and captured decent sunlight for reading. Giles, a voracious reader, stacked his precious books all around on the floor next to his reading chair positioned near the opened window. His manor on Kent Island held even more books.

She should go visit but not until this Susquehannock and islander squabbling settled.

Giles begin to tidy his reading pile. He glanced at his sisters, then at the small red-leather bound book in his hand before setting it on his desk.

"Oh, sit and stop fidgeting." Mary sat near his chair. "Talk to us."

He scowled. "You two build a ridiculous fort for no need and then come to scold me."

"We act preemptively." Margaret stood before him. "You act from frustration."

"I did the best I could." He regarded Mary then turned back to Margaret, his face heated red. "You have no right to judge me. The other day you even said I deserved not to be judged by you so harshly."

"I clearly remember our conversation. I promised you I would be more temperate. We do not come to scold as a parent, nor to judge as your peers. We come as sisters who love you. When they call you to court you need to have your mind and thoughts in order. If not, your anger will dictate what words you say, and you will be the worse for it."

"She's right, Giles, what happened? Let Margaret help you prepare for your defense."

He looked long at Margaret, then motioned for her to sit. He sat, rubbed his face, and shut his eyes. Neither woman said anything.

"I made mistakes. When we got to Kent, I told the men I wouldn't press any of them into service. Yet, I needed twenty men, and none stepped forth to volunteer."

He stood and paced, ending at the window overlooking the St. George.

"I've been their commander for over two years now. I thought some of them would take up arms with me because of our association and good will. These natives will continue to raid if we don't do something. When none stepped up to join, it forced me to select men and require them to commit. This took much of the fight out of me, especially when they started saying they needed to stay and care for their crops. They had a whole cartload of excuses,"

"Goodwin told me something else." Mary leaned forward. "Leonard appointed Brainthwaite as the new commander. You must have felt diminished and betrayed."

Margaret looked at the two. "Leonard would believe it reasonable to take your title and position away because of your failure to enlist men to fight."

"Unfortunately," Mary said, "he made Brainthwaite commander before Giles even arrived on Kent."

The replacement of his command would bother Giles more than his failure to enlist volunteers. No wonder he looked so distraught. He coveted his commander title along with his leadership role. Margaret imagined Giles's thoughts as he sailed to what had been his domain to gather up Brainthwaite's men to fight for him. She knew how despondent and impulsive Giles became when he could not realize his dreams.

"No matter, Giles. Let us prepare for your trial. The men's crops would rot this time of year if they did not have time to get them in the drying sheds and take proper care of the tobacco. You have a strong point there. Now tell me about the other excuses they piled in that cartload."

Chapter 49

The true soldier fights not because he hates what is in front of him but because he loves what is behind him.
- G. K. Chesterton

FOR SOME REASON, THE governor had not been in any hurry to try Giles until several months later. Margaret and Mary wove through the crush of standing spectators and found a bench against the wall near the front, giving them a good view without anyone standing in front of them.

A planter leaned over and said, "You ladies built a mighty fine fortress around your home. 'Tis but a sad waste of your time and money, I say. No savages sail our river but look to your brother's country that be raided."

"My good man," Mary said. But Margaret placed her hand on Mary's arm, to quiet her.

Margaret cocked an eyebrow at the man and hinted a smile.

Lord Governor called for silence, then summoned Giles forth to explain his actions and answer for them.

Giles started off declaring the timing of the expedition would bring great financial harm to the planters of Kent Island because their crops would rot. He then went on to say the men feared reprisal from the Susquehannock, and if the men went to war, they wouldn't have enough gunpowder left to defend themselves.

Naturally the prosecution asked him questions dealing with his ability to persuade, but in the end, Giles apologized. They accepted, and he was acquitted.

The sisters waited for Giles outside Pope's house. The chill in the winter air felt pleasant to Margaret after the stuffy and crowded meeting hall. When Giles appeared, Mary congratulated him.

"I agree," Margaret said. "Giles, your explanation and apology seemed to come from your heart, and you even sounded humble. This becomes you."

"Walk with me to my home," Giles said. "Rather, I should say since October— your home. I would appreciate the company." He took Mary's arm and nodded at Margaret. "I miss our family and enjoy having you two by my side. Have either of you heard anything from our young Empress?"

Margaret glanced at Mary.

Mary raised her eyebrows. "With our priest not being allowed to travel to her territory, we have no information."

Giles looked out across the St. George, as if deep in thought.

A moment later he said, "Our governor making Brainthwaite's appointment as Commander of Kent Island brought me great offense. Sisters, we must never underestimate the good governor's judgment. Leonard wisely waited months to have this trial to give me time to tame my anger and control my tongue."

"A good possibility." Margaret had never seen Giles give weight to his own actions like this. "Leonard must have written Lord Baltimore of your failure to raise troops. Perhaps he also held up the trial to wait for further instruction from England."

"I'm such a goose. Did I not mention the governor wrote Lord Baltimore, and he in turn offered to fund another march on the Susquehannocks?"

"Good heavens, Giles." Margaret grabbed his arm. "You will not be doing this all over again, I beg not."

He laughed. "Captain Cornwallis has agreed. After all, as a captain in the military this makes more sense. I haven't had his training, and I've never been in a battle."

Mary squinted at Giles. "Last fall Captain Cornwallis walked out and refused to even serve on the council."

"As I said, dear sisters, our governor is not to be underestimated. Cornwallis has set aside his rage with Leonard and agreed to lead the troops. He told the soldiers the march would not interfere with planting time, any who volunteered could keep what they plundered, and collection of their debts would be postponed. I should have had such incentives to offer my volunteers."

Margaret sighed. "Someone needs to stop the raiding and murders." Having the fort at Sisters Freehold somewhat settled her. "When will this take place?"

"Up to Cornwallis, I'd say."

"So much fighting." Margaret watched the clouds, wondering if it might snow. "Ann Greene told me back in October King Charles flew the royal standard over Nottingham Castle and called for action against Parliament. The English Civil War has started."

Margaret decided they should sew a flag to fly and call their fort St. Thomas's Fort.

"England." Mary shook her head. "Whatever will they do? I heard the king has sent the queen abroad for her protection. I worry about our family."

"Sweet sister." Giles smiled. "Charles has thousands of Cornish fighters considered to be the fiercest soldiers of all. King Charles will soon control the Parliament's uprising."

Ah, Giles. You will always be our dreamer.

Chapter 50
March 1643

I gave my decisions on the principles of common justice and honesty between man and man, and relied on natural born sense, and not on law, learning to guide me; for I had never read a page in a law book in all my life.
- Davey Crocket

AFTER THE CHRISTMAS SEASON of 1642, Margaret spent most of the next three months going to and from provincial court to make demands of payment on debts, mostly for other people.

Sometimes the only purpose for her appearance in court was to be certain the transactions or the claims were set in record. In her court appearance last October, she made sure Secretary Lewger had on record Giles's transfer of all his estate to the Brent sisters. Giles stated the purpose of the transaction was his need of funds to pay debts to his uncle and others in England.

Franc Stowre had been correct about the Indian raid on Thomas Charinton's estate. The tobacco shed had not been burned, and so the administrator of the murdered estate owner paid Franc Stowre his due, and he in turn paid Margaret. Lewger again dutifully recorded these transactions in his ledgers.

I suspect no one now laughs at our building a fortress.

Margaret, during breakfast that morning, discussed the business she would present before the provincial court.

Missus Taylor interrupted, saying, "Ladies, I've heard a perplexing story of interest. Last night it seems a group of Virginians caused a fuss at the ordinary."

"Indians raiding, burning, and killing and now Virginians." Mary scowled at Margaret.

"The Virginians posed no threat," the maid said. "They claim to have been kidnapped. Stowre found this information most perplexing."

"He didn't see or talk with them?" Mary asked.

"Robert Clarke told him thus as he passed by earlier this morning. The *Reformation* has docked, may we be excused to go see what news it brings from England?"

The sisters agreed they could all go after caring for the animals. Mary and Margaret walked together. The huge ship rode deep in the waters of the St. George.

"Evidently they didn't unload much cargo in Virginia last night," Mary said.

Margaret wanted to wait and see what goods could be purchased, but said, "I must scurry on to Pope's house, but I hope we have news from home."

"Why would a ship need so many cannons?" Mary frowned. "Pirates, I suppose. Look. They're getting ready to unload. I'm going down to see. Enjoy your morning in court."

Margaret saw Leonard coming up the path to the cliff from the ship below. She strolled over to bid him a good morning. The creases above his brooding eyes and his set jaw told her his mind overflowed with problems.

"Kind sir, what troubles you this breezy, cool morning?"

On seeing her, Leonard's smile spread wide. He took her hand and kissed it, then tucked his arm over hers.

"Walk with me to Pope's manor."

She sighed. "You never change. I heard about a disturbance at Pope's ordinary last night. Do you know of this?"

"Captain Ingle's doing. He accosted Commander Yeardley of Northhampton County and his brother, Francis, when Ingle's ship docked at Accomac yesterday evening. I presume Ingle had invited a group of these Virginians on board and entertained the more important visitors in his cabin." Leonard chuckled. "According to Ingle, Francis Yeardley called Parliament a bunch of roundheads. You can imagine how that incensed Ingle."

"Captain Ingle would never let such remarks pass."

"He called the Yeardleys rattleheads, so Commander Yeardley arrested Ingle in the name of the king. Ingle drew his cutlass, yelling something about king and Parliament, and held it at Yeardley's chest, ordering all Virginians ashore. All went, including the Yeardleys, except for some forgotten twenty to thirty Virginians partying below deck who sailed here because they hadn't heard the order. They entertained the ordinary with tales of their kidnapping over ale last night."

"Leonard, it bothers me greatly that a ship named *Reformation* carries our goods to and fro and the captain of the ship openly announces he has no tolerance for our king. He frequently sails from Gravesend, where we both know Parliament instigates much turmoil against King Charles."

"Look at his ship. Thirty crew, twelve cannon, and the means to not let pirates make off with our hard work. His reputation stands for exacting the best prices." Leonard held her hand and looked into her eyes. "Margaret, I care for neither his politics nor religion, nor he mine. Yet we have no better way to enjoy the convenience of trading and transporting our tobacco and wares. He's a consistent and competent trader."

"I do not consider him competent and do not trust him one whit. He has treated Giles, Mary, and me rather poorly."

"We can't depend on the Dutch. You know how they are."

"All I know about the Dutch is they sell arms to the natives." She withdrew her arm from his. "I am curious, my good governor, when I found you this morning, you seemed distraught."

Leonard studied his boots, then turned his gaze on Margaret. "I expected an important letter to come on this passage—from your sister, Ann." He held up his packet of letters. "Lately, she writes me not."

Chapter 51

...And this Assembly on behalf of the inhabitants do pledge the faith of the colony for a continuance of a free and peaceable trade....
- The House of Burgess, St. Mary's City

WEEKS LATER, WITH A hint of spring buds appearing on the trees, Margaret strode out to attend court. This time she would face Captain Ingle for an unpaid bill he owed her for an exchange made in London over a year ago.

She arrived promptly at the opening of the doors and found a place to sit near one of the back tables. She watched the men file in and greet each other. As usual, Leonard stood at his place in front preparing for the morning, his eyes intent on whatever lay before him. John Lewger sat at the desk beside Calvert with ledgers, ink, and quills.

She hoped her case against Ingle wouldn't be called until late because, if she stayed, she might learn precious information. A familiar voice surprised her. Giles entered, cheerful and talking with another man she did not know.

After being arrested and fined for the failed military march on the Susquehannock, she never expected him to be at court again, unless someone filed a complaint or debt against him.

Captain Ingle swaggered in, removed his hat, and looked around.

Please, Dear Lord, let him find a place far away from me.

He grinned, marched over to Margaret's table, and sat down next to her.

"Good morning, Lady Brent. We have an interesting time before us. Regardless, I wish you a pleasant year with abundant crops of which you will commission me to transport to England."

Margaret smiled at the rogue. "Interesting, indeed, Captain Ingle. I wish for the calming of tumultuous waves in stormy seas reserved for sailors of integrity."

The seaman squinted at Margaret a moment before shooting her a toothy grin. Then he stood to hail a scrawny man unknown to Margaret. The man scurried over, as if beholden to this scoundrel. They cheerfully greeted each other.

Ingle grinned. "Tell, did Lemmon make my apology to Yeardley? I am quite disposed to submit whatever I can to right any offense I may have caused."

"Captain Ingle, those Virginians you kidnapped haven't stopped talking about their night on your ship." He guffawed. "I am quite sure a man such as Richard would do whatever you bid."

Margaret shivered. This man Ingle played the world. Ready to plunge his cutlass into a man who defended the king, he then offers who knows what kindness to right the wrong. Her mother once said not to ignore twinges of emotional reactions to others. She had preached to her daughters their ears, head, and heart knew less than deep internal senses. Margaret knew well the truth of their mother's words.

Lord Governor rapped his knuckles on the table and called the meeting to order. When all had quieted in their places, he read an announcement proclaiming additions to his council. As lieutenant governor, he often had as few as three but today he listed six.

He named Giles in the fourth position on his council, leaving Margaret aghast. After having Giles arrested, he now declared him a member of his council—not high up on the list, but still valued. Captain Cornwallis also received appointment to the council, though he had refused to take the oath of loyalty and had not served since last September. A new man, James Neale, made this coveted list. Next, Leonard announced since no action had been taken on Lord Baltimore's January offer to fund a military attack on the Susquehannock, this offer had been withdrawn.

She found such action baffling. The raids and murders continued to increase up and down the Chesapeake and Patuxent River.

Others must have felt the same as this caused some murmurs within the group. Captain Cornwallis had waited too long. Perhaps, like Giles, the captain couldn't raise enough volunteers to fight. Margaret shuddered. One day only fools will laugh at Sisters Freehold building their St. Thomas's Fort.

Chapter 52
April 11, 1643

History, like love, is so apt to surround her heroes with an atmosphere of brightness.
- James Fenimore Cooper

AT THIS MORNING'S COURT, Margaret argued against the issue Ingle had presented two weeks earlier. His bill due to her, a total of 20 pounds of silver, involved her dealings with George Ludlow of Virginia and Ingle's inept trading with a London merchant. The governor requested his own attorney to obtain depositions before he ruled.

What most interested Margaret came from watching the governor's sense of urgency. He quickly asked Lewger questions, then shuffled through his own notes. As if he needed this business all behind him. Though his movements seemed in haste, his facial expression sustained good cheer by an unrestrained smile glued fast on his lips.

When all had finished presenting their business in front of the court, the governor asked Nathaniel Pope to rise.

"Here ye all. This problem with the Susquehannock and with the other tribes they have incited against the English will not diminish unless we take action. You each must be diligent in your servants mustering and marching. I, your Lieutenant General of Maryland, in the name and for the sake of Maryland, exempt Nathaniel Pope and his nine servants from attending any muster or march, as he shall keep watch over Pope's house to guard our records and house of meeting."

Men clapped and muttered words of cheer, but some shook their heads and grumbled. Margaret saw this house quite divided and wondered the consequences.

Leonard Calvert raised his hand for silence. When he had regained everyone's attention, he said, "Before we adjourn, know that in the next few days I shall sail to England. With the turmoil there and the unsettled nature of our land here, a personal consultation with Lord Baltimore seems necessary. We both shall return in the fall when we can better discuss the troubles of our beloved England and may have some answers for difficulties we face here."

No one spoke. They, just as she, worried for their English families' wellbeing.

"Gentleman Giles Brent, please rise." Calvert waited until the voices quieted and Giles stood waiting. "In my absence, I appoint you the Lieutenant General of the Province of Maryland. You shall act as governor until my return."

This announcement brought an eruption of jovial remarks and discussion.

'Tis clear I have no understanding of the rules these men use for their dangerous games.

Leonard adjourned the session, but requested Giles stay behind and discuss some matters with Lewger and him. Leonard also signaled to Margaret to come forward and join them, then Leonard turned back and conferred with Lewger.

Giles smiled broadly at his sister. A lock of dark hair fell forward, and he brushed it aside, holding out his hands to take hers. His eyes sparkled with delight.

"Congratulations, brother mine." She grinned. "I wish Mary had come with me today for this occasion. Father would be proud of you."

"I hadn't expected this." He lowered his voice so only she could hear. "After all, I was only fourth on his list of councilors."

Leonard straightened and Lewger stood. "Giles, I'm confident you will be wise in handling this responsibility. However, you are not to call Assembly, grant any lands, or interfere in the ongoing dispute between Lord Baltimore and the Jesuits. Lord Baltimore will send you written instructions on these matters in a couple of months. I probably won't be returning until the fall. In the meantime, you have the marauding Indian situation to resolve. Be as creative as you must in finding a solution for this difficult problem."

"I will endeavor to be your diligent servant, Governor, and not cause you or your brother disappointments."

"As far as the Jesuit problem, Giles," Leonard said, "my brother's solution appears to be near. We cannot have others seeing Maryland partial to or owned by Catholic priests. The extensive land the Jesuits now control has caused resentment among the Protestants."

"Leonard," Margaret said, "a few months ago you had Giles arrested, confined to his home, and standing trial. Now you have bestowed the highest honor of the land on his shoulders. Forgive me for being suspect, but there is much more to this than you have told."

No pasted grin this time, but a genuine smile of joy covered his face. "The letter I didn't receive weeks ago, it was on the ship just arrived—weeks late. Your sister Ann has agreed to marry me. I'm off to England to be wed."

"Giles, we have a new brother!"

Giles, mouth open and with eyes wide, glared at Calvert.

He smacked his fist into his palm and with teeth gritted, growled, "The bloody hell—"

Chapter 53

We cannot all do great things, but we can do small things with great love.
- St. Mother Teresa of Calcutta

HER BROTHER STRODE AWAY from Calvert, her, the meeting house, and on down the road toward his home. Margaret dashed after him.

"Your rude behavior puzzles me."

He ignored her.

She walked alongside him in his silence. Thomas Greene strode past on his way home. He nodded a good day to them.

Giles would not even give him a glance.

"I do not understand this anger. Our governor bestowed a great honor on you, and you curse him."

Giles said nothing.

She glanced down at the dock full of shoppers, buying merchandise from the English shipping merchant.

"I shall go with you to your home."

Giles didn't slow his pace but curled his hands into fists at his side.

"Enough, little brother. Tell me what makes you thus?"

He spat. "Fulke runs back to England to marry. Calvert absconds with our sister so he can have a wife. What am I left with? A murderous country where I find my business divided between Kent Island, playing at Governor, and killing marauding Indians. I'm doomed to live a single life, but you would not care about that."

The silence now belonged to Margaret. She strode along beside him.

Finally, he said, "You usually nag me. Tell me what to do. Most of the time you scold me like a naughty child. Your silence unsettles me."

She laughed. She didn't expect to... it just slipped out. "I had no idea you found me so predictable."

He grumbled something.

"Giles, in your current mood you will make this a long, long summer. You have much to do and think, being our governor. Keep your mind on the tasks ahead."

He stopped and squinted at her, then said, "I am, and I have been inventing plans. Cornwallis will take every third man in the province, and each community will donate supplies, and the men will march on the Susquehannock."

"Dear brother. If your plan to attack the natives doesn't work, we will all be slaughtered."

"Here's another thought. We could create a garrison on Palmer Island—that might work. We place cannons there, with the sharpest shooters, and supplies to last a year."

She looked back at the docked ship and wondered if Mary had boarded the ship. Margaret had so much to tell her. Even though Leonard had forbidden his substitute governor from calling Assembly, granting lands, and interfering with Lord Baltimore and the priests, he had bestowed a great honor on Giles.

"Tell me of this dispute between Lord Baltimore and our priests."

Giles huffed. "Nothing new. The priests have acquired abundant land from the Indians. Lord Baltimore expected the priests who came over to become land-holders like gentlemen using the headright system. Yet the Jesuits operate as a sect. Mattapany and all the Chapel Land is Jesuit land. According to English law, Jesuit land belongs to the Pope, even our chapel."

Margaret smirked. "Lord Baltimore tries hard to keep Catholics from being Catholic."

"For a good reason, dear sister. This country has ten times more Protestants than Catholics. Many of our indentured servants have obtained freeman status. Your Protestant servants and merchants may smile and say kind things to you. But beware. That skirmish between Ingle and the kidnapped Royalist Virginians reflects the plight of England's civil war. Parliament no longer tolerates King Charles allowing the Church of England to keep rituals that mimic the Catholic Church. And yet the Pope owns a goodly part of our lands."

"Leonard and his brother will find a solution." Margaret said, "The Pope might agree to release the land and chapel back to Lord Baltimore if someone buys it."

"Land, land, land." Giles threw his hands in the air. "Everyone wants the larg-est piece of dirt they can grab. Eternal damnation. You can have your land, the priests can have theirs, but unlike my virgin sisters and chaste priests, I care not a whit about land. I want a wife."

"Senses, Giles. You would do well to apologize and congratulate Leonard. Your situation isn't his fault. And you are now governor of his province."

* * *

As Margaret approached her home, Thomas Greene, running toward her, shouted, "Lady Brent—Lady Brent!"

She could see terror on his face.

"Thomas, what—?" She dashed to meet him.

"My wife, Ann—oh, dear God. Please come."

The quarter mile distance flew past as she kept pace with Thomas. When they reached the sheds, Margaret could see and smell foul air filled with smoke. Ann Greene's maids clustered around something on the ground between the house and the outdoor kitchen. They had been in the soap making process. Melted fat, now burning, had splashed in the dirt from a heavy kettle. Beside the fire, smoldering stirrers lay. Margaret slowed, unsure of what she was to find.

One of the maids looked up, tears streaked her face. She moved aside for Thomas and Margaret. The other maids did the same.

Sprawled on the wet, ash-covered ground—a person—unrecognizable—filled Margaret with horror. Unconscious, yet Ann's face covered with wet, wild locks of hair held the distorted look of disbelief. Her dirt-covered, charred gown and petticoats melded into the grotesque leathery, red, and scorched skin of her hands, arms, and legs.

Without warning, Margaret's stomach lurched, flooding her throat and mouth with bile.

God, grant me strength—I know not what to do.

"Ann, Ann, my dear Ann." Thomas fell to the ground and cradled his wife's head in his arms. His shoulders shook from his sobs.

Sweat dripped from Margaret, though frost coated her insides, causing shivers. She must not vomit.

"You." Margaret pointed to a maid, "Run to my home and fetch my sister. Tell her what has happened. Thomas, tend to your boys. They must not see their mother like this."

He ignored her. God had mercifully let Ann's mind escape the torture of her burning, but Thomas would receive no such kindness. Margaret had to get him away.

The maids muttered explanations about Ann's petticoat lace catching on fire, a stirring stick caught in the tangle and burning grease splashing. One of the maids shuttled the boys into the house as someone threw water, which scattered the flames. Others more wise tossed dirt, covering and smothering the fire.

Margaret looked around and pointed to one of the men servants. "Saddle two horses. Ride with your master to fetch Father White or Father Fisher. Hurry now. Pull him away and take him with you."

Life, precious and fragile—as wisps of smoke, carrying away all we are meant to be.

Leaning near to her friend's face, Margaret whispered, "Sweet Lady Ann, Mary and I will watch over your dear boys and care for your family. You shall go to rest now."

Everything inside Margaret floated and churned unsettled like a river in the storm while the silent noise inside her head howled in anguish. She would keep talking to her friend until the priest arrived. She had nothing else to give but this simple gesture.

"In my heart you hear me, so I will pray with you until Father White comes and prepares you for your eternal journey."

Chapter 54
Late Summer 1643

To have a right to do a thing is not at all the same as to be right in doing it.
- G. K. Chesterton

THE TRAGEDY OF ANN Greene's death weighed on Margaret throughout the summer. Combined with Giles's anger over Leonard sailing off to marry their little sister and worry about the increased raids up and down the Patuxent River country, the hot, muggy months gave little cheer.

Margaret and Mary caught themselves in fretting over the safety of young Mary because of news that the Piscataway's enemy, the Susquehannock, prowled near their tribe's village.

Good news came early fall. The widow Winifred Seyborn agreed to marry Thomas Greene. Everyone rejoiced, except for Giles. Goodwin watched him climb into his pinnace. With his jaw set, Giles sailed away. No one knew where he went or when he would return.

* * *

"Margaret, Mary!" Giles's voice called. "Come greet my new bride!" A loud rap sounded on their oak door. Mary hastened to open it.

Giles, with a silly grin and his arm around young Mary Kittamaquund, said, "Meet your new sister-in-law, Empress of the Piscataway tribes."

Air flew away, leaving Margaret dizzy and her mouth agape.

This must not be.

"Won't you welcome the newlyweds into your home?" Giles guided young Mary through the doorway. "After sailing all the way from Piscataway, certainly you would offer ale or cider." Giles, looking quite giddy, touched young Mary's cheek.

Young Mary, her shoulder leaning into Giles, blushed and searched her auntie's faces.

"Giles—your actions have preceded your judgment." The young girl watched Margaret. She must not cause the child concern. Any reprimand necessitated careful consideration. Yet, this could not be justified to Leonard.

Mary seemed confused over her own emotions. She guided the couple to the dining room then back to the living room. Margaret followed, muttered something, and called sharply to Missus Brookes.

Giles just grinned.

Margaret glared, placed her hands on her hips and, controlling her voice, said, "You cannot be married. Our Governor forbids any priests to go to Piscataway. I

207

know you. You would not think to marry on Kent Island or anywhere else where there are no friends. You would never marry without your family."

Missus Brookes interrupted with cider and motioned them into the dining room. Before she left, she smiled at young Mary. The girl blushed, frantically looking from Mary to Margaret. Mary indicated they all should sit.

"We have missed you, Mary." Margaret took a deep breath. "I am curious as to how your tribe is and about you and Giles."

"Auntie Margaret, since my father died, my husband tied our arrangement with advisor John, who be Mosorcorques before Father White baptized him. John treated Giles Brent. He gave him pork and bacon, tobacco, and a length of white shells—our finest roanoke—to seal our marriage. Since my husband's home not be there in Piscataway Village, Captain Giles Brent used John's house as his. All our family and friends came, bring food, and gifts as is the Piscataway tradition."

"We did marry with family." Giles pulled out the string of white shells and handed the roanoke to Mary.

"Husband Giles sat at the head of the house. The women take me to sit by him. Everyone sits and waits. Women get up and serve food. I serve my new husband first. After we eat everyone sings and dances until night. Then everyone leave my husband and myself and go to their homes. This our manner of Piscataway marriage."

"I see." Mary eyed Giles. "What will you say to our governor about the great gifts your new wife and the Piscataway Tribe bestowed on you?"

"Gifts? Some woven mats, two carved wooden bowls, and a bearskin cloak seem little to discuss." Giles scrunched up his face and glanced back and forth between his two sisters.

"What Mary wants to know, as I do, is how much land did you receive from the tribe by marrying their Empress?"

He slapped the table, startling young Mary. "You two always look for something untoward. I get no land. I do not want their land. I could not have their land no matter who I married. Mary has no brothers, so she and her sisters have created, according to their tradition, a matriarchal society. In this society the women share advice—even about war. The women plant and care for the land, and these women own the land. Any land Mary had would have passed down to her sisters. This topic is indisputable now, anyway. Since Mary will be living with me, the tribe has appointed Wahocasso as their new Tayac. She'll be carrying on their matriarchal lineage."

We have behaved shamefully. The newlyweds came to share their happiness, yet we scold them.

Young Mary gazed downward and waited. The room held silence. Margaret stood and stepped over to the new bride and put her hands on Mary's shoulders.

"Empress Mary, welcome into our family. I can tell by how Giles looks at you he loves you deeply. If I remember correctly, Father White married your mother and father in a Christian ceremony even though your parents had been previously joined in your traditional ways. Your union with Giles should also be sanctified by Father White."

Marriage ceremonies in St. Mary's City, even though few, had become quiet affairs as Lord Baltimore limited the involvement of the clergy. Several years earlier these matters had become the task of the provincial secretary. Lewger, as secretary, now issued and recorded marriage licenses, estates probations, and wills. Even deciding issues of immorality had been taken from the church.

Evidently, Lord Baltimore had faced increased animosity from those in England who believed Catholics ruled Maryland.

The Empress gazed into Giles's eyes and said, "I would like that. Would it please you?"

Margaret sighed. "We have a problem because our proprietor has taken marriage from the hands of the church. We shall ask Father White how your marriage might still receive God's blessings."

* * *

Two days later, Lady Mary gathered late summer wildflowers and greenery to weave a wreath to adorn the young bride's ebony hair. Margaret helped the girl finish sewing her new doe-skin smock. The elegant young woman had grown even taller.

The previous day Father White had sent Giles and Mary to John Lewger's home to obtain a marriage license. John Lewger had been hostile at first, but then he settled down and congratulated them. Father White could perform a blessing ceremony, but the real marriage happened when John Lewger recorded it in his ledger.

"Auntie Margaret, you be unhappy I marry your handsome brother." Sitting cross-legged on the floor, Empress Mary selected another cockle shell to sew on the hem of her dress.

"We adore you." Margaret sorted red and yellow beads for the neckline of the dress. We hope you will be happy being married."

"Husband makes me laugh. We hunt and fish together. He be kind. How you say—*sweet*— to me. I hope we have many children."

Giles, as acting governor, marrying a Piscataway Empress in their chapel brought everyone out. Father White officiated, while Father Fisher and two new priests stood near, looking pious in their vestments. Margaret knew if Leonard had been there, he would have bellowed like a bull, first over the marriage, and next about the priests being overly public with the Catholic ceremony in their vestments.

The gathering of townspeople would not fit inside the small chapel. With doors and windows open, many stood outside around the nearby trees. Margaret took note that Protestants, rather than be inside with the priests, had been the ones who stood outside and watched.

Stowre and some of the men and maids from Sisters Freehold went to Giles's large white manor and laid an outdoor table full of food and decorated it with wildflowers and forest greens for the newlyweds and their well-wishers. Late in the afternoon, guests stood on the bluff above Giles' dock ready to cheer him and young Mary when they sailed for Kent Island.

Before they stepped onto his pinnace, Margaret stopped the couple and said, "Giles, if Kent becomes dangerous, you must bring Mary to live with us."

"Dear sister, I am capable of protecting my new wife. Besides, my home is a fort."

"However, brother," Mary said, "This has been a horrid summer for Indian raids. How many villages and plantations have been burned along the Patuxent and the Chesapeake? How many men did Cornwallis lose during his raid up the river from the fort you had built on Palmer Island?"

The young Empress's glances darted from Giles to Mary and back. Arguing did little to help this occasion.

Fort Conquest—a misnomer if I ever heard one.

However, Margaret would not mock his attempts. Even when impulsive, he did his best.

"Whenever you come to St. Mary's, you must bring Mary with you." Margaret's throat closed, making it difficult to talk.

Young Mary grinned up at Giles.

Mary said, "Your wife still has much to teach me about the herbs and mushrooms in the forest."

"Ridiculous." He smiled. "You know more about the woods than the rest of us. Yet, I shall bring my bride whenever I come."

He took young Mary's hand, waved to the crowd on the banks, and helped the Empress into his pinnace. To the cheers above, they sailed away from the dock, and off down the river.

Margaret's frogs sat uncomfortably up in her throat. She caught sight of Mary dabbing at the corner of her eye. Feeling miserable, she slipped her arm around her sister's shoulder and watched until the pinnace sailed from view.

"Oh, Margaret. I mourn to see her leave. A young bride should have other women around."

Margaret murmured, "No place on Earth could be as awful for her as Kent Island."

Chapter 55
Winter 1643

...To declare War, grant Letters of Marque and Reprisal, and make Rules concerning Captures on Land and Water....
- Constitution of the United States of America. Article II, section 8.

IN NOVEMBER THE BRENTS strode down to greet a Dutch ship at the dock. Tales of pirate deeds from privateers, often sanctioned by a King or Parliament needing monetary support, had spread quickly among the colonies. Margaret wondered if this possibly caused the *Reformation* to sail in other waters.

The small Dutch vessel didn't usually trade with Maryland because of the *Reformation's* diligence as a consistent merchant of Maryland's goods. She hoped this ship had come by way of England, bringing passengers and news.

Lord Baltimore and Leonard Calvert had sent word months ago they would arrive in Maryland this fall. What a joy for her and Mary to be united with their younger sister. Yet, when all had disembarked from the vessel, Cecil Calvert, Leonard, and Ann had not. Ten pounds of stone slid into her heart.

The sisters, with Giles and young Mary, walked to the ordinary. They could visit awhile before Giles's meeting. Then the sisters would take young Mary home with them.

"I am pleased we will have some time together." Margaret, relieved to see young Mary happy, was still unsettled about Ann and Leonard not arriving.

"Lord Baltimore has never set foot on Maryland soil." Giles signaled for four ales. "I suspect he has to be disappointed. Do you care for something to eat?"

Young Mary shook her head. "Some foods—fish and clams—do not agree with me, Auntie Margaret. I do not know why."

She has gained weight. Maybe Giles will be a father.

Giles continued. "The civil war must be the cause for Cecil's absence. The communication I've received from him dates back to July."

"Good morning, Governor Brent." One of Pope's men nodded and set four tankards of ale in the middle of their table. Every seat at the ordinary had filled. Men visited amicably over food and drink before convening in the large meeting hall.

"Regards to your master, Biggs." Giles distributed the tankers. "I hope to see him later at our meeting."

Young Mary touched her husband's sleeve. "Kind husband, this great man, Lord Cecil Baltimore Calvert, who sent you to our country has not first come to

211

study the land and water and its food? Of this strangeness I do not understand."

Mary smiled at the young woman. "Your tayac would study all before your tribe could settle in a place. The expanse of the ocean sets England far from Maryland, and now with his attentions on a civil war it may not be possible for him to come."

"Lord Baltimore's letters cause me to worry," Giles said. "His communications no longer tell his location. In the past, they've always stated, *Given under my hand and seal* at wherever he was, and then *in the Realm of England*, and then the date."

"He must be hiding." Margaret's worry extended to her father, Ann, and siblings. "The war has caused delays in shipping and our communications."

"'Tis a sickly mess." Giles glanced at one of his letters, saying, "Englishmen fighting in Ireland signed a ceasefire, raised arms there to support the king, and left the Irish to enjoy whatever they had plundered. This strengthening of their army has frightened Parliament rebels. They secured the service of Scotland's powerful army. Doesn't bode well for King Charles."

Young Mary touched her husband's arm. "You talk about fighting across the ocean. Why we worry about far away when we have dangerous raids near our lands?"

Taking her hand and kissing her fingertips, Giles grinned. "You bring me comfort in all you say and do. Yet the war in England has become our problem. When people in England battle each other, the English here may engage in similar acts, being loyal to the conflict."

Glancing around at others in the ordinary, Mary leaned in close and said, "I suspect because of being Catholic, our governor, his brother, and Ann could not find a safe passage. Giles, with your communications being months old, their ship might have to sail who knows where before it arrives here. The ability to move freely in England must be impossible."

"The Susquehannock terrorize everyone." Young Mary's chin quivered. "We need many brave men to make them stop the war with us. I worry about my people."

"We do have similar worries here as in England," Margaret said. "The Susquehannock mostly raid in the spring and summer. Do they now attack Kent Island this time of year?"

"Not in cold months. They sailed up and down burning, killing, and stealing until a few months ago. Unfortunately," Giles lowered his voice, "we have other eastern shore Indians tribes joining in these raids. I have appointed James Neal to hire a small group of men to help him patrol the Patuxent River. Also, Captain Cornwallis will tax colonies for men and supplies and lead an offense against the Susquehannock this spring."

Mary shrugged. "Cornwallis again, you say. He's failed twice with some of his men killed. What would be different this time?"

"He's the most experienced."

Nudging her empty tankard away, Margaret said, "My men tell me interesting stories about some of the London ships sailing the Chesapeake. Any ship, trading in a port hostile to Parliament, may be seized by another if holding a Letter of

Marque. I suspect the king holds the same true for ships trading in ports hostile to him."

Her sister sat straighter. "If so, we are in serious trouble with securing our needed supplies. We may have no trading because the English Civil War no longer stays in England."

Chapter 56
Early March 1644

Wherever women gather together, failure is impossible.
- Susan B. Anthony

THE THREE BRENT WOMEN with Winifred Greene, carrying bundles of rag strips, knocked on Ann Lewger's door. Her man welcomed them and escorted the ladies into the parlor where two fireplaces roared with freshly set fires.

"Winifred, Margaret, Mary, and our precious Empress, I barely slept last night with anticipation. Let my maid take your cloaks. The room will warm shortly. Oh goodness—" Ann Lewger stopped and grinned at young Mary. "Your rounded form tells me we have much to celebrate."

"Thank you, Lady Lewger. I have something akin to ague, though my aunties assure me I do not. Celebrations do not enter my thoughts this morning."

Lady Greene said, "You have nothing to worry about, young one. The sickness comes to most of us who carry a baby within."

"I wanted to eat all the time," Lady Lewger said, "but then I couldn't keep anything down. After a while you'll feel better. Come sit by me. Have you ever made a bed rug before?"

"Most of our rags," Mary said, "come from this young woman's petticoats and gowns. She grew out of them faster than we could assemble them."

Margaret mumbled, "We kept adding ruffles to the hems, but pretty soon it all looked ridiculous. Our young Mary has grown into a lovely woman."

The women piled the cloth strips onto the tabletop and started sorting. Lady Lewger said, "My John identified a widow with two daughters. Their home has little heat."

"Then our assignment," Winifred pulled out four lengths of different colored cloth, and said, "this day is to make three bed rugs to cover their cots."

"I took a stew to John Morton last week." Margaret selected her colors. "The wind howled through walls even after he chinked the cracks with mud. His home sits poorly—quite exposed. Little John appears puny."

Already braiding strands, Mary said, "That child has not done well since the death of his mother and the infant."

Young Mary studied what the other women did with the strips of cloth, then she selected four. When her nimble fingers surpassed them all in length of braided cloth and she reached the end, she stopped. Margaret showed her how to tie in more strips.

Lady Greene's hands worked deftly "What happened with the latest Ingle trouble? Thomas said the court called it *ignoramus*."

214

"I do not know this word, aunties."

Margaret continued braiding. "It means *unknown to us* or *overlooked*. Both could apply in Ingle's situation. The court, at least four times, decided *ignoramus* for Ingles, and for Cornwallis, Neal, Packer, and another in aiding Ingle. I suspect they did not want any disruption of Ingle's trading their tobacco with England."

"That William Hardige." Mary scowled. "He causes trouble wherever he goes. Ingle seemed to have been his friend before the Virginia kidnapping incident. Yet now Hardige has turned against Ingle. He well knows Giles, Margaret, and I have unsettled financial dealings with Ingle. He probably hoped our ill feelings would encourage Giles to retaliate."

"Ann," Margaret said, "How does your John regard the sheriff? Sheriff Edward Packer seems to have a disloyal side to him."

Ann sighed. "I don't know but I wish Giles had left Robert Ellyson as sheriff."

"I also question," Margaret said, "the loyalty of Captain Cornwallis. Yet Captain Cornwallis did compel Hardige to go back to northern Virginia."

Winifred selected more strips of cloth. "Thomas tells me little. He says there's no need to put worry in my head about the doings of the men. Of course, that incites my curiosity."

Winifred watched for a response.

Smiling, Margaret said, "Remember last year when Ingle brought a group of Virginians to Maryland by mistake? Kidnapped, they said. Hardige said Ingle had called out against the king. Giles told Hardige this happened in Virginia, so Maryland had no business with it. Hardige insisted Ingle be arrested for treason because Ingle said he was Captain of Gravesend for Parliament, had a Letter of Marque, and he could capture ships sailing for the king. Hardige said Ingle told someone on Kent Island King Charles is no king."

Winifred, mouth agape, shuddered. "Treasonous words. Ingle could lose his head and his ship."

Lady Lewger spoke up. "My John agrees. Why no one has arrested this man before now—"

"Captain Yardley and his brother tried, as did Giles." Margaret untied a knot and retied it. She glanced at young Mary. Pale and sitting still, she had placed her work in her lap and folded her hands over it.

Poor child. This baby within has greatly upset her humors.

Smirking, Mary said, "The *Reformation* is our only dependable lifeline to England, and Maryland is the *Reformation's* only dependable income. The posturing and fisticuffs shall continue."

"Actually fighting?" Winifred stopped braiding. "I want to hear the whole story about this court your brother held at your home."

"The incident began when Giles and Captain Cornwallis boarded the *Reformation* one morning. They could not arrest Ingle on board because that ship is heavily armed and guarded. So, Giles invited Ingle to dinner. Later that morning Ingle went ashore with some of his men, and Giles handed him a warrant because of his Kent Island treasonous words against the king. Secretary Lewger had signed the warrant as advisor to this act." She nodded at Ann. "The governor then had Captain Cornwallis and Hardige arrest Ingle and turn him over to our sheriff."

Winifred held up her hand to stop Margaret. "Wait, I'm confused. Captain Cornwallis and Ingle are close friends. The captain sails to England often on the *Reformation*."

"He does," Margaret said. "This makes everything quite complicated, but Giles puts no trust in Sheriff Packer. He told the two men to keep the arrest a secret and return to meet him at the ship later." Margaret glanced over and said, "Young Mary, I am concerned. Your cheeks have no color."

"Perhaps if I had something to drink."

Ann Lewger summoned a maid to bring them all cider and goat milk for young Mary.

Continuing, Margaret said, "I cannot remember all the events, but some Marylanders boarded the ship to trade. Most of the crew had gone on land. When the Marylanders learned Ingle had been arrested, they captured the remaining crew. The ship had been taken."

Tying off a knot, Mary said, "This is the night Giles held court at our home. Everyone talked at once, men accused each other of falsehoods, but eventually everything settled."

"Earlier, our brother," Margaret added, "had offered some of the crew double their pay to sail the ship with her goods to Bristol for the king, not Parliament. He tacked a notice to the mainstay stating Captain Ingle's treasonous acts. At the meeting that night, James Neale told Giles he would keep the prisoner. Giles refused, probably because of Neale being a Protestant and friend of Ingle. Captain Cornwallis volunteered to take Ingle, and Giles agreed. Cornwallis took Ingle back to his ship and told the guards to return all the weapons to the crew and go to their rest."

Young Mary had taken only a tiny sip of milk. Her brow furrowed and her face appeared to be somewhat grayish.

"I am worried about you." Margaret stood and moved around the table.

Rising, Ann Lewger felt the girl's forehead. She said, "She doesn't have a fever. You might feel better if you lie down." Ann led her from the room.

When Ann returned, she said, "We'll look in on her in a while. Please continue, Margaret."

"Maybe we should take her home," Mary said. "But then, maybe she shouldn't travel."

"Let her rest in bed," Ann Lewger said. "We'll keep a watchful eye on her. Go on, Margaret. I've only been privy to so little of this story."

"This is where it all becomes a mess. Captain Cornwallis stayed in the ship's Great Cabin with Ingle. Most of the Maryland guards climbed below to go to their rest. The *Reformation*'s crew returned from shore and seemed friendly, until they confronted the remaining guards with violence. They tied and nailed the hatch secure to keep them below. When the ship had been completely retaken, the Marylanders were put off, and Ingle had his ship back with a hostage, Captain Cornwallis."

Scoffing, Winifred said, "Cornwallis could be no hostage because his and Ingle's friendship goes back years. What trick is this?"

"What happened afterwards—" Lady Lewger said, "I cannot understand a whit of it."

"Confusing, indeed." Margaret looked around at the women. "Ann, your husband, John, acting as His Lordship's Attorney, filed charges again against these same men. This last hearing, held at St. Inigoes manor, extracted a fine against Captain Cornwallis for a thousand pounds of tobacco and Ingle for four hundred pounds of lead shot and a barrel of gunpowder."

"Well, that seems appropriate compensation for the troubles they caused." Ann said.

"Then Captain Cornwallis bonded Ingle's fine with four hundred pounds of tobacco," Margaret said. "Cornwallis promised Ingle would deliver the gunpowder and shot, or the court could keep Cornwallis's four hundred pounds."

Ann shook her head. "Is this when my husband issued a certificate to Ingle, giving him a year of calm passage for his trading in Maryland?"

Margaret sighed. "With all of God's goodness, I do not understand these men. They play at life like little boys with toys. This is when my brother, the court, and by your husband Lewger's hand decided they would give Ingle a certificate granting him free and unmolested trade in Maryland. Next, I learn Giles has also loaned his pinnace to Ingle, as well as giving him an island near Kent Island."

"What fiddle faddle." Lady Greene said, "Thomas has not been the least pleased about Ingle's Island. He believes we Catholics have been quite mistreated and too many give obeisance to any Protestant who whines."

Margaret nodded as she set aside her work and said, "Mary, come with me. We should look in on young Mary."

Chapter 57
March 1644

Naked I came from my mother's womb, and naked I will depart. The Lord gave and the Lord has taken away; may the name of the Lord be praised.
- Job 1:21

THE MORNING'S COURT PROCEEDINGS exhausted Margaret. On her walk home, she planned to clear her mind, but instead she replayed their effort to protect what remained of Leonard Calvert's estate from Captain Cornwallis.

A few days earlier Captain Cornwallis had threatened to bring suit against Lord Baltimore. Cecil Calvert refused to pay Cornwallis in honor of their agreement when Cornwallis purchased the priests' lands in St. Mary's, including the church and its land. Taking funds to pay this suit would seriously diminish the Calvert estates.

Much fuss and many arguments later, Lewger, Giles, and Margaret consulted privately.

Lewger made an inventory of the Baltimore and Calvert estate. For years Margaret had watched over the Baltimore cattle. Since Leonard had sold his newly constructed house to Nathaniel Pope, the Calvert estate mostly comprised of tobacco, acres and acres of land, cattle, and Leonard's original home.

Early on, Leonard had agreed to pay Mary and Margaret for their guardianship of the Piscataway Empress. As of yet he had not paid them, and it would come to a robust sum. His delay created an opportunity for Margaret and Mary to lock up those funds, preventing Cornwallis's suit from being paid.

Margaret filed suit to attach 7,000 pounds of Leonard Calvert's tobacco until Leonard Calvert returned to answer her suit, pertaining to the guardianship of Mary Kittamaquund. Also, she demanded the price of four cows and four young cattle and three calves due to the said orphan, as much of young Mary's estate remained in Governor Calvert's hands because of his guardianship. Now there would be little left for Cornwallis to take. All this finagling and plotting drained Margaret's spirit.

If the laws they created protected people and property, then should not these matters be simple?

The doorway to her home in St Thomas's Fort brought a hint of memory from Margaret's childhood. When she placed her fingers on the door handle a warmth of expectation for comfort and love filled her. Once inside she would see and smell the goodness of her life.

Quiet—empty. Cold. She hung her cloak on the peg by the door and called out to both Marys.

Missus Taylor rushed into the room—lines twitched around the corner of her mouth.

"Young Mary has left—your sister is in her room." The maid clutched and unclutched her hands. "Thanks be given you are home."

Everything within trembled with confusion. Margaret's ears filled with mewing sounds of her own fear as she rushed to Mary's room. She rapped once on the door and opened it. Mary sat, dabbing her eyes with a piece of linen. Her face, blotchy from crying, told what Margaret feared. Young Mary no longer carried the unborn infant.

The night before had passed slowly. Both Mary and Margaret took turns sitting with young Mary through her pains. When dawn came, her fitful dozes lengthened into a restful slumber. The sisters prayed this meant the unborn child and mother had experienced the worst. Margaret had talked with Giles at the ordinary before court and assured him that perhaps now all would be well.

"Where is she? Where did she go?" Margaret's insides went in every direction. She willed the leaping frogs to still.

Her sister shook her head.

"You must know." Margaret called out, "Missus Taylor!"

The maid scurried into the room.

"Tell me where young Mary went. How could you let her out of the house in that condition?"

Missus Taylor looked down at the floor. Mary remained silent.

Margaret's head filled with rage, she set her jaw, turned, and rushed through to the front room. The girl couldn't be far, not with all she had endured the past eighteen hours. The woods, that's where she had gone. Margaret flung the door open.

"Stop, please." Mary grabbed her. "You must not go. Leave her to her own." She tugged her sister inside and closed the door.

"It is not like you to not care. We cannot leave her alone—not now of all times. She needs us."

Grabbing both of Margaret's hands, Mary said, "Our Indian Empress has different needs than what we can give her. Deep seated within generations of traditions—traditions not erased by Father White's baptism—our young native woman must do what her mother, aunts, and grandmothers do when they miscarry their unborn. I argued and pleaded I should accompany her during this time, but she refused to let me."

"You should have gone anyway." Margaret did not like feeling so hateful toward her sister, but this was inexcusable.

"A mother, in her grief, has a right to care for herself and what would have been hers in the way she finds appropriate. Would you deny this young woman her birthright to find comfort in her tribe's customs and her own heritage? I believe not. Piscataway mothers, alone, must perform the ritual that prepares the child's spirit for the journey it must take. When she has found the right place to bury the evidence of the life expelled from her body, and she has conducted the ancient rituals, then she will return to us, Sisters Freehold, and her loving husband."

Margaret's energy, fight, and passion wilted into goose down, leaving a deep ache in their vacated place. She swallowed her grief, nodded, opened the door once more, and stared out beyond their stockade toward the forest.

Chapter 58
Late Summer 1644

Never make a defense or apology before you are accused.
- King Charles I

MARGARET, DURING THEIR TIME of grief, had watched barren winter plants bud out with new growth with the warmth of spring. Then in the heat of summer, Margaret's heart sang. Like a promise from nature, young Mary again carried a child within. Now August, the three Brent women spent the morning at a newly docked Dutch merchant ship.

They strode down the gangplank carrying baskets laden with fabrics, frying pans, pewter, nutmeg, lemons, and some peculiar, lovely items. Dutch ships carried porcelain from China and special leaves to make a hot beverage called tea. Empress Mary often used leaves and blossoms stirred into heated water to heal but the Dutch used these leaves for a beverage to serve at the table.

Their men, Stowre, Gedd, Pursell, Stephans, and Delanhey carried mallets, axes, and adzes to make more bowls. They loaded gunpowder and lead shot in the wagon. As women landholders, she and Mary would not be left unprotected and forgotten by the men of Maryland.

The ladies handed their baskets up for the men to stow in the wagon, then strolled up the path to St. Mary's. When they reached the top, Giles stood there, smiling at them, or more specifically at his young bride. Margaret enjoyed seeing her brother in love.

She glanced at the men still on the dock, preparing to drive the loaded wagon back to St. Thomas's Fort. With Indians raiding everywhere, their additional gunpowder and shot purchased from the Dutch felt heartening. The sisters' armament included flintlocks and some wheellock muzzleloaders, but they still had to fuss with a few matchlocks. Giles, Leonard, and their friends had continually teased the women about their stronghold.

"Brother dear. I noticed many others have purchased gunpowder and shot today. I suspect they no longer laugh about our Sisters Freehold becoming St. Thomas's Fort."

He shrugged.

"Did you just say they all wished they had a grand fort like the Ladies Brent?"

Her sister and young Mary giggled.

"Margaret, do not jest about grave matters. The Susquehannock raids have devastated the Mattapany missions. Catholics in the area fear for their property and life. Even the Dutch in Manhattan and the Swedes in Delaware suffer numerous casualties. The worst of it, a prisoner in Virginia, after the slaughter along the

James and York Rivers, said tribes for hundreds of miles have now joined together to drive Europeans into the sea."

Mary cocked her head, scrunching up her eyebrows. "I had understood the tension with the Patuxent Indians and the Maryland settlers had calmed."

"Not in the least true. I sent settlers in the Patuxent area a letter asserting these Indians enjoyed the protection of Lord Baltimore and must be treated with respect and humanity. Then I had to follow with a letter to the Indians telling them to avoid all settlements along the Patuxent River."

Young Mary smiled. "It must please you not to worry about my people."

Giles's cheek twitched. He slid his arm around her shoulders. Holding her tight against his side, he stared out over the St. George.

Mary's glance caught Margaret's attention. Mary nodded toward their brother. Margaret shrugged. She had no clue what slid through his mind. She drew in a breath and waited for him to speak. Young Mary, content, remained silent as was her nature.

"Giles," Margaret finally said, "something unspoken troubles you. As family, you should tell us."

He took a few breaths, then said, "A few days ago I replaced John Lewger. He acted without my knowledge. Until Leonard returns, William Brainthwaite occupies the office of secretary and serves as judge with Thomas Greene and Cuthbert Fenwick."

"John Lewger? There can be no act so egregious to warrant this punitive treatment." Margaret said, "And Cuthbert Fenwick—the overseer of Cornwallis's manor?" Refusing to let Giles look away, she moved in front of him. "I fear you once again have acted hastily without due mindfulness."

"Giles," Mary said, "Secretary Lewger has held that position since before we arrived in St. Mary's. Leonard Calvert will not tolerate this nonsense."

Giles's face grew inflamed. "For weeks, while away attending to my own affairs on Kent Island, Lewger attempted to negotiate peace with the Susquehannock and the Piscataway. He said not a word to me. Over a month ago he sent Captain Fleet with armed men to deliver conditions for peace. The least of which was for the Susquehannock to return our two cannons they had captured. If they didn't agree, Fleet had authority to take prisoners or kill any who spoke against the English. Fearing these two tribes would attack us, Lewger established a garrison at Piscataway—all under my name without my knowing or consent. What would you ladies have me do?"

The Empress jerked away and stood staring at him. The wildness in her eyes showed she fully comprehended what he had said.

"My sweet Mary, I won't let anything happen to your people." He clutched her hand and held it. "Lewger got involved when he heard the Susquehannock planned a peace treaty with the Piscataway. We know the Susquehannock would do anything to stop the Piscataway's cooperation with the English."

"When Leonard returns," Margaret said, "he will be outraged and not tolerate what you have done concerning Secretary Lewger. We already expect him to be furious when he learns Cornwallis has sailed away to England to make his claim against Leonard and Lord Baltimore's estate. Considering this, I doubt if

Leonard will even give a whit that you, John Lewger, and I protected his assets."

Pointing toward the river, Mary said, "A pinnace arrives. Look! It's the *Trewlove* returning from England. We shall receive news about the war."

The pinnace tied up on the other side of the merchant ship. With much trading happening on the dock, the Brents could not see who disembarked.

Young Mary placed her hand on her small, rounded belly, smiling even more broadly.

"I heard from one of the Dutch seamen," Mary said, "our king has lost the north of England to Parliament and the Scots. Oh—look who comes." Mary pointed at the path.

They watched Leonard Calvert as he strode up to them with smiles and his eyes twinkling.

"Leonard," Margaret rushed to him and took his hand. "Where is our sister? I had hoped you would bring her back with you. Now I am worried."

"Your sister Ann and your family enjoy good health. We shall celebrate, because you have a beautiful nephew, William, with another sibling on the way."

Margaret had never seen Leonard's face so full of joy.

Leonard's gaze landed on young Mary and his smile vanished. His eyes grew large and dark. "Mary Kittamaquund, you are with child." He glowered at Margaret and Mary, then saw Giles, holding young Mary's hand.

"You!" Leonard lunged at Giles, clutching him by the arm. His face red with fury, he pulled his fist back.

"Leonard—" Margaret thrusted herself between the two.

He lowered his fist, shoving around Margaret, and with his face inches from Giles's, he shouted, "You bloody damned bastard—you unforgivable bedswerver!"

PART THREE

ST. THOMAS'S FORT

Chapter 59
February 1645

...that he hoped there would be nere a Papist left in Maryland by May Day.
- Anonymous, Kent Island, Maryland

BITTER, ICY STORMS KEPT fireplaces devouring logs. Where the walls of homes could not be adequately chinked, winds whistled ghostly songs of winter, while white chimney smoke swirled and danced against dark clouds.

Thankfully, today the sun appeared to everyone's joy, leaving snow only in places of constant shadows. Dressed in their warmest woolens, Margaret and both Marys discussed the promise of warmer days on their walk from the chapel's social back to St. Thomas's fort. The sisters insisted young Mary not rush because birthing seemed only days away.

Giles and Leonard, best of friends once more, strode on ahead with the Greene family. The oldest Greene boy, young Thomas, ran circles around his younger brother, Leonard, and the slow walking adults, while the elder Thomas carried their toddler.

The Dutch ship *Looking Glass*, after weeks of trading, continued riding near the mouth of St. Inigoes Creek not far from Cornwallis's home. However, Patuxent men during this morning's gathering had told Giles they spied the *Reformation* sailing their waters these past few days. This worried Giles and Leonard.

Ingle had stormed away in a fit last month, so this afternoon Leonard decided it would be prudent to discuss the ongoing Ingle dilemma with the Dutch captain. Any ship found in what Ingle claimed as his trading territory might be a target for harassment.

"Why is my husband concerned about Captain Ingle?" Young Mary said, "No one made him leave Maryland."

"Curious man, that Ingle." Margaret shook her head. "I heard a story about Cornwallis's overseer, Fenwick. He was in the middle of receiving the *Reformation's* delivery of merchandise Cornwallis had shipped from England a few months ago. Ingle stopped unloading, mumbled something, then pulled up anchor and sailed away with part of Cornwallis's cargo still on board."

"These men baffle me." Her sister said to no one. "Cornwallis evidently sailed off to England with the traitor, Ingle. Now Ingle's back without Cornwallis. This fall Leonard talked as if he wanted to hang Giles or at least lock him up, but instead kept him on as counselor. Then Leonard runs off to Virginia to get support for his commission from England to capture disloyal ships. Rather than put Giles back as governor in his absence, he selected William Brainthwaite. But look at Leonard and Giles now."

Young Mary, striding out as if she had no baby within, laughed. "These men talk, talk, talk, get angry, fight, then be friends again like little woodland fawns. In my tribe if angry and fight, one must leave or die like wildcat or bear. No talk, talk, talk, and no friendship again."

"I would vote for that." Margaret grinned. "Last month that old debt from Lord Baltimore came up again. Cornwallis, still in England, demanded to be paid for buying up Lord Baltimore's church land and chapel to keep it from becoming property of the Pope. Giles, Lewger, and I decided to file claims on Lord Baltimore's remaining assets, so Cornwallis would see Lord Baltimore had nothing of worth left here. We knew Cornwallis had planned to sue him."

Mary huffed. "How does Lord Calvert justify not paying someone who acted as his agent in purchasing land?"

"I suspect with the civil war in England, Cecil Calvert no longer has funds in England either. He says nothing is lost because Cornwallis now possesses the lands and church in place of money."

"Another angry man." Young Mary caressed her rounded stomach. "I do not want our baby to be full of anger. We must fill everything with happy."

Young Mary stopped. She placed her hands on her back.

"Something pulls hard." She slid her fingers around to the lower part of her stomach.

The sisters looked at each other. Then Mary placed a hand on the Empress's tummy.

"Your stomach has tightened to prepare to give you a baby. I am pleased we are almost home."

"My husband thinks this should be a boy, but I think it would be better to have a girl. My people let the women own the land. We women get to say if there will be war. I believe our way might be better."

Laughing out loud, Margaret said, "I agree after this last month's court. I watched men so riled they decided to file suits against everyone. Giles sued Leonard for what he still owes you, young Mary. Then Leonard sued Fenwick. Fenwick sued Leonard and Lewger. Giles sued Cornwallis, and even Father Fisher started suing. Heaven help us all."

Her sister stared at her, saying, "They act like children at play, fighting over taking turns."

There stood the truth. A sad hollowness filled Margaret. "It does seem so. Our brother, because of his passion and fondness to be noticed, often finds himself in disfavor with Leonard. Yet this week he sits in court as a judge and on the provincial council next to Lewger and Leonard. Their inconsistencies give me a headache."

Perhaps underneath their folderol something grander is happening. These men argued and struggled fiercely but still must find a way to hold this fragile land and its people together. Perhaps these attempts at harmony becomes their glue.

Mary said, "Our Empress is right. We should send these men off into the wilderness."

Young Mary giggled.

Gratitude swept over Margaret. Our good Lord had decided this delightful person would have health and good cheer to take her through the birthing of this child.

In December, Leonard had heard Claiborne plotted to take Kent Island, do away with Giles, and plunder his manor. Leonard immediately had warned Giles and sent for young Mary. He insisted she stay safely with Margaret and Mary while he and Giles devised a counterattack. For now, all on Kent seemed quiet.

"Oh my, see the sails." Mary pointed down the St. George River. "I fear the *Reformation* has come."

They had a clear view of the St. George to the south. Yet with the ship's sails billowing, it did appear to be the size of the many-cannon merchant warship belonging to Captain Ingle.

"Margaret," her sister said softly, "tell us of Ingle's intentions."

Young Mary looked from sister to sister with her brow knitted.

"Only our Lord knows. The man left Maryland in a fury in January, without even collecting his trade permit. John Lewger said he sailed up the Potomac where men of questionable character boarded his ship—such as William Hardige and the Sturman men."

"If the *Reformation* sails this way—" Mary glanced around. They stood alone. "I must warn our men." She hitched up her skirts and headed toward the *Looking Glass*.

"I run faster." Young Mary started after her.

Margaret caught her arm. "You do run faster but not when you have a baby within. You and I will let Mary do what she must." If the *Looking Glass* was still moored not far from the Cornwallis place—at the mouth of St. Inigoes Creek— then Mary would not get there in time.

Several minutes later Margaret and young Mary arrived at St. Thomas's Fort. Their men servants stood in the courtyard with their flintlocks, listening to instructions from Stowre. After the storms, Margaret and Mary's men consistently practiced mustering out. Leonard required this, but few landowners bothered, except at St. Thomas's Fort. The sisters, concerned about the increased Indian raids, decided the men should train and drill whenever the weather allowed.

After all, men agree delicate women, landholders or not, must be protected.

Before the women entered the house, Winifred Greene, walking up the path with her children, called to them.

"Ladies Brent, my husband told me to come and stay until he returned. He didn't take time to explain. I suspect it's because the *Reformation* is nearby."

Margaret held the door open. "Missus Brookes will make us a treat. Have you ever had tea?"

Young Mary, squatting on the polished floor, engaged the boys in a game she used to play with some seashells and sticks. Margaret and Winifred sipped tea with honey and milk from blue and white porcelain cups and watched.

Within the hour, Margaret heard men's voices mixed with Mary's. She donned her cloak to meet them. Leonard, Thomas Greene, and Mary, inside the fort's entrance, chattered with Stowre and the men. Leonard strode back and bolted the gate.

What agitates them so? Where is Giles?

Margaret marched over and unbolted the gate to watch for her brother.

"Come away, Margaret." Leonard's commanding voice irritated her. "I must leave. Bolt the entrance after I'm gone."

"I shall not until you have given me good reason." She didn't see Giles anywhere. "Where is my brother?"

"He's on the *Looking Glass,* as I was. They said Ingle sent letters to Protestants of Maryland, complaining about the papists and telling those who would join with him against the Catholics could share in plunder. Secure the lock."

"Goodness. But Giles—"

Leonard threw his hands up. "He visits with the captain of the *Looking Glass.* No need to fret. Cuthbert Fenwick and I both wrote Ingle a letter guaranteeing his safety along with my signed license for his free trade in Maryland. With the storms last week, we haven't given him these yet, but Fenwick will today. All will be well."

Mary and Thomas Greene carried their conversation with them into the house, leaving Margaret to argue with Leonard.

Something skittered in Margaret's mind.

"Leonard, if there is no need to fret then there is no need to bolt our fortress."

He huffed. "Woman, the man is irrational and has been busy recruiting. He'll settle when Fenwick gives him our papers, but until then I must hurry and warn the others. The rest of you remain here until we know what Ingle plans." Leonard hurried out the gate toward St. Mary's, shouting back, "Margaret, bolt that gate."

"Men." Margaret huffed. She lifted her petticoats above her shoes and strode out leaving the gate open for others to bolt. She would go south to see about the *Looking Glass* and the *Reformation* moored at St. Inigoes Creek.

Chapter 60

Public reformers had need first practice on their own hearts that which
they purpose to try on others.
- King Charles I

WHEN MARGARET APPROACHED ST. Inigoes Creek, she sought a place for a clear view of both ships. The Dutch ship flew the colors of the Prince of Orange from her mast with the cross of St. George flying from the stern. When St. George's white with a red-cross flag flew, everyone knew the ship sailed as an English merchant ship.

Ingle's ship, *Reformation,* curiously flew a white peace flag next to its England colors. Margaret's skin prickled. Knowing Ingle, this screamed of trickery. She secured herself behind a large oak to watch. Ingle and the Dutch captain hollered back and forth. The Dutch ship slowly lowered her colors.

This can't be good, whatever it means.

A wherry from the Dutch ship was dropped into the water and three crew with the captain rowed to the other ship. The captain and the sailors boarded the *Reformation.* Margaret caught herself holding her breath. The two captains talked, then Ingle tore up papers and flung them into the water. Some of Ingle's men climbed into the wherry and rowed it back to the *Looking Glass,* leaving the Dutch captain and his crew behind.

Those Dutch have been taken captive. I must not let this stand.

But she had not a clue what to do. Giles, with others, stood on the deck of the *Looking Glass* and watched Ingle's men in the wherry approach.

Oh, Giles, leave. Get out of there.

"Look to ye selves!" Someone in the wherry called back to the *Reformation.* "They in the *Looking Glass* have cannons loaded and fire set."

Giles drew his sword. A deafening blast shook the world. Margaret yelped, holding her ears—eyes shut. When she next looked, puffs of smoke rose from one of the *Reformation's* cannons. Ingle's men scurried up out of the wherry and boarded the *Looking Glass.* Her heart leaped against her ribs, knowing not what to do.

Dear Mother in Heaven, a war has begun.

She, a woman, had no counterpart to swords and cannons. Worse, she could no longer see Giles. Ingle detested him. Margaret, heart still lurching, stumbled backwards, hitched her petticoats, and with untied hood fled the way she had come. She must get help to Giles and warn the others.

Her breath came hard, cramping her side. She passed through Thomas Greene's property and slowed, gasping for air as she approached St. Thomas's

Fort. Before she could bang on the gate, Stowre opened it.

"Been watching for you, my Lady. All have been worried with your being gone and the governor nowhere around." He stood aside. She entered, and he threw the bolts into place. "Everyone's inside waiting. We heard ordnance fire."

Thomas Greene evidently had been watching for her too. He rushed out of the house, shouting at the others to stay inside.

Margaret leaned forward, working to calm her breathing. The men held patient.

"I fear Ingle will murder Giles." She told what she had seen.

Thomas Greene scratched his well-trimmed beard. "I'll take some of my men and go keep watch as you did, Lady Margaret. We will see what we can do."

"Where did the governor go?"

"I suspect to Pope's Ordinary to trade news. Tell my wife I'm off to talk to our servants, then to St. Inigoes Creek. Assure her I shall keep well hidden. If we can move and take your brother, we will."

He unbolted the gate and hurried off.

"Stowre," she said, "some at St. Thomas's Fort keep strong to their Protestant faith. Would you tell everyone I am safe but say no more. I shall return, but I must talk to our governor." Margaret started through the gate, then stopped. "Please assign men to be ready with arms, raise our St. Thomas's Fort flag, and see at least two stand constant watch."

St. Thomas Aquinas, and his beliefs, held dear to Mary and Margaret's hearts. He more than anyone in the world, understood vows of chastity. Their white flag with a red "T" edged in gold, resembling the savior's cross, would remind all of the virtues practiced by St. Thomas and those behind the walls of this fort. She and Mary often renewed their pledge to hold reason in their self-governance, to practice forgiveness and humility, to avoid excessiveness and arrogance, to understand people receive what they deserve, and to be courageous and brave. Most importantly, they strove to be charitable to all in speech, thoughts, and actions.

Behind her, Margaret heard the guard bolt the gate. Pulling her hood over her head, she tied it, then hurried to Pope's Ordinary.

When she came in sight of Pope's establishment, she saw Leonard outside, talking with a small group of planters and tradesmen. Goodwin stood listening. Robinson bellowed something, waved his hand in the air, and stomped off. Three others followed him, leaving only Goodwin and one other man.

"Lord Governor," Margret called. The early evening air brought a chill to her face and hands but left the rest of her hot and damp after her rushing about. She slowed her breathing.

Ladies should not gasp air through their mouths like fish.

He looked in her direction, and she saw the little smile he always wore whenever she appeared. She started toward him. When she came closer his smile faded. He must have recognized her worry. She swiped a long tendril of her reddish hair from her face and tucked it back under her hood. The sadness of it all. Giles and the Dutch and the other Marylanders, who may have been murdered—Her legs stopped. Just stopped. Her feet stood anchored to the ground. Her emotions bubbled up ready to spill out any moment. She looked up to see tenderness in

Leonard's handsome, sleepy-looking eyes.

Shoulders back, stand tall. Be the woman I must be… no matter how difficult this Maryland is.

"You have great concern. Tell us." He motioned Goodwin and his friend to be a part of their conversation.

She told what she had witnessed. "Leonard, Ingle dislikes you as much as Giles." Her voice shook, imagining a cutlass at Giles's throat. "Come stay at St. Thomas's Fort. Thomas Greene has gone to spy and rescue Giles. In any measure, he will come back with information."

Leonard studied the two men. "With Ingle's firing his cannons, we must assemble a militia. Of all the men I talked with this afternoon, only Goodwin and Greenhold agreed to help."

"Ye cannot count on indentured." Goodwin glanced around. "Most be Protestant."

Leonard shifted his weight and said, "Truth of it. With four hundred strong in Maryland only a few of us are Catholic, probably no more than forty. I shall not be raising a militia against Ingle here." He sighed. "I must get men from Virginia."

Margaret, hands on her hips, shook her head. "No matter how you go, Leonard, you would invite your death. Going on foot would be dangerous and take too long. Yet, with the *Reformation* riding at the mouth of St. Inigoes, Ingle's guards will capture any ship or pinnace sailing into or out of the St. George River. You have found yourself trapped."

Chapter 61

Life is a flame burning itself out, but it catches fire again every time a child is born.
- George Bernard Shaw

GOODWIN DECLINED TO GO to St. Thomas's Fort with Margaret. He said he and John Greenhold would hunt for some honest men to fight.

Leonard and Margaret walked together in the cold twilight. He talked of his new son, William, of his dreams for the unborn baby, and his dear wife, Ann.

"We hoped Ann would come back with you. Yet, with Ingle fighting, maybe it is best she stayed in England." Margaret understood the difficulty in leaving England. Seven years ago, one October dawn, fighting tears, she and Mary had kissed their sweet sisters and father goodbye.

Leonard took her hand. "You've heard stories about women crossing the sea with unborn children. Even young children rarely survive. As difficult as the voyage is, getting Ann and our son safely on board a ship during this civil war posed a problem. The king's guard and the Committee of Sequestrations patrol every port to keep watch over ships transporting Catholics."

The sun had set when they neared St. Thomas's Fort. Still, they could see a figure—a
man hastening toward them.

"Thomas Greene?" Margaret looked up at Leonard. He nodded. They hurried to meet him.

"A moment." Greene bent to catch his breath. "Crushing news. Ingle's men are ransacking Cornwallis's great home. I watched them cart off furniture, tapestries, tools, and pots. They whoop and holler and run about like shaved hogs in a thunderstorm."

"Giles." Margaret's voice caught. "Have you seen him?"

Greene faltered before saying, "No sign of him or Fenwick.

Leonard sighed. "Cornwallis and Ingle had a close friendship. If Ingle loots friends' homes, our troubles grow beyond what we imagined."

Ingle will murder Giles.

"Who goes there?" The call came from inside St. Thomas's Fort.

"'Tis your governor, Thomas Greene, and Lady Brent," Leonard shouted back. Someone slid the bolt and pulled the gate wide.

Lantern light shone from the windows of the home. Greene and Margaret started through the gate, but Leonard stopped, pulling them aside.

"The darkness hides much. Give me your pinnace to sail to Virginia. No one caught up in the excitement of looting will see me on the river this night."

"I must take it for a trip to Kent Island. Now without Giles, I have to tend to his estate and livestock. You might be gone for weeks." She heard the gate close and bolted.

Greene said, "Take mine, Governor. It's not as large and will be faster."

Leonard nodded.

"May God's eye watch over you, Governor." Greene said. "We pray for your success and a speedy return."

"I smell smoke." Margaret moved farther away from the fort and scanned the countryside. "A house or shed has caught fire on Oliver's place." She shuddered. Roger Oliver's property stood to the south and east of Greene's.

"Leonard, go." Greene pointed. "I'll go to Oliver's."

"You shall not." Margaret snatched Greene's arm. "The fire was probably started by the rebels. You go nowhere without your arms and someone beside you who carries a flintlock."

"You had best listen to the lady, Thomas Greene." Leonard waved back.

"Thomas, talk to Stowre. He will loan you a rifle and an armed man. You can get your own later." She called out to her guard. "Open the gate for Thomas Greene and Lady Brent."

Entering, Greene said, "There stands Stowre with men over by the well. Tell my wife all. I shall return after we extinguish the fire."

The candles, glowing from within, welcomed her. When she reached the door, she could hear women and children's mixed voices. She stepped inside.

A tiny cry came from a bedroom—that special slight guttural sound newborns make.

"The Brent family has a beautiful little girl." Mary drew Margaret into the house. "Come see."

Margaret's insides tingled, canceling her fear. She untied her hood and pulled off her cloak, shoving it toward Missus Taylor, and followed her sister into young Mary's room. The new mother, grinning and wide-eyed, cuddled her little bundle. A tiny tuft of coal-black hair stuck out from the wrapping. Margaret moved in close and saw the little fawn-skinned child. The mother handed her baby to Margaret.

In awe, Margaret savored the weight of this tiny, warm bundle in her arms. Her whole being filled with blessed ecstasy.

Young Mary looked past Margaret, then at Margaret's face. Her brows furrowed.

"My husband is not with you." Tears appeared.

"Do not worry, dear." Margaret slipped the infant back into the mother's arms.

Her own distress about her brother stirred greater fear than all other concerns. Still, this was not the time to alarm a new mother.

"God smiles and looks after him."

Young Mary grinned. "I cannot wait for him to hold his beautiful little Piscataway princess."

Chapter 62

Sustain me, my God, according to your promise, and I will live; do not let my hopes be dashed.
- Psalm 119:116

Hearing unfamiliar voices in the front hall, Margaret left the young mother and child to their rest and sought to determine who had come to St. Thomas's Fort. Two men had brought their wives and children, asking if they could stay at the fort while they fought.

All evening long the rebels burned buildings and fired shots. Goodwin appeared near midnight with John Morton and his young son, John. Goodwin and Morton, covered in grime and ash, smelled of smoke, death, and gunpowder. Little John, way beyond the age, clutched his braided-bed rug, sucked his thumb, and hid his face when anyone talked to him. Margaret's heart hurt for the loss of Bess and the damage this child and his father suffered. She assured Morton little John would receive the best of care.

Missus Brookes had served everyone a portion of stew sometime during the evening. Missus Guesse, in turn, took the children to the loft where she and Missus Taylor made sleeping pallets on the floor for them. The mothers sang softly or told stories and kissed them goodnight. Missus Taylor decided she would be the one to feed, bathe, and tend to little John's needs.

Shortly after midnight Margaret, fearing the harm of rumors, and worrying their servants would not be alert and ready for the next day, called them together in the large dining room. Once they quieted, she, Mary, and Winifred Greene told them what had happened with the Dutch ship and Ingle's ship. Margaret did not mention Leonard.

"Some of you are Protestants. Winifred, Mary, and I can respect your loyalty to Parliament and England, but we cannot have you here if you are disloyal to us. If you pledge your allegiance to protect and uphold St. Thomas's Fort, by staying and bearing arms, if need be, Mary and I will grant you freeman status when this is over. We have been assured the Greenes will do the same for those who serve them. If after all of this, you wish to continue in our service, we will pay your hire. If you, as a Protestant do choose to stay, and the Protestants win this war, the Greenes, Mary, and I will swear we held you against your wishes. We will say you were unwilling participants. No punishment will be meted. If you decide against this, then you must leave tonight."

Years ago, Margaret had promised God she would not let falsehoods take purchase in her heart. Tonight, a lie to keep the Protestants safe did not feel wrong.

Perhaps on occasion not all falsehoods hold the weight of sin as do the people who force their telling.

No one spoke.

Margaret looked at Mary and Winifred. "Please take each person into another room and hear their personal testament of allegiance. While you do so, the rest of us will form a plan of defense. When all is done, everyone should find somewhere to sleep until your turn to stand watch. The morrow will make many demands."

Most seemed too excited to settle and sleep. As maids extinguished the candles, one by one, the house grew quieter. Thomas Greene still hadn't returned, and Winifred paced about. Margaret encouraged her to take sleep, assuring the wife she would awaken her when Thomas returned.

Margaret walked through her home, stepping around near strangers who whispered, coughed, snored, and slept. Tomorrow, the five men who stayed to protect the fort would sleep in the barn. She counted the number of people Missus Brooks would need to feed, including Greene's servants whenever they arrived—six maids, six women, eight children, and five or six men who would remain as guards.

She donned her cloak, stepped outside, and asked the guard to unbolt the gate. She told him she would go but a few feet, and he should close and lock it after her. Margaret could see numerous buildings burned. The flames shone bright in the dark, and the smell of the smoke carried to her on the breeze. She scanned the countryside for Thomas Greene.

Alone in the darkness, her eyes adjusted as her ears listened to night sounds. She waited. Her mind filled with thoughts of Giles. An owl's nasal hooting frightened a cottontail. It scurried under a bush. A few minutes later a doe and fawn strolled near, heading to the forest. Still, no Giles or Thomas. The breeze from the river brought a chill not unlike her hurting heart.

She started back to the fort but stopped. Her skin bristled. Someone approached.

"Lady Brent. I must talk to ye."

"Who calls to me?" The night shadows revealed only sounds and smells— sharp smells of smoke and rum. "I shall not talk to drunkards."

She had been foolish to leave the fort. Yet, the guard could still hear her if she called out.

"Nay, I not be the least drunk, only had me a nip or two." A skinny, unshaved sailor stepped into the rising moonlight.

Peter Coates.

"Ye saved me from hanging. Though ye don't care for me, I owe ye me life."

"You owe me nothing, Peter Coates. You sail for Captain Ingle on the *Reformation*, and you could use a decent stew with soda bread. Come in and partake." Missus Brookes would have left the huge iron pot still hanging over the coals.

"Naw. I say me due to ye then be off. I come to tell ye to watch out for raiding and plunder. 'Tis my payment for your kindness in Gloucester." He paused. "Nay, I see ye no need for me warning with ye fort. Ye did not have a fortress here last time captain came. Aw, me debt can nere be paid."

"Peter, I forgive your debt, yet I have a question. Have you seen my brother, the gentleman Giles Brent? I worry he may be dead."

"Captain Ingle gives orders to nary harm any of those gentlemen. He will be taking them to London to prove his case."

"Gentlemen? Are there more?" Perhaps he referred to Cuthbert Fenwick, Cornwallis's overseer.

"Aye, they brought the governor's secretary on board this night. Dragged him out of his bed in his nightclothes with no stockings or shoes. We had a good laugh about that."

Poor John Lewger, always so proper.

"The secretary's wife and son?"

"Nay. They be left behind. No use to the captain."

"Are there more prisoners?"

"Aye, the factor—Fenwick—from that huge mansion belonging to Cornwallis, but they left Fenwick's wife and children stay in the house. Captain Ingle be all excited when they captured two priests and others from a mission. The two priests be prisoners in chains. They take some of the captives to Cornwallis's house on St. Inigoes River because it be surrounded with palisade and many cannons. They throw the other priests in a pinnace. Me hear they be left upon Virginia shores for the savages." He stopped talking for a minute, then said, "I have told ye much. In turn, if ye could tell me this one thing, Captain Ingle would bestow me respect."

"What do you want to know?"

"We be given orders to hunt and seize your governor, Leonard Calvert. Can ye tell me where he be?"

Her heart quickened. "I understand he has left the country."

Peter Coates nodded.

"Peter, this life you have of murder and plundering is not good."

"I do not murder, and ye see I pay me honest debts. This be me life even if it may well be me death. Goodbye, Lady Brent."

He loped off into the darkness. She stood staring until the damp night air cut through her cloak.

Goodbye, indeed.

More fires visible in the distance told Margaret these raids happened in earnest. She welcomed knowing Giles and Lewger would not be harmed, unless hanged by the courts in England. The priests? Father White and Fisher? Those other sacrificed priests… Sickened with helplessness, she forced her feet to take her back to the safety of the fort.

The guard called out, "Who comes this night?"

"Lady Brent." She could manage no more.

Chapter 63

Nobody cares how much you know until they know how much you care.
- Theodore Roosevelt

SHORTLY BEFORE DAWN MARGARET woke to the sound of gunfire. She rushed through the dark house and hurried outside. Mary followed.

Samuel Pursell called down from the parapet, "No need for concern, Ladies. Two ruffians with torches said to give up the Lord Governor or they would burn the fort down. Gedd's big gun chased away them scallywags. Suspect they'll return later, but for now they hold their scared arses in high esteem."

He and Gedd broke loose with guffaws.

The sisters started back indoors when they heard Gedd shout.

"Halt and declare who you be!"

"Thomas Greene with my men and maids." He added, "Please do not shoot our posteriors."

His tobacco had been stolen before the rebels had burned the drying shed. They had looted his home and made off with their chickens. He and his men overtook the disorganized pillagers, running them off. Knowing they would come back better prepared, Greene brought his horses with feed to St. Thomas's Fort along with flintlocks, swords, powder, shot, and other salvaged valuables. He turned his pigs loose to forage in the woods. Their maids had gathered contents from their larder to help feed those within the fort.

Winifred peeked out the door. With a squeal, she ran into Thomas's arms. Margaret had her maids assist the sorting and storing of the Greene's contributions. Then Winifred, Margaret, and Mary settled to hear more of Thomas's night's events.

Margaret sighed. "It's time I go to Kent. I need to protect Giles's valuables and livestock. I shall leave after dark."

"You've not sailed the Chesapeake, and you must not travel alone." The corners of her sister's mouth tightened. "What should we tell young Mary about her husband?"

Everyone looked at Margaret.

"Let me tell her the truth. He's a prisoner, being treated like a gentleman, and will be taken to England. I fear once in England he will stand trial and may be hanged. Yet, with Lord Baltimore's connections, all may be well, and he could soon be home."

Mary frowned. "Your truth will make me feel better if you leave out the trial and such."

The women in St. Thomas's Fort had many tasks to keep them busy. Some

238

entertained children while others did laundry duty, mended clothes, fed the animals, prepared the vegetable garden for spring planting, and helped Missus Brookes by plucking feathers from chickens or sorting beans. The noise level, inside and out, grew as the children became accustomed to their new living spaces.

Margaret cut cheese and meat, then wrapped the food she would take on her trip to Kent.

"Listen to those children," Mary said, "no concern about this rebellion. I worry about Ann Lewger and young John. I shall go and bring them here."

Stowre, eating a shriveled apple from last fall's barrel, said, "Nay. You must not, Lady Mary. There be shots fired now and then, and there be lots of burning and looting. We have no report on the state of the countryside."

"We need more spies." Margaret glanced at the men guarding their palisade. Some slept in the darkened barn before taking their turn at watch.

"Let me go," said Stowre. "I'll give Lady Lewger your invitation, then escort her and her son to St. Thomas's Fort."

"One more thing, please." Mary nodded to Margaret. "If our home has become the garrison against the Protestant rebels, we need a strategy for ending this chaos. All the men who fight for our cause should work together. Stowre, if you see anyone who fights against these raiders, would you tell them to come to St. Thomas's Fort today. With their information we can build a plan and even reinforce their supplies as long as we are able."

Margaret packed her food into a basket. "I will be at the dock readying the pinnace to sail this evening."

Mary started to protest, but Margaret waved her words away.

"Let me walk with you." Stowre grabbed his flintlock and waited for her to lead.

Together they strode through the gate. Margaret heard the reassuring chunk of the bolt being set. Stowre talked about some men who might be willing to join the cause.

Margaret listened, but her mind found it difficult to concentrate on the meaning of his words. Something looked amiss. She gasped. She could not see the mast top of her pinnace. Margaret ran to the edge of the cliff where the trail led down to the dock.

"My pinnace—gone—" A painful lump in her throat stopped more words.

A blast from Stowre's gun ended her thoughts. She swirled—dropped low to see Stowre on one knee, preparing to shoot again. Another shot came their way. It thunked into a tree. She froze, staring between the trunks at three rough looking men—Hardige, Sturman, and Baldridge.

"Run!" Stowre called out to her.

They scout, looking for Leonard.

Hardige shouted something but she didn't know what. More shots.

"Go!" Stowre yelled.

A tremor shook through her. She dashed—holding low. More gunfire.

Margaret reached the gate. It slid open. Men on the top of the palisade hollered, returning shots. Stowre pushed through the gate behind her. One of Greene's men closed and bolted it.

Furious, she made a vow to never again leave the fort without her gun. *Running in fear will not become my way.*

She had to get to Kent Island before raiders did. They would steal Giles's livestock, and he kept a library filled with treasured and rare books dear to him. Margaret feared his men would join the Protestant rebellion.

With Leonard taking Greene's pinnace, and her pinnace gone, Giles's pinnace most assuredly had been stolen too. Kent Island might as well be as far as England.

Stowre ran fingers through his gray and brown-haired beard. "Sorry, Lady Brent. I should nay let you be out there."

"Nonsense. I refuse to be a prisoner in my own home. The sounds of shooting have stopped. They must have decided to find easier targets."

He scowled. "They think the governor here. I be off to talk with Lady Lewger."

"Be careful, Stowre. I find you a valuable man."

* * *

Within the next few hours, a man here and there would appear at their gate saying Stowre sent them. Goodwin and Greenhold came too. Mary and Margaret gathered all the men. Mary questioned the new ones about what they had seen or heard. Margaret could not figure out any systemized plan of the rebels except harass all Catholics, plunder their homes, slaughter their livestock, steal whatever tobacco they had stored from last year's crops, and burn outbuildings and maybe homes.

Whoever owned a home, no matter their faith, it still might be burned. Many Protestants and Catholics, not wanting to take sides or have their homes pillaged or destroyed, had fled from Maryland.

A stranger named Rabley who joined their group told the sisters how Nathaniel Pope had a gang of Protestants erecting a fort with a moat around Leonard's manor, now Pope's Ordinary. They imprisoned the Jesuit captives there who had been taken from St. Mary's mission. After the rebels had removed the expensive household items and precious metals and jewels that filled the Jesuits' two large houses, the rebels burned the structures.

"Nathanial Pope?" Margaret's insides burned. "How presumptuous of him to use our government house as their fort."

"Everyone listens," Rabley said, "and does what they're told by Mister Pope and Baldrige. Pope's Fort's full of Catholic prisoners."

Mary grew red in the face. "Maybe we should take captives."

"The drying shed could hold them." Gedd said.

Having the fort built around some of their outbuildings as well as their home seemed excessive at the time, but now Margaret saw good reason.

Giving the situation more thought, Margaret shook her head. "We would have more to worry over and feed. Let us be frugal with our supplies."

"Ingle's ship still rides at the mouth of St. Inigoes River." Mary looked around and said, "if my brother, John Lewger, and the two priests are still being held on Ingle's ship, they must be rescued. Do we have any strong swimmers?"

Stowre arrived in their yard with Lady Lewger and young John. The growing youth carried a flintlock and seemed distractible. He kept looking all around, and his face twitched.

Margaret drew them aside and welcomed them.

"We appreciate the invitation to be here," Ann said. "I understand you have a new baby in the house."

"Mother." John said. "This isn't social. It's war."

"War," his mother said, "should never be the cause of displaced niceties."

"So Stowre, what are the plans." Young John hefted his rifle higher.

"Young John Lewger," Margaret said. "You have grown into a man since we last talked. To be a part of this, give your respect and attention to the one who instigates our strategies, Lady Mary." She pointed toward her sister who, surrounded by armed men, discussed possibilities.

Mary nodded to young John and continued talking to her soldiers. "Tell us of any knowledge you have concerning Pope's Fort. Give us suggestions on how it might be breached. If we free his prisoners, then we might have more to fight with us."

Young John stepped up and said, "Yet, Lady Brent, I fear these captives will not fight. They are but priests."

Chapter 64

Courage isn't having the strength to go on—it's going on when you don't have the strength.
- Napoleon Bonaparte

GREENHOLD, WHO HAD COME with Goodwin, stepped over to Margaret. "I told Stowre I can get you to Kent Island by tomorrow morning and back the following day."

Margaret's heart filled with gratitude for him and Stowre.

Greenhold and Margaret left on foot at twilight. She carried a basket of food, her flintlock, powder, and shot. They skirted around farms and any commotion they observed, walking due east to the Chesapeake, seven miles away. There they met Greenhold's friend who had a small shallop. He helped them aboard, and they sailed off into the dark up the bay.

Greenhold leaned over to Margaret and said, "I would not be so brave to do this at night, but my friend knows the Chesapeake well. Give thanks to our Lord your pinnace was stolen. Our good Lord has many ways to keep you safe."

The intimidating night at last gave way to day. The sun appeared above the horizon as a dark-red orb. Its light sparkled on the water through breaks in darkened clouds. Kent Island came into view. Even before sunlight, she could smell acrid smoke. It billowed into the cool, heavy morning air from small fires along the coastline. Only a few farmhouses stood untouched. An hour later, with Margaret's eyes smarting and lungs laboring, Giles's dock came into view. Through the haze she could tell much of the fort and outbuildings had been burned.

The shallop clunked against Giles's pier. Margaret leaped out with her flintlock ready before Greenhold could tie the man's vessel. She strode to a large pile of burning rubble in front of the home. Some of Giles's men stood talking and laughing. When Margaret approached, they shifted positions, removing their caps. Their faces held bushels of guilt.

"Tell me of this burning ash heap."

No one answered. They looked around as if for someone else to do the talking.

"I demand to know what you burned here."

A bull of a man said, "We dunut burn nuthin'."

"And the livestock—what about the animals?"

"Slaughtered, runoff, or stolen, Lady." She knew him by the name of James.

"Of course, none of you had any part in this, am I correct, James?"

Still silence. Then another man spoke, "Cummins be the one who threw all Master Brent's books in that pile, and he be the one who burned them. Nary one

242

of us."

Cummins equals the devil in doing evil's work. Those beautiful books—

"I see." Margaret set her jaw. "So here you five stand letting Gentleman Brent's home be ransacked. You have no food, no means of income, and no thought of tomorrow. I guess thieving must become your way."

Two shifted their rifles. Another slid his hand down to his cutlass.

Greenhold and the boatman had come up behind her. They, too, raised their flintlocks.

"Pfft. Enjoy the rest of your wretched lives." She marched back down to the wharf and stepped back into the shallop.

"Take me home, please, good man."

The gentle rocking and swaying of the shallop might have been pleasant except for her internal seething, combined with sitting on a bench designed for— crabbing, she supposed. Its roughness left splinters in her gown and hands. Her ruined shoes rested in pools of fish-smelling, muddy water. Acrid smoke permeated everything, including her hair, and cutting pain into her heart.

Greenhold offered her a sip of his fresh water. She took the flask, appreciating the wet, sweet taste. He nodded. She sipped again, then handed him the basket of food. Margaret's emptiness left no room for sustenance.

Staring at the tiny waves rolling away from the boat, her mind sorted through the last few days. Nathaniel Pope—building a fort around the Governor's House—Giles, John Lewger, Father White, and Father Fisher being hauled off to England to stand trial—Ingle, capturing a Dutch ship, setting men to raid, plunder, and murder the Catholics of St. Mary's County. Then there was Ingle's audacity in looting his friend Cornwallis's manor. Thinking about Pope and Ingle, she found herself equally angry with both. Leonard had given Nathaniel Pope the opportunity to rise in status. How disgraceful his disloyalty.

For what purpose? Wealth? Revenge? Power?

The rising sun glared in her face. Her head hurt.

Simple. Ingle and Pope will replace our Maryland government with Protestant rule and continue their religious intolerance.

Chapter 65
April–August 1645

Success is not final. Failure is not fatal. It's the courage to continue that counts.
- Winston Churchill

"TWO MONTHS, MARY. I am inside out with concern for Giles and Leonard."

"Ingle's ship still rides in St. Inigoes River." Mary glanced southward. "He still hopes to capture our governor."

Margaret and Mary had joined the vexed women at St. Thomas's Fort who fretted about sons and husbands. Occasionally a messenger would come to tell of recent events—hordes of Virginians and rebelling Protestants far outnumbered the Maryland defenders.

Mary's plans to rescue the captives from the *Reformation* or Cornwallis's Cross Manor had failed for lack of willing militia and, in the trying, one man drowned in the St. Inigoes River.

They simply could not take Pope's Fort unless they had more support. In their feeble attempts, several of their soldiers had been captured. No one knew how many men had been killed.

What in Heaven's name has happened to our good governor?

Throughout the weeks, gunshots pelted their fortress, unnerving the adults as well as the children. Last night rebels with torches, shouting, "We demand Calvert!" charged at the fort in attempts to burn it.

The guards' shots deterred them.

One afternoon Margaret stood high on their parapet, assessing the country-side and damage. Scorched marks on the corner posts of the fort unsettled her.

"Mary, if a guard dozes, they will burn our palisade to the ground."

Inspecting the damage, Mary shrugged. "Oak is dense and slow to burn when fresh cut. During hot summer months, when it dries, we shall worry."

Stories began to spread over the countryside about Ingle being incensed because they had not captured Governor Calvert. Weeks later, guards, standing on the top of the fortress, called everyone to look south down river.

The *Reformation* sailed out of St. Inigoes River into the St. George with the *Looking Glass* following. Ingle sailed off to England with his prisoners and the Dutch ship as his bounty—his gift to Parliament, leaving Maryland in ruin.

Reports came back to St. Thomas's Fort about a mood shift of the rebels. They continued to loot and raid, hollering insults about Catholics, the king, and all who supported papist ways. Yet a larger concern for everyone fixated on food.

With the uprising, no ships docked in Maryland to bring supplies, and since spring crops had not been planted, the food situation became dire.

* * *

On an August morning Mary stacked wood for winter that young Mary had just split with her axe. Margaret minded the baby, playing finger games and singing to her until she fell asleep. Young Mary had refused to name the child until her father returned.

After cuddling her precious niece, Margaret placed the child in the large Piscataway basket and positioned it on the wide, wooden bench in the corner of the kitchen. She reminded the women working near to not let the other children bother the sleeping baby. Protective, she knew, but the child fared better out of the way than on the floor where some ill-mannered lad might trip over her.

Providing for this child and everyone at the fort had drained their resources. She found Mary and young Mary still working alone outside. "We have no tobacco crop or corn this season, we have uncollectable income from owed debts, and I cannot plead court cases for anyone. Our income suffers."

"We do have some tobacco reserves in our drying shed."

"Reserves, Mary. Our wealth is in unplanted land. With a shortage of men, we have only worked a fraction of what we own." She watched young Mary deftly swing the axe and hit her mark each time. "We shall never plant it."

Mary didn't respond.

"Agreed then? I shall draw up documents of sale for some acreage."

"Most of our countrymen worry about getting food." Mary continued to stack the split wood in neat rows. "No one wants our land. Young Mary, you need to stop chopping. Margaret, look at this woman. She wears me out."

"We can sell land to Virginians. When Leonard returns, I can take the Greene's pinnace to Virginia."

"Leonard needs to bring us militiamen, or there will be no need to trade our land." Mary frowned. "If he doesn't, you know all of Maryland will belong to Virginia."

Chapter 66
Late August 1645

Start by doing what is necessary; then do the possible; and suddenly you are doing the impossible.
- St. Francis of Assisi

STOWRE CAME TO THE fort periodically to give the Brent sisters information. On one particularly hot day, he appeared. His hair oily, his face and hands black with grime, he looked malnourished and exhausted. Flies gathered around him. The three stood in the shade of a walnut tree where others could not hear.

"What men we have left run low on powder and shot."

Mary asked, "How many have been killed?"

He shook his head. "I have no count. At least a handful taken prisoner."

"Pope's Fort." Margaret fumed. "I fear our Maryland's leader is now Nathaniel Pope. This farmer, planter, freeman has risen to the status of Mister, and now this Protestant seems to have become the official head of government. His new position must be the intention for all this fighting."

"James Baldridge stands beside him." Mary set her jaw. "These Protestants emulate the Parliamentarians in England. They fight to take over our government and our country."

"Have you heard from Governor Calvert?" Stowre's face told her he had not.

Margaret stared at nothing. "Our Governor must be ill or dead. Come, you must be starving."

They walked toward the house as Missus Brookes approached them. "Forgive me. I would not intrude on your conversation except I fear we face an emergency. I have finished an inventory of our vegetables and meat. With these people to feed, we haven't enough to last the month."

"Grain and corn?" Margaret waited.

"Less than a month. With no meat I now serve pottage."

Stowre said, "I leave now and will come back in a few days."

Margaret held her hand up for him to stay. "Missus Brookes, we do have enough to give this man something of nourishment."

"We do. Follow me."

A good woman, Missus Brooks knows we have no food to spare.

Sighing, Mary said, "We should send some men out again. Maybe this time they will find some kind of game or even fish."

"Clams might be fine. It is almost September."

"To save powder and shot we could send young Mary out with her bow for deer."

"If something happened, who would nurse her baby?" Margaret felt a headache coming.

* * *

In the early morning darkness, a week later, Margaret heard a familiar voice answer the guard's query. She raced out, wrapping a shawl over her nightdress to find Leonard—his face pale and drawn.

"Come, eat some pottage and tell us what success you have in raising a militia."

Leonard shook his head. "Men, some of you go to Greene's pinnace and bring the munitions we've brought. One of you stand guard until I return."

"You brought no men?" Margaret's heart sank. "We can't hold out without a militia. Most have fled the country or have joined the Protestants or have been killed or are now prisoners of Nathaniel Pope." She hated feeling emotional, but this disappointment swept her beyond caring.

Mary woke Missus Brookes, then sat Leonard at the table. When Missus Brookes entered, she twisted her apron sash and murmured in Mary's ear. Mary patted the woman's hand, waving her to the kitchen.

Missus Brookes, flushed, then a short time later returned to ladle hot meatless pottage into Leonard's bowl, and give him a half tankard of ale.

Leonard consumed the meal without talking. He had lost weight.

Missus Brookes, eyes avoiding everyone, took his bowl away.

"Spend the day here and rest." Margaret put her hand on top of his.

"They hunt for me. I shall sail to the Potomac and be well up it before the sunrise. Some in the north may agree to join us."

"Please—not north." Margaret, without thinking, held tight his hand. "I hear terrible tales about the northern neck of Virginia. The most ferocious fighters come from there."

He stared into Margaret's face, shook his head, and thanked Missus Brookes for her pottage. Margaret followed him to the door, winding around the sleeping women with young children. Leonard would say no more. He opened the door. Emptiness filled her. She stared motionless as he walked away.

He stopped before he left the fort and said something to Greene's men. They took their guns and walked out with him. The guard closed the gate and bolted it.

How strange. Maybe the pinnace held more for them to carry back.

Margaret shut the door and stepped over a little girl about to bite her baby sister. The mother woke and intervened before crying started. Missus Brookes and Mary planned the rations for the morrow, while Margaret left to dress for the day. When she returned to the kitchen, she sat and listened absently to Mary and the cook's soft voices.

A gun fired. Margaret jumped, holding her breath. The firing of shots had calmed the last few days. Without the constant noise, this one shot put them on high alert. She rushed out into the dark yard.

"Guard, tell me what you see."

"M'lady, I make out some men. They come from the south with something. 'Tis our governor with our men—they haul forth a cow, m'lady—a quite dead cow."

Holy Mother of God, Leonard has shot our neighbor Oliver's cow.

Chapter 67

You have power over your mind, not outside events. Realize this and you will find strength.
- Marcus Aurelius

THEY BUTCHERED AND SKINNED Oliver's cow that same day. If one could ignore the circumstances of her death and enjoy what the beast provided, all would have full bellies with hopeful hearts. Yet, Margaret's heart filled with worry over Leonard.

On this sunny day everyone found work to do outside. Margaret cringed at young Mary's work. Determined, the girl scraped out the brains of the cow to use in the tanning process of the hide. With the messy work finished, she wiped her hands on her skirt, left the beast to the men, and took her baby inside to nurse.

Women of the fort chattered in good spirits as they performed their morning tasks. The children, making mischief and dashing underfoot, provoked Lady Lewger to insist they follow her into the barn. She would tell enchanting stories and let them tumble in the straw. Perhaps the younger ones would fall asleep in the darkened, peaceful barn. The promise of tiny sassafras or lemon sweets bestowed from Mary's hoard sent them dancing eagerly behind Lady Lewger. Margaret shuddered and hoped Mister Wiggles kept hidden.

The two guards up on the parapet watched the children. One yelled, "We like sassafras and stories too."

Those who heard laughed. Margaret grinned and stopped to tell the women doing laundry to be frugal with water. Two maids weeded the garden. Squash was almost ready to harvest. Pumpkin would soon follow.

"I nursed the little princess." Young Mary said to Margaret. "Auntie Mary and I chop-stack more wood." Margaret happily carried the baby inside to rock, coo, and sing to her until her little dark eyes closed and tiny fingers stopped clutching. When asleep, Margaret placed her gently in her basket on the bench.

Men shouted.

The air stilled with silence—too much silence. Margaret's skin tingled. She strained to hear. The soft chunk of splitting and stacking of wood continued from the back of the house.

Two shots shattered the moment.

Margaret rushed from the kitchen, through the dining hall, into the great hall, and grabbed her flintlock, holding it down beside her skirt. With the crook of her thumb, she pulled the cock of her flintlock full back. She jerked the door open. Men poured through the stockade gate. The new soldier, who Margaret hadn't seen since the day the Lewgers arrived at the fort, Rabley his name, stood inside the opened gate, waving for others to enter. They whooped into the yard with their weapons at the ready.

Her heart stopped at the sight of St. Thomas's two fallen guards.

What has happened to the women, the children?

She prayed they stayed safely hidden in the barn.

A sweaty, unshaven brute charged from the gate toward the house. He saw Margaret, slowed, chuckled, and relaxed the hold on his gun. Licking his lips, he grinned.

The rebel stopped, eyes widened, as the flintlock emerged from the folds of her gown, her finger firm on the trigger.

She aimed at his chest and squeezed.

The baby's scream pierced through the blast.

Heart skittering, Margaret fled to the kitchen. The child sat wailing, wide-eyed with red, wet cheeks. Margaret, hands shaking, struggled to reload her powder and shot.

The back kitchen door flung open. A soldier loped over and snatched the sobbing baby. His gun pointed at Margaret as she inserted the ramrod down her barrel.

"Would not do tha, woman." He held the screaming child crooked, dangling over his elbow, in front of his chest. Sounds of others stormed into the front hall, searching rooms.

The infant gasped for a breath then shrieked to the skies.

He shall not take Giles's child.

"'Tis over woman, lower ye gun."

A sickening thud—blood, tissue, and bone sprayed everything nearby. The rebel crumpled to his knees. Margaret swiped her forehead and cheek and raised her rifle, but the man dropped the screaming child then toppled to the floor.

Margaret, forgetting her rifle, scooped up and hugged the sticky, sobbing baby.

Sounds of others flooded through the dining hall, heading toward the kitchen. She glanced at the soldier on the floor—Young Mary's axe was embedded deep into the back of his skull.

The empress, jaw set hard, stared at him. She put her boot on his back, yanked out her axe, wiped the remnants of carnage on her petticoat, then held out her arms for her child.

Mary stood frozen in the doorway. Soldiers had stormed into the kitchen with guns aimed to kill.

Someone snatched the axe and Margaret's flintlock. Then the men marched the Brent women with sobbing child to the barn to join the other captives.

Margaret did as she was told.

The soldiers tried to control the chaos, but these men knew not how. Margaret saw her fear echoed in her sister's face. A soldier shot his pistol in the air. Everyone quieted except the wailing children.

The rebels argued. Then they corralled the inhabitants of St. Thomas's Fort into a tight knot, and after much discussion, herded everyone south. They would march their prisoners to Cornwallis's looted and damaged mansion. Margaret knew this decision meant for now these rebels had no plans for a mass murder. *Dear Lord, what will become of Maryland, Leonard, and us?*

Chapter 68
August 1646

One Year Later

I can't go back to yesterday because I was a different person then.
- Lewis Carroll

LAST YEAR, AFTER DAYS of imprisonment in the Cornwallis's ravaged Cross Manor, the Catholics and their followers finally pledged an oath of loyalty to those in power. Margaret smirked. The one in power was *the* Mister Pope. And that was that.

Then the Brents, Greenes, and their servants returned to what was left of their homes. All valuable, moveable objects had been plundered. Part of the fort had been burned.

Surprisingly, the capture of St. Thomas's Fort had ended the raids. The Brents and Greens' loyal and hardworking men and maids spent the autumn months laboring to repair the damaged properties and restore what they could of their larder. The loss of crops, livestock, and shortage of provisions had turned their winter into one of cold and hunger.

Maryland, your peacefulness betrays what the rebels have done to you.

On this sultry August morning, Margaret, holding the toddler, looked over to the garden where the two Marys picked peas and beans. The child, chubby and energetic, made Margaret smile. What didn't make her smile was her inability to figure out the government of Maryland.

Last March a Virginian, calling himself Captain Edward Hill, had been sent to find and bring back two men. He stayed and became governor.

"Heavens, Mary, to think a Virginian Protestant has become governor of Maryland, and under whose authority?" Margaret carried the toddler over to the garden.

"The Protestant Assembly duly elected him. Margaret, the child can walk."

Margaret stood the baby in the garden. The child wobbled, then toddled forward, falling into the cabbage.

After righting the child, Margaret said, "Maryland is reverting back to becoming part of Virginia. This year of worry with no word about Giles, Leonard, and the priests exhausts me. They may have been hanged or slaughtered."

Goodwin with his donkey at his side strolled through the open gate of the fort. The baby squealed and her little fat legs stumbled toward the donkey. Margaret and the Marys waved him over.

"Me bring ye news, m'ladies. Ye brother and Gentleman Lewger have arrived in Virginia. There they be attending to business afore coming home. But home they be soon."

A lump in her throat and tears rising, Margaret grabbed Mary and hugged her.

"Come, tell us more." Mary said, laughing.

"Naw, me must go north and tell Lady Lewger."

He picked the child up and set her on the donkey. She giggled, patting it. The gentle beast twitched his ears and held stone still.

"One more thing to tell ye. Your governor has sent a message to all of Maryland."

"Captain Hill?" Margaret looked at Mary to see if she understood.

"Naw, Leonard Calvert, our real governor. He sends a message from Virginia to Marylanders, telling them they would be pardoned for their rebellion. First, they must pledge loyalty and agree to Lord Baltimore's rule."

Butterflies or bumble bees, real or imagined, buzzed and fluttered around Margaret. Without thought she whispered, "He lives."

We won't become part of Virginia.

"Leonard—" Mary said. "Thank the heavens, but where has he been?"

"Nay." Goodwin shook his head, lifted the child down, and bid his goodbye. The princess toddled after them as best she could before tumbling over a tree root.

"Goodwin," Margaret called, "he is alive, and his giving pardons must mean he plans—"

He and the donkey stopped. He turned to her and said, "There be things me must not say. Be patient, m'ladies."

Chapter 69
December 1646

A real man smiles in trouble, gathers strength from distress, and grows brave by reflection.
- Thomas Paine

SINCE THE REBELLION, CAPTAIN Hill had held only one court. Margaret elected not to attend court, nor would she have been welcomed. Widow Oliver brought charges against Pope's Fort because they had also killed one of her cows. The widow, having two children, would feel the loss of even one cow most distressing. Her husband, Roger, had been killed by a Susquehannock, during one of Cornwallis' attacks on the tribe. Margaret sighed. The Brents must compensate the Pope family for the cow Leonard shot.

Approaching Goodwin's smithy at daybreak, she wondered why Goodwin had asked her to come. He said she might enjoy something most unusual this morning. It had been four months since he visited them in their garden. His being so secretive intrigued her, so she left the house in the predawn chill and stood waiting for him to appear.

While gazing over the St. George River a pervasive heaviness settled deep within her. Months ago, on St. Inigoes River—when Captain Ingle captured the Dutch ship—their world had changed. She swallowed hard and glanced toward Pope's Fort.

Pope's Fort had not suffered damage as did St. Thomas's Fort. Still, no flag flew. Margaret had a twinge of sanctimonious pride about their beautiful, symbolic flag. Three men stood outside Pope's Fort talking. Nathaniel Pope had reopened his ordinary. Catholics who entered would not be welcome.

And there it was. The problem that would not leave.

All hope for religious tolerance and political equality had been erased. With Protestants in control, their Assembly filled with Protestant burgesses, and with England in the hands of Parliament, Lord Baltimore's grand plan would evaporate. Maryland's dream would be no more.

Virginia has burned our land and murdered our ideals. Soon there will be no place left for pious groups as Catholics—or other extremes—such as the Puritans.

"M'lady Brent, ye came." Goodwin strode up the hill toward her, a grin wider than the river. "And jest in time, me would say. Look ye out there on the river."

She glanced beyond the dock.

"Nay, to the south."

Two pinnaces sailed the breeze toward St. Mary's—one she recognized.

"Thomas Greene's pinnace. Leonard comes!" She wrapped her arms around herself to contain her joy and kept her eyes on the vessels. "And my pinnace—the *Phoenix*—they've found my pinnace."

"Aye, he brings troops to rid those Protestants of their pretend governor."

"Oh, Goodwin. Please, no more fighting."

"You be not saying such if Governor Calvert gets his way. Pope's men be lazy and unawares. The rebels gone home or on their farms without arms. Me think this battle be quick. You and me, we stand here and watch."

The pinnaces docked and Calvert's militia filed out of the two pinnaces and down the gangplanks and stood silent, waiting instructions. Margaret counted twenty-nine armed men.

She gasped. Leonard had emerged with Giles and John Lewger.

The statesmen, talking quietly, disembarked from Margaret's pinnace.

Clasping her rosary, fearful something might destroy this moment, she said, "Goodwin?"

If they go to battle and die, I shall be wont to die too.

Calvert addressed his men, then silence prevailed. The militia followed the three statesmen up the path to the cliff, marching with guns at the ready, to Pope's Fort.

Goodwin stood frozen as did Margaret. Her breathing felt nonexistent.

As Calvert's militiamen neared, Pope's men, enjoying their conversation, looked up. One shouted something back toward the ordinary. Margaret could not make out the words. Nathaniel Pope emerged.

Calvert's militia had spread out and around the fort with lookouts who watched for other attacks. Leonard, Giles, and John strode up to Nathanial Pope. They exchanged words. Then the four of them strode into Pope's house. Two of Calvert's armed soldiers accompanied them.

Margaret looked at Goodwin. "What will happen?"

Goodwin shrugged. "Guess you and me wait."

Margaret leaned against a big oak, and Goodwin sat on his haunches.

An hour later, Giles and Lewger strode out and spoke to the cadre of soldiers. The men laughed, talked, and put themselves at ease. Giles looked toward the smithy and waved. He headed up the hill. John Lewger waved too but turned up the road to his home.

Goodwin stood. Margaret ran to greet her brother. She hugged him, which he had never liked. Her hug was required to be certain of this reality—of his being here.

Pulling him to Goodwin, she said, "Tell us all."

"Hoot-hoot. Good to be home." Giles sniffed the air, looked out at the river, then smiled at his sister. "Goodwin, thank you for bringing her here. Now my eagerness to see my wife and new daughter engulfs me."

"Tell. What happened down there."

"They put up no resistance. Leonard arrested Pope, the rebels in Hill's council, and some soldiers. Pope no longer owns the governor's house. Leonard will take up his residence there." Giles laughed. "One no longer needs a house when in prison. Our governor plans to call Assembly next month at St. Inigoes Fort. He will pardon rebels who pledge fealty, but he intends to discover who plundered, and they must return what they can or pay three-times the value."

Margaret tingled with happiness.

We will be strong and still hold the dream of our Maryland.

"Giles, my pinnace—"

"We knew the Virginian ruffian sailing it did not have your permission. We shall use it for our transportation to your home."

"But why did you and John Lewger go to Virginia before coming home? What was Leonard doing all this time?"

"So many questions. Dear sister, Leonard did not return earlier because he had no success in raising troops. That truth is half the matter. The other half pains me to say."

He had been in prison? Nonsense.

"Our Lord Governor has been quite ill."

Chapter 70
Later That Day

Democracy is the power of equal votes for unequal minds.
- King Charles I

AFTER WELCOMING GILES HOME and enjoying a sensible supper by Missus Brooks, in spite of their still diminished larder, they took their ease in front of the fireplace to watch Giles play with his toddler. The child with long dark straight hair, light tan skin, and eyes shining black would soon be two years old. They named her Mary, but to avoid confusion they would call her Elizabeth, after the Brents' mother.

Giles, ever the child himself, is recapturing some of his playful childhood pleasures.

Laughing, he got up off the floor and stretched. Elizabeth clung to his leg, saying, "More-more, peese."

Her mother picked her up, saying, "Nap time. Your father needs to rest." Ignoring Giles and the child's protests, young Mary took the child away.

He stretched out his long legs, arched his back, and rubbed his arms.

"Romping thus has caused me to use muscles I seldom use."

Nodding, Margaret said, "My back and hips feel the years from carrying your child hither and yon."

He stared into the fire. "This business of falling into our Proprietor's disfavor disturbs me. Cecil's decision be damned for the things I should not need give a single apology. Ingle should have been called on his traitorous ways long before I did so. Even Lewger agrees. After seeing what part Baldridge played in this rebellion, I should not have been surprised at his letting Ingle escape. However, Cornwallis's disloyalty did surprise me. Our Lord Proprietor does not see him as disloyal, but I do."

A chill overtook Margaret. More logs on the fire wouldn't warm her. She could not guess Giles's future.

"Lord Baltimore accused me of unthinkable things when I married. Bloody hell. Fulke returns to England for want of a bride, Leonard rushes off to England to marry our little sister, and they leave me here, no wife to console me, and with a pig's arse of a mess."

His sisters kept silent.

"With what funds I have left I shall purchase lands and build a manor in Virginia around Aquia Creek. My family and I will live there—to retire." He stretched and said, "Margaret and Mary, your life here will change. Maryland requires rebuilding. Most of her people have fled to other colonies or have been

257

ruthlessly murdered. What have we left? Maybe a hundred or so out of four hundred? Restoring equality and tolerance in a new government, when the majority of citizens are angry Protestants, will near be impossible."

"You are the dreamer of grand ideas," Margaret said. "No one may practice Catholicism in Virginia. Protestants dominate their colony, too. Even their Puritans are harassed."

After a moment, Mary said, "We could go back to how father had resolved the problem of living in a land of Protestants and being Catholic."

Giles nodded. "Many do so in Virginia, and no one gives them mind because they live out beyond the settlements and towns. Inconvenience has advantages. I shall build my own chapel on my lands and employ our own family priest."

Her father's priest had lived at Lark Stoke and tutored them, until the king's men abolished this practice. Margaret sighed. Giles had given up on their beloved Maryland.

But not so. Giles had not given up but been driven away. Lord Baltimore had seen to it that Giles would not be welcomed in this province.

"Giles," she said, "I wish you would reconsider. Often tempers settle, and all is well again."

"Virginia will bring us peace that you sisters will not find in Maryland. Sell your land to Virginia Puritans. Many wish to live here. Buy land in Virginia with me."

"I cannot. If Leonard's ill, he needs me." The emptiness inside came back.
Maryland is my land, my home, my dream. Only here I have a voice.

"No need to fuss about Leonard. He's sought medical care in Virginia and takes medication. You saw him today, leading a charge against our foe."

"Hardly a charge, brother."

"He tells me he plans to send his troops to settle Kent Island and then north to Virginia—to Chicagoan and the trouble-makers—and quell threats. Those rebels in the north continue their plot to murder Catholics."

"Kent Island—after what Cummins did there—now Claiborne is back. Those of us whom they plundered will need representation for our recompense." She shook her head. "The courts will be quite busy. I shall stay, but Mary need not remain."

"Dear sister, we started this together, and we will end this together. I live where you live."

Chapter 71
January 1647

If you are silent, be silent out of love. If you speak, speak out of love.
- St. Augustine

WHAT MARGARET WANTED MOST was to talk to Leonard. He had lost much weight and looked exhausted, but he insisted he must spend his time restoring Maryland. He had no idle time for chatting, yet a month later he did invite her to sit in Assembly at St. Inigoes.

This pleased her. What did not please her came from Lord Baltimore. Her brother's handling of the Ingle matter, along with his marriage, dissatisfied him. Giles would not be on Leonard's new council.

Leonard specifically requested Margaret to sit in Assembly because he needed insight on reactions to his proceedings. She would sit silent and observe, watching the gentlemen of the council with their governor mend the broken and create new laws.

Margaret, at the back of the large drafty hall at St. Inigoes Fort, hoped to be discreet. This sad environment swept away any joy. She shivered and pulled her cloak tight. Once this had been a grand place with tapestries, gleaming fine wood furnishings, and sacred brass and silver relics, but the rebels had destroyed St. Inigoes' splendor. Now the cold, dusty hall held sparse furnishings—just tables, benches, and a few chairs.

The gentlemen and burgesses greeted each other, showing scant civility to those of opposition during the rebellion. All appeared impatient to get on with business.

A familiar internal bristling returned—Margaret recognized her feeling of exclusion. She had not been allowed to partake in the discussion long ago, when Lord Baltimore talked to her father and brothers. They had gathered around the table to study maps of the new world. She could not count the numerous other times she had been excluded. Exclusion from information and discussions followed her through life.

Yet Leonard has been generous to include me.

She had attended many of these august gatherings of the great landholders and the freemen. Here assembled those men who might own a few acres or many acreages titled as hundreds. Kindly, Leonard had opened these legislative doors of Maryland to Margaret where she participated and acquired knowledge.

Still, I hold lands—more land than many who vote here today.

She folded her hands. willed her frogs to stop tussling, and waited.

Governor Leonard Calvert stood and called Assembly to order. He did not need to ask for quiet this time.

Standing tall, looking thinner but as handsome as ever, and with a strong voice he said, "You have been called hither as freemen to treat and advise. You may touch all matters in Assembly without fear—freely and boldly. If you have experienced any crime since my last general pardon, we will address such business later. For now, I have six witnesses who will testify on my behalf. Before their coming out of Virginia, I did declare to all soldiers, in public, if the inhabitants of St. Mary's accepted my pardon for everyone's part in the rebellion and are obedient to these lordship's soldiers, these soldiers should expect to serve with no pillage. I told the soldiers I would receive these inhabitants in peace and only take aid for the soldiers from the inhabitants to quell the troubles in Kent."

Margaret listened as each of the six men repeated what Leonard had said. Many of these men in today's Assembly had been part of Captain Hill's Assembly last year.

Governor Calvert's greatest opposition in this Assembly came when he proposed a sixty-pound duty on each hogshead of tobacco to pay Lord Baltimore's soldiers.

Margaret cringed. These citizens, after a year of raiding and burning, scarcely had enough food to feed their families. Some called out they would abandon Maryland because of this cost to pay the soldiers.

Obviously frustrated, Governor Calvert said, "If the soldiers' pay requires more than sixty pounds per hogshead, then I and Lord Baltimore will pay the rest from our estates."

The bill passed.

Margaret mentally crossed herself in hopes the expensive soldiers would soon be dispersed back to their homes.

After the Assembly adjourned, governmental functions began to improve. Margaret gave Leonard due credit for his leadership.

A few days later the Provincial Court resumed hearing cases. One of the first cases involved several men who spread seditious rumors. John Lewger addressed the court in these matters.

"I charge these men who are well known to all in this province. Thomas and John Sturman, Francis Gray, John Hampton, Robert Smith, and Thomas Yewell, each who have received previous pardons for crimes of rebellion, have without permission fled to Chicagoan to plot against this province. They plan to burn, steal cattle, and do away with our governor, Leonard Calvert. Some of these men are spreading rumors of an invasion of Maryland by Claiborne, Virginia, and even Parliament. Lastly, some of these men have stolen and killed our cattle in the night and taken the meat."

Governor Calvert asked, "What evidence do you bring before us."

A man stood and said, "My name is Edward Thomson. I live in Chicagoan. I heard Taylor and Gray speak they would go to kill ye, Governor. When ye go for Kent, these Chicagoans will go and burn and destroy as much as they be able here in St. Mary's."

Lewger's court revelation would now delay the Kent assault. Margaret could see Leonard's concern for needing to pay the soldiers for longer service.

When the court adjourned, Leonard told Margaret his plans for Kent would have to wait until April. Captain Price of the militia approached them, removed his hat, and bowed to Lady Brent.

He said, "I overheard your conversation, Governor. There is disquiet among my men. They must be fed, and they must be paid."

"The next shipment of tobacco will benefit your soldiers, captain. I personally will see to it your men will not go hungry, and they will receive compensation for their efforts."

If you do not hold to this, my dear governor, we all shall suffer mightily.

Chapter 72
April 1647

Don't be pushed by your problems. Be led by your dreams.
- Ralph Waldo Emerson

HER GOVERNOR HAD MANAGED in four months to put Maryland back into order. Leonard called Assembly and held courts with Protestant rebels and Catholic loyalists working together. When Calvert finally landed his troops on Kent Island, he again pardoned those on Kent who pledged fidelity to Lord Baltimore.

As Governor, he appointed Robert Vaughan to be commander of Kent Island. The island settled into a congenial calm. For those who refused to make the pledge, their estates were seized until they did. The worst of the usurpers stood to face whatever justice the courts handed out, including Cummins, who had slaughtered Giles's cattle and burned his books. Unfortunately, the most disruptive agent of all, Claiborne, had fled to Virginia.

This should be celebrated. Yet Margaret's frogs sprawled in a stupor.

Under Leonard Calvert's forgiving leadership, Maryland had a chance for a stable government, with tolerance for an individual's religion, and where people could produce crops for food and income.

Numbness refused to let Margaret be comforted by Leonard's accomplishments. The citizens disliked his duties—fees placed on the sale of their tobacco to pay the soldiers. Even her friends and neighbors argued over this new tax.

"We've given our share—powder, shot, our looted farms, seem plenty pay for our country."

"Yah, and me son's life."

"What aboot me livestock and me corn—'tis gone. We barely have enoof ta feed the wee ones."

These voices played in her head during court this morning. The news of Kent Island had created a jovial atmosphere for all except Margaret. The soldiers had not been paid, they needed appropriate meals, and they must be sent home. Yet Leonard would not send them home until they had been paid. These troubles nagged her all the way back to St. Thomas's Fort.

She opened the door to find Giles and young Mary hustling around, packing their belongings in bundles. Little Elizabeth pulled and chewed at the cords holding leather packages together. Slobber dripped from her chin and in her other hand she clutched her tiny straw dolly Margaret had made and dressed from scraps of calico and lace.

Missus Brooks had prepared their afternoon meal, placing dishes and servers on the table.

"Come partake." Mary called from the dining room to Giles and young Mary. "Tell us about your morning in court, dear sister."

Margaret stood staring at the bundles. Giles and young Mary sat at the table and waited for Margaret to come say grace. Instead, Margaret picked up Elizabeth, wiped her chin, and laid her cheek on the plump, warm head of the toddler. This tiny person nuzzled close to her auntie, laid her head on Margaret's chest, and stuck her fingers in her mouth. She smelled of dried milk, leather, and wild strawberries. Margaret remembered a day, long ago, when she and Leonard had picked and eaten wild strawberries... the day he had proposed.

I do not know which might be holier—our way of chastity or their way, bringing this precious one to life.

"Margaret," Mary called, "come say grace."

The tied bundles told all. The couple, with Margaret's heart, would sail to Virginia. She turned toward the window and stared out blinking hard, not wanting anyone to see her face. The baby, warm and heavy, gurgled words too soft to understand.

"Say your words again, please." Margaret put her ear down against the child's dark locks of hair.

"Bye-bye aunmarger."

"Bye-bye my dear heart."

Chapter 73
June 9, 1647

He was a man, take him for all and all. I shall not look upon his like again.
- William Shakespeare

A SUCCESSION OF RAPID knocks brought Mary and Margaret to their door before Missus Taylor could open it. Already hot, the early morning June sun poured into their muggy home as the ever-present flies hummed around the doorframe. Their neighbor Thomas Greene, face lined in concern, stood before them.

Hat in hand, he said, "Forgive me ladies. We have an urgent summons to appear at the Governor's home. One of his men just left the message at my house and rode off on his horse."

"You've elected to walk." Margaret said. "If it's urgent we saddle—"

"Walking will provide time to sort things out."

"Heavens, Thomas, sorting things out requires information. I find this unsettling not knowing more of what brings you here full of unease." Margaret pulled the door shut behind them.

The three hurried up the path to St. Mary's. Leonard had held two courts since returning from Kent, one the middle of May and one a few days ago. His face had a grayness about it, and he appeared considerably thinner, but he had presided with his usual alertness.

"We've never been summoned like this before." This troubled her. "Tell us why he has called us. Something decisive must have happened."

"The militia grows more impatient." Thomas kept his brisk pace while talking. "They've been housed at St. Inigoes Fort since the first of the year, and their only conflict of any merit happened a month ago at Kent Island. They run low on food. They will have to wait until this year's crops come in for hardier meals."

Margaret glanced over at him. "The province must provide them with corn from last year's crops."

"Not receiving their wages presents a greater concern. Leonard promised them pay in place of their looting." He scowled. "If they decide to loot—we have no defense. We used to be four hundred strong in St. Mary's City. The rebellion has left us less than a hundred."

"Those who fled should have returned by now." Margaret shook her head.

Greene set his jaw. "If we have an insubordinate militia, they will destroy Maryland."

"Lord Baltimore," Mary said, "still has the charter from the king—the one giving him entitlement to Maryland."

Thomas Greene huffed and squinted at her. "Unfortunately, with our own war we have taken our eyes off England. The Scots handed King Charles over to the Parliamentarians, who will behead him. Lord Baltimore's charter may not be viable much longer. If we do not demonstrate a strong government, we will lose our right to govern and any semblance of religious tolerance."

This twisted mess more than provoked Margaret. "We cannot have the Protestants of Virginia reclaiming Maryland."

When they arrived at the Governor's House, Peasley, quite grim, bowed. He ushered them into the main hall and back to Leonard's bedroom.

Margaret hesitated. Mary reached over and clutched Margaret's hand.

Stars in heaven, this is most improper.

Thomas Greene placed his hand on Margaret's back and nodded toward Peasley, standing at the bedroom's open door. The three entered the darkened room. The drapes had been closed against the heat of the morning. East India spiced incense burned—its heavy scent pretended to cover objectionable smells. Leonard, wearing night clothes, and propped in a great bed surrounded with numerous down pillows smiled weakly at them. He beckoned them forward. No longer did a handsome face and shining dark eyes welcome her. This morning he appeared thin, with a sickly yellow hue.

Margaret dropped Mary's hand. She dashed to his bedside. "Leonard—I—" She shuddered.

Death invites this man into the realm of no return.

Glancing at Mary, Thomas, and Peasley, Margaret had no words for the turmoil and questions in her mind.

Peasley had escorted the Governor's two closest servants to join them. He offered Leonard a sip of water, then stepped aside.

"As you can see," Leonard said in a clear and quiet tone, "the time has come for me to sort out my affairs and those of the province. I must be sure they are in order. My men and friends, you have been asked here to witness my instructions. In the next few days, you will be called to verify what I say here."

This cannot be so. His mind sharp—his age young—he still has much to contribute. My dear Leonard, my dearest...

Leonard's words jumbled in her ears. She studied the people in the room. Here lay Maryland's Governor, leading the country with his wisdom for the last time from his deathbed.

This particular event, happening at this exact moment, would alter the citizens of Maryland's lives. Margaret willed her mind to be silent. She swallowed uncomfortably—her mouth dry. Across the ocean, dearest Ann and her two babes would wait for a father who would never return.

Oh, dear Lord, someone must make him well.

Winter stormed into her soul. She forced herself to listen. Soon this would be revealed as a great show—like one written by their long-ago neighbor William of Stratford. One of these men, in any second, would declare this scene a farce. Then all would have a good laugh.

No one laughed. She needed this to end now.

She shut her eyes and worked to put Leonard's well-executed words into something she might understand. He expected this of her.

"With that business settled, I now appoint Thomas Greene," Leonard cleared his throat and said, "to be the next governor of Maryland under the authority of the second Lord Baltimore and by the Maryland Charter given to his father and him from King James and his son, King Charles."

Both kings now dead or as good as dead, and the charter—

"Lastly," he coughed, wiped his mouth, then said, "I appoint Lady Margaret Brent to be the sole executrix of my estate."

Margaret held back a gasp. Her eyes opened wide.

Could this even be—the meaning of it all—?

The governor's unprecedented move would raise questions among the men of Maryland.

Show no emotion but listen intently.

"Margaret, the soldiers—Lord Baltimore's and my estate—take all and pay all."

Leonard sunk deeper into his pillows.

With his eyes half closed, he said, "The fears of Marylanders have started to settle as they look to the future. These citizens will not survive another siege."

The only noise in the room was the cacophony of unintelligible sounds in Margaret's mind. She wondered if only she had privy to it.

Leonard—St. Mary's needs a priest. A priest—give us a priest.

Realizing everyone stared at her, she swallowed, then bowed her head.

"Let us pray."

She crossed herself and willed her voice to remain strong and say words.

"Almighty and merciful God, who hast bestowed upon mankind Thy gift of everlasting life, we beseech you to bless our dear Governor, Leonard Calvert and be gracious unto us Thy loving servants. Comfort our souls which Thou hast made, that, in the hour of our passing, wipe away all stain of sin, so we may deserve to come forth and stand before Thee. Through Christ our Lord. Amen."

Everyone echoed, "Amen."

Leonard motioned for Peasley to come bend nearer. He spoke quietly into his ear. Peasley straightened and looked at those around Calvert's bedside.

"Your governor would speak in private with the Lady Margaret Brent. The rest will accompany me into the dining hall for some beverage, where you might discuss matters of concern."

When they had left and shut the door, Leonard said, "Dear sweet lady, come sit. Bring the chair close where I can easily look upon your beauty that gives me comfort."

She tugged the heavy chair until placed next to his bed.

"Much better. I need to clearly hear your answers to what I must ask of you."

Margaret could hold silent no longer.

"You have totally befuddled me, sir." Her voice, uncooperative, caused her to cough. "When I inquired as to your health several times these last months, you refused to acknowledge anything serious betook you. Now I see for myself, and it pleases me not in the least. Giles mentioned you saw a physician in Virginia who had prescribed medications. Giles told me all would be well. Leonard, I—this surprises me—and breaks my heart." Moisture filled her eyes. She shut them and turned away for a moment to dab them.

"Giles told the truth. I took treatment from a chirugeon, Doctor Hooper, but after months of bloodletting I fared no better." He closed his eyes and rested for a few moments. His breathing appeared quite shallow. "I consulted next with Doctor Waldron who prescribed mithridate. I have taken it faithfully. These last few weeks it continued to lose its value."

"Mithridate—for the plague, no—others would be sick too. Doctor Waldron must believe you had been poisoned." This could be so. Many Virginian Protestants would be pleased to see him and the other Marylanders gone.

"Doctor Waldron questioned me about snake bite," he cleared his throat and said, "but I cannot recall having been bitten. Besides, if a snake had bitten me," his voice rasped, "I would be dead from Doctor Hooper's bloodletting long before I even took Doctor Waldron's mithridate." He struggled to breathe more air, but it brought on a coughing spell.

"Maybe Doctor Gerrard from St. Clemmons—"

"Margaret, leave this be." He wiped his mouth. "I have no vigor for such discussion."

She could see this truth.

"My time on Earth slips quickly. Please, let me say what I must."

Her inner frogs jittered, heated, and lurched about. On the outside Margaret sat straight and presented tranquility with attentiveness. She folded her hands in her lap and waited for him to speak.

"If the soldiers do not receive compensation for their employment," his voice barely audible, said, "you will see an uprising, one Maryland will not survive. The customs imposed on the tobacco exports will not be sufficient. Take my brother's cattle and my land and whatever of value in our estates and sell them for the soldiers' pay."

As the minutes progressed, Leonard's energy dwindled. He continued to give her instructions on the affairs of Maryland and then he turned to his personal instructions.

"Please send a tender note to my dear wife. I know not what to say to her."

His eyes shut, watering at the corners. Tears of grief or illness, she did not know.

"You, dear lady, know words to soothe. I have a small carved wooden box. Send the contents to Ann for her and the children as my remembrance." He hesitated. "I should not ask, but if you might keep a small parcel of any part of my estate to transfer to my eldest son, William, it would be God's blessing." He shut his eyes. He whispered, "Promise me—you will save Maryland first."

She leaned close and said, "I shall. How I do wish Maryland had a priest to give you comfort."

His boney fingers waved her words away. "Call the others in. I have personal items yet to dispense."

She bit her lip, worked the large chair aside, and stared down at him.

He reached for her hand. She leaned in and gave it to him. "My dear, dear

Lady Margaret." He kissed her fingers. "I forever hold you close in my heart and in the highest esteem."

Chapter 74
June 1647

Subtlety may deceive you; integrity never will.
- Oliver Cromwell

IN HER GRIEF, MARY took on the task to pen notes to those who lived beyond the ears of the governor's home, telling them of Leonard Calvert's death and funeral.

She looked up from her work and said, "For heaven's sake, Margaret. Quit pacing and do something productive. No matter your troubles, they have never driven you this mad before."

"We have no priest, Mary. We don't even have a church with a roof. This cannot be a proper funeral. I say we have not one person who can even pretend to be a priest. What to do—what to do?"

"We do as we must, dear sister. St. Thomas believed all receive what they deserve. You must take comfort in knowing it is not what you do, but what God wills. Now please busy yourself with what may be within your capabilities and stop bothering God about His will."

Margaret huffed. "I am off to purchase dozens and dozens of waxed votive candles and will hire a seamstress. Please do see to it our maids start preparing the feast. Remember you promised to gather baskets of wildflowers and cut greens for the service."

Carpenter and planter Daniel Clocker, one of Cornwallis's freed men, encountered Margaret on the path to St. Mary's. Upon hearing the news, his grief was such he insisted on constructing a fine wooden coffin for his Governor, thus helping to ease Margaret's dark brooding.

She knocked on the door of Missus Todd and hired her to sew a luxurious black hearse cloth edged in white silk that bore the Calvert arms. From the seamstress's prior work, this hearse cloth would match any of even the finest English gentlemen.

The muggy and warm air made her clothes uncomfortable and sticky. Walking these distances to procure these funeral items had not settled her mind. There would be no proper goodbye without a priest.

Winifred Greene and her maids helped plan the funeral feast. They would lay an elaborate table with beef, mutton, venison, quail, vegetables of all sorts, fruit, and the most tempting of sweets. The attendees would be served fine wine and ale. Still, without a priest there would be no comfort. Margaret let her gaze sweep along the St. George River.

This beautiful outdoors holds God's church, but how can we manage without a priest?

Her rambunctious frogs curled into themselves and wept.

* * *

Margaret and Mary watched Giles and his family sail up the St. George and dock their pinnace at St. Thomas's Fort. The sisters rushed down to welcome the little family.

"Hi aunmarger. Hi." Elizabeth pranced up and down on the deck waving her little straw doll.

Their men carried the family's bundles to the house, and Margaret snatched the child into her arms, hugging her until the child squirmed.

"Down peese." She, with her dolly, patted Margaret on her cheek.

Margaret laughed, set the child on the dock, and turned to greet Giles and young Mary. Beside them, wearing a black and white cassock stood a thin, young priest.

Margaret blinked. There stood a real priest, waiting. Trickles of tears might stream down her cheeks. She would not allow it, but then, she could not stop them. She coughed, swallowing hard.

Giles placed his hand on the man's back. "A manor close to our land hired this pious and learned man to be their family priest. I requested permission, and they agreed. He will officiate at Leonard's service. Margaret and Mary, please welcome Father Taitte."

Chapter 75
St. John's Hall
January 21, 1648

In grave difficulties, and with little hope, the boldest measures are the safest.
- King Charles I

TODAY IN ASSEMBLY, MARGARET wore a bold green gown with a buttercream silk petticoat. These colors complemented her red hair and the green of her eyes. Silk against her skin calmed her. She draped her black woolen cape across the bench where she sat and watched the burgesses and gentlemen.

Six months ago, after Leonard's death, the captain of the militia informed Governor Greene his men had no food. Greene embargoed all exports of corn and assessed part of the planters' crop to be given to the soldiers.

"Lady Brent," a gentlemen landholder addressed her. "How goes the inventory on Lord Baltimore and Governor Calvert's estate? The militia will not stand much longer without pay."

"I assure you, sir, the inventory has been completed, and I shall address this matter today."

After Leonard's passing, Margaret received her Letters of Administration for his estate. In court a few days later and before her brother returned to Virginia, Governor Greene appointed Giles as the sole member of his council. Then Greene posed a question.

"Since Lord Baltimore's Maryland attorney John Lewger has returned to England, Lord Baltimore has no one to represent him." Governor Greene then asked Giles, "Should Leonard Calvert's administrator serve as attorney for Lord Baltimore in Lewger's place?"

Their act made sure Margaret's authority to disperse Lord Baltimore's property would be written in the official record. She sat straight and clasped her hands.

This appointment has placed me in a most untenable situation.

These angry planters must pay assessments on their tobacco shipments. Such revenue would help cover what Maryland owed these soldiers. Margaret shuddered. After six months of no compensation, the militia had been threatening to plunder.

Thomas Greene decided to keep the soldiers here for his protection because the former governor from Virginia, Edward Hill, demanded he had the right to be reinstated as Maryland's governor.

Margaret's dilemma on how to pay the soldiers could be resolved if she had time to collect the many debts owed to Leonard. Without payment of these debts, the only way to prevent an uprising would be to sell Leonard's and Lord Baltimore's land and cattle.

One of the first court cases today came from a soldier demanding his due.

Governor Greene called Margaret forward to respond.

"Burgesses of Assembly and Gentlemen of the provincial court, any demand on the Calvert estates for payment will not be recognized as yet. I claim the privilege of administrator, and this custom declares the estate not to be troubled within a twelvemonth and a day. Administrators need unhindered time to receive bills, put accounts in order, and organize payments."

Twelvemonth and a day comes quickly—the tenth of June, but for now these hungry beasts shall be held at bay.

Having thought that, a wave of guilt swept over her. These men could have started looting. They deserved compensation.

Greene called the Assembly to come to order several times before the men settled.

He lacks control, unlike Leonard.

Margaret listened to the proceedings with her ears, but her mind replayed her quandary.

Even bestowed the legal authority of Lord Baltimore's attorney, if she sold anything of Lord Baltimore without his permission, his ire toward her would be greater than any anger toward Giles. Unlike her brother, she did not want to flee to Virginia.

Lord Baltimore must grant approval before she sold any of his holdings.

Yet time prevented this. A rebellion could erupt before the next ship sailed. His being weeks away across the Atlantic would not allow for the formality of please, may I, and thank you.

Assemblymen's frenzied discussion over possible tariff percentages imposed on exported tobacco in order to pay the soldiers caused her stomach to grip. The way this tariff argument seemed to be going, she would have no choice but to send her request to Cecil Calvert and wait for him to respond with his blessings.

Blessings—hardly. But then if he knew the dire and honest predicament befalling his Maryland entitlement, one which Catholic's enemies might snatch away, he would give approval. He surely knows, with King Charles in prison and about to lose his head, no one in England will protect his father's charter.

Now voices grew loud in argument about the required amounts of corn to be forfeit for bread to feed the militia. They talked in circles. Someone must straighten this out.

Governor Greene knows not how to lead this discussion to any good end. These landowners each have a vote, and the result could well destroy our province. These arguments are muddled without forethought.

Burning with annoyance, Margaret lurched up, standing tall.

"Lord Governor."

"Assembly recognizes Lady Brent."

Margaret strode forward. Her indignation melted as her sense of exclusion and long-denied entitlement grew.

"Lord Governor and Gentlemen of Assembly, I am one of the largest of landowners in Maryland with over 120 acres, in addition to 2,000 acres entitled to me through headrights. My interest because I am a woman landowner does not receive representation in your governing body. As the administrator of Lord Baltimore's estate and the executrix of the former Governor Leonard Calvert, their financial holdings and responsibilities are at the mercy of decisions made here today.

"I, Margaret Brent, stand before you as a landowner. I seek a vote in this Assembly Hall. I also request a second voice in this Assembly Hall as the personal representative for your former Governor, Leonard Calvert."

The hall erupted into debate then punctuated with shouting, mirth, and guffaws.

Standing straight and staring into the governor's face, Margaret waited.

After much chaos, Governor Greene finally stood, and slammed his hand down on the table.

"Quiet!"

Margaret knew what his ruling would be.

When the hall settled, he said, "Lady Brent, your service to Maryland cannot be denied. That you have acquired more lands than most is well known." He set his lips and picked up some papers. He looked back at her and shaking his head, said, "We, in this Assembly and in our Provincial Court owe you great respect. With regret, I must remind all any vote given by a woman can only be accepted if she be our Queen."

And there it was, like her brothers a long time ago, these gentlemen would not step aside to let her stand at their table.

Margaret continued to stare into his eyes as she spoke in a calm but commanding voice. "Let your record show that unless I be given voice, I do thus protest and disavow all proceedings here today."

She plucked up her skirts, turned, and strode to the back bench, not thinking of anything except she had voiced what her heart required. Wrapping the warm wool of her cloak around her, her hands began to shake. Margaret set her jaw, silenced her frogs, and marched out of the hall.

She gave Peasley a nod. He bowed and escorted her to the door, gently bidding her good day.

The echo of the men's words splintered and cracked around her in the winter-chilled air.

She and her sister owned more land than most. These men had no right to exclude her. Leonard had charged her to *sell all and pay all* to prevent another uprising. Two votes would not have changed much, but this loss cost her the privilege to negotiate with them—to reframe the case for tobacco and corn tariffs to pay the soldiers.

Margaret buried her hands into the folds of her cloak to warm them. She could not do anything about the cold biting into her toes and heart.

They must replenish powder and shot and renovate the damaged St. Thomas's Fort. Leaping frogs unsettled her stomach. Margaret would send her message to Lord Baltimore and wait for his reply.

Still, she would not hear from him until long after the raiding and looting destroyed Maryland. Regardless, she must obtain his permission.

Without it, she could not remain in her beloved Maryland.

My Maryland, I have sailed your waters and worked your soil and watched your people die for their love of you. My allegiance to you flows through my heart and blood. What to do?

Leonard's home and surrounding land should be preserved for his son's inheritance. She must not sell even one item, one calf, or one piglet belonging to Lord Baltimore, war or not, he would never again welcome her in his province.

She rubbed her temples. Like those Assemblymen, her thoughts scurried around in circles.

Could she have saved Maryland from all this chaos? Even though she couldn't let him know, her heart did belong to Leonard. If Margaret had unselfishly given it to him, and they had married, the end would not be such as this. The frogs pounced in nervous tiny hops. She and Leonard would have lived in his glorious new home.

Nathaniel Pope could not have derived any power.

The two of them would have found a way to keep Ingles from rebelling. She shuddered at her next thought. If they had no need for a militia, Leonard would not have gone to Virginia where he became so gravely ill.

If she had married him, she would have lost her land and her voice, but all of this dissention would have been avoided and Leonard might have lived.

A lump formed in her throat.

Maybe Giles and young Mary hold the greatest of God's blessings—a blessing I do not know except through my love for Elizabeth.

This morning at St. Thomas's Fort, before she started out into the gray morning's cold, something behind the drapery had caught her eye. Her glance told not what it might be. Curious, she moved the fabric aside and saw Elizabeth's forgotten dolly. Margaret, with aching heart, held it to her cheek, remembering warm, sweet baby smells.

Oh, the sight of that wee dolly pours sadness into my heart—remembering my dear little one far away in Virginia.

Virginia Puritans had paid a good price to purchase Maryland property. She sighed. She would visit her brother and return Elizabeth's dolly.

Further up the lane, Leonard's home appeared—casting a sensation of abandonment—no longer promising her a future full of hope. She trod along the worn trail and turned to the path that would take her home. The sight of Mister William Whittle distracted her thoughts as he trudged up toward Goodwin's smithy, shouldering a heavy-looking piece of metal. Goodwin always cheered her.

Mister Whittle and Goodwin discussed the piece of metal. She smiled, knowing the people of St. Mary's valued Goodwin and his business.

Margaret shivered, but not from the flakes of snow drifting down from the pillowed sky. Seeing these two men recalled her discussion with Mister Whittle and his wife a few days earlier. Her angst over starving soldiers and her predicament with Lord Baltimore reignited.

Lord Baltimore's permission, if it came at all, would not arrive in time to pro-

tect his *Maryland legacy. All will be lost—citizens, homes, livestock, crops, and even Lord Baltimore's grant. Whatever he might approve, being late would make it all worthless.*

Goodwin's donkey munched on a breakfast of hay. Margaret approached the gentle beast. He glanced toward her, swished his tail in contentment, and continued eating. She scratched the wee animal behind his ear and whispered, "You have endured so much, but now you live in love and peace."

Goodwin's impulse to rescue this creature speaks well of him. What did Sir William Shakespeare say? If we are true to ourselves, we cannot be false to others.

Standing at his forge, Goodwin smiled and nodded at Margaret, then took Whittle's metal and positioned it with great concentration over the hot coals.

"Mister Whittle, a word with you if you please." Margaret called to him.

"Ah, Lady Brent. My wife asked about you yesterday."

"Please do give her my regard. My sister and I wish her well."

As I do for each citizen of this fine land.

She glanced out over the St. George River and swallowed hard. Her asking for rights in Assembly didn't bother her, but now she couldn't bring any words forth for Mister Whittle, who stood and waited for her to speak.

He does not know he waits for me to save, and also forsake, my beloved Maryland. My lands shall soon become lands owned by Puritans.

"Tell me, Mister Whittle."

Margaret hesitated to shush her frogs. She lifted her chin and forced a strong voice.

"Since I now have a rather large herd of Lord Baltimore's cattle to sell, do you still wish to purchase a cow?"

-End-

Afterword

August 1648
Governor Edward Stone
Protestant

General Assembly of the Province of Maryland
Letter in response to Lord Baltimore's
Communication

Proceeding and Acts of the General Assembly.

...we do Verily believe and in Conscience report that it was better for the Colonys safety at that time in her hands then in any man's else in the whole Province after your Brother's death for the Soldiers would never have treated any other with that Civility and respect and though they were even ready at times to run into mutiny yet she still pacified them til at the last things were brought to that strait that she must be admitted and declared your Lordships Attorney....

When Margaret sold a cow to William Whittle within the hour of leaving the General Assembly in January of 1648, she knew Lord Baltimore would not forgive her. Upon hearing of this sale, he wrote the Assembly a scathing letter announcing her actions as invalid. For political harmony in August 1648, Lord Baltimore replaced Governor Thomas Greene, a Catholic, and appointed Captain Edward Stone, a Protestant, Governor of Maryland. Above, is a segment of the Assembly's reply, under Governor Stone, defending Margaret Brent's actions. This was excerpted from the Maryland Historical State Archives. Governor Stone and his assembly composed the above response to Lord Baltimore's letter concerning Margaret Brent selling his cattle. It is said every man in the Assembly signed this document.

Margaret Brent pled for herself and others at least 134 cases in the Maryland provincial court, and with selfless action, as Leonard Calvert's executrix. She prevented the destruction of the first Lord Baltimore's great dream, which has become our Great American Dream. Had Margaret not paid the militia, and forfeited her welcome to remain in Maryland, the ensuing uprising by angry soldiers would certainly have cost Lord Baltimore his charter over the province. The Lords Baltimore had set in motion a place where all could worship freely, along with two significant unintended consequences. To maintain the semblance of a non-Catholic controlled province, Cecil Calvert instituted the separation of church from state. Also his headright system caused the demise of the old English manorial system and created the ability of servants to rise as landholders and even become lawmakers. Margaret Brent, after paying the governor's militia, moved to Westmoreland, Virginia with her sister. They named their new estate Peace and acquired approximately 10,000 acres of land, including where Alexandria, Virginia now sits. Mary died in 1658 and Margaret died in 1671.

Giles Brent and Mary Kittamaquund Brent moved to Stafford County, Virginia to their estate named Retirement. Much controversy surrounds Mary Kittamaquund Brent and Giles Brent's number of children because Giles only mentions two children and not his wife in his will dated 1671. Margaret Brent's will in 1663 mentions three of Giles Brent's children. The couple may have had only three children, but others insist they had seven children. This author takes issue with both sides of the current argument concerning the children born to Giles and Mary Brent for various reasons best left for another discussion. Some records indicate in the short years of the Giles and Mary Brent marriage they had Mary (c. b. 1645) Richard (c. b. 1646) Henry (c.?) Margaret (c.?) Katherine (c. b. 1650) Giles (b. 1652) and Nancy (c.?). Some researchers speculate all but two children died before Giles Brent's will was written. Did Mary Brent die in childbirth with Nancy? Some ask why Katherine, (c. b. 1650 d. 1670) at age four would be sent to Calvert County, Maryland to live with Baker Brooke's family. It seems logical there would be no record of Mary Kittamaquund's death, probably around 1654, because Giles would have taken his wife back to tribal lands for the traditional burial ceremony. This author finds the current research and DNA information insufficient to come to any definitive conclusion concerning the children born to Giles and Mary Brent.

Richard Ingle expected the courts of England to reward him for his capture of the Dutch ship and his notable prisoners. Instead, the courts ruled against him.

Father Andrew White and Father Philip Fisher (Thomas Copely) could have been hanged for being Catholics who had returned to England. They pleaded it was not through their own volition that they returned. The court released them and the other prisoners, but later recaptured Father White and held him in the terrifying Newgate Prision awaiting a martyr's death. In 1648 Father White had been released and was living in Antwerp. He never returned to his beloved Maryland.

Author's Notes

ONCE A YEAR, THE American Bar Association awards five deserving women attorneys the Margaret Brent Award. Margaret became a powerful force in pre-colonial Maryland but is known only through the records of Maryland's court cases and those who refer to her as *attorney*. Since we know little about her personal life, I wanted to use this incongruent research to humanize her.

For centuries before and after the 1600s, documented history has followed men, mainly men of note. For the most part, women's voices remained silent and obedient unless they left personal written records of their lives. Their diaries, journals, and letters created possible opportunities for them to be included in today's history, such as in Eliza Schuyler Hamilton (*My Dear Hamilton*, by Dray and Kamoie) and others like Alice Bradford (*Beheld* by Nesbit).

Diaries, letters, or journals written by or about Margaret Brent have not yet been uncovered. Little is known about her except she came from an aristocratic Catholic family in Gloucestershire, England, born in 1601, as one of thirteen children. The only original source documentation available to us comes from over 134 court-recorded appearances by Lady Margaret Brent. Court records started a year or so after she became a resident of pre-colonial Maryland. These court cases, organized and catalogued by Dr. Lois Green Carr, are housed in the Maryland Historical Society's Archives.

Margaret Brent, her sister, and two brothers dared to make the note-worthy adventure from England to North America in 1638. Here her name began to appear in documents. Giles Brent's history is better known. Giles, Margaret's younger brother, presided as temporary governor of Maryland for many months. He stirred up controversy when he married a young Indian princess, and his name and his son's name are frequently associated with major conflicts.

I found only one way to hear Margaret's voice and know her heart. This came from studying her legal cases and from evaluating disparate information tangential to her. I needed to understand the political events of the time, both in England and in Maryland, learn about her family, research who her friends and neighbors were, and determine the hardships and happiness she would encounter in Maryland. Only then would I know what deep, internal conflicts might explain the unpredictable actions of Margaret Brent and others who lived in pre-colonial Maryland.

Questions researchers have ask about Margaret Brent and may have offered assumptions:

-Why did only Margaret and one sister go to Maryland with just two of their brothers?

-What caused her older brother to return to England after a few months?

-What caused Maryland settlers to become sick and die more than in other colonies?

-Why did Margaret and her sister never marry when Maryland had an extreme shortage of women?

-Were Margaret Brent and Governor Leonard Calvert lovers or just friends?

-Why did Giles Brent marry a very young Indian princess?

-Why did Margaret Brent and Governor Calvert allow this marriage?

-Why did Giles and Margaret Brent say Captain Ingle treated them badly?

-Why wasn't Captain Ingle held accountable for his questionable behaviors?

-Why did Captain Cornwallis, whose actions were often disloyal, maintain his good favor with the Calverts?

-Why did some men in Maryland fall out of favor with the governor, then later be rewarded?

-How could a fort be built during a rebellion around Margaret and her sister's home, which would be strong enough to withstand attacks and be known as the main garrison for Catholics?

-What caused the sisters' fort to fall?

-What could be the purported violence within the fort when it fell?

-Where was Leonard Calvert, the governor, during the rebellion?

-What caused Leonard Calvert's death?

-Why did the Brents move to Virginia?

When researchers stitch together history with bits and pieces of information from various sources, they often make suppositions based on sparse data. Some of these questions still have no answers.

In this historical biographical novel, *The Spinster, the Rebel, and the Governor,* an understanding of the characters' actions evolved from examining peripheral, historical facts along with documented social conditions. For example, in Protestant England during Margaret Brent's time, women had prayer books to study, written expressly for them and were discouraged from studying the bible used by men. Wouldn't some women, like Margaret Brent, resent this? What might they do in turn? Using facts and social mores could create a historically correct story. I wanted to bring the reader an engaging tale based on strong probabilities, rather than on simple and obvious assumptions. I explored wider and deeper into my research in order to examine motivations borne out of plausible internal conflicts the characters faced. With this, I needed the help of a few fictitious characters.

Two other historical fiction biographies have been written about Margaret Brent. One was written over sixty-five years ago in 1957 and appears to have been written for school children. Another, *Mary's Land* by Lucia St Clair Robson, was written in 1995. This story features a fictional, London street urchin and her association with Margaret Brent. Over time, all of our writing becomes outdated because archeological data advances, new research emerges, and more evidence evolves.

The St. George River is now St. Mary's River. A group of men who didn't punch timecards and had no union to answer to in the 1600s slapped up a house in days. Builders did not pour foundations or install such time-consuming items as plumbing, heating, electrical wiring, and insulation. St. Mary's City developed into something much different over hundreds of years.

Historical facts are the foundation, the bones, of this story. To breathe life and eliminate the mundane, events and timelines were compressed, but not twisted. Because this story is written in third person point of view, the reader will learn only what Margaret knows. Fictional Carrie Wells became the impetus for Margaret to become involved in the court system. Fictional Peter Coates became eyes for Margaret to absorb what happened during the initial part of the rebellion. These imaginary characters helped give substance and flavor to enhance our scant knowledge about the few, brave historical people who populated pre-colonial Maryland.

In Appreciation

When writing this book, I asked other minds and eyes to play with me to help ensure the truthfulness fashioned in this almost 400-year-old revived world.

Susan Hettema, you kept my characters true to their own voices and values. Your rewrite suggestions created stronger, emotional scenes.

Mary Ann Domina, overall, you discover the joy in my writing. When you send me back to do a rewrite, your sensitivity opens new possibilities for my characters.

Elizabeth Anonia, I'm honored by your asking to read my draft. You directed me to places where I needed to smooth transitions and clarify events. Most of all, I cherish the generous time you, Douglas Greth, Astrid, and Theo spent to show me around Maryland and Historic St. Mary's City. This let me breathe the air, walk on soil where the settlers had walked, and delight in the beauty of the river, when all the while I could write at my computer in New Mexico.

Ann Zeigler, as an attorney, a cerebral thinker, and a wordsmith your proofing and guidance added polish to my work. Sir William Blackstone stood by my side.

Paul Zeigler, a voracious reader and a man who willingly read this story about a determined, independent woman, you brought up pertinent questions about this historical period. I appreciated your suggestions. However, your final comment meant the world to me when you said, "This is a really good book."

Leah Rubin, your added value to my writings can't be ignored. Not only are you an excellent copyeditor, but you brought forth a questioning intelligence that required me to deliberate and reconsider.

Sharon Miller, goodness, where would I be with my mess of references if you didn't straighten them up and make them march as they should?

Henry Miller PhD. RPA, Maryland Heritage Scholar, your quick response to my inquiries delighted me. Your passion for uncovering the history of St. Mary's City and your willingness to share will benefit all who read this book. Thank you for taking time out of your busy life to enrich the telling of Margaret Brent's life. The reasons for "seasoning" and illnesses unique to St. Mary's City bothered me, then I read your article. What a comfort to me and my research to know I haven't been off track, including the supposed portrait circling about, which neither of us believes is Margaret Brent.

PARTIAL LIST OF HISTORICAL PEOPLE

Altman, Father John, (b. d. November 1640) one of two Jesuit Priests to arrive in Maryland with the first colonists. Worked closely with Father Andrew White. Their mission was to attend to the Catholic colonists and convert the Native Americans. Father Altman spent much time on Kent Island and assisted with distributions and assignments at Mattapany, involving their mission's storehouse at the mouth of the Patuxent River.

Baldridge, James, (b. d.) sheriff of St. Mary's City, Maryland, c. 1638.

Brainthwaite, William, (b. d.) commander of Kent Island and deputy governor. Relative of Calvert family.

Brent, Ann, (b. 1612 d.) daughter of Richard and Elizabeth Brent and a sister of Margaret and Mary Brent. She married Leonard Calvert between 1642-1644. Two children: William, Ann. Ann (daughter) married Baker Brooke (d. 1678/9) of Calvert County, Maryland. Remarried Henry Brent (d. 1694). Remarried Richard Marsham (d. 1713). The marriage of Ann Brent to Leonard Calvert has been questioned. This author believes motivation arising from researched facts eliminate the controversy.

Brent, Catherine, (b. 1612 d. 1639/40) daughter of Richard and Elizabeth Brent, a sister of Margaret and Mary Brent, and a nun who died in the convent English Abbey of Our Lady of Consolation in Cambrai. Some have her death dated much later.

Brent, Edward, (b. d.) one of six sons of Richard Brent and Elizabeth Brent and a brother of Fulke and Giles.

Brent, Eleanor, (b. d.) daughter of Richard and Elizabeth Brent became a nun and was one of seven sisters of Richard Brent and a sister to Mary and Margaret.

Brent, Elizabeth, (b. d.) daughter of Richard and Elizabeth Brent became a nun and was one of seven sisters of Richard Brent and a sister to Mary and Margaret.

Brent, Fulke, (b. 1595 d. 1656) one of six sons of Richard Brent and Elizabeth Brent, departed from Plymouth, England and immigrated to St. Mary's County, Maryland on the ship *Charity*, November 1638. Member of the Maryland Assembly, returned to England, March 1638/39. No researcher knows why he returned. This author uncovers motivation for probable reason. Married Cecily___. Died before January 1656/7. No children.

Brent, George, (b. 1602 d. 1671) one of six sons of Richard Brent and Elizabeth Brent and a brother of Fulke and Giles. George married Anne Peyton in 1635. George Brent, age 21, was granted administer of his father's estate in 1652

Brent, Giles, [Col.] (b. 1604 d. Feb.1671/2) one of six sons of Richard Brent and Elizabeth Brent, departed from Plymouth, England and immigrated to St. Mary's County, Maryland, on ship *Charity* November 1638, member of the Maryland Assembly, granted land and status. Commander of Kent Island. Deputy Governor of Maryland 1643-1644. Married Piscataway Empress, Mary Kittamaquund. This marriage seems to baffle and shock researchers. This author uncovers likely motivation and acceptance for this marriage. Four children lived: Mary, Giles, Jr., Katherine, Richard. He moved to Aquia Creek, Stafford County, Virginia c. 1649. 1654 deeded everything for the second time to his sister, Margaret, to educate his children and take care of his wife, Mary. Remarried Frances Whitgreaves ___, no children.

    Brent, Jane, (b. d.) daughter of Richard and Elizabeth Brent is a sister to Mary and Margaret.

    Brent, Margaret, (b. 1601 d. May 1671) daughter of Richard and Elizabeth Brent is the protagonist of this fictionalized biography. She left no known letters, diaries, or journals. Most information about Margaret comes from the records of court cases and genealogy research. Knowing who she was and what she did stems from tangential information about events and people around her. Only her birth date and family information is known until she arrives in Maryland in November 1638 with her sister, Mary, and two brothers, Fulke and Giles. They left Plymouth, England on the ship *Charity* in October 1638. Margaret and Mary owned Sisters Freehold (70 acres and a manor south of St. Mary's Fort) and had titles to other lands. Research shows the Brent sisters built a fortress around their home and it became the Catholic garrison during the Protestant rebellion. No one knows when the fort was built, and other researchers believe it was erected for protection against the rebellion. This author believes the motivation establishing the fort came long before because of what Maryland experienced prior to the rebellion. Margaret presented over 134 legal cases to the governing body of Maryland, and in the records that survived after 1642 she's often listed as "Attorney". Leonard Calvert appointed her his executrix after Ingle's rebellion while on his deathbed. He told her to take all of his possessions and Lord Baltimore's to pay the soldiers their wages. After Leonard Calvert's death, Margaret asked to be allowed to have two votes in the courts. This denied, she settled Leonard Calvert's estate and paid the militia. Margaret, with her sister, moved to their Virginia estate, Peace, in Westmoreland County, Virginia.

    Brent, Mary, (b. 1603 d. 1658) daughter of Richard and Elizabeth Brent. Little is known about Mary. She arrived in Maryland in November 1638 with her two brothers, Fulke and Giles, and Margaret. She and Margaret moved to their estate, Peace, in Westmoreland County, Virginia. These two sisters remained unmarried.

    Brent, Richard, (b. d.) one of six sons of Richard Brent and Elizabeth Brent and a brother of Fulke and Giles. On occasions, he was imprisoned because of his controversial writings.

    Brent, Richard, (c. b. 1573 d. 1652)) Gloucestershire, England. Lord of Lark Stoke and Admington Manors. Married Elizabeth Reed, (c. b. 1594 d. 1631) and had six sons and seven daughters: Fulke, Giles, Edward, Richard, William, George, Margaret, Mary, Catherine, Elizabeth, Eleanor, Ann, Jane. Three daughters went to a convent in France. Mary and Margaret went to Maryland. Ann and Jane stayed in England. Fulke and Giles went to Maryland with their sisters. Fulke returned a few months later. Son Richard was imprisoned in London off and on for his political writings.

Brent, William, (b. d.) one of six sons of Richard Brent and Elizabeth Brent and a brother of Fulke and Giles.

Calvert, Cecil or Cecilius, (b. 1605 d. 1675) first son of George Calvert and became the Second Lord Baltimore. He married Anne Arundell of Lord Arundell of Wardour. They had three sons and six daughters. He was granted his father's title and the proprietorship of the province of Maryland by King Charles I where he governed as Lord Proprietor from afar. This author discovered through his passion to preserve religious tolerance and peace in Maryland, the second Lord Baltimore created three major founding principles of our country: religious tolerance, separation of church and state, and the Great American Dream where a citizen may rise from deprivation and poverty to own land, acquire wealth, and become part of the governing body. Cecil Calvert never voyaged to Maryland.

Calvert, George, (b. 1578 d. 1632) Yorkshire, England. King James I, on 16 Feb. 1624, created the title of Lord Baltimore for George Calvert, thus making him Irish nobility. George Calvert, after resigning from most of his political assignments, resided at the Baltimore Manor in County Longford, Ireland. He had six sons and five daughters. This story starts after his death. The vision of his religious and political Maryland social experiment, sanctioned by two kings, places the foundation for Margaret's story. Their vision inadvertently formed the great American Dream. Margaret's part assured Calvert's grant of Maryland did not revert back to practicing religious intolerance and become once again under the governmental control of Virginia.

Calvert, Leonard, (b. 1606 d. June 1647) appointed Governor of Maryland by his brother, Cecil, he immigrated to Maryland in 1634. There he diligently followed his brother's mandates to the best of his ability. He had to juggle tensions between the different populations such as Catholic (and the powerful Jesuits), Protestant, Native American tribes, landowners, indentured servants, and the Virginians. Researchers speculate on Leonard Calvert and Margaret Brent's relationship. Some insist they were lovers, others say they were only good friends. All wonder why they didn't marry. This author believes the research reveals strong motivation that uncovers their true relationship. On one of his many trips back to England, Leonard Calvert married Ann Brent, Margaret and Mary's younger sister. They had two children, William and Ann. He appointed Margaret Brent his executrix while on his deathbed. He told her to, ". . . take all and pay all."

Claiborne, William, (c. b. 1600 c. d. 1677) Virginia's Secretary of State. First English settler of Virginia's Kent Island between 1627-1630. He built a mill, fort, store, and enjoyed generous trading permits. When King Charles affirmed Kent Island to be a part of Maryland, Claiborne refused to acknowledge the authority of Leonard Calvert, second Lord Baltimore, or Maryland. Claiborne and his Kent Island followers frequently stirred up the Native American's distrust of Marylanders, traded without license, and prepared to attack Maryland trading vessels with their own armed ship. When the king and the governor of Virginia would not support Claiborne, and England became even more hostile to Catholics, he joined forces with Richard Ingles to rid Maryland of her Catholics.

Cornwallis, Thomas, Captain, (b. 1605 d. 1675) Cornwallis along with John Lewger and Leonard Calvert played a major part in the founding of St. Mary's City and Maryland. He did as he was bid but was often at odds with Leonard Calvert. He married Penelope __. Thomas Cornwallis, as the second son of noble family (either Royalist or Roman Catholic Recusant) arrived in Maryland in 1634 on the *Ark*. He built a mill for St. Mary's and a small church. He had as many or more than twenty servants, and the largest of all Maryland mansions (made of timber and brick). The brick probably came from the James River area in Virginia. His household goods included linens, beddings, plates, brass, pewter, and other finery. He also had abundant livestock. Cornwallis is spelled several ways in the early records including Cornwalley. One source states he married in England sometime after 1645. Another source states clearly his wife was in charge of his Maryland servants and property when he was gone from Maryland prior to 1645. It makes sense he had someone, like a spouse, in Maryland to oversee his large holding while he was away on his many different trips. For the sake of this story, he's married when the Brents arrive in Maryland. Fenwick and family were also named as overseers of Cornwallis's estate.

De Sousa, Mathias, (b. d.) a free black who sat in the Maryland Assembly as a legislator (burgess). In 1641 he traded with the natives and used Lewger's and Jesuit's pinnaces.

Fenwick, Cuthbert, (b. 1615 d. 1655) overseer of the Cornwallis estate and appointed to sit on council by Giles Brent. His wife and children stayed at Corwallis's estate during the Protestant Rebellion. It seems Fenwick appeared on the scene around 1640.

Fisher, Father Philip, aka Thomas Copley, (b. 1595/96 Madrid, d. 1652 Maryland) real name, Thomas Copley. Eldest son of esteemed William Copley of Gatton, England. Changed his name from Thomas Copley to Philip Fisher probably to protect his parents from his illegally going abroad. Grandfather and father were exiled under Queen Elizabeth. William returned when King James I gained the crown, but as a recusant, he never gained the family's former stature. Father Philip Fisher worked with second Lord Baltimore to establish the Jesuit Mission in Maryland in 1637. With more than a dozen priests and large holdings, this required someone with Father Philip Fisher's business sense.

Gray, Francis, (b. d. 1667) (probably from England) married Alice Moreman 1637.

Freeman. Immigrated to Maryland by 1637. A Protestant, carpenter, he showed antagonism to Catholics and was involved in a court case against a Jesuit. Moved to Virginia 1647. Assisted Richard Ingle in his rebellion against Maryland.

Greene, Thomas, (b. 1610 d. 1651/2) settled in Maryland 1634 arriving by *Ark* and *Dove* with Leonard Calvert and about fifteen other gentlemen. Married Ann Cox (formerly married) and a sister to Dr. Gerard. They had two sons, Thomas and Leonard. Greene was a strong supporter of the Jesuits. Before 1647, as a widower, married Winifred Seyborn. Much genealogical contention abounds around Ann Greene, the birthdates of Thomas's children, and when Ann died. Thomas Greene was named second Provincial Governor of Maryland by Leonard Calvert from his death bed. The second Lord Baltimore replaced Thomas Green with William Stone as Governor. Later Greene served as Deputy Governor and declared support of Prince Charles, prompting parliament to place Maryland under Protestant control. His widow married Robert Clarke. This Thomas Greene should not be confused with the Thomas Greene who was the pilot of Ingle's ship *Reformation.*

Hawley, Jerome, (b. 1590 d. 1638) 2nd wife, Eleanor, arriving in Maryland in 1634 on the *Ark* and *Dove*. Hawley, Cornwallis, and Leonard Calvert were appointed by the second Lord Baltimore to organize the settling of Maryland. Two years later the second Lord Baltimore sent Lewger as a significant party to assist. Hawley is on record as having a questionable past as an assistant or in service to the Queen. There is an unsubstantiated account he may have been involved in a plot to poison a Lady at a palace banquet. In Maryland, Hawley evidently was assigned to influence the Virginia Assembly. He must have lived in both Maryland and Virginia, and traveled much. He died in Virginia in 1638. A doctor's account said his death might have been an accident. At one point the Virginia governor told Leonard Calvert that Hawley would steal them both poor. Hawley and Cornwallis seemed to do much business together; capital gain drove their motivations in most everything. They appeared to have a similar attitude about Leonard Calvert being a weak leader. Hawley and Cornwallis wrote a document, *A Relation of Maryland*, which Cecil Calvert (second Lord Baltimore) used to promote the settling of Maryland. Some sources incorrectly state Hawley and Lewger wrote the document. It was written in 1635. Lewger didn't arrive in Maryland until 1636.

Hill, Edward, (b. d.) A Virginian, in 1646 during the insurrection, was sent to Maryland with Thomas Willoughby to demand return of Virginians. The party in power selected him as governor. When Leonard Calvert returned with troops, Calvert reclaimed his position as governor. Hill continued to fight for the governorship after Calvert's death.

Hooper, Doctor, (b. d.) A Virginian chirugeon (doctor-surgeon) who attended Leonard Calvert.

Ingle, Richard, (b. 1609 d. 1653) Merchant seaman from Virginia, trading goods and tobacco up and down the coast and to England, apparently had successful negotiation skills. Even with a ship named *Reformation*, Ingle garnered the majority of Maryland's shipping imports and exports. He was an anti-Catholic who tussled with Maryland founders from 1642 until he instigated a rebellion against them. The rebellion left only about 100 of 400-600 Marylanders in the province. Ingles seemed to have been a good friend of Captain Cornwallis.

Kittamaquund, Chitomachen, (b. 1607 d. 1641) Chitomachen may be a first name or a different spelling/pronunciation of Kittamaquund. He is also referred to as Chitomacon Kittamaquund. He negotiated the selling of St. Mary's City to Leonard Calvert, after Chitomacon killed his brother who was unfriendly to the English. His daughter was named Empress (later Queen) Mary Kittamaquund, Tayac of the Piscataway Indians. He ruled close to 7,000 people, was baptized in 1640 by Father Andrew White, and given the name of Charles Kittamaquund in a village about 15 miles south of present-day Washington D.C.

Kittamaquund, Mary (c. b. 1631 c. d. 1654) Daughter of Chitomachen Kittamaquund, was baptized in 1641, became the wife of Giles Brent (married c.

1644) and had six children. They lived in Virginia after Ingle's rebellion. Father Andrew White estimated Mary to have been born about 1634, but Porter & Porter in *Daughters of Princes Mary Kittamaquund* (3/2014) DNAeXplained-Genetic Genealogy, believe Mary was born more likely around 1631 because of her life experiences. A Jesuit Priest in a letter to the Pope also mentioned this girl seemed older than what Father White had said. There is no record of her death but in keeping with tribal traditions, there would be no documentations. Her next to the last child, Katherine, (c. b. 1650) is recorded as an indentured in Calvert County, Maryland as a very young child (age 4 years) living with the Thomas Brooke family, possibly because of the death of her mother. Giles and Mary's last child, Nancy, probably was born in 1654 and may have been the cause of the mother's death. It would be expected that Mary Kittamaquund would have been returned to her people for a quiet tribal burial.

Lewger, Ann, (b. d.) Arrived in Maryland 1636. Wife of John Lewger. Son, John, age nine. Her husband, John Lewger returned to England 1648.

Lewger, John, (b. 1601/2 d.) arrived in Maryland 1636 on the ship *Unity* with his wife, Ann, and son, John, age nine. John Lewger the elder, close friend of second Lord Baltimore, attended Trinity College, Oxford. He was named Secretary of the Province in Maryland and Lord of two manors. Leonard Calvert respected this man and thought him loyal. Lewger was kidnapped by Richard Ingles in 1645 and taken to England.

Lewis, William, (b. d.) Catholic overseer at St. Inigoe's Mission, found guilty in court by Leonard Calvert, Captain Cornwallis, and John Lewger (all Catholics) of depriving Protestants Francis Gray and Robert Seagrave of reading a Protestant book that disparaged Catholics. The court imposed heavy fines on Lewis.

Mosorcorques (John, baptized**)** In 1640 was principal councilor to Tayac Kittamaquund, probably because Mary Kittamaquund married, in 1644. **Wahocasso** is listed as Tayac until 1658.

Neal, James, (b. d.) served on council of Governor Leonard Calvert and also for Giles Brent, who was acting governor. During the rebellion, Neal fled Maryland, and Nathaniel Pope gave his property to a Virginian.

Oliver, Roger, (b. d.) A landowner with wife and two children, Oliver was killed during combat with the Susquehannocks. Some believe a Dutch knife found near him was used for his murder. Later, his two cows were shot for food during the rebellion.

Pope, Nathaniel, (c. b. 1603 d. 1660) In 1638 as a free man, transported himself to Maryland. He brought no servants. He worked his 100 acres given him as a Maryland adventurer. In 1642 he purchased Leonard Calvert's newly built manor, which served as an ordinary that housed and fed visiting burgesses and as a meeting place for the Assembly and Provincial court. By 1644, he sat on juries and had achieved the title of Mister. During the rebellion, he had a fort built around the manor and became the most prominent Protestant in Maryland.

Revell, Randall, (c. b. 1613 d. 1685) arrived 1634-1636 from England. A cooper, who acquired lands, a boat, and seemed to be in the good graces of Cecil Calvert. This man is probably the same Randall Revell in Virginia after 1644. Married to Rebecca (from London) and had a son, Edward (b. 1638 in Maryland).

Smith, Thomas, (b. d.) Kent Island, March 1638, indictment for piracy and hanged after pleading Benefit of Clergy (meaning he could read and write). Calvert denied him this because his plea was after his trial and the sentencing. (This happened just before the Brents arrived in Maryland.)

Stone, William, (c. b. 1603 c. d. 1660) Puritan Governor of Maryland, 1649-1652, invited Virginia Puritans to settle in Maryland.

Sturman, Thomas and **John,** father and son Marylanders became part of Ingle's rebellion against the Catholics.

Vaughn, Robert, (b. d.) Protestant from Kent Island. Loyal to Lord Baltimore. Commander of Kent Island 1646 and became one of Calvert's councilmen.

Waldron, Doctor, (b. d.) a Virginia doctor who attended to Leonard Calvert.

White, Father Andrew, (b. 1597 d. 1656) The Reverend arrived in Maryland on the *Ark* and *Dove* in 1634 with Leonard Calvert. Wrote detailed account of the 1634 crossing on the *Ark* and *Dove*. Personal mission to convert Native Americans. Baptized tayac and members of Piscataway tribe c. 1640. Handwrote Catechism prayers in Piscataway and Latin and English. Taken to England in chains with Father Fisher, held for a time in Newgate Prison, and never allowed to return to his beloved Maryland.

Whittle, William, (b. d.) Purchased one of Lord Baltimore's cows from Margaret Brent an hour after Margaret left Assembly in January 1648.

Partial List of Mentioned Servants in Early Maryland

Little is known about these motivated and hardworking people before they came to Maryland, so their England backstories are fictionalized. Information about their trade skills comes from court records or incidental references. Their names often bear a variation of spellings, a huge problem for any genealogist. These men and women listed below represent others, like themselves, who became the force of change, turning the English Manorial System into the great American Dream. Bearing a powerful initiative to risk all, many rose above servitude, acquired land, property, and secured stature in shaping their communities.

Brookes, Elizabeth. Passage paid for by Margaret and Mary Brent 1638.

Clarke, Robert. Passage paid for by Father Philip Fisher. Trader, surveyor. Freeman who owned Clarke's Freehold.

Clocker, Daniel. Arrived in Maryland c. 1636. Passage paid for by Captain Cornwallis. Freeman, acquired land, grew crops, respected as a councilor. Married widow, Mary Lawne Courtney in 1645. Carpenter, planter, held Clocker Hold, changed to Clocker Marsh.

Courts, John. Passage paid by Fulke Brent 1638. Fulke returned to England March 1638/9. Court purchased his early release.

Delanhey, John. Passage paid for by Margaret and Mary Brent 1638.

Gedd (Ged) Thomas. Passage paid for by Margaret and Mary Brent 1638.

Goodwin. No record of his first name. Blacksmith written beside Goodwin. Passage paid for by Margaret and Mary Brent, 1638. Giles Brent had a smithy built on his property.

Guesse, Elizabeth. Passage paid for by Margaret and Mary Brent 1638.

Hardige, William. Accuses Ingle of treason, then becomes part of Ingle's rebellion.

Lawne, Mary. Passage paid for by Margaret and Mary Brent. Married James Courtney, a free immigrant who had purchased Mary Lawne's indenture time. Mary and James had one son. Mary was listed as a midwife and then a widow in 1643. She later married a man named Clocker. She and several other women years later were sentenced to be hanged for theft, but Cromwell's rise to power prevented it.

Peasley, William. Brother-in-law of the Calverts and lived on Drury Ln. in London. He plays no part in this book, but he played a large part in establishing Maryland. He seemed to be the distributer of Hawley and Cornwallis's promotional booklet, *A Relation of Maryland*. People were told if they wanted to go to Maryland, tell Peasley and he'd see their passage arranged. I thought Peasley deserved some recognition, so I borrowed his name and gave it to Leonard Calvert's most trusted man servant.

Pope, Francis. Passage paid by Fulke Brent 1638. Fulke returned to England March 1638/9. Pope purchased his early release. Francis Pope should not be confused with Nathaniel Pope, freeman, who purchased Calvert's manor.

Pursell (Pursall), Samuel. Passage paid for by Margaret and Mary Brent 1638.

Price, Captain John. Head of the militia Leonard Calvert acquired to fight for Maryland.

Robinson, John. Passage paid for by Margaret and Mary Brent 1638. Referred to in a court document as barber. His court record stated he had a surly disposition. D. Richardson *Sidelights of Maryland History.* Vol. 1. Page 106 mentions a John Robinson at a Provincial Court proceeding in the year 1637. This probably would be another John Robinson or an incorrect date.

Stephans, John. Passage paid for by Margaret and Mary Brent 1638.

Stowre (Stower) (Slower), Franc (Francis). Passage paid for by Margaret and Mary Brent. 1638 or later.

Taylor, Mary. Passage paid for by Margaret and Mary Brent 1638.

Todd, Thomas. Passage paid by Lewger. Todd, a glover, agreed to make deerskin breeches and gloves for Lewger in return of release.

Todd, ___. Woman who sewed the silk funerary cloth said to be finer than anything found in England. She may have been the wife of Thomas Todd.

SELECTED REFERENCES

"CXII: Act of General Assembly of the Kirk of Scotland concerning episcopal government (1639)," in *Charters and Documents Relating To the City of Glasgow 1175-1649 Part 2*, ed. J D Marwick (Glasgow: Scottish Burgh Records Society, 1894), 397-400. *British History Online*. Accessed 8 May 2019. http://www.british-history.ac.uk/glasgow-charters/1175-1649/no2/pp 397-400.

Ancestry.com. Thomas Greene. 1634-1777, *Maryland, U.S., Compiled Marriage Index, 1634-1777* [database on-line]. Provo, UT, USA: Ancestry.com Operations, Inc.

Blackstone, William, Sir, *Commentaries on the Laws of England.* 1723-1780 4 v. 2 general. Tables: 27 cm. (4to) First Edition. Oxford: Printed at the Clarendon Press, 1765-1769.

Britannica, T. Editors of Encyclopaedia. "William Claiborne." *Encyclopedia Britannica*, November 18, 2011. https://www.britannica.com/biography/William-Claiborne.

Brugger, Robert J. *Maryland, A Middle Temperament, 1634-1980*. Baltimore: Johns Hopkins University Press, 1988.

Campbell, Bernard U. "Historical Sketch of the Early Christian Missions Among the Indians of Maryland: Read Before the Maryland History Society, Jan. 8th, 1846. Baltimore, 1847." *Maryland Historical Magazine* 1, no. 4 (December 1906): 293-316.

Carr, Lois Green, Louis Peddicord, and Russell R. Menard. *Maryland at the Beginning* Annapolis: Maryland State Archives, 1984.

Carr, Lois Green. "Margaret Brent—A Brief History." *Maryland State Archives*. 2002. http://msa.maryland.gov/msa/speccol/sc3500/sc3520/002100/0021.

Carr, Lois Green. "St. Mary's County Career Files: Biographical files of 17th and 18th Century Marylanders." *Maryland State Archives, Special Collections.* 2008. http://speccol.msa.maryland.gov/carr/.

Charles I, 1627: "An act to restrain the Passing or Sending of any to be popishly bred beyond the Seas" in *Statues of the Realm: Volume 5, 1628-80*. Accessed 8 May 2019. https://www.british-istory.ac.uk/statutes-realm/wol5/pp25-26.

Chroust, Anton-Hermann. "Legal Profession in Colonial America." *Notre Dame Law Review* 33, no 3, Article 4 (1958): 373-374.

Cornwallis, Thomas and Jerome Hawley. *A Relation of Maryland: reprinted from the London edition of 1635*. New York: J. Sabin, 1865. Pdf. https://www.loc.gov/item/01021595/.

De Lisle, Leanda. *After Elizabeth, the Rise of James of Scotland and the Struggle for the Throne of England*. New York: Ballantine Books, 2005.

Drake, Paul, J.D. *What Did They Mean by That? A Dictionary of Historical and Genealogical Terms Old and New*. Westminster, MD: Heritage Books, 2008.

First Roman Catholic Settlement in Virginia. Virginia Historical Marker, E 76. https://www.hmdb.org/Photos/6/Photo6075.jpg.

Earle, Alice Morse. *Home Life in Colonial Days*. New York: Dover Publications, 2006.

Fraser, Antonia. *Faith and Treason, The Story of the Gunpowder Plot*. New York: Anchor Books, 1996.

Gies, Joseph and Frances Gies. *Life in a Medieval City*. New York: Harper Perennial, 1969.

Goodman, Ruth. *How to be a Tudor: A Dawn to Dusk Guide to Tudor Life*. New York: Liveright Publishing Corporation, 2015.

Great Britain & Ireland, Tourist and Motoring Atlas. Greenville, SC: Michelin Travel Publications, 2004.

Helmes, Winifred G., ed. *Notable Maryland Women*. Cambridge, MD: Tidewater Publisher, 1977.

Herbert, N. M., ed. *A History of the County of Gloucester: Volume 4, the City of Gloucester*. London: Victoria County History 1988. *British History Online*, http://www.british-history.ac.uk/vch/glos/vol4.

Holliday, Carl. *Woman's Life in Colonial Days*. Garden City, NY: Dover Publications, 1999.

Ingle, Edward, A. B., "Captain Richard Ingle, The Maryland 'Pirate and Rebel.' 1642-1653: A paper read before the Maryland Historical Society. May 12, 1884." Baltimore: John Murphy and Company for the Maryland Historical Society, 1884.

Kimberz, Edward. "18th Century Maryland as Portrayed in the Itinerant Observations of Edward Kimberz." *Maryland Historical Magazine*, (1956): 325-326.

"Kittamaquund, Tayac of the Piscataway (d. 1641)." *Exploring Maryland's Roots*. http://mdroots.thinkport.org/library/kittamaquund.asp.

Krugler, John D. *English & Catholic: The Lords Baltimore in the Seventeenth Century*. Baltimore: The Johns Hopkins University Press, 2004.

Laurence Lux-Sterritt. "Mary Ward's English Institute: The Apostolate as Self-Affirmation?" *Recusant History*, 28, no 2 (2006): 192-208.

Martin, D. "The states of Maryland and Delaware, from the latest surveys." Map. 1796. *Norman B. Leventhal Map & Education Center.* Accessed October 08, 2020. https://collections.leventhalmap.org/search/commonwealth:6t053p48c.

Milam, William F. "Francis Gray and Ingle's Rebellion" *Milam in Virginia.* http://milaminvirginia.com/Links/RUSH/francis_gray.html.

Morse, Glenn Tilley. "The Ark and The Dove Ancestral Ships of Maryland." *American Antiquarian Society*, 49 no 1 (April 1939): 102-120.

Norton, Elizabeth. *The Hidden Lives of Tudor Women: A Social History.* New York: Pegasus Book Ltd, 2017.

O'Neill, Therese. "15 Historic Terms for Crime and Punishment, Defined." *Mental Floss, From the Archives* (May 15, 2015). https://mentalfloss.com/article/63819/15-historic-terms-crime-and -punishment-defined.

Pettegree, Andrew. "The English Reformation." *BBC History* (February 17, 2011). http://www.bbc.co.uk/history/british/tudors/english_reformation_01.shtml.

Potter, Shawn Henry, and Lois Carol Potter. "Daughters of Princess Mary Kittamaquund." *DNAeXplained—Genetic Genealogy: Discovering Your Ancestors-one Gene at a Time* (March 4, 2014). https://dna-explained.com/2014/03/04/daughters-of-princess-mary-kittamaquund.

Richardson, Douglas. *Royal Ancestry: A Study in Colonial and Medieval Families, Vol. I.* Salt Lake City: The Author, 519-521. 2013.

Richardson, Douglas. *Royal Ancestry: A Study in Colonial and Medieval Families, Vol. II.* Salt Lake City: The Author, 64-64, 2013.

Richardson, Douglas. *Royal Ancestry: A Study in Colonial and Medieval Families, Vol. III.* Salt Lake City: The Author, 118-119, 2013.

Richardson, Hester Dorsey. *Side-Lights on Maryland, History, Volumes 1 & 2.* Baltimore: Genealogical Publishing Co., Inc., 1997.

Riordan, Timothy B., *The Plundering Time.* Baltimore: Maryland Historical Society, 2004.

Sloan, Eric. *A Museum of Early American Tools.* New York: Dover Publications, 2002.

Sperry, Kip. *Reading Early American Handwriting.* Baltimore: Genealogical Publishing Co., Inc., 1996.

Steiner, Bernard Christian. *Beginning of Maryland, 1631-1639.* Baltimore: The Johns Hopkins Press, August-September-October, 1903.

Stone, Garry Wheeler, "Secretary John Lewger." (PhD diss., University of Pennsylvania, 1982.

Swinden, Cara. "Crime and the Common Law in England, 1580-1640." (Honors Thesis, University of Richmond,1992). https://scholarship.richmond.edu/honors-theses.

Taylor, Dale. *Everyday Life in Colonial America, from 1607-1783.* Cincinnati: Writer's Digest Books, 1999.

Thompson, Harry F. "Richard Ingle in Maryland". *Maryland Historical Magazine* 1, no. 2 (June 1906): 293-316.

Ulrich, Laurel, Thatcher. *Good Wives: Image and Reality in the Lives of Women in Northern New England, 1650-1750.* New York: Vintage Books, Random House, Inc., 1991.

Book Club Questions

1. What was your initial reaction when you first started reading this book? What was your reaction after you finished this book?

2. Margaret kept secrets from her father and brothers, making them believe she must not love them. Has a secret in your family been misconstrued?

3. Cecil Calvert, encouraging them to go to Maryland, changed the Brent family's life. Have you ever had a cousin, aunt, or uncle impact your life?

4. Margaret did not want to leave a wrong until righted. Have you ever stepped out of your comfort zone to make something a little better for another?

5. If you had to move away with no chance of replacing what you leave behind, what would you select, not for survival, but for your own comfort?

6. Which scenes from the events in Maryland stayed in your mind?

7. Did you uncover something you hadn't really thought about from the Brent's settling in the New World?

8. Did this story remind you of any other books? If not, how did it seem different?

9. What prior knowledge did you have of the English conflict between Protestants and Catholics? Does "religious tolerance" bring a different understanding for you after reading this book?

10. England's landed gentry system deteriorated in Maryland, causing Maryland's society to often be on an unsettling edge. Can you see how policies, events, and concerns that occurred in England shaped Maryland?

11. Cecil Calvert, the Second Lord Baltimore, found it necessary to remove some traditional responsibilities from the church. He also insisted Protestants and Catholics could equally participate in governing. Several years after the first Maryland settlers arrived, the head-right system brought about consequences Lord Baltimore never expected. How did these three actions give rise to the founding of our nation and the Great American Dream?

12. Often the endings of stories are not what we would wish or expect. Considering the historical facts, can you see another choice for Margaret?

About the Author

Charlene Bell Dietz's award-winning mystery novels *The Flapper, the Scientist, and the Saboteur* combines family saga with corporate espionage, and *The Flapper, the Impostor, and the Stalker* propels readers back into 1923 in frenetic Chicago. *The Scientist, the Psychic, and the Nut* gives readers a frightening Caribbean vacation. Her latest novel *The Spinster, the Rebel, and the Governor* is a historical biography about Lady Margaret Brent, the first American woman to be called an attorney, whose integrity and intelligence saves pre-colonial Maryland from devastation. Charlene lives in New Mexico.